#700

FAITH
AND
COURAGE

TAPESTRY OF LOVE SERIES

RIBBON OF LOVE – Book one

FAITH AND COURAGE - Book two

FAITH

AND

COURAGE

by

Donna R. Causey

Copyright © 2012 by Donna R. Causey
All Rights Reserved
This book, or parts thereof, may not be reproduced in any
form without permission
Published by Donway Publishing

ISBN-978-0-9838998-1-5

DEDICATED

To my two daughter-in-law's Becky & Lori
and my grandchildren
Parker, Emma and Ella.
May you always be proud of our heritage

ACKNOWLEDGEMENTS

Faith and Courage is a fictional story about real pioneers who lived on the Eastern Shore of Virginia. This novel is based on actual court records and historical events that took place in England and the Eastern Shore of Virginia around 1650. I consulted historical books such as *Ye Kingdom of Accawmacke* by Jennings Cropper Wise, the journal of Col. Norwood, *Voyage to Virginia*, and many others on 17th century England and the Eastern Shore of Virginia. The number of books is too numerous to include here, but essential to historical accuracy in *Faith and Courage.*

I'd especially like to thank all the wonderful genealogists, historians and members who contributed information to the Delmarva Settlers website, http://nabbhistory.salisbury.edu/. The website was an invaluable resource while writing *Faith and Courage.* Other helpful websites include: http://www.ghotes.net/ and http://www.tyaskin.com/handley/

The extensively, researched biographies written by James Edward Jensen, Timothy Robinson, and Ryan Charles Cox on Ambrose Dixon, Stephen Horsey, Alice Traveller Custis, William Coulbourn and the Johnson family on the Delmarva Settlers website were invaluable in telling a complete story of these characters in *Faith and Courage.*

As always, I must give special thanks to my husband Wayne and son's Mike and Brian as well as my good friends, Jackie Shugart and Gayle Farris who cheered me on, helped edit and provided suggestions. Your support and encouragement are beyond measure.

Last but not least, I am grateful to all my ancestors who recorded and documented records of their lives. This novel would not exist without them.

Donna R Causey

TO THE READER

The timeline and setting of this novel is 17th century England and the Eastern Shore of Virginia. This novel is a work of fiction and a product of my imagination. While 90% of the historical events actually occurred and the names of the characters came from court records of the Eastern Shore of Virginia, literary license was used to tell George Willson's and the Dixon's story.

In historical fiction novels, it is sometimes difficult to separate actual history from fiction. I've included an Appendix at the end to delineate and clarify some of the questions the reader may have.

If you are a descendant or would like to learn more about Ambrose Dixon's life, be sure to visit Ambrose Dixon's facebook page http://www.facebook.com/groups/360246826459/ sponsored by Eric B. Borgman.

Ribbon of Love is the first in the Series, Tapestry of Love, about my ancestors. Faith and Courage is the second book. I am currently working on the 3rd book in the Tapestry of Love Series and hope to have it completed in 2013. Follow my progress on facebook: http://www.facebook.com/ribbonoflove and visit my websites: http://www.alabamapioneers.com http://www.donnacausey.com

Donna R. Causey

CHAPTER ONE

January, 1649 Cranbrook, England

The walls of the cottage shook violently. Alarmed, George Willson jumped to his feet and scanned the small room as he tried to determine the source of the explosion. The letter he was reading slipped through his fingertips and drifted slowly to the floor.

The blast came again, louder and closer this time.

"Ka-Blam! Boom! Boom!"

Is that gunfire?

George was a soldier for King Charles' Army and all too familiar with the report of the matchlock and blunderbuss. He peered out the front window and watched a horse-drawn carriage race swiftly down the street. Several hatless men chased after it, shooting weapons in the air. He looked toward the town square. His view was partially obscured by a dust cloud created by men running and shouting among the citizenry with their weaponry raised toward the sky. Children and women screamed as they scrambled for safety.

Has everyone gone mad? What's this about?

A tall, lean man with long hair, ran in front of the cottage. George stuck his head out his open window and hollered at him.

"William, what has happened?"

The man halted a moment to reply, "You haven't heard, George? 'Tis posted in the square! Parliament plans to behead King Charles!"

"What? You cannot mean it!"

"'Tis true...'tis true! King Charles is to be executed! What will become of us?" the man exclaimed. He glanced back at the men on horseback barreling in his direction and continued down the street at a faster pace.

George drew his head back in the window and collapsed into the worn chair by the fireplace. His mother died a week ago and George was on a brief leave from the King's Army to take care of her affairs and make living arrangements for his younger sisters,

1

Elizabeth and Sarah.

What will become of us indeed? I never thought Parliament would go this far.

He ran his fingers through his curly hair as he contemplated the situation. George's deep blue eyes, auburn locks and freckled complexion belied his serious nature. Before he had been involuntarily forced to fight with King Charles' Army, George was drawn to the ministry and planned on a much different career as a village parson. This war against Parliament's Army was not consistent with his personal beliefs. He held no great love for the King, still...he did not wish him dead.

I thought once Parliament's Army captured the King they'd reconcile and we'd be at peace....but now....they should not behead our King! This is wrong! What am I to do? I'm still a King's soldier in Parliament's eyes. Where will I go?

Forced to sell the family home to pay his mother's debts, an inheritance was nonexistent. George stood and glanced around his mother's small Parlour where he'd spent his childhood. The spindle-legged chairs were stained and worn from years of use. An old, scarred table was on one side of the room. Above the fireplace on a mantel shelf were two pewter candlesticks.

I have nothing. Even this is no longer mine. At least Anne will be able to provide for herself as well as my two sisters in her position as a midwife...but where will I go? Everyone here knows that I fought with the King's army. What shall I do now? I didna see how I can remain in England.

He noticed the letter lying on the floor and bent down to pick it up.

Mayhaps there's a chance for me in Virginia. Mary writes such cheery letters about the Colonies.

A knock at the cottage door interrupted his thoughts. He walked over and grasped the knob just as someone forcefully pushed the door from the other side and burst into the room. George lost his balance and nearly toppled to the floor.

"What in the deuce, Richard? Why did you push like that?" George growled.

Richard was tall and thin. He had a long scar between his eye and ear that he received from a saber cut. "Sorry, George....I didna realize you were standing so close. Have ya' heard the news?"

"About King Charles? Aye, Logan told me as he ran down the street in a panic...like everyone else in England it seems!"

"What opinion do ya' have?" Richard whispered. He peered apprehensively out the door before he finally shut it and walked in an agitated manner to the center of the room. Richard was George's best friend in the Army, but he tended to talk too fast and become fidgety when excited.

"I really didna know what to think, Richard. I only recently heard. When and how did it happen? I know the King had a trial but I assumed Parliament would work out a reconciliation." George sat down and stared at his distressed friend.

Richard anxiously paced the floor. "I did as well. I understand that King Charles challenged Parliament at the trial. He said they had no authority over him...and I agree with the King. I heard there was not even enough members of the House of Lords at the trial to constitute a Parliament! I believe many thought the trial decision would be reversed!"

"I wish it had....an agreement should have been made with the King."

"I agree...nonetheless, Cromwell rules now and after his barbarity these last few years and with us being the King's soldiers...I fear we'll not be in good favor with Parliament's Army."

George stood and faced Richard. "Then we probably should not remain here. Cranbrook is a Parliament stronghold. I suggest we make haste for London. Mayhaps we can connect with others in the King's army and yet save him."

"I s'pose 'tis the best thing to do but not dressed as soldiers. It would be too dangerous. When do ya' want to leave?"

"I'm ready today. Elizabeth and Sarah are settled with Anne and the new owners will take possession of this place soon. I only returned to gather my things. We could leave on the coach for London this afternoon."

"I'll square things with me family and meet ya' at the coach," Richard retorted and briskly walked to the door.

George joined him and put his hand against the door frame, "Then I'll see you soon. Let's hope we can do something to stop this madness."

George waited at the entrance and watched his friend leave.

3

He glanced toward the racket in the square and gave a heavy sigh.

It took only an hour for George to gather his meager belongings. Dressed in his old tattered clothes in the hope that he'd be inconspicuous, George studied the room for one last time and tried to imprint the image to memory. Thoughts of his family flooded his mind and he became overwhelmed by emotion so he sat down a moment to regain control. Once there were ten members residing in this small cottage. Now only he and his three sisters were left.

We were never wealthy...but we were always happy.

George focused on a chair by the fireplace. A vision flashed before his eyes of Grandpapa Willson sitting there telling stories to his brothers and sisters while Mum sat across from them spinning yarn. He looked toward the door and half-expected his always jubilant father to enter the room in high spirits. Grandpapa Willson had been the first to die, succumbing to a brief illness. Within two short years, the war claimed Papa and his his two brothers. Then his sister died in childbirth and finally, consumption took the life of his Mum. George stood and tried to regain his composure. He stared at the door and envisioned a scene of soldiers bursting through the entrance and announcing that he was their prisoner.

I dare not remain much longer. Should I venture out. What if someone reports me as a King's soldier? Thank goodness Anne's provided a home for my sisters. They should be safe here and my sisters will be a comfort to Anne since my brother, Robert, died. Being a widow at so young an age has not been easy, I'm sure...especially since she has no other family left to rely on.

George approached the window to assess the activity in the street. He looked in the direction of his sister-in-law's house.

'Tis still too early to meet Richard. Mayhaps, there's time to see them again. I hope I'm doing the right thing. Oh Anne, how I wish I could bring comfort to you...but you only see me as ye're husband's younger brother. Now that he's gone, could you ever look at me the way you looked at Robert?

George shook his head trying to banish his thoughts.

What kind of person am I? My brother's gone and I'm coveting his wife...yet..I..I cannot help it. She's been in my heart and uppermost in my mind since the day Robert brought her home. How could anyone not be captivated by her beautiful blond, silky hair, diminutive statue and winsome smile? And now...mayhaps I'll never see her again.

George turned away from the window in anguish.

'Tis useless to hope...she'll never be mine. She still loves Robert...and what do I have to offer her? I no longer even have a home.

He studied the small cottage again. Restless and wanting to focus his mind on something else, George picked up his bag containing his only belongings and abruptly walked out the door.

George Willson and Richard Johnson reached London late in the evening. The next morning, they immediately set course for the Mitre. The Inn was frequently visited by the King's soldiers. Dan Rawlinson, the owner, was a staunch Royalist so it would be the best place to connect with some of the King's Army. The two friends walked the bank of the Thames and tried to avoid the ever present muck. The stench from the garbage littered streets filled their nostrils. They passed two young boys playing marbles.

"Ye're cheating, James!" one of the boys shouted.

"I am not!" his scrawny companion retorted. "I'm just a better shot than ya'. I've been practicing while ye're chasing after Amanda."

"Stow it...or I'll knock ye're head off," the bigger boy replied.

George chuckled as he and Richard crossed the street. "Remember our carefree days when all we had to do was worry about marbles and lassies, Richard?"

"Aye, seems like just a short time ago we were like those lads...I'd give anything if thats all that plagued me now."

George opened the door to the Inn and stepped down into the dimly, lit tavern with Richard following close behind. The two men waited a moment by the door while their eyes adjusted to the darkness. George studied the people in the room. A bearded man was seated near the door with his back to the entrance. He was surrounded by several flush-faced young men intently listening to the man's words.

The man panted heavily and spoke in a raspy voice as if he

had difficulty breathing. "Virginia is a bountiful land if ye desire a place of safety. We're not bothered much by Parliament and a man can grow rich in a short time, growing 'backy." The man took a slug of ale from his tankard.

"What about the savages? I heard they massacred whole towns," countered one of the young men sitting at the table.

"Aye, 'tis true. They did once, but Virginia's much safer now. Most of the Indians moved further north. Any that remain quieted down after Claiborne attacked their towns and put the fear in 'um. 'Sides, it appears to me that ye didna have much choice. Ye'll not be safe if ye remain in England. Ye said Parliament's army will probably arrest ya' soon." He picked up his mug and downed the last of the golden liquid. A few drops dribbled down his chin which he sloppily wiped away with the back of his hand before continuing.

"Of course there's always the chance the Indians will rise up again...still, with the opportunity to become rich...'tis worth the risk. We do pretty much as we please without government breathing down our necks....unlike here." The man suddenly lowered his voice and cautiously surveyed the room. He became aware of George and Richard behind him and rose to his feet. The other young men sitting at the table also stood. The man's eyes rested on George and he nodded. George returned the nod.

The bearded man whispered something to the man beside him. George was no longer able to discern his words.

"Welcome men," Rawlinson recognized George and Richard. "Tis good that some of the King's soldiers are not 'afeerd' to show their face in London. I'd heard most left for Ireland, leaving our poor King to fend for himself with Cromwell's men."

"Ireland, ya' say....what pray tell do they hope to accomplish there?" Richard asked Rawlinson as the two men approached the owner.

"Regroup for a plan of attack, I s'pose...at least that's what some say...but who knows? Why aren't you two with them?"

"We've on leave," George quickly responded as he searched the room. A table down the middle was filled with various shaped loaves of bread placed at intervals along its length. Salt shakers were placed beside the loaves of bread. George spotted an empty table in a corner and walked toward it. After George and Richard sat, the other men in the room sat down as well and quietly continued their discussion.

"A tankard of ale, Dan, and we'll have some of ye're wife's good venison...we're a bit peckish," Richard ordered.

"Certainly...I'm glad ye're not like the other cowards that left ...mayhaps there's hope for the King yet," Rawlinson added grudgingly. He directed his words to a woman clearing some pewter mugs off a table, "Margaret, these men want some of ye're venison."

"I heard 'em," she replied wryly. She smiled at Richard and George, then left the room briefly, and returned with two steaming bowls. One was filled to the brim with venison stew and another with buttered beans. Margaret placed the bowls on George and Richard's table, then walked over to the long table and picked up two trenchers, along with a loaf of bread and spoons. After tucking the bread under her arm, she returned to their table.

"Have ye come to view the terrible crime to be perpetrated on our King?" she peppered, not waiting for an answer. Margaret shook her head as she spoke. "Tis a sad day...with Parliament in charge now and the King to be executed today...who will they go after next?"

"He's to be executed today?" asked Richard in astonishment.

"Aye, I just heard word. 'Twill be this afternoon." She glanced back at her husband then whispered, "Dan is so distraught; he plans to drape our Mitre sign in mourning."

"Doesn't he fear Parliament's Army?" Richard inquired.

"Aye," she replied gravely. "Still, he feels he must show his respect for the King in some way and will not be dissuaded. We thought about closing but he said that he wanted to provide a place for the King's supporters to meet...just in case there's a chance of a rescue."

"Where will this travesty on the King take place?" asked George.

"Last I heard, 'tis to be at the Banqueting Hall at Whitehall. I could not bear to see it...even if we were closed."

"Has there been any talk of saving the King?"

"Some talk...but that's all it's been is talk. Most of the King's soldiers are in Ireland like Dan said."

George noticed a tear trickling down her chubby cheek

before she moved abruptly toward another table.

"Need a refill, mates?" she asked.

"Fresh pints all around on me, Maggie, and make sure ye're mindin' ye're P's and Q's" on that slate. Last time ye put down quarts and nearly broke me," a short, stocky man answered.

Maggie picked up her chalk and held the slate so the man could see it. She boldly marked the numeral 5 under the Q instead of under the P in the other corner for pints.

"There ya' go again. Now ye treat me right Maggie or I'll be going somewhere else."

Maggie winked back at him, "Ah...ye'll never do that James, ya' love me too much." Then she hollered at her husband, "Need 5 pints for these gentlemen, Dan, and didna fill them tall....they're getting right snooty."

The men at the table chuckled at her brashness.

George smiled at Richard and commented, "Good old Maggie...nothing keeps her down long."

While wolfishly eating the first decent meal he'd had in two days, George cautiously studied the men in the small room. Other than the group they'd overheard when they entered, most of the guests appeared to be gentlemen.

After sopping up the last drops of stew with his bread, Richard said, "Let's head to the Banqueting Hall...seems no one here is interested in forming a plan to save the King. Mayhaps we'll find some of the King's soldiers there."

London was extremely crowded. George and Richard were frequently jostled while they briskly walked the few blocks to Whitehall palace. The muddy streets, cluttered with smelly rubbish and offal on the sides, overflowed with people walking, riding horseback, or traveling in all manner of carriages; all headed toward Whitehall palace.

The two men proceeded past closed shops with ascending stories projected over the street above the ground floor, sometimes two to five stories high. Additional stories provided a roof for lower levels. The fronts of the shops were made of brick or timber and a few even had rich carvings. All businesses were closed. George glanced at the beggars' chalk marks on the front of some of the houses indicating it was worthwhile to beg from the residents. He frowned when they approached a parish church with most of it's carved work destroyed and painting defaced.

"Whew...would ya' look at that crowd," Richard exclaimed as they neared the Banqueting Hall.

A sea of people, covered the street in front of the scaffold. It was a particularly cold and gloomy winter day. Nevertheless, those closest to the platform were in danger of suffocation as many in the mob pushed forward in search of a better view.

George's eye ran over the crowd and he commented, "Didna seem to be any of the King's soldiers about...'course they're probably not dressed as soldiers...like us."

"Mayhaps this was not such a good idea. Someone might recognize us." Richard whispered.

"Let's see if we can move near the front. Mayhaps we won't be noticed with our backs to the crowd."

George and Richard maneuvered among the people until they found a location near the scaffold that allowed them a fairly, clear view. Both men were tall and this was a benefit since the platform was built at a good height off the ground.

Guards and tables of food surrounded the scaffold and separated them from the decking. The scaffold was draped completely in black. Even the floor was black. The axe and the block lay squarely in the center.

George studied the people near them. Some were talking quietly while others seemed exuberant and even gleeful. A few fashionably-dressed ladies, further away from the main crowd, dabbed tears from their eyes with handkerchiefs.

"He was allowed a walk through the park this morning," declared an elderly man with rheumy eyes standing next to George."

"Did ya' see him? How did he appear?" asked Richard.

"Nay, I didna see him. I was at home...me wife saw him when she went for water. He was surrounded by many people and soldiers. His colors were flying, drums were beating...'twas quite a commotion according to her. I never thought I'd live to see this day. Imagine, beheading our King...'tis hard to fathom."

"Aye, 'tis a day we won't soon forget."

The assemblage suddenly grew silent as King Charles appeared on the platform with Col. Hacker and Col. Tomlinson. The King walked defiantly to the center, observed the axe and block then spoke to Col. Hacker.

George strained to take in his words, but 'Boos' mingled with 'Hurrahs' from the multitude prevented him from making out what was said.

"Pity, I don't imagine we'll hear much," remarked Richard.

George nodded.

King Charles stood at the front of the platform and surveyed the boisterous crowd. He turned toward Col. Tomlinson and scowled, then returned his gaze to the congregation. Silence fell over the assemblage as the King began to speak.

"My duty is to God first and then to my country for to clear myself both as an honest man and a good King, and a good Christian. I shall begin first with my innocence. In troth I think it not very needful for me to insist long upon this, for all the world knows that I never did begin a war with the two Houses of Parliament."

Boos rang out from the crowd drowning out the King's voice, but he continued speaking and it gradually became quiet again. "I hope in God...that God will clear me of it...I will not, I am in charity. God forbid that I should lay it upon the two Houses of Parliament; there is no necessity of either. I hope that they are free of this guilt. For I do believe that ill instruments between them and me has been the chief cause of all this bloodshed."

King Charles' words stirred the people. Shouts muffled the King's voice. George leaned forward and cupped his hands to his ears as he tried to catch the King's words.

"That an unjust sentence that I suffered for to take effect, is punished now by an unjust sentence upon me...to show you that I am an innocent man."

"Humph, I wouldn't call meself innocent if I were him...being so close to meeting me maker," the elderly man whispered.

The multitude quieted and the King's words could more easily be heard.

"I have forgiven all the world, and even those in particular that have been the chief causes of my death. Who they are, God knows...I do not desire to know...God forgive them. But this is not all, my charity must go further. I wish that they may repent, for indeed they have committed a great sin in that particular...I pray God."

A voice from the crowd yelled, "You forgive them? God needs to forgive you!" Others joined in the shouts.

"May God forgive you!"

"God forgive the King!"

The King paused briefly, then continued, "My charity commands me not only to forgive particular men, but my charity commands me to endeavor to the last gasp the peace of the Kingdom."

King Charles focused his attention on the men to his left of the platform. "So, sirs, I do wish with all my soul, and I do hope there is some here that will carry it further; that they may endeavor the peace of the Kingdom." The King's words were again suppressed by grumblings in the crowd.

George leaned toward Richard and spoke softly, "I wonder if we will ever be at peace again."

"We can only hope the spark has gone out of the fight with the King's death," Richard replied under his breath.

George returned his gaze toward the scaffold.

The King said, "You must give God his due by regulating rightly His Church which is now out of order. For to set you in a way particularly now...I cannot, but only this. A national synod freely called, freely debating among themselves, must settle this, when that every opinion is freely and clearly heard..."

"Why didna we have a synod before ye went to war?" mumbled the old man. "It would have saved a lot of lives."

The King appeared to be finished and addressed the men standing beside him. The Bishop conversed briefly with him and the King nodded then faced the people before him, "I thank you very heartily, my lord, for that I had almost forgotten it. In troth, Sirs, my conscience in religion I think is very well known to all the world; and, therefore, I declare before you all that I die a Christian, according to the profession of the Church of England, as I found it left me by my father. And this honest man," King Charles pointed to the Bishop, "I think will witness it."

King Charles directed his officers, "Sirs, excuse me for this same, I have a good cause and I have a gracious God. I will say no more."

Then the King approached Col. Hacker and said, "Take care that they do not put me to pain. And Sir, this, an it please you---"

The masked executioner moved toward the axe and the King suddenly exclaimed, "Take heed of the axe. Pray take heed of the axe."

The executioner moved back from the King.

King Charles stared at him a moment and said, "I shall say but very short prayers, and when I thrust out my hands, then I am ready."

The executioner nodded.

The Bishop walked over to the King and gave him his nightcap. King Charles covered his head with it then asked the executioner, "Does my hair trouble you?"

The executioner nodded and said something to him. The Bishop helped King Charles push some straggling pieces of hair under his cap.

Silence pervaded among the assemblage of English citizens as they watched King Charles. George shifted his position and edged closer to the scaffold as he tried to hear the King's last words.

King Charles turned toward Dr. Dobbs, to his right of the platform. "I have a good cause, and a gracious God on my side."

The Bishop replied, "There is but one stage more. This stage is turbulent and troublesome; it is a short one. But you may consider, it will soon carry you a very great way. It will carry you from Earth to Heaven. And there you shall find a great deal of cordial joy and comfort."

King Charles raised his hands, focused his eyes toward Heaven and declared, "I go from a corruptible to an incorruptible crown; where no disturbance can be, no disturbance in the world."

"You are exchanged from a temporal to an eternal crown, a good exchange," the Bishop gravely added.

The King looked at the Executioner and asked again, "Is my hair well?"

The executioner nodded. The King took off his cloak and the Jeweled pendant of the Order of the Garter from around his neck and gave his cloak to the Bishop and said, "Remember to give it to the Prince." He took off his doublet and revealed a silky blue waistcoat.

The Bishop returned the cloak and helped the King put it back on. King Charles stared grimly at the block for a moment, then fixed his eyes on the executioner, "You must set it fast."

To which the executioner replied, "It is fast, Sir."

King Charles demanded, "It might have been a little higher."

"It can be no higher, Sir," countered the executioner.

The King nodded. "When I put out my hands this way," King Charles stretched his hands out and said, "Then."

King Charles bowed his head, said two or three words and lifted his eyes upward. He kneeled and put his head on the block.

The executioner moved toward the King again to tuck a few stray hairs under the King's cap, when the King shouted, "Stay for the sign!"

"Yes, I will your Majesty."

The spectators waited in silence. Tortuous moments went by before the King finally stretched out his hands. Instantly, the executioner, at one blow, severed King Charles' head from his body. Blood spattered everyone on the scaffold and covered the block on the black-draped platform. Not a sound was heard for a few seconds. Then a collective groan spread throughout the crowd. The groan soon became a thunderous roar from the people in attendance. The executioner raised the King's severed head, dripping with blood. He held it high for all the spectators to view and declared, "Behold the head of a traitor!"

George dropped his head in prayer. Many hid their eyes or turned away from the gruesome spectacle.

The soldiers immediately lifted King Charles' body and placed it in a coffin. The executioner placed the King's head in the coffin. Two soldiers carefully covered it with black velvet. Two more soldiers joined them, lifted the coffin and carried it inside the Banqueting Hall.

A soft misty rain fell. However, the congregation continued to stand in a state of shock for some time.

Richard whispered cautiously, "What shall we do now? We can't stay here. 'Tis not safe. Should we go to Ireland and join the other King's soldiers?"

"I didna know, Richard. I didna wish to continue to fight. I need to take a walk to clear my thoughts."

"I'll come with ya'. We need to stay together."

"Nay, Richard. I want to be alone for a while. We should be safe, dressed as we are. I'll meet you at the Mitre this evening and we can discuss what to do."

Richard stared after his friend for a few moments then turned and walked in the other direction.

Depressed over the event he witnessed, George trudged heavily toward Charing Cross and down the streets of London for over an hour. His mind was filled with unanswered questions.

Where is justice in this? What good will executing the King do? What will become of this great Kingdom now? This is not yet over. If our King is sentenced to death, others will follow!

The excited anticipation displayed by English citizens in George's earlier walk had given way to chaos. It was as if turbulent storm clouds enveloped the city, bending and twisting people's emotions at will. Angry men shouted at each other in the streets.

"They killed our King! We are doomed. God will punish us," screamed a woman as she tore down the street.

Women openly cried while still other's appeared euphoric. Children dashed about, ignored by mothers in deep discussions with other women. Fights broke out among some of the men and were not subdued. Pickpockets were rampant. Men on horseback dashed about unchecked by distraught soldiers.

Few shops were open. Worried owners sat on their stoops guarding their stores and sometimes argued with anyone standing near. George heard snatches of conversations as he walked.

"They should not have killed him!"

"He deserved to die! I lost all my sons in the War!"

"Have ye heard who'll be next?"

"The King was wrong...but he didna deserve death!"

"What will become of us? Surely, God will punish us for killing the King," screamed an elderly woman as she fell to her knees in prayer.

Many people flocked in front of churches, wailing loudly. Disorderly lines formed as they tried to gain entrance. Closed carriages bolted down the crowded streets. People scrambled for safety and tried to avoid the horse's hooves.

George halted briefly when he became aware of disturbance in front of him. He watched a constable shove an old woman to the street. She was dressed plainly in gray cotton and held pamphlets in her hand. A tall, thin man, also dressed in plain clothes and leather breeches, was being led away by two officers. The thin man exclaimed, "Friend we have done nothing wrong."

The constable shouted after him, "Ye're a Quaker and a scoundrel and we'll not have the likes of ye're kind around here. 'Tis people like ye that caused the death of our King. Mayhaps a little time in the gaol will convince ya' to leave."

The officer, turned to the woman lying on the street and ordered, "Off with you or ye'll have the same."

The woman pulled herself up by her cane. She watched the constable and officer depart with the man. Once they were out of sight, she began offering pamphlets again to anyone who passed.

George walked over to her. She handed him a pamphlet and greeted him with a smile, "God Bless you, son." He took the pamphlet, nodded and continued down the street. After putting some distance between them, George stopped to read the pamphlet.

'This is the Spirit, or Father, which dwells in man. He it is by whom everyone lives, and moves, and hath his being.....and he is perfect when he is taken up in the Spirit and lives in the light...the Spirit of Light dwells within everyone and may rule the mind and actions of every man....True happiness, complete satisfaction, which is Heaven, can only be gained by following the promptings of the Inward Light. God can speak to you, through his risen son, without the need to heed churchmen, pay tithes, or engage in deceitful practices.'

Spirit of Light that dwells within every man...true happiness by following the promptings from the Inward Light...God will speak to me without the need of Churchmen...I've seen what some Churchmen do in war and God could not be a part of it.

George stared back at the woman on the corner and advanced toward her.

CHAPTER TWO

A few months earlier, Eastern Shore of Virginia
Ambrose Dixon was an imposing, muscular man with regular features and deep-set eyes that could be stern and fierce one moment, then become soft and gentle the next. He had dark hair, straight brows and a firm chin uncovered by a beard which was indicative of strength and intelligence, though there was something of hardness and obstinacy as well. It was difficult for him to sit and wait, especially when he was worried and he was concerned about what was transpiring in the adjoining room. He glanced restlessly around the Parlour, stared at the flames in the fire for a moment, then his gaze returned to the direction of an adjacent room. Ambrose frowned.

"Do ya' think we'll have to wait long, Papa?" asked the young boy sitting across from him.

"I didna know, Henry, Jr. This is the first time I've had to wait like this."

Ambrose stood and placed a log in the fireplace. Flames leaped, danced and sparks began to fly.

Joanne Custis ambled into the Parlour carrying an empty pail. Joanne was not tall. Still, she was somehow imposing-looking in her full-skirted black gown and they both took note when she gave an order.

"Henry, Jr.," she spoke to the restless, young boy, "Would ya' be a good lad and fetch me some more water?"

"Certainly, Mrs. Custis." the boy replied as he jumped up quickly. Henry, Jr. was nine years old and it was hard for him to sit idle for very long. It was apparent he wanted to leave the room and venture outdoors and relished the opportunity to leave. His lanky build indicated he would one day become a tall man but for now, Henry, Jr. was all arms and legs. He recklessly grabbed the pail and banged it loudly against the door frame before running out the entrance.

Ambrose watched him leave then asked, "How is she?" The

circles under his eyes revealed the strain he was experiencing while waiting.

"Mary's doing fine Ambrose. It shouldn't be long now but I didna envy her the next few hours. She's reached the hardest time."

Joanne Custis was the Dixon's nearest neighbor and even though she and her husband were Royalists and the Dixon's were Nonconformists, she was still a close friend of Ambrose's wife. She walked over to a table made of halved logs, placed squarely in the room. She studied the table, laden with biscuits, fruit and cheese for a moment, then picked up a biscuit and took a bite. A few crumbs fell on her dress and she brushed them aside.

"I think I'll have a little tea while I wait on Henry, Jr. It's been a while since I've eaten. 'Twas a long night."

"Aye, it has been at that. I think the boy is the only one who managed some sleep. I do appreciate ye're coming so quickly. I know Mary does too. Of course, our servant, Maria, is here, but I hated to leave the two of them alone while I went after the midwife and Mary's cousin, Priscilla."

Joanne pulled a pewter cup from the shelf and addressed Ambrose "Did you want some tea?"

"Aye, I believe I do," he said as he sat down on the bench next to the table. "I forgot to eat." He picked up a piece of cheese and a biscuit.

"Did the boy have something to eat?"

Ambrose nodded, "Maria prepared his victuals while I was gone this morning."

"Have you decided on a name yet?"

"Well, Mary insists that it should be Ambrose if 'tis a boy so I insisted it should be Mary if a girl," Ambrose replied. "'Tis hard to believe I will have me own bairn soon...of course, Henry, Jr.'s like me own; he was so young when his Pa died. But this bairn will be me own flesh and blood...and there's something special about that."

"Aye, 'tis true. I sometimes forget, Henry, Jr isn't ye're own... especially the way he follows you everywhere."

"Aye...he's never given us a day of trouble."

"Don't ye think he looks a lot like his Pa?" Joanne asked.

"Aye, he does and if he turns out to be half the man Henry Pattenden was...he'll make us proud."

A piercing scream came from the back part of the house and both Joanne and Ambrose rose to their feet.

"Well, I 'spect the time is close for ye're bairn to be born," Joanne declared. "Why don't you take Henry, Jr. outside? It's going to become quite noisy around here for a while and I don't imagine it will be good for him to hear his Mum in pain."

"That's probably a good idea," Ambrose stood and gave a nervous cough. Hearing his wife in pain was not easy for him either. "We'll be in the carpentry shop if ya' need me...be sure to let me know when the bairn's here."

Henry, Jr. barged into the room, struggling with the heavy water pail.

"Thanks, lad. Bring the pail over here. I need to heat the water before taking it in," Joanne said.

Ambrose reached down, took the pail from his son and deftly lifted it to the table. "Henry, ye've done a fine job, but I think this is women's doings in here and I'm behind on my work. Why don't we work on the shallop instead of waiting here?"

"What about Mum? Won't she need us?"

"Joanne says she's fine and there's nothing for us to do but wait. We can do that at the carpentry shed. They'll come for us if we're needed. Let's get out of their way."

Henry, Jr. gave a worried glance at his mother's room then reluctantly followed Ambrose out the door.

The man and boy walked slowly to the carpentry shop, each deep in thought. Ambrose stood a moment to admire the large stack of shaped lumber loaded neatly in his wagon and the many out buildings surrounding the house.

I built everything on this place...from the house to the barn and the out buildings. Now, mayhaps I'll have a son of me own to give it to. 'Tis hard to imagine. Of course, I have Henry, Jr. Still, there's nothing like having a son of me own.

"How many people will the new shallop hold, Papa?"

"About twenty-five, I guess. It's the biggest one I've built yet."

"What do we need to do now?" the inquisitive boy asked.

"We need to make a few more planks then we'll be ready to add the ribs to the keel. Do ya' think ye can help with that?"

"I think so Papa, I'm a lot stronger now." Henry, Jr. shouted

19

as he bounded for the carpentry shop.

"You are that, son." Ambrose laughed as he followed Henry, Jr.

He may look like his Pa but he acts more like his Mum. I hate she's having so much pain. Mary's had too much suffering already.

Ambrose smiled as he recalled the first time he met Mary. Her husband, Henry Pattenden asked him to build their first home while they were living with her Aunt Alice Willson.

I don't think I'd ever seen a more beautiful woman...Little Henry, Jr. was only a month old. Mary's large gray, expressive eyes were eyes a man could drown in. I think I was in love with her from the start. I wonder if she realized how I felt....of course she was Henry's wife.....I doubt she even noticed me.

Henry, Jr. broke into Ambrose's reverie with a question, "Why are they called ribs, Papa?"

"'Cause they hold the skeleton together, just like your ribs," Henry laughed as he reached down to tickle Henry, Jr's ribs.

A loud scream came from the house, startling them both.

Henry, Jr. asked, "Is Mum alright, Papa?"

"Aye, lad. 'Tis just a hard and painful thing to bring a bairn into the world, but I'm sure she'll be fine. Now lets get started. We need to complete this shallop for Mr. Scarburgh before he pays us another visit complaining."

A couple of hours later, little Mary Jane Dixon was born. Joanne walked out on the porch and called for Ambrose and Henry, Jr. to meet her.

Mary's cousin, Priscilla Willson, and their indentured servant, Maria, left the crowded bedroom. They met Henry Jr. and Ambrose in the Parlour.

Priscilla arrived the previous night and had remained with Mary throughout the ordeal. She appeared exhausted but excited as she announced, "You have a beautiful daughter, Ambrose!"

"A daughter?....well, I'll be. How's Mary?"

"She's well....tired...but well. I'm sure she's anxious to see you both."

Ambrose walked briskly toward the bedroom while Henry, Jr. followed in his footsteps. Mary was propped up in the bed with a small infant nestled in one arm. Her long dark, disheveled tresses fell softly around her face. Joanne and Barbary moved to the other side of the small room so Ambrose and Henry, Jr. could inch closer to the bed.

"We have a daughter, Ambrose. I'd hoped to give you a son. Are you disappointed?"

Ambrose took three large steps toward Mary and gently clasped her free hand in his. He tenderly smoothed her hair with his other hand while he gazed at his daughter.

"She's a prime lassie, Mary. I already have a son with Henry, Jr.....we need a daughter now."

Henry, Jr. sat down on the bed next to his mother and stared at his sister. "She's awfully little, Mum."

Ambrose touched Mary Jane's hand and the infant quickly circled her small hand around his thumb.

"She's small now son, but she'll grow fast," Mary responded. She looked up at Ambrose's beaming smile.

"She looks like you, Mary," Ambrose said. "I'm glad she didn't take after her Papa."

"I didna know who she looks like, but I hope she will be as strong as her Papa," Mary countered.

Barbary interrupted, "She's a fine bairn, Miss Mary....still, you and the bairn must both get some rest....so gentlemen...I'll have to shoo' ya' out for now."

Ambrose smiled at Mary and said, "You do need ye're rest." He leaned over and gave Mary a gentle kiss on her cheek, then turned to Henry, Jr. "Let's see if we can make a few more ribs for the shallop before nightfall, son."

Ambrose and Henry, Jr. reluctantly left the room while Joanne Custis and the midwife remained.

"Mary, do ye want me to place her in the crib?" Joanne inquired.

"Not yet, I want to hold her a little longer. We'll be fine for now. You must all be exhausted. Ye've been with me for hours."

"I admit I'm tired and I might take a spot of tea....and even, a biscuit. I'll check you again before I leave," Barbary announced. I s'pose I need a little break since Miss Bailey's bairn will probably be born this week."

Joanne clucked as she examined the infant. "She is a

beautiful bairn, Mary...nonetheless, you of all people know that 'tis never good to grow too fond of a newborn. It's up to God whether she lives past the first few years."

Joanne followed Barbary out of the room, and Mary cuddled her daughter closer, "I don't care what Joanne says, Mary Jane, you are truly a blessing...and I love you...and I'll become as fond of you as I want."

The infant made smacking sounds with her mouth. "Are you hungry?"

Mary pushed herself into a sitting position and cradled her daughter in the crook of her arm. She guided Mary Jane's mouth toward her breast. The infant latched on and began eagerly sucking.

"Very good, Mary Jane. You have a good appetite." As the infant suckled, Mary's mind wandered to the child she had lost a few years before, when her husband, Henry was alive. Tears began to trickle down her cheeks as she recalled the day her child died.

Mary Margaret, you were such a wee thing and when that fever came, you just could not fight it. I thought ye'd be safe since Henry was a doctor, but even he could not save you. God, please let this one live. I couldn't bear to lose another child.

Mary Jane lost Mary's nipple for a moment and began to whimper. Mary guided her mouth back to her breast and stroked the infant's forehead.

So much has changed in such a short time. Henry and I came to the colonies with such high hopes. Now most of the people we knew and loved are gone. When Henry died, I didna know how I'd manage...I loved him so much....why did he have to leave me?

Mary's eyes clouded with tears making it difficult to see. She wiped them away with her free hand.

I must stop thinking like this...that life is gone and now I have a new life with Ambrose. What would I have done if he hadn't proposed marriage after Henry died?...I really had no other choice. I couldn't manage the plantation by myself...Will I ever be rid of this guilt?...I feel like I betrayed Henry....'Twas only a few months after his death when we married....and....I didna love Ambrose.....Still, he's a kind man...especially to Henry, Jr.

Mary Jane stopped sucking and drifted off into sleep. Mary gently placed the infant on the bed, then scrunched down and encircled her child in the crook of her arm while she continued reflecting on life.

Oh Papa...how you would have loved seeing ye're granddaughter....ye're gone too...and now Mum's ill in England. Oh....I wish ye'd come to the Colonies with us. Mary Jane will never know what a wonderful grandpapa she had. Ambrose was truly sent from God. Mayhaps, I will grow to love him....he said I would....I hope he's right...at least he seems happy enough for now.

Barbary returned to the Mary's room and asked "How are ye feeling, Mary? 'Tis there anything more I can do for ya'?"

"Nay, I'm quite well...thanks to ye're care...and Mary Jane suckled some before she went to sleep. Did you find something to eat?"

"Aye, we're all sufficiently satisfied," Barbary laughed as she patted her plump stomach. "That was quite a feast ya' prepared. Joanne and Priscilla left. They thought it best to let you rest some. Since ye're doing so well...I'll return home. Mayhaps I can catch a few winks before Mrs. Bailey's 'lyin in.'"

"Thanks again and I'll pray for Mrs. Bailey."

"Me too, Mary. Her last two were quite difficult and the one before that was stillborn."

"Aye, I remember."

"Get some rest now. Those two men of yours will be coming round soon. Maria is preparing their victuals for tonight so sleep while ye can."

"I won't argue with ye, Barbary. I do admit I'm tired."

Barbary shut the door and Mary closed her eyes and drifted off to sleep with her small infant cradled in her arm.

CHAPTER THREE

Spring, 1649, Eastern Shore of Virginia

Fluffy clouds billowed in the misty, blue sky and a soft breeze caressed the sloping land as Ambrose stood at his front door and sipped his morning tea from a pewter cup. It was a promising day for a trip across the bay. He glanced back at Mary as she pounded bread dough. Her apron was covered with flour and sweat was above her brow. A few straggling curls escaped her rochet, framing her face like a halo.

"Mary, I think I'll take the new shallop on the water to check for problems before turning it over to Scarburgh. Would ya' care to join me? Ye deserve a break once in a while," Ambrose added.

Mary gave a heavy sigh and took a minute before answering while she inspected her husband. He wore a dark shirt and his pants were tucked in high boots. A small felt hat shaded his eyes. He was a handsome man and a fine figure of manhood intent on a task before him that was very much suited to his taste.

She wiped her hands on her apron before she answered, "Nay, Ambrose. 'Tis baking day and I'm afraid I cannot put it off, especially since Maria's busy outside making candles. There's no one available to watch Mary Jane. I'm sure Henry, Jr. will enjoy going with you."

"Nothing keeps that youngun' off the water...sometimes I think he's half fish," Ambrose laughed. He threw the remaining tea in the yard, placed the cup on the table near Mary and gave her cheek a quick peck. "I'll stop by Hungar's Mercantile and see if a packet arrived from ye're brother."

Mary quickly lowered her head so Ambrose would not see the moisture in her eyes, threatening to fill with tears. Her emotions were hard to control when she thought about her family in England.

"Thanks Ambrose. It has been a long time since he last wrote and I'm worried about Mum." Mary replied with a voice full of feeling.

"Aye, well it's settled then. Henry, Jr. and I will leave right away."

After Ambrose left the cottage, Mary stepped over to a small window and watched him call her son from the barn. Henry, Jr. waited for no second invitation, but snatched his hat from a post and dashed across the short distance to catch up with Ambrose. In a fever of excitement, he gleefully loped along with Ambrose down the path toward the quay where the boat's crew waited.

It would be nice to leave all this never-ending work behind and enjoy a beautiful day with them, but that would only mean twice as much work tomorrow. I'd better quit day-dreaming. Mary Jane will be awake soon enough and I'll never get this baking done.

Mary glanced back at the dough she was pounding, She returned to the table and attacked the dough with a vengeance.

Ambrose skillfully glided the large shallop around the islets in Plantation Creek and was soon on the Chesapeake. The crew lowered the leeboard into the water to keep the boat sailing straight. A gentle breeze blew against the canvas billowing the sheets to full sail. The water shimmered and reflected the sun's rays.

Henry, Jr. observed a flock of wild geese returning home after their winter migration. He asked, "Papa, do you know where the geese go when they leave here?"

"I know they head south, son, but I'm not sure exactly where. It's strange how they always seem to make it back home to the same place."

Henry, Jr. watched Ambrose for a while, then asked, "Papa, may I try sailing her?"

"Sure, son. She seems to be handling fine. Stay close to the bank though."

Ambrose smiled as Henry took hold of the tiller.

He will be an expert on the water soon. I couldn't ask for a better son, even if he's not me own.

Ambrose walked around the shallop. He examined the shrouds, stay sail and main sail. Everything seemed to be in working order.

"Let's head back toward Hungar's, son. I'd like to see how

she rows. I don't imagine we'll have much wind on the creek."

When they entered the creek, the crew lowered the sails and manned the oars as the shallop glided along toward Hungar's quay. When they arrived, one of the crewmen climbed on the pier and tied off the shallop.

Ambrose watched a determined looking man dressed in a dark blue waist-coat, tan breeches and carrying a plumed hat beneath his arm, rapidly walk toward the quay to meet them. Col. Edmund Scarburgh was considered quite wealthy among the citizens of the Eastern Shore. He was also noted for his fiery temperament.

"It appears Scarburgh's here," Ambrose commented. "I guess we can turn the shallop over to him."

"Aye, Papa...but how will we get back?" Henry, Jr. asked.

"Hopefully, he'll take us home...but ye never know about the Colonel," Ambrose laughed.

Henry, Jr. eyed Col. Scarburgh warily as he approached.

"Is that my shallop, Ambrose?"

"Aye, Colonel. I was giving her a final check."

"She looks mighty fine, Ambrose. How many men do you think she'll hold?"

"About twenty-five. She's the biggest one I built yet."

"If she's as good as you say...mayhaps I'll have more built. Do you know anything about the Bermuda sloop? Argoll Yeadley was telling me about them. Seems they're easier to navigate and don't require a large crew."

"Aye, sir. John Custis described the sloop to me, but I've never seen it. He said they were fast, sturdy and could carry quite a bit of goods. Are ye interested in building one?"

"One...I need more than one if they're that good. Let me gather my crew and we'll follow you to ye're plantation."

"Aye, sir. First, I need to pick up some items and check for packets in the store."

"Well then...ye'll find me in the Ordinary when ye're ready to go...I believe I fancy another pint of ale first, anyway," Scarburgh said as he walked rapidly down the pier.

Ambrose climbed the riverbank with Henry, Jr. trailing close behind. "You men wait here," Ambrose shouted back to the crew. "We shouldn't be long."

Hungar's Mercantile was only a small log building on the quay but the center of all activity in the small community. Nearby, Hurgar's Church and the Ordinary completed what could be called a town on Plantation Creek. Most people received supplies and sent products from ships anchored just offshore their personal quays. They used the ship's boat and shallops to ferry supplies and men ashore. However, the citizens of Eastern Shore depended on the Mercantile for news, packets and items they ran out of before ships arrived.

Alex Mountney, a ruddy, jovial man, was the owner of Hungar's Mercantile. He greeted Ambrose warmly when they entered the store, "Looks like ye've built a fine shallop for Scarburgh, Ambrose. He's been talking about it for weeks....brags it will be the largest on the Bay and it sure looks like it from here."

"Aye, she's a good-looking ship...kind of hate to give her up. Here's a list of items we need. Are there any packets for us?"

"Aye, there's one for Mary."

"Is that right? I know she'll be happy. She's been expecting a letter from her brother."

Alex handed the packet to Ambrose and glanced at the long list Ambrose held in his hand. "I may not have everything ye need today, we're due another shipment soon...and I'm low on stock right now."

"Well, fill what ye're able. Henry, Jr., stay here and wait on the order...let the crew know when it's complete and they can help load it on the shallop. I'll settle up with Scarburgh," ordered Ambrose as he walked out of the store.

The Ordinary was a short walk from the Mercantile. The small wooden building was dark and crowded as usual. After his eyes adjusted to the dim light, Ambrose glanced around the sparsely populated room and spotted Rev. Nathaniel Eaton, the former Church Clerk, in his usual place, at a table gambling over cards while he nursed a pint of ale. Ambrose frowned.

Nathaniel Eaton was well-educated but destitute when he arrived on the Eastern Shore a few years back. He related a sad story about mistreatment at Harvard College in the Massachusetts colony. Rev. Rozier quickly took him under his wing and gave Eaton a responsible position as Church Clerk so Rev. Eaton would have means to send for his wife and children he'd been forced to leave behind when he escaped the officials in Massachusetts.

Doubts about Rev. Eaton's story began to rise among many in the community when he was often seen at the Ordinary, gambling and drinking heavily. He soon became indebted to several citizens on the Eastern Shore. Tragedy followed, with news that Eaton's family had been killed in a ship-wreck on their way to Virginia. A few months later, the whole community was shocked when Rev. Eaton pursued and married Anne, the wealthy and recently widowed wife of Rev. Cotton. However, the marriage did not stop his gambling and drinking. Rev. Eaton still spent most evenings at Hungar's Ordinary.

Poor Anne really picked a loser when she married Eaton. I warrant there is little left of the estate Rev. Cotton and her father left her.

Ambrose saw Scarburgh seated at a table in a corner of the room. Scarburgh appeared to be providing an earful to a unknown gentleman sitting next to him.

Ambrose approached his table.

"Join me in a pint of ale before we leave," Scarburgh addressed Ambrose. "John here has just arrived from England and he's updating me on events there. It appears England's being ruled by barbarians after they executed our King."

"Executed the King!" Ambrose was stunned. A moment went by as he tried to take in the astounding news before he exclaimed, "That can't be true! I heard he was captured but...but...how could they execute our King!"

"I'm afraid 'tis very true." John replied. "That's why I left...too much turmoil in England right now. Everyone who supported him is in danger. I heard only good news about Virginia...so I decided to see it for meself."

"Who is ruling England? Who's King now?" Ambrose questioned.

"There's not a King. England's now a Republic, called the Commonwealth of England and Parliament has executive and legislative powers," the man said as he took a handkerchief from his coat and wiped his brow.

"What happened to the King's army?" inquired Col. Scarburgh.

"I hear they're regrouping in Ireland...Cromwell's planning

an invasion...the War never seems to have an end...so I sailed for Virginia. I've had enough."

"Does that mean that ye'll be staying?" Ambrose asked.

"Mayhaps...and I'm sure there will be many more like me to follow. No one on the King's side during the War is safe in England now. I might even take a turn at planting the sot weed. Col. Scarburgh, here, was telling me about his success as a tobacco planter...though he says the Indians are a plague."

"Are ye having more trouble from the savages, Col. Scarburgh?" Ambrose asked. "I thought they'd calmed down since our recent raids."

"I always have trouble with them, you know that...thievin' savages steal me blind. Things will never be better until every last Indian is killed or at least forced out of Accawmacke and I aim to do my part in making that come about," he said loudly.

"Aye, aye," some men in the Ordinary cheered.

"Just say the word and we'll join you in another foray. We'll be ready anytime," exclaimed a pock-faced man playing cards.

"Then we'll plan one soon," Scarburgh announced.

Henry, Jr. arrived at the door of the Ordinary and Col. Scarburgh declared, "Ambrose, I'd like to try the new shallop first and see if it performs as ye say. Let's take her out and then we'll settle accounts. John, would ye like to join us? I want to know the particulars of how the King came to be executed and it'll give you a chance to survey the land in Accawmacke. I can also give you a tour of my plantation."

"Certainly, Col. Scarburgh mayhaps it will help me decide about this place. Thanks for the offer," the man replied.

The three men followed Henry, Jr. out the door toward the quay.

Ambrose, Henry, Jr. and his crew disembarked from the shallop when they returned home. The crew carried supplies to the house while Ambrose and Henry, Jr. remained on the pier and watched Scarburgh maneuver the shallop away from the quay.

"I hate to see that one leave...kind of enjoyed building such a large vessel."

"But won't ya' be building another one, Papa? Col.

Scarburgh said he wanted another right away."

"He did, son. Guess I'll be needing some help around here with the number of ships, Scarburgh says he wants. I can't manage this tobacco plantation and build those shallops too."

"I can help, Papa."

"You certainly can Henry and why don't we start now. I believe ye're capable of helping with some of the curing. Let's head up to the drying barn. I'll show you how to work the vents."

"Sure Papa."

While they followed the rugged path to the barn, Ambrose instructed Henry, Jr., "The vents are very important, son...they help create the right conditions for the curing process to take place...you have to adjust them just right so as not to get mold."

Once they reached the barn, Ambrose pointed to the empty hooks. "The tobacco leaves will be hung on the hooks so they can shed water for curing. After the tobacco leaves have cured, we'll strike them and let 'em sweat for a couple of weeks. After that, they'll be ready to prize and roll into hogsheads for transport to England."

"I watched the oxen pull the hogsheads down to the creek, Papa. Is that why the barn is on the rise so they'll roll down hill?"

"Aye, son, and 'tis good we have our drying barn near the creek...the oxen didna have to pull the hogshead so far. Once they're at the creek we can easily roll the hogsheads to the bay and onto the shallop at the quay."

"Aye Papa" Henry, Jr. nodded. "Will we have a good crop this year?"

Ambrose laughed, "The Lord only knows, son. If we can make it through preparing that new field, planting, thinning, unpredictable weather, beetles, worms, weeds, topping, diseases and avoiding frost, then we might be lucky enough to have a crop to cure. After that, we're lucky if the 'dang' crop cures right and we didna have mold. That's why I'd rather build boats and ships...I have more control."

"I like building boats too, Papa."

"That's good, son...cause it seems that we'll have plenty to build."

A man of medium height with straight, dark hair and deep-set eyes rode up on horseback and greeted them, "Hallao,

Ambrose...it appears ya' have some mighty good help there."

"Aye, Horsey," Ambrose replied. "Henry, Jr.'s a fine boy. What brings ye out this way?"

Stephen Horsey's land neighbored Ambrose's plantation. The community respected him even though he was still young. At times, friends were a little shy of him since he was known to have a quick temper. Ambrose and Stephen were Nonconformist and both were around thirty years of age so they soon became fast friends. Though muscular and vigorous, he remained unmarried and was a frequent guest at the Dixon's.

"Thought I share a bit of news with you and catch ye're thoughts about it," Stephen said as he dismounted.

"News...huh...must be important for ya' to come all the way out here."

"'Tis. You know I was in court at Hungar's yesterday and William Finley was there."

"He was? I thought he left for good with Stone and those others who set out for Maryland two years ago. What's he doing back in Accawamacke?"

"He said he had some unfinished business. He's on his way back to Maryland today. I asked him how he liked Maryland and...well...he gave me some mighty interesting information."

"What information?"

"It seems Stone had some agreement with Gov. Calvert about resettling in Maryland before he left...cause...believe it or not...he was named Governor of the colony after he arrived."

"I thought he might've had another reason for going there other than the regulations our Commissioners passed. I never understood why he left, being sheriff here and all...seems such a waste to start over again."

Horsey removed his hat and wiped his forehead with a handkerchief before continuing, "I agree. But that's not what I came to tell ya'. It seems that Stone managed to persuade the Maryland Assembly to pass a Religious Toleration Act."

"Religious Toleration Act? What's that?"

"Well, as I understand it...the Act allows everyone freedom to worship however they want as long as they believe in Christ, but anyone who denies the divinity of Christ will be sentenced to death."

"Sentenced to death? That's a bit harsh. I wonder how he managed something like that."

"I didna know. I thought most everyone in Maryland was Catholic and was against Nonconformists. Anyway, according to Finley, anyone who insults the Virgin Mary, the apostles or evangelists could be whipped, jailed, fined or even lose their land."

"Wheewwww." Ambrose gave a low whistle. He looked off for a minute into the woods before he spoke again. "I don't imagine our Gov. Berkeley will think much of the Act...still...I like it. A man should be allowed to worship in his own way, but I agree, every man should believe in the divinity of Christ."

"The news got me to thinkin...with the way things have been around here lately.....mayhaps moving to Maryland might not be such a bad idea. Lord Baltimore is clamoring for more settlers and has plenty of good land available. Evidently, he doesn't have enough people to support the colony."

Ambrose surveyed his plantation a moment before answering..."Seems like an awful lot to give up."

"How about offering me a cup of tea and we can discuss this new Act...mayhaps something can be done here in Accawmacke along the same line."

"Sure thing, Horsey...and I'll see if Mary can rustle up a little of that custard pie she made last night."

"Mum's custard pie's the best," chimed in Henry, Jr.

"Sounds great...I always enjoy some good custard pie, especially one that's cooked by ye're Mum."

Henry Jr peppered Stephen Horsey with questions as they walked toward the house while Ambrose lagged behind.

Maryland does sound like they're headed in the right direction with this Act...but how could I ever leave this place.

The large sprawling house perched on top of a rise like a bird preparing for flight. Two rooms on either side appeared as wings attached to a large central room. Several out-buildings surrounded the house.

Ambrose smiled to himself as he recalled the day he made final arrangements with Mary's husband, Henry Pattenden to build the main part of the house.

She was so beautiful...it took my breath away....nonetheless, she was another man's wife....but now she's mine!...I know she still hankers for her first husband...but there's always hope...one day, mayhaps her feelings will change. At least we have a daughter....and of course, there's Henry, Jr....and he's like my own son...I'm satisfied with that for now...how could I ever think of leaving here?

CHAPTER FOUR

September 1649 – Eastern Shore, Virginia

It was September 12th, Mary Willson Pattenden Dixon's twenty-eighth birthday. She stood at her bureau and studied her face in the mirror. Lines were beginning to creep around her mouth and the dark circles under her eyes revealed lack of sleep. Her infant daughter suffered with an earache so Mary was awake most of the night tending to her. Mary Jane was now sleeping quietly in her crib.

Mary pinched her cheeks, trying to bring some color in her face but to no avail. She felt nothing except sadness since Ambrose brought home the packet containing the letter from her brother, George.

How could Mum be gone? I mustn't think about it or I'll start crying again.

Mary attacked her long dark hair with her brush, as she tried to control her emotions. She twisted her tresses into a tight bun on her head with one hand and absentmindedly reached for a ribbon with the other. Her eyes fell on a tattered and faded ribbon. Tears began to flow down her cheeks as she picked it up. Memories overwhelmed her. The ribbon had been a gift from her family before she left with Henry for Virginia. It was given as a reminder of their love and always brought her comfort. She sat on the side of her bed and recalled the special day her Papa presented her with the ribbon.

What were his words? It's been so long now that it's hard to remember. Let's see....The nine colors in the ribbon represent each member of her family in England who loved and would be praying for me. Oh...I wish I could bring that day back. It was the last time we were all together as a family. Now so many are gone forever...Mum, Papa, Grandpapa, two brothers and a sister. All that's left are Elizabeth, Sarah, George and me...since they're in England, I may never see them again.

Mary fingered the ribbon for a few moments then stood and

used it to tie up her hair. She covered her head with a lace-trimmed rochet. Mary's birthday was also the anniversary of her marriage to Henry Pattenden. On each morning of her birthday after Henry died, she made the sad trek to the nearby cemetery at High Meadow where both Henry and her infant daughter, Mary Margaret, were buried.

How naïve I was to believe my birthday would always be a day of happiness...now it brings me only pain and heartache. What did Papa say before I traveled to the colonies? 'Mary, you and Henry are forging a new path.. You are creating a new tapestry of love for our family. Henry and I were so full of hope. I never thought I'd be on this path alone...and now....I'm married to a man I didna love...I should be happy...at least I'm married to a kind, understanding man...not like poor Anne Eaton.

Mary sat on the edge of the bed and reflected on her marriage.

Really, I should not be sad. My life could be much worse. Ambrose was quite surprising. I was worried that he'd be difficult since he had a reputation as a fierce Indian fighter...but he was quite understanding and patient with me....even when I was reluctant that first night...and then....well....he was so gentle and caring for my feelings. It was quite a different experience than it was with Henry..I actually enjoyed it a little...still, how could I when I didna love him...Oh, what am I thinking...how can I betray Henry with these thoughts.

Mary blushed and abruptly stood. She gazed at her reflection in the mirror, tucked a few stray hairs in place then walked over to her daughter's crib. She reached down and gently touched her child's forehead to check for fever and thankfully found none.

Now....we have this beautiful baby girl and soon, mayhaps....another child...I cannot believe I'm to have a child so soon after Mary Jane. Henry always said, children are little miracles and that is true. Henry, Jr. has his father's smile and Mary Jane has Papa's eyes and mother's mouth. My children keep my family near. Enough with this wool-gathering. I need to stop looking back. Papa would be disappointed in me...I have a kind, decent husband and two beautiful children and must look ahead to the future. I'll not go to the cemetery today. Mayhaps I'll make a cake. Ambrose and Henry,

Jr. are busy with the harvest and I'm sure they'd appreciate a cake.

Mary walked down the hall and found Maria preparing the noon meal. She studied the tall slim woman as she stirred the large vat over the fire.

I should be ashamed of myself. Maria lost her husband and children in England to typhoid. Yet, she was brave enough to come to the Colonies by herself and start a new life as our servant. Why am I feeling sorry for myself? Ambrose is a good man...I should count my blessings...still...I just didna love him as I loved Henry...I wonder if I ever will?

Maria glanced at Mary and smiled. "How's the wee one? Better I hope."

"Aye, she's sleeping peacefully. She had a fitful night but is much improved...no more fever...I believe she's over the worse."

Maria nodded.

How will I manage without Maria? She's been with me almost seven years now and is like a member of my family. Her indenture is up this year and I know she has plans to marry...she's more than a servant...she's my dear friend....

Mary moved behind Maria and reached for a pewter cup on a shelf. "I should have awakened earlier...I was up all night with Mary Jane. She cried incessantly. When she finally went to sleep, I fell asleep as well."

"Ye're in need of rest yeself, Miss Mary...and deserve it today, of all days...'tis ye birthday! Didna ya' plan to go to the cemetery?"

"Not this time, Maria.....I think I'll stay here and make a cake. I'm sure the men would probably appreciate it after a long hard day in the fields and I want to be sure Mary Jane's over her illness."

"Certainly, Miss Mary....still, we should celebrate ye're birthday," Maria declared as she winked at Mary. "What can I do to help?"

"Just continue with the men's meal...I'll feed the chickens and gather some eggs." Mary rushed out with the pail of feed, a little embarrassed by Maria's mentioning a celebration.

Mary studied her house as she fed the chickens.

Henry would be so happy with our home if he were still alive. He always wanted a large house and with the expansion Ambrose built last year, our home now has seven rooms.

"I wish you were still here to enjoy it," Mary said softly to herself as she looked in the direction of the cemetery.

Has it really been eleven years? It seems such a short time since we arrived, filled with dreams of our future...dreams shared with many good friends...now so many of those friends are gone, lying in the cemetery with you...now I'm here alone...Oh, I must stop this...I must look forward, not backward....

Mary's reverie was interrupted as she watched a woman walk toward her from the quay. She shaded her eyes with her hand and squinted as she focused on the woman walking up the path. She was fashionably attired in a long gray dress with a white apron. The outer skirt of the dress was gathered up on the sides to reveal a white underskirt. She traipsed carefully up the path, trying to avoid throwing mud on her clothing as she walked.

"Why, Joanne...what brings ye this way so early?" Mary shouted when she recognized her friend.

John and Joanne Custis had only recently arrived on the Eastern Shore. When fighting started in England, they fled to Holland for safety. Later, they joined their daughter, Anne, in Virginia when she married Col. Argoll Yeardley, Commander of the Eastern Shore. Joanne frequently visited Mary since they were close neighbors on the opposite side of Plantation Creek.

"I came to wish you a happy birthday Mary...'tis a special day. I know ye've always spend it at the cemetery and I said to myself that ye're birthday is not the day to spend at the cemetery. I hoped to catch you before you left and talk you out of going."

"As it happens, I decided to stay home this morning...Mary Jane's ill and I didna want to leave her today."

"Mary Jane, ill? I hope it's not serious."

"Nay, 'twas just an earache. Her fever broke last night. She seems to be better now...though...I thought it best to stay home to be sure. I'm glad you've come. Is that ye're new sloop at the quay?"

"Aye, 'tis. John is very proud of it's speed."

"Ambrose will want to see it. He's talked about little else since he heard it arrived. I know he's anxious to build one."

"Well, when he returns...he can look at it as much as he wants. I brought my spinning wheel and thought I'd visit a spell, if ye've time."

"Sounds great. I planned to bake a cake so mayhaps you can stay to enjoy it with us. Go on in and tell Maria to have James retrieve ye're spinning wheel...while I check for some eggs."

When Mary returned to the house, Joanne was busy spinning and chatting with Maria.

"The air is becoming a little cool outside already...'tis nice to come in and join you by the fire," Mary said. She carried a basket loaded with eggs and set it on the table.

"It appears the hens were very generous today, Miss Mary," Maria said. "Let me take that basket while you warm up. I know ye'd like to visit with Mrs. Custis."

"Thanks Maria. Is Mary Jane still asleep?"

"She is Miss Mary, and appears to be in a restful sleep. I'm sure she's over her earache."

"That's good. Would you like some tea, Joanne? And I believe we might have a few biscuits left," Mary asked her guest.

"Aye, tea would be fine, 'twill take the chill off, however, I didna care for any biscuits."

Maria said, "I'll bring ye're tea right away. Would you like a biscuit Miss Mary?"

"Nay, Maria...tea will be sufficient. I think I'll spin a little with Joanne while we catch up on the news...then I'll start the cake."

"Certainly, Miss Mary," Maria said as she left to prepare the tea.

Mary unknotted her thread and began to spin.

After a few silent moments of companionship enjoyed by good friends, Joanne said, "I didna know what you think Mary, but I'm heartsick over the execution of our good King Charles...'tis hard to understand what those men were thinking. How could they kill our King? I grow despondent every time I think about it. What will become of our home?"

As Nonconforminsts, Mary and Ambrose had differing views from the Custis family concerning the Civil War in England. Mary and Ambrose generally sided with Parliament's army.

Mary paused a moment to decide how to respond. She chose her words carefully. "I'm heartsick too Joanne. Ambrose and I do not condone such violence. Executing our King is unbelievable."

Joanne was not one to mince her words and plunged into the subject boldly, "I wondered how you felt...I'm aware of ye're

39

views though I didna truly understand them...at least 'tis good to know that ye're against his execution."

Mary smiled at the unusual energy and feeling in Joanne's tone. "We agree completely with you about the King, but let's not discuss our differences...that's men's business and usually results in unending quarrels."

"Ye're right about that," Joanne chortled. "John is always in one argument or another with someone about something."

In an attempt to change the subject, Mary asked, "Did you hear about Peter Walker's seven year-old servant being found dead behind his house?"

"Aye, John told me.....does anyone know how he died?"

"'Tis said he was found by the barn after that horrific storm. Some say the boy was running away and was struck by lightning. Others say Peter Walker found him and punished him. There's talk that he beat him to death. Ambrose said there will be a court inquiry as to how the child died. I know Peter Walker has a temper...still, do ye think he could have beat the boy to death?"

"I hope not.....but you never know.....'tis always hard to deal with an insolent servant.....yet...one so young.....I just didna know." Joanne stopped spinning a minute and stared off in the distance thoughtfully.

Her face took on a serious demeanor so Mary asked, "Is something troubling you, Joanne?"

"Aye, Mary, there is another reason I came to see you today. I didna know how to approach you about it knowing how you feel about the King's supporters. You know we had an Inn and Tavern in England where many of the King's Army stayed...and of course we still have many friends in England who are quite panicked since his execution. I received a packet this week from our good friend, Col. Norwood. He informed me that he and other close associates of ours will be traveling to Virginia soon on the *Virginia Merchant* and plan to settle here."

"How many people will be coming?"

"That's what concerns me...I understand 'tis close to 350 people. If it 'twas only a few, then we could make room for them, but...350...'tis impossible..."

"Three hundred and fifty people!" Mary stared at Joanne with a look of astonishment. She slowly responded as thoughts ran through her mind, "That's quite a lot...it will put demands on everyone to find lodging for them....especially this time of year...and we need to consider food as well....there won't be time for an additional planting since winter is approaching. Most people have some extra for new settlers, though...not for that many."

Joanne looked timidly at her friend, "I know 'tis quite a lot...and I wouldn't ask....knowing how you feel, but I just didna have a choice....I can not accommodate so many...and...and..since the King was executed...they fear for their lives..."

Mary realized that she had upset Joanne with her comments so she asked more gently, "When will they be arriving?"

Reassured by Mary's tone, Joanne replied with more confidence, "'Tis my understanding that it will be this month. They want to leave immediately."

"Then we should start planning now....with favorable trade winds....they could be here before Christmas. I'm glad you received a packet notifying us......'twill give us time to make arrangements."

"I agree. Ye've resided here longer than me, Mary......what should we do? I told my daughter Anne and her husband Argoll. Since he's Commander....I thought he'd make arrangements. Yet....well...I feel there's more needs to be done."

"I'm sure your son-in-law, Col Yeardley, is probably making plans for their housing, but he'll need everyone's help. We need to tell Rev. Rozier...mayhaps we can meet with others after church this Sunday."

"That sounds like a good plan Mary. I knew you'd know what to do."

CHAPTER FIVE

Fall, 1649 – Atlantic Ocean from Gravesend, England

George Willson leaned his arms on the ship's railing as he stared toward the distant mainland receding in the east and reflected on what he was leaving behind.

Ah, dear sweet Anne. Will I ever see ye again?...and my sisters... this is the best opportunity for me right now. Mayhaps one day I can return a success and Anne will agree to be my bride. I wonder if that will be enough to win her love or should I just give up. Will she ever have feelings for me?

Richard Johnson, standing beside George, took a draw on his pipe and asked, "Having second thoughts, George?"

"Not a one. I'm thankful to be leaving, what with all we've seen. I just never thought we'd leave this way."

George glanced back at a well-dressed man in a red doublet and tan breeches wearing a red-plumed hat. He was laughing with a beautiful young lady, who was perched on a crate, wearing a sky blue silk dress delicately brocaded in silver; the waist was long and sharply-pointed. The lady's face was hidden behind a brilliantly detailed fan she held in her hand and from time to time, she gave the man a flirty smile as they chatted.

"Not as nurse-maid for a bunch of Royalists," George continued harshly under his breath.

"Aye...'tis a strange predicament we've found ourselves in," Richard glanced up at the sea gulls diving toward the ocean. They squawked loudly making conversation difficult. "Thank God we met up with Major Morrison at the Mitre. We'd be hard pressed to find an easier transport to Virginia. If we hadn't served under him during the War...we'd probably still be searching for a way off the mainland."

"Ye're right about that...'twas a lucky break running into him. I hope everything is well with my sister, Mary. She'll be surprised since I didn't have time to send her a packet and let her know we're coming."

"How long has ye're sister lived in the Colonies?"

"Around eleven years now. She paints a good picture of Virginia in her letters...I hope she's not exaggerating...though I'm sure it won't be up to some of these dandies' standards," George whispered and gave a laugh. "I imagine they'll find keepin' up with the latest fashions a problem since all supplies have to be shipped from England. They didna have fashionable shops for fancy dresses in Virginia."

"They'll be in for a surprise, that's for certain, but at least they'll be alive...unlike our King."

"Aye, that is true enough. England's plagued with rascals willing to take a life right now. Why do you think they wanted to go to Virginia instead of the Leeward Islands, Barbados or Antigua? I've heard, many fortunes have been made there in the sugar trade...almost a sure thing. What do you suppose made them decide on Virginia?"

"I understand that Major Morrison had the King's commission to be captain of the fort and Col. Norwood is related to Sir William Berkeley, the governor of Virginia, so they just talked 350 family and friends into joining them in their adventure."

"Well, at least Captain Locker is a good enough sort...seems to be treating us fair. I hope we have an easy trip, compared to some I've heard of...I know Mary and her first husband had a terrible storm on their first voyage to the colonies."

Richard studied the puffy clouds dancing in the sky. A strong southwest wind blew hard against the sails of the *Virginia Merchant*. The ship was large, 300 tons with three masts. It had 30 plus guns, plenty of fire power to fight pirates if need be. It was one among a fleet of ten ships on it's way to the Colonies.

He commented, "Aye, well, everything seems agreeable for now....'tis all we can hope for, I guess." George turned his face hopefully towards the west, then glanced back at the receding English mainland. The land became a dim, uncertain line against the horizon, till it was swallowed up in the boundless ocean.

The next day, the *Virginia Merchant* experienced a severe gale that blew itself out after three days. However, it forced the ship off course. After twenty days sailing, the cooper notified the

Captain that the water cask was almost empty, so Captain Locker set sail for the nearest western Island of Fyall and thankfully arrived on October 14th.

The King of Portugal authorized the governor of Fyall to treat all ships that belonged and were faithful to the King of Great Britain with more than common courtesy. English merchants from the town came on board and invited the weary travelers to refresh themselves with fruit and all the island produced. Major Morrison, Col. Norwood and Major Fox were invited to dine at the home of a Mr. Andrews with Captain Tatum, who recently arrived from Brazil.

At Major Morrison's request, George and Richard escorted the men to the mainland. They were dismissed once they reached the town and took the opportunity to explore the island.

The town of Horta was approximately a half a mile from the shore and nestled in an amphitheater of hills, three hundred to seven hundred feet high in a semicircular bay. The well-fortified castle of Santa Cruz stood at the end of the town on the peak of the island. It had a wall of stonework that extended along the seashore.

"Would you look at those steep hills?....I imagine they would be hard to farm...yet...they appear to be covered with plants," remarked George as the two men walked toward the town.

In the market-place, rows of tables were laden with specimens of various vegetables and fruits, freshly picked from the gardens. Beautiful tropical flowers provided a fragrant scent to the air.

"I don't think I've ever seen so many oranges and peaches. We should be able to stock up on them for the rest of our trip. They'll be a nice break from that swill we've been eating," Richard commented.

Many churches and convents with their ornamental towers sat atop elevated spots and looked over the city and harbor. The narrow streets leading to the market-place and custom house were thronged with people and donkeys. The whole town had a festive appcarance, basking in the October sunlight. Richard pointed to a rowdy group of drunken seamen who were taunting the natives as the they drew near the center of Horta.

"Look at those men." he commented. "I imagine their Captain won't be too happy if they plan to set sail soon. Those men won't be in any condition to leave."

"I imagine, Captain Locker will be upset because I recognize them from our ship. I wonder how they arrived here so fast."

"Didn't Captain Locker order a few men out with the longboat immediately after we set anchor? He told them to acquire water to fill the cask since we were dangerously low. It looks like they didna waste any time arriving on land, but they didna seem to be seeking water."

"'Tis unlikely the cask will be filled any time today unless 'tis with ale."

"It appears so. Mayhaps we should see if we can access some water and return it to the ship. There are many women and children in dire need still on board."

"True. I hate to have them wait another night because the crew was derelict."

It took all evening, but George and Richard managed to collect water and return a filled keg to the ship. When they arrived, Captain Locker had returned from dinner and was happy to see George and Richard, especially since they had also managed to secure a small boat to carry the water.

"Thank God for ye're help men. My confounded drunken crew has caused the longboat to be staved to pieces!" Captain Locker shouted angrily. "I need to return to the island and find some boats to load our supplies! Thanks be to God that ye're here. The cask is completely dry."

"We'll be happy to assist ye, Sir," Richard replied.

"Good....it's late tonight. I'd appreciate it if ye'd return with me and my officers to the island tomorrow to find more boats and my missing men."

The next day, boats were obtained and supplies brought on board by the still drunken crew who continued to taste liberally of Horta's famous wine. By evening, the crew was ordered to remain in quarters. They presented no difficulty since most were still in a dead-drunk stupor. However, it did present a problem to the passengers invited on shore for dinner. Captain Tatum, from the neighboring ship in the harbor, came to their aid offering the use of his longboat to transport the passengers. Captain Locker ordered

46

his officers to assist the passengers in the borrowed longboat.

Col. Norwood and his traveling companions were invited to dine that evening on Captain Tatum's ship. Richard and George accompanied them again.

Col. Norwood was seated at the back of the boat with George and Richard. He was a ruddy, stalwart man in his late forties. His corpulent size and fashionable attire indicated that he'd had a life of ease and enough worldly goods to be accounted rich among his peers.

As the small boat glided over the water, Col. Norwood exclaimed in a loud hearty voice, "George, the Captain said that you and Richard have been most helpful retrieving our water and supplies. I want ye to join us as we dine with Captain Tatum tonight. You deserve it."

"Why, thank you, Captain Norwood. 'Twould be an honor.," George responded.

"Aye, Captain Norwood...a real honor," Richard said as he emphatically nodded his head. "But we didna do that much."

"That's not what I heard, men. The Captain was very insistent that there would have been no water last night without ye're help."

The boat arrived at Captain Tatum's ship and they were welcomed with a firing of guns. Col. Norwood and Major Morrison were seated next to Col. Tatum at a long dining table. Beside Col. Tatum sat a tall, willowy and beautiful young woman. She had very clear skin and large dark eyes. On each cheek was a touch of red. A young boy was on her other side.

"I wonder who she is?" Richard whispered to George as they seated themselves.

Col. Tatum stood and addressed the group. "We are most honored to have the Queen of the Island of Fyall and her son, the future King to share our meal with us tonight. Dear Queen, we welcome you to our humble repast."

After an interpreter told the young lady what was said, she nodded toward Col. Tatum and he sat back down. Several toasts were made to King Charles and the boy King of Fyall. Once the meal was finished, another rich wine from Brazil was served and more toasts were made. The Queen wished the party a happy voyage and they departed for the *Virginia Merchant*.

Upon their arrival, Captain Locker discovered that his crew was again missing and had continued their debauchery onshore so he ordered his officers to immediately retrieve the seaman. Once all were on board, Captain Locker made plans to stock and depart the Island of Fyall as soon as possible before he lost complete control of his crew.

The ship was provided with black pigs, peaches and fruit, and a considerable portion of beer. The *Virginia Merchant* set sail on the 22nd of October, but soon found themselves in the midst of another vicious storm.

CHAPTER SIX

November 1649 Eastern Shore, Virginia

The citizens of the Eastern Shore were ready for the Royalists. However, they began to worry when the ship had not arrived by November. Other ships reported terrible storms crossing the Atlantic and a violent snowstorm occurred early in the month. Even 'hog killing' days, which normally took place in the fall, were put off until fairer weather. The citizens of Accawmacke were forced to remain indoors.

After many snowy and cloudy days, the sun finally came out, but a stiff wind continued to sway and bend the trees across the land. Growing impatient, Ambrose decided to take advantage of the sunny day to build a few more trestle legs for makeshift tables that would be needed by Mary and the other women to prepare the freshly killed and cooked hogs on hog-killing day. Ambrose and Henry, Jr. spent the morning building the supports. It was grueling work in the brisk breeze that penetrated their layers of clothing.

The fierce wind whistled eerily around the corner of the cozy cottage while Mary and Maria busied themselves rubbing salt in trout for pickled fish. Mary picked up a stack of salted fish and carried it to the barrel full of brine. Her hands were red and raw so she rubbed butter on them while she glanced out the small window at her son and husband working together.

I know, he's working hard because I crave some fresh cracklings. He's afraid this child I'm carrying will be marked if I don't fulfill my craving soon. Ambrose is such a good husband.

She glanced at her bulging tummy.

I wonder if ye'll be a boy this time. I'm sure Ambrose will be happy with either a lad or lassie....he just wants more children.

Mary heard laughter outside. She caught a glimpse of Ambrose's felt beaver flying off his head from a strong gust. Henry, Jr. set out after it while Ambrose laughed and trudged close behind. Their footsteps made loud crunching sounds as they crossed the hard-packed snow. Finally, Henry, Jr. caught up with the beaver. He tramped back and handed it to Ambrose. Instead of placing it back on his head, Ambrose shook the snow off and laughed. They slowly walked toward the house.

"I 'spect Ambrose and Henry, Jr. would like a nice cup of hot tea, Maria. It looks like they're coming this way," Mary commented.

"I imagine it's a bit cold out there with all that wind," Maria added.

"Aye, I think they're probably frustrated too, with this bad weather. Ambrose wanted to kill the hogs before December. Do we have any of that apple pastry left? I'll serve them some soup. I'm sure they'll be plenty hungry."

"There's a little left and we have lots of bread and cheese to go with it. We made a considerable amount since we were expecting all those Royalists."

"Aye, we'll be eating bread, cheese and corn for a while if they don't arrive soon. Still, 'tis better we prepared for them. I'd hate to have another winter with dwindling food supplies like we did when the Dutch arrived a few years ago."

"True. That time worried me some too. I was afraid our food would be gone before spring, but thanks to Big Tom and the Assateagues suppling us with that additional corn, we were able to manage."

A cold blast chilled the room when Ambrose and Henry, Jr. opened the door.

"Something smells awfully good in here. We've worked up powerful appetites, haven't we Henry?"

"'Tis about time ya' both came in. I was afraid ye'd freeze out there with that wind howling around something fierce."

"Papa said if we kept working hard...we wouldn't freeze," Henry, Jr. responded. "'Tis still awfully cold though."

"But wasn't I right about working hard? We didn't freeze, did we son?" Ambrose chuckled.

"Nay, Papa...ye're right."

Well, the two of you get washed up, I'll have some hot soup waiting for you." Mary ladled the soup into two bowls and filled two pewter mugs with hot tea.

When Ambrose and Henry returned, Ambrose gave Mary a peck on the cheek before sitting on the bench beside Henry, Jr. who was almost finished with his bowl of soup.

Ambrose smiled at Henry, Jr., "Ya' seem to have worked up an appetite young man. Ye'd better slow down or ye're belly will be burst with that hot soup."

"'Ah, Papa....ye're joshing. My stomach won't burst and Mum said this is the best way to get warm," Henry, Jr. grinned as he halted a moment to tear off a piece of warm bread.

"Are you two going to join us?" Ambrose asked Mary and Maria. "Ye've been working hard all morning too."

"Aye, but we've been in the warm house," Maria replied.

"We need to finish this salting first," Mary added.

"Well, it looks like you two have certainly prepared enough food for the winter...I didna believe we'll go hungry."

"We shouldn't...but we did make a bit extra for that ship of Royalists we were expecting. Have ye heard anymore about the ship, Ambrose?"

"Nay, Mary. It should've been here by now...it must have been lost at sea or we'd have heard something."

"I know Joanne is upset. She had a number of close friends traveling on it. I should go see about her when this weather improves. I believe I need a break from all this food preparation."

"Aye, you may not want to come back from Joanne's since I plan to kill those hogs as soon as we have fair weather. 'Hog-killing' day is a mighty hard one to endure."

"Ye're right about that, Ambrose. If we didna have Maria here to help me as well as our good neighbors, I might think about staying at Joanne's," Mary smiled.

"That reminds me, Maria." Ambrose took another bite of soup and continued, "Ye're indenture contract will be complete next month. Have ye thought of what ye plan to do?"

"I know what she plans to do. She plans to wed...haven't ye noticed Col. William Coulbourne visiting us a lot lately," Mary teased.

Maria's face flushed as she stammered, "Miss Mary, why...why...how did ye know?"

Ambrose laughed heartily at Maria's embarrassment. He tried to speak between chortles, "Ye're right, Mary. I wondered why the Old Colonel went so far out of his way to visit us...now it makes complete sense."

Henry, Jr. was listening closely to the conversation. Suddenly, he exclaimed loudly, "Maria, ye can't leave us...ye're family!"

"Shush, Henry....ye'll wake Mary Jane...ye're right son, Maria is like our family and will always be welcome in our home, but ye must remember...she'd like her own family. Maria's time with us was always temporary." Mary looked at Maria and declared, "I do hate to see ya' leave. How will I ever manage without you? We've been through so much together." Mary's voice broke and she hugged Maria's neck.

Tears filled Maria's eyes. "Miss Mary, I'm not leaving right now....I'll stay at least till the wee one's born. William has to build us a home....I have no place to go just yet. He's been so busy traveling back and forth between the Colonies and England that he's had little time to build us a fit house. I told him I'd not be content in that little shed he calls a home."

"Then that will be our gift to you, Maria!" Ambrose said with excitement. "I've been in a quandary of what to give ye after ya' left. As Mary and Henry said, "Ye're family."

Maria dropped the fish she had been salting and stared at Ambrose in astonishment, "Why Mr. Dixon....that's too much. Ye're too generous."

"Nonsense, I build houses for everyone else....I can build one for you too. I'll talk to Col. Coulbourne as soon as this weather clears. Mayhaps I can start on it by spring if ye didna mind staying with us a while till it's built."

"As I said, I wouldn't leave Miss Mary this close to the new bairn's birth...spring will be a wonderful time to wed."

"Then I guess, we need to start planning ye're spring wedding then," Mary laughed.

"Ah, Mr. Dixon and Miss Mary, "Ye're too good to me," Maria cried. "A spring wedding...I never dreamed I'd be happy again after the loss of my family in London...but it seems I've found happiness with all of you and now with Col. Coulbourne. God has truly blessed me."

CHAPTER SEVEN

November 8, 1649 Atlantic Ocean

Food supplies were again dangerously low on the *Virginia Merchant* and wearied passengers were becoming increasingly impatient to land. In the interest of saving time, Captain Locker decided to utilize ocean currents and risk sailing the *Virginia Merchant* near Cape Hatteras, along the eastern seaboard, always a treacherous part of the shoreline. The shoals and turbulent water created danger, but Captain Locker became even more worried when the ship sailed into a blanket of dense fog. He was discussing the situation with Major Morrison before dawn broke when suddenly a seaman cried out, "All hands aloft! Reefs all around! We'll be breached. All hands aloft!"

The alarmed seamen arrived on deck quickly, but when they saw the cause of the alert, immediately fell to their knees and commended their souls to God. Captain Locker was so astonished that he was unable to voice a command. One seaman took heart and shouted, "Is there no good fellow that will stand to the helm, and loose a sail?"

Thomas Reasin and John Smith took action. Thomas frantically loosened the fore-topsail to put the ship in steerage way, while John stood to the helm and shifted it in just in time to avoid dashing the starboard on a ledge.

"Good work, men," Captain Locker shouted. But the escape was for only a moment; another jutting rock was about to befall the ship on the larboard bow. Captain Locker regained his composure and took charge of his crew now energized by the initial success. They set about to assist in the second attempt and were again rewarded by avoiding danger.

At first light, the fog lifted; the suns rays flooded the deck and revealed a dismal picture. The ship was deep in the shoals without a clear channel in the water to avoid the sandbar. The men continued to work diligently, but the ship soon struck ground.

Seaman Tom Reason shouted, "She's still afloat Captain...we

just need deep water."

"Get the chains men!" shouted the Captain. "Find that water!" "Aye, sir," a crewman replied.

Tom Reasin noticed the ship advance a little toward a distant channel.

"She's moving Captain!" shouted Mate Putts.

"Aye...heave the lead again, Tom. We'll get out of this yet."

Tom heaved the lead and the ship advanced a little further toward the channel. Finally, the *Virginia Merchant* drew a good deal of water and after the next cast they were in the channel. By mid-morning they had cleared the shoals of Cape Hatteras. The ship was on her way out to sea and safely away from the dangerous shoreline.

Col. Norwood had been watching the crew work and walked over to congratulate the Captain.

"That was a right good piece of work ye're men did there, Captain. I thought we were done for when I saw those reefs."

"Aye, I had the same feeling. The men made up for all that trouble they caused at Horta."

"I'll drink to that," Col. Norwood laughed.

Captain Locker stared off toward the horizon. "Still, I didna like what I see in the northwest there...hope we're not in for another gale."

Col. Norwood looked in the direction the Captain pointed. "Mayhaps it will blow over. We can always hope."

"I've found hope is often in short supply when ye're on the Atlantic during these storms," Captain Locker said grimly as he pulled out his pipe and tapped it on the railing. "We're so close to land now too...'tis mighty discouraging."

By mid-afternoon the gale was upon them and separated the ship from land at the rate of eight leagues a watch. The Captain ordered the ship about and the sails furled, but the towering waves were so high and the sea so unruly that they were not successful in turning the ship about.

Blinding flashes of lightning continually forked the sky and peal after peal of thunder crashed over the ship while torrential rain fell.

The passengers below deck prayed and screamed with each new wave that pounded against the ship. Finally, by late afternoon, the winds began to die down and the sea gradually calmed, but a stiff breeze continued to blow from the west sending the ship further out to sea.

George and Richard climbed the ladder to the deck. They joined the captain as he ordered the men to unfurl the sails and raise the mainyard.

"Did that gale push us very far from shore, Captain?" asked George.

"Aye, men...I'm afraid so...and 'tis not over yet. If we didna get around it, we'll be pushed even further...Nay, Nay, man...hold that sheet, put ye're back into it," the Captain shouted as he ran over to help a seaman struggling with a sail.

George studied the threatening skies and the sea foaming with rage, "I believe the Captain is right. I didna think this gale is over...will we ever reach land?"

Col. Norwood accompanied George and Richard on the deck. "'Tis it over men?"

"The Captain said he doubted it," Richard responded.

"The women on this ship are really angry at me. Many haven't been above deck in days because of this weather. They started packing when we reached Cape Hatteras believing we'd be on land soon and now it appears that it may be a lot longer than a few days. I didna know what I'm to tell them. They had not planned on such troubles," Col. Norwood complained.

At that instant, a loud snap from above interrupted their conversation. They glanced up just in time to see the foremast head under the cap break off and fly away from the ship. The whole foremast was threatening to break.

"If this wind gets any worse, we may have more to worry about than just when we will land...mayhaps we'll be worried about our lives," George retorted.

"True....true. I guess I need to be thankful that we're not suffered more."

The gale picked up again late that evening. Once during the night, the sea broke so strongly over the deck where a seaman was walking that when he returned, he was up to his knees in water, reciting short prayers. He thought the ship was foundering and at its last gasp.

All passengers remained below deck during the storm. They lay on their platforms, trying to remain calm, but children cried and could not be consoled. No one was able to sleep. Suddenly the ship stood still, with her head under water as she seemed to bore her way into the sea. A loud craaacck was heard.

"My God....what is happening!" shouted a woman

"The Lord be with us!" a man shouted.

"All hands aloft!" declared the Captain.

Water began to pour into the hold through a gap in the hull. Men jumped from their platforms and pulled the attached platforms to cover the gap.

Col. Norwood rushed on deck to ascertain the cause of the break in the ship. When he returned, the hole was sealed. Col Norwood sat down hard on a remaining platform.

"What is it Norwood? What has happened?" asked Major Morrison.

"We no longer have a ship...'tis just a hull. The forecastle is gone, bowsprit gone, mainmast gone...all that is left is the mizzenmast."

"God help us!" screamed a woman. "We should never have made this trip!" she glared angrily at her husband.

"We'd have died at home....what choice did we have?" he growled.

"All is not lost.....the Captain assured me he could bring the ship about with the mizzenmast," Col Norwood stated.

The gale continued for two more days. At it's worse, several seamen were washed overboard with no attempt for rescue since every man expected the same fate.

After the storm ended, excitement flew throughout the ship briefly when the crew spied an English merchant ship. Captain Locker ordered the crew to fire off the salute cannon to signal their distress, but the other ship for some reason would not return the communication and soon disappeared from sight.

Captain Locker's thoughts turned to feeding the passengers and crew. His men had been without rest or food for most of the days they fought the storm. Many of the passengers did not have an appetite due to all the fright they had experienced, but the Captain knew it was important to try to establish some semblance of normalcy.

The bread supply and cook room were soaked with sea water. Two cooks had been swept off the ship. Meat could not be dressed without the cook room and all the cookery was damaged beyond repair. There was no way to start a fire for hot food which everyone needed.

George approached the Captain with a suggestion.

"Sir, mayhaps we could saw a cask in the middle and fill it with ballast. That might make a rough fire pit."

"Aye, good idea. I'll have one of my crew help ye."

"Nay, they've had enough work these past few days. Richard will help me."

"Thanks, George. I'm sure everyone will appreciate some hot victuals, even if is just peas and salt beef."

George and Richard made the makeshift firepit and it worked fairly well, but sometimes the rolling of the ship created problems, sending the cask topsy-turvy. A meal of parched peas and broiled salt beef rejuvenated the passengers and crew, and a calm sea lifted their spirits.

A week later, on November 15th, the Captain evaluated the condition of the ship. Despite losing so many parts, the foremast still stood but was without a sail and was of no use. Without rigging it was almost impossible to climb the greasy pole. However, Tom Reasin decided to attempt it.

"Tom, if ye can attach a sail to that foremast, I'll give ye 10 pounds of tobacco when we reach Virginia," shouted a planter.

"Aye, Tom, I didna have a plantation yet, but I'll pledge 20 pounds when I have me first crop," Col. Norwood exclaimed.

Major Morrison and Richard Fox, not to be outdone by their friend and companion Col. Norwood, pledged 20 pounds each. Others joined in and Tom stood to be a very rich man indeed if he succeeded.

Tom found some iron spikes in the ship's stores and drove one into the mast as high as he could reach. Then he took a ten foot rope and threaded it in a pulley which divided it in the middle and knotted the ends at the spike. This made a stirrup for him to stand on as he drove another spike up the mast. In a few hours, with the help of others in the crew, he had a sail attached so the ship could head for port. When Tom came down the mast, everyone cheered.

Tom looked at the men on deck and exclaimed, "Well Captain. It appears I'll be leaving ye soon. With all the tobacco pledged...it seems I'll be able to start a new life as a planter."

"It appears so, Tom," the Captain laughed. "But I'll certainly not be happy with losing such a good man. Ye've come to our rescue more than once this trip."

"That's exactly why we'll need him with us in Virginia," exclaimed Norwood.

"Aye," to that Norwood," retorted Major Morrison.

Tom grinned and shook hands with Col. Norwood.

All the *Virgina Merchant* needed now was a favorable wind and it would be none too soon as all that remained of their food was a biscuit cake a day for each person.

CHAPTER EIGHT

December, 1649 – Atlantic Ocean

After Tom raised the sail on the foremast, the passengers on the *Virginia Merchant* had high hopes that they would soon be sleeping on warm beds with their friends in Virginia but it was not to be. Days went by as they drifted just offshore. A biscuit cake a day became half a biscuit a day. Only Malaga sack was left to quench their thirst which inflamed rather than extinguished it.

Each night the gale blew and carried the ship further away from land. In a week's time, the ship drifted at least two hundred leagues away from shore. Around the 19th day the wind shifted to the east only to change to the west later that evening. The bilge pumps failed and the crew was forced to bail water with buckets. The tackle holding the guns was rotting creating the fear of one falling and pulling the ship over since the guns carried considerable weight.

Col. Norwood and the Captain evaluated the situation with the guns when Mate Putts, walked up to them to offer a suggestion.

"Suppose we place timber in the hatchway. That way the weight will be more in the center of the ship."

"That just might work, Putts," the Captain responded. "And it sure couldn't hurt. It'll give the crew something to do as well....and provide some relief from worrying."

The Captain ordered the timber moved and the ship had more ballast where it was needed which solved the problem. However, the lack of provisions could not be overcome. Woman and children were crying for food. Rats became commodities. A well-grown rat sold for sixteen shillings. Death visited the ship each night with burials at sea the next morning. Sometimes passengers missed the make-shift funerals, especially if there was more than one a day.

George and Richard stood on the deck staring at the unforgiving ocean.

"Did ye hear about that nice Mrs. Grayson?...the lady that

invited us to share meals with her family when we first boarded?" George asked Richard.

"Aye, I know she's having quite a problem since she was great with child. What about her?"

"She tried to buy a rat yesterday from Darby for twenty shillings and he refused her. She died last night."

"Ach, how sad. I really liked her. If we didna reach land soon....I'm afraid we'll all follow her in death."

"So much water around us, and none fit for drinking. Sometimes, I wish we'd have another gale. At least we were able to drink the rainwater...now we have nothing but wind."

The ship's navigation instruments were destroyed in the last gale, so the Captain and crew had only the North Star to rely on and due to the changing winds during the night they were often unable to determine exactly where they were. They decided to attempt to sail for the first American land they could spy. The desperation continued with each passing day.

Christmas was fast approaching and the Captain wanted to lift everyone's spirits. He ordered all the meal tubs scraped and the women made a pudding from the scrapings. They added Malaga sack, sea water with fruit and spice, all well fried in oil. Col. Norwood, Major Richard Fox, and Major Morrison as well as a few others enjoyed this small Christmas repast.

Finally, the westerly wind began to blow the ship closer to shore and on the evening of January 3rd, the water changed color. News spread fast throughout the ship and when morning arrived, all the passengers and crew stood on deck searching for land.

"I wonder where we are?" George asked Richard as they tried to catch a glimpse of the glorious land in the distance.

"Doesn't matter to me....long as we reach it. We've been tempted too many times."

"I'm going to kiss that ground if'en we reach it," a wizened old man said who was standing beside him."

Three or four hours later the ship drew within six or seven miles of the shore. Everyone urged the Captain to drop anchor, but he hesitated.

"We have only one anchor left...if I drop it too quickly...we could have a sudden storm and lose it and it's too short a cable to anchor us in the ocean...not strong enough," Captain Locker said to

Col. Norwood.

"Ye're right, of course, but to take the chance of drifting back out to sea with a shift in the wind tonight....I can't say it doesn't worry me some...I didna think we will survive much longer without food or water," Col. Norwood replied.

"Just a while longer and we'll be a little closer...safe enough to drop the anchor," Captain Locker declared.

Around two o'clock that afternoon, the Captain ordered the anchor dropped. He directed Mate Putts to go on shore to discover what they might expect, most importantly if there was food and water available. Major Morrison and twelve sickly passengers accompanied him. Putts returned alone three hours later.

"Tis nothing but good news I bring," he shouted as he climbed on the boat. "There's a creek large enough to harbor the ship, fresh water and considerable fowl."

"Where are the others?" Captain Locker asked.

"Waiting for everyone to join them on shore. Major Morrison said that the whole ship will probably want to follow him so he was leaving space in the boat."

Everyone on the ship was ecstatic. It seemed their prayers had been answered at last.

Captain Locker was still skeptical. "You say the creek is large and deep enough for this ship? This I must see for myself before I risk this ship. Who wants to join me?"

Col. Norwood, Major Fox, George Willson, Richard Johnson as well as some others joined him in the wherry.

"My greatest desire is to drink my fill of fresh water," George declared.

Col. Norwood said, "That's all I've dreamed about for the last three weeks. I have visions of cellars and taps running down my throat."

"Aye, well, I wouldn't mind the taste of roasted fowl, as well," Richard added. "I'm so starved....my stomach has given up growling."

Dusk was setting on the land when the wherry neared the shore so the passengers were thankful for the fires set by Major Morrison and their friends welcoming them to the land.

As soon as the group set foot on land, Major Morrison led them to the running stream of water and everyone drank their fill.

Major Morrison, Captain Locker, Richard Willson, Richard Johnson and Col. Norwood crossed the creek in the wherry with two crew members so the Captain could ascertain its suitability as a harbor. Some wild fowl were startled by the men's approach and Captain Locker killed a duck. He gave it to a member of his crew to roast while they continued to search the shore.

They discovered an oyster bank and added a few oysters to the duck repast. After giving thanks for their good fortune, the men sat around the fire and feasted on the duck and oysters.

"What do you think of the creek, Captain? Is it deep enough for you?" George asked.

"'Twill do. I wish it was somewhat deeper, but 'twill do. I'll return to the ship and wait for light to sail for the harbor. Does anyone want to return with me?"

"Nay," they all replied.

Col. Norwood laughed. "I didna think any of us savors being on a ship again after this experience."

Major Morrison chuckled, "I'll say Amen to that."

"Aye, well...I'll rest a spell and return at first light with some victuals for the ship. Then we'll head for the creek," the Captain said.

The winds picked up at nightfall and everyone awakened stiff and cold as the fire had nearly died during the night. The Captain was gone and all on shore assumed the ship would soon head toward the harbor at the creek.

George looked out to sea toward the ship and was astonished to see it at sea under sail heading for the Capes rather than the creek.

"Captain Norwood, do you remember what Captain Locker said last night? Isn't the ship sailing away from us?" George pointed toward the ocean.

"What is the meaning of this?" Col. Norwood exclaimed. "Are they leaving us here?"

"Surely not....the Captain said he would head for the creek harbor last night, I'm certain of it." Major Morrison declared.

"The ship's out to sea...what are we to do now?" George shouted above the wind as he voiced the others thoughts. "How could they abandon us like that...in this strange country....with no provisions. We don't even know where we are!"

CHAPTER NINE

January 2nd, 1650 Accawmacke

"I think we woke the dead yesterday with all the screeching of Littleton's hogs, Ambrose," Stephen Horsey declared.

"Ye're right about that...Argoll said their noise could be heard clear to Hungars," Ambrose laughed.

The two men and three of Ambrose's servants were building a large tripod used to lift the hogs into the huge kettle for 'hog-killing' day.

"At least, Mary's craving for cracklings was satisfied. I was feared that our bairn might be marked before I could kill my own hogs."

"Aye, 'tis good we had a break from the snow," Horsey said as he sat down on a stump to catch his breath.

Ambrose looked at his friend and laughed, "Too much work for ya', Horsey? Didna tell me you need to stop already?"

"I was just 'bout worked to death, yesterday....I deserve a break," Stephen retorted with a big grin on his face. "I imagine you could use one yeself. How many hogs did Littleton cook? I lost count."

"Five.....Littleton wanted some extra meat in case the *Virginia Merchant* arrived."

"Ah...I wonder what happened to that ship. John Custis told me last week that it left around September or October at the latest."

"That's what I heard...mayhaps they stayed in the Isles for awhile. Several ships reported storms on the ocean. The Captain may have wanted to wait out the storms."

"Tis possible, I guess. John Custis was at Hungars almost everyday last week seeking word on the ship...but to no avail."

"Ye were at Hungars last week?"

"Aye, I had to be a juror on James Hughes trial."

"What was the decision?"

"It was an accident. James didn't know the gun was loaded

when he picked it up at Charlton's. It discharged accidentally and killed little Elizabeth Pope. We found him guilty of manslaughter."

"I always thought well of James. I couldn't believe it when he was accused of murdering that poor child."

"I heard another bit of news while I was at court ye might be interested in."

"What's that?" Ambrose walked over to the fence and leaned against the post.

"Seems our Commissioners are not happy with the Commonwealth Government in England. They issued a proclamation last week."

"What did it say?"

"Basically, it said that Charles II was King of England not the Commonwealth and they pledge their allegiance to him."

"Ye didna meant it!" Ambrose exclaimed.

"Aye, 'twas a shock to me too. I couldn't believe they'd actually go as far to issue a proclamation."

"Who signed it?"

"They all did!"

"Well 'tis sure to open a can of worms...I wonder how it will affect us?"

"I wonder too, Ambrose, but you know all the Commissioners have leanings for the Royalists. I imagine thats why the *Virginia Merchant's* coming to Accawamacke."

"Ye're probably right. Well, it appears I'm not going to get much more work out of ya'...mayhaps some victuals will give you energy. Let's see what Mary can scratch up for ye."

"I wouldn't mind a little of her custard pie," Horsey grinned as he stood up.

"Sounds like ye're in need a wife."

"As a matter of fact...I've been thinking the same. I hope to marry a widow like you did...seems to have turned out pretty well for ya'." Horsey laughed.

"I'll agree with that. But I doubt ye'd ever find as good a wife as me Mary. Have someone particular in mind?"

"I've asked Sarah Williams to be me bride."

"Michael Williams widow? One that lives across the creek from ya'?"

"Aye, the very one."

"She has three young'uns."

"Two sons and a daughter. I'll have a ready made family."

"You picked a handsome woman, Horsey...I'll have to say that. But has she agreed?"

"Aye, we're to be married in a couple of months."

"'Tis great news! There'll be quite a few weddings this spring. Our Maria plans to marry Coulbourne in May."

"The old Colonel?"

"Turns out he's not so old...just looks that way," Ambrose chuckled. "At least that's what Maria told Mary."

As the men approached the house, Mary opened the door and greeted Stephen, "Nice to see you again so soon, Stephen!"

"Ye're good cooking draws me, Mary.....like water to a man dying of thirst."

"How nice of you to say....come on in...I'm sure I can find something tasty for ye're appetite."

CHAPTER TEN

January 6, 1650 Virginia

The small group of people, numbering twenty, left behind by the *Virginia Merchant*, elected Col. Norwood as their leader. He immediately sent his cousin Francis Cary to investigate the land while the rest of the party discussed what to do.

"We'll need shelter and a good source of food, immediately" Major Morrison said. "We know there is water from the creek. Mayhaps we should build our shelter there."

"But we might not see the ship when it returns if we are too far inland," George commented.

"That's true," Col. Norwood replied.

The men were still sitting around the fire discussing their options and making plans when Cary came rushing back. As he approached, all manner of ducks and fowl suddenly took flight, squawking loudly, and nearly drowned out his voice.

"There's a a small creek, only a short distance from here, with a number of oysters such as these," Francis exclaimed as he dropped the oysters he was carrying on the sand. "The tide has exposed a whole bank of them...there for the taking. We have fresh water and food only a short walk from here."

"Did ye see any Indians?" asked Norwood.

"Nay, nary a one. It appears that we're on an island."

"That's not good. We may not have much game," said George. Could ya' see how far away we are from the mainland?"

"'Tis too far and deep to wade, but some may swim."

"Mayhaps we will not starve at least. Oysters and fowl should feed us for a time...at least until the ship returns," George commented. "Surely, they cannot leave us here forever."

"I agree. I didna believe they have entirely forsaken us. Not after Captain Locker said he would return. I always considered him an honorable man," Norwood added. "We must simply survive until then."

"I hope ye're trust is warranted, Norwood," Major Morrison

declared. He picked up a couple of sticks from the brush and threw them on the fire, sending sparks flying into the sky.

"We should shoot some of the fowl at once. We may not have a chance later." Richard pointed inland at dark clouds. "It appears a storm will overtake us soon."

"We need to set about preparing shelter now," Major Morrison said. "No telling how bad that storm will be. I'll stay here with some of the men and work on that...Richard, you and George are good shots. I say ye take the fowling guns and shoot some birds...though from the number here...it shouldn't even take a good eye to bring them down."

"We could probably bring them down with a few good stones," Cary Francis declared as he chased a couple of gulls who seemed intent on investigating his truck.

Col. Norwood smiled and said, "We should be thankful for them...at least we'll not starve with the oysters and numerous fowl, we'll have food until the ship returns. We have our plan...let's implement it before the weather comes in and hope our ship returns tomorrow."

"Amen to that," said a gaunt old man.

"Shouldn't we ask for God's help, Col. Norwood," George commented.

"Of course, George.....thanks for reminding me. Everyone gather round and we'll pray for His guidance and blessing."

Richard and George returned with a number of fowl and everyone went about the task of removing feathers and preparing the meat. Two rough, makeshift huts had been built in their absence, one for the women and children and another for the men. Col. Norwood returned with with his arms full of fallen branches and dropped them on the sand by the fire. He rubbed his ears, trying to warm them.

"Seems we're in for a cold night," he commented.

"Aye," Morrison responded as he added another log to the fire. I hope we'll not have a fierce storm as well. 'Twill make it hard to tend the fire."

Soft snowflakes began to fall on the the small party while they sat around the roaring fire, eating cooked oysters and quietly discussing their situation. Several ducks, skewered with sharp sticks roasted over the fire. Three women watched the ducks closely and moved them whenever there was danger of flaming up or dropping their succulent repast into the fire. Drops of fat from the birds dripped and made sizzling noises as they fell.

George swallowed an oyster whole and stared at the fire. He watched the little tongues of flame wrap themselves round a log then gradually the whole log was lit creating a glowing light in the dark night. He thought about his visits with the Quakers before leaving England. It seemed so long ago and so far removed from their situation now.

What did they say about light? Each man has an Inner Light where God speaks to him and we need only listen to God through our Inner Light. Mayhaps, this Inner Light is like these flames. If we only seek God in our Inner Light...we will be filled with His Light and saved from the darkness that besets us now.

Before they completed their meal, the snow flakes changed to a snow storm and a fierce wind with hail and snow soon raged over the campsite. Many rushed to the respective huts for shelter. Richard and George remained with Col. Norwood and Major Morrison to maintain the fire with the brush and short pine trees on the island.

"I wish we had a windbreak of some kind. I fear this strong wind will blow out the fire," Richard commented.

Col. Norwood stood and began to remove his great coat as he said, "Here men...see what you can do with my coat."

Being quite corpulent in size, his coat was extremely large.

Major Morrison took the coat from him and remarked, "This may work. George, you and Richard see if you can find some sturdy posts to support it."

The coat was soon staked with pine sticks and blocked the wintry blast, but the wind proved too strong and it frequently blew down.

After chasing the coat and staking it again several times, Major Morrison exclaimed, "I fear the coat will be blown away so let's leave it down, at least until this wind dies some."

The snow storm continued all night, making sleep difficult.

The following day, everyone woke stiff and extremely cold. Four inches of cold, wet, snow covered the ground. Cary left to collect fresh water from the creek and investigate the oyster bed. He returned a few minutes later.

"The bed is completely submerged by the tide. This is all I could dig up on the bank," Cary said as he dropped twelve oysters from his cold, stiff fingers onto the sand.

"At least we have some of the fowl we killed yesterday left. We'll manage today," Col. Norwood said. "Mayhaps the tide will subside or the ship will return."

Major Morrison ordered, "Everyone must gather firewood. We need to keep this fire going strong so we won't freeze."

A strong gusty wind blew the remainder of the day. Snow and hail fell at times during the day forcing the people to stay in the tiny huts when the pounding of the hail became too hard. The men took shifts attending the fire. The storm remained throughout the night and the following day.

On the third day, Richard and George hunted for game to replenish their meat but found little. They returned, nearly frozen, with barely enough to make a meal for the group. George and Richard stood by the fire chatting and trying to warm themselves while the women prepared the sparse meal.

"I wonder what happened to all the fowl. This island was teaming with birds when we arrived," Richard commented.

"Mayhaps the storm made them seek shelter on the mainland. I wish we could fly there as well. If this weather doesn't let up soon. I'm afraid we're doomed."

Richard gazed at the cloudy sky. "It doesn't look like the snow will leave today...so I guess we're faced with another rough night."

Days went by and the cold and snow soon became unbearable. Everyone wrapped themselves with all their clothing, but could not get warm in the freezing temperatures. The pine burned hot and smoked extensively making it hard to remain close to the fire for any length of time.

"I didna know if we'll last 'til the ship returns if this storm keeps up," Richard declared as he huddled close to the fire. For the past two days, Richard and George had been giving half of their portion of food to the two young boys in their party. George had a

70

sturdy build and seemed to manage with the decreased rations, but Richard was very lean and now his already gaunt frame was a bag of bones.

"You won't survive if you keep sharing ye're food," George said with a voice filled with anguish as he studied his friend.

"Those boys didna have much of a chance...starved as they are, George. They remind me of my two brothers back in England."

"Still, you'll not live long on reduced portions. I wish I knew why the ship left," George shouted.

"Hopefully, we'll live long enough to ask them that very question," Col. Norwood commented as he walked over and threw a few logs in the fire. "Major Morrison is having particular difficulty today. I'm worried about him."

"What seems to be his problem?"

"He's very weak....has difficulty standing. I've never seen him quite so affected."

"These conditions will test the best of us," George said. "I'm amazed Mrs. Brown and her two children are still alive."

"I agree. We need a break from this weather."

Ten days went by, and the food situation became even more dire. The continuous winds plus the gun-fire from their hunting, drove all the fowl further inland. An old women died during the night and no one had the energy to attempt a burial in the frigid cold. They simply placed her body some distance from their camp. The men assembled around the fire and considered their grave situation.

"You know we'll all soon follow her in death if we don't have a source of food soon," Major Morrison said.

"I'd welcome death at this point...a quick death...rather than this slow one from starvation," mumbled an emaciated man lying close to the fire.

"I didna know which death would be better...one from starvation or freezing. I wish this blasted storm would abate," a man complained. He sat cross-legged by the fire with his cloak wrapped tightly around him. "I didna think I've ever been so cold."

"The ship should have been here by now. They knew we didna have provisions," remarked Major Morrison.

"Aye, I fear we are on our own," Col. Norwood acknowledged.

"Then we'll surely all die because there is nothing left on this island for game," George bitterly expressed. He picked up a stick and angrily threw it into the fire sending sparks flying high into the sky.

"Not unless God provides a miracle," Richard uttered in a weak voice.

Col. Norwood suddenly stood and walked toward the ocean. He stared at the roaring waves for a time then returned to the fire and declared, "Men, you have elected me to lead and I believe God has provided a miracle."

"What do ye mean?" inquired Major Morrison.

"Why with this woman's death...God has provided for us. We have no alternative but to convert her corpse to food."

"Nay, nay...I'd rather starve!" George exclaimed

"I as well," shouted another man.

"How can you say such a thing?" an old man bellowed. "We are not animals, Sir."

"That does seem rather barbarian, Norwood," Major Morrison affirmed.

"I do not make this choice lightly, Morrison," Col. Norwood said in a voice full of anguish. I know how it appears, but I was elected leader and as such I must make this arduous decision for our survival. I see no other way for us to live through this ordeal."

"But to be reduced to dining on a corpse? How can you believe God wills this?" George screamed in the whistling wind.

"I believe God has provided for us....but suit yeself...I will not force my solution." Col. Norwood collapsed on the sand, spent by the emotion he felt.

Richard pushed himself to a sitting position and whispered, "Col. Norwood is right. 'Tis a miracle from God. We must accept what God has provided."

"But...but...'tis not right," George moaned. "I didna believe you are saying such a thing,"

"Nor I, Sir," announced a younger man sitting by Major Morrison. "How could we even talk of doing such a dastardly act?...I prefer to die first...I do not wish to be associated with such vulgar savages and such talk." He stood and walked toward the men's hut.

An old man with a long gray beard watched him leave then countered, "He may well have his preference fulfilled soon. For me, I agree with Col. Norwood. God has provided for us and we would be foolish to refuse."

Richard continued, "Certainly, it no longer matters to Mrs. Dodd. She is with God and free from this suffering. 'Tis only her corpse that remains."

"Ye're all right," Major Morrison acceded gravely. I see no other remedy for our circumstances and I too do not believe God wishes us all to die here. However offensive this decision may be, I reluctantly agree with Col. Norwood."

"Col. Norwood is right. We will all die and I can not believe God desires this when He has provided a means for us to live," Cary supported.

Another very feeble man spoke somberly, "I'm in agreement with Col. Norwood, but we should take a vote. That way, no one person will be made responsible for our decision."

Col. Norwood focused his eyes on George, "Will ye accept the group's decision if we bring it to a vote?"

George stood and circled the fire for a moment. He stared at the woman's corpse some distance away. In a voice filled with pain, he said, "Aye, Sir. I will accept the group's decision....with the condition that we include the women in the vote as well."

"That's fine with me. Everyone should be in total agreement," Col. Norwood nodded.

The women were called to the fire and informed of the men's decision. After more emotionally charged discussion, a vote was taken and the desperate party, bonded by their collective survival instincts, agreed to use the woman's corpse as food. However, it was too late for four of the men, including Richard who died during the night.

CHAPTER ELEVEN

January 15, 1650 Accawmacke

It was near blizzard conditions most of the month of January. The extended cold spell required a great deal of wood for the fireplace. Since it was too cold to do much else outside, Ambrose decided to chop wood. After putting in a full morning, he took a break to warm up.

The frigid air outside marked a drastic contrast to the warm interior of the cozy house. Ambrose smiled at Mary as he entered. She sat by the fireplace humming and rocking Mary Jane in her cradle. A huge fire leaped and danced in the wide fireplace and the light from the fire fell upon her joyful face. Without a word, Ambrose crossed the room to her side, took her hand and kissed it tenderly, then drew up a chair near the fire and seated himself. She smiled and began humming again. Ambrose studied her face and tried to trace her features in the flickering light. A pleasure of mere existence stole over him.

Oh, Mary. I never thought I'd could be so happy. I have you, Henry, Jr. and Mary Jane to come home to everyday. Life was so different only a few short years ago.

Mary looked at Ambrose and whispered so as not to disturb Mary Jane, "I bet you're hungry. I'll dish up something warm to take the chill off your bones."

"Sounds good to me," Ambrose whispered back.

"Me too," Henry, Jr. added quietly as he entered the room.

"Then both of ye wash up while I prepare ye're food."

Henry, Jr. and Ambrose left the room and Mary heard horses hooves outside.

I wonder who that could be in this weather?

A loud pounding at the door soon followed, waking Mary Jane and she started to cry. Mary frowned. She walked over to greet the impatient visitor.

"Why Stephen Horsey? What brings you this way in such terrible weather?" Mary asked in astonishment.

"I have some news, Mary. Is Ambrose here?"

"Why, yes...he's washing up. Do you care to join us?...'tis just rabbit stew...but 'tis hot."

"Nay, I need to reach some other plantations before dark to alert them, but I'll sit by ye're fire a minute to warm up."

"Alert them of what?" Ambrose asked as he appeared in the doorway.

"We've had word from Nathaniel Littleton. It seems some Kinkotanks braves found a few Englishmen nearly starved to death on Assateague Island. Littleton sent Jenkin Price to guide them to his plantation. From the way the Indian described their dress, they could be our missing Royalists."

"Did he say how many?" queried Ambrose.

"Around a dozen were still alive. Some of them died before the Indians found them. The Indian indicated there was only a small number that landed on the island. I don't know anymore."

"If they are from the *Virginia Merchant,* I hope the others were not lost at sea," Mary said intently as she dished the stew into a bowl. "Wouldn't you like some tea Stephen? 'Twill warm you some."

"Nay, Mary. I need to be on my way. I have yet to inform John and Joanne Custis of the news. I know they've been worried. They had many friends on that ship," Stephen replied as he stood and began to wrap his scarf around his throat.

"Would you like me to tell Custis for you, Stephen? That ride is pretty long by horseback in this weather and ye've already traveled quite far to reach us," Ambrose said as he followed Stephen out of the house.

"Nay, but I should be on my way in case this storm decides to kick up again," Stephen replied.

After they reached the porch, Stephen leaned over and whispered to Ambrose, "I didna want to say this in front of Mary and Henry, Jr., but the Indian reported the people survived by eating the corpses of their dead."

Ambrose, astonished by the comment, did not respond at first. He gazed off toward the woods before asking, "Do you know how long they were on the island?"

"Nay, I didna have any more information. I'm sure, we'll learn what happened once they arrive at Littleton's. Can you imagine being brought so low as to eat ye're friends' dead bodies?...I can't fathom it."

"I wouldn't say anything about this to John and Joanne. It may not be true...mayhaps the Indian didna communicate correctly. Let's leave it up to the survivors to tell their story."

"That's a good idea...'twill be enough hard news for John and Joanne if these people are their friends...especially since it seems so few survived."

Stephen studied the gray clouds overhead and said, "It looks like we might be in for more snow...I'll be on my way so I can return home before dark."

"Take care friend."

Ambrose stood for a minute on the porch watching Stephen ride off.

Those poor people must have been pretty desperate...I heard old stories that some of the early settlers survived a winter that way. I didna know if I could do such a thing, but 'tis not for me to judge. I've never faced starvation.

Mary opened the door and said, "Ambrose, ye're going to freeze out here. Come inside....ye're meal is waiting."

Ambrose smiled at Mary and followed her inside.

The small group of survivors arrived at Littleton's plantation where they were fed and from there they traveled to the plantation of Stephen Charlton who gave them fresh clothing. Word spread and people throughout Accawmacke prepared to assist them. The women met at Hungar's church to make plans.

"Do you have any names, Rev. Rozier? Our good friend Col. Norwood was supposed to be on that ship," asked Joanne Custis.

"Aye, here is the list" Rev. Rozier said, as he waved a piece of parchment. "I believe there were almost twenty that landed on the island, but only twelve remain...let's see...Aye, there is a Col. Norwood listed."

"Oh, thank goodness! He survived!" Joanne exclaimed. "I'll send my carriage for him at once."

"And here's another name that might be of interest to you Mary," Rev. Rozier continued. "Didna you have a brother named George Willson? I thought I heard Ambrose say ye were expecting a packet from him."

"Aye, Rev. Rozier...but he's not written that he was coming to Virginia...of course, I haven't heard from him for a while...surely, he would let me know if he was coming to Virginia," Mary asserted. "The last I heard he was in the military."

"Well this does say that he is military. I don't suppose it's him though from what you say."

"I'll have Ambrose pick him up from the Charlton's plantation anyway...we can certainly take care of him. Does ye're list include anything about his age or condition?"

"Nay, Mary. Only his name," replied Rev. Rozier. "There are three women and two children. God bless them. I didna know how children could survive such as they've been through."

"That's true. Did the children's parents live?" asked Anne Yeardley.

"Aye, it says she's the mother of both children."

"Thanks be to God...they won't be alone in a strange country."

As the group of women and Rev. Rozier continued to discuss the survivors, Mary's mind was elsewhere.

Could I dare think that this is my brother? Oh that would be wonderful...to have him here with me. Why wouldn't he let me know he was coming...and why would he be on a Royalist ship?

"Mary, did you say that you and Ambrose would take care of this George Willson?" Rev. Rozier asked.

"Hmm...Oh, Aye, Rev. Rozier. We'll send a carriage for him today. We'll be happy to take care of him at our plantation."

"I believe that takes care of everyone. Here's hoping none of them need more than time to heal from their ordeal. Let's pray for their recovery...please bow your heads. Father, we come to you today asking your blessing on these poor individuals needing our care. Lead us and guide us as we administer to their needs. Bless each lady here today and protect us all. Amen"

The ladies stood and began chatting among themselves. Mary decided to return home immediately.

I must tell Ambrose to send our shallop at once for George Willson. I can't wait a minute more wondering.

CHAPTER TWELVE

January 16, 1650 Accawmacke

Ambrose and Henry, Jr. were working in the carpentry shed when Mary arrived home. She gingerly climbed the snow-covered embankment to the shed after disembarking from the shallop and excitedly told them about George Willson.

"Dare I hope that he might be my brother?" she cried to Ambrose. "Surely, he would have sent me a packet. Why would he arrive unannounced?"

"I don't know Mary....but Henry, Jr. and I will go immediately to bring him home," Ambrose answered as he began to put away tools. "That's the only way ye're questions will be answered. How old is he? Did Rev. Rozier have any more information about him?"

"Nay, only his name and thank you Ambrose. I didna think I can wait any longer...not knowing. Maria and I will ready up a room. There is no telling what condition he's in," she said as she walked out of the small wooden shed.

Mary continued toward the house while Henry, Jr. and Ambrose and two servants descended down the embankment to the waiting shallop. Thoughts flooded her mind as she traipsed the slippery path to her house, wet from melting snow. She tried to avoid the puddles of water and mud as she walked and pulled her cloak tightly around her.

Why would George come here without sending me a packet first? Could something have happened to my sisters and he didn't want to share it in a letter? I can't lose another member of my family...so many are gone....first Grandpapa, then Papa, my brothers, Anne and last year, Mum. Only twelve years ago we were so happy together sitting in my parents' home in Cranberry.

Tears filled Mary's eyes as she reached the house and reflected on that day. She stood at the door a minute to regain her composure and recalled her father's words when he gave her that special ribbon.

Remember this as a ribbon of love that ties and forever binds us to ye no matter how far the distance. We will always love and be praying for ye even though distance keeps us apart.

"Ye're no longer here to pray for us, Papa, but I still feel ye're love," Mary said aloud to herself. She glanced toward the water at Ambrose and Henry, Jr. as they reached the shallop.

You said something else....what was it? Oh, I remember, now...Each member of our family will follow a different path in their life, but when the strands are woven and tied together a strong bond is created resulting in a beautiful design making a tapestry of our love.

Mary continued to stand at the door and watched Ambrose and Henry, Jr. guide the shallop away from the pier.

"I've certainly continued the tapestry here....first with my first husband, Henry...and now with Ambrose...I have Henry, Jr., Mary Jane and now this wee one to continue our family's design," she said aloud as she patted her swollen tummy.

Mary's father's words penetrated her thoughts again and overcome by emotion she leaned against the porch post for support.

Always remember God's love ties ye to us, Mary...a family that has been here for generations, long before Grandpapa's time. With His love in ye're life, our family's design will remain beautiful and strong and our hearts will be forever bound just like the strands in this ribbon.

"Oh Papa, I miss you so...what will God have in store for me next? There has been so much sadness and loss in my life already...if this is George and he brings bad news...will I be able to stand it?"

The front door opened suddenly and Maria asked, "Miss Mary, are you alright? I heard ye're voice, but you didna come in...I was worried."

Mary stood up straight and smiled at Maria. "I'm fine Mary....just doing a little too much thinking, I s'pose. We must prepare for a guest. One of the survivors will be staying with us."

"Aye, Miss Mary. 'Tis the survivor a man or a woman?"

"Man...and uh, Maria...there is a chance that he might be me brother, George."

"Ye're brother, George? How?...What? Did ye know he was coming? I didna remember you mentioning him visiting," Maria asked in astonishment as she helped Mary take off her cloak.

"That's why, I'm not sure 'tis me brother, Maria. I've received no word of him coming, but this guest is named George Willson...my brother's name. Ambrose and Henry, Jr. are on their way to collect him...then we'll know. We must make his room ready...they shouldn't be long."

"Aye, Miss Mary. Right away. Is he...George...ill? Do we know anything else about him?"

"Nay, Maria. I'll guess we'll just have to wait and see. How has Mary Jane been?" Mary inquired as she walked over to pick up her daughter, who was playing on a rug by the fire.

"Like an angel, that little one never gives a day of trouble."

"She is like an angel, isn't she? And she looks so much like my sister, Anne. I was thinking about my family out there on the porch, just now. It has been such a long time since I've seen anyone from home. I guess I was quite overcome with memories."

"Memories give us comfort and keep us going through bad times, Mam...even the bad ones...especially when that's all we have," Maria said with emotion in her voice.

"Ah, that's so true," Mary said as she brushed her hand down her daughter's hair "Sometimes that is all we're left...well, I guess we'd better get started on that room...it's not going to ready itself," Mary said as she stood then leaned over and sat Mary Jane, back down on the rug.

Mary Jane instantly began to cry and reach for her mother, but Mary said, "Be good Mary Jane...we've lots to do."

Maria patted Mary's arm. "Miss Mary, you stay and visit with Mary Jane...ye've been working hard all day and 'tis close to ye're 'lyin in'...with a wee one on the way, you need to rest some. I can ready the room for our guest."

Mary smiled at Maria then picked up her daughter, "I do admit...I am quite tired today. I believe I'll take ye suggestion and sit with Mary Jane and catch up on my sewing for a spell. I certainly didna want this bairn to arrive too early."

"I agree, Mum...we have enough goings on with ye're brother's visit...that is...if our guest is ye're brother."

"Oh...I hope so, Maria...I sure hope he's me brother...but I also hope he isn't bringing bad news...otherwise, why didna he send me a packet? Ah well...I guess we'll find out when he arrives."

"Aye, Mam." Maria answered as she left the room.

Mary placed her child on the rug and sat in the straight back chair nearest the fire. She picked up her sewing basket, but Mary Jane cried and hugged her mother's legs.

"Now Mary Jane...you need to stop ye're crying. You may have an uncle coming and what would he think of all this crying."

Mary set the basket down and pulled Mary Jane into her lap. She could no longer hold back her tears as she held her daughter close and stared into the flickering flames of the fire.

Mary was pounding bread dough, three hours later, when the door burst open and Henry, Jr. ran into the house with a shout,"'Tis him Mum...'tis Uncle George! Can ye believe it? Papa said ye'd be pleased."

Mary stared at her son...speechless...then suddenly began sobbing and collapsed on the bench by the table.

Henry Jr. rushed over to his mother and put his arms around her shoulders. "Mum, didna be sad. Papa said ye'd be happy. Why are ye crying?"

"Oh, Henry, Jr," she exclaimed. "These are tears of joy...I'm not sad....these are tears of joy. How is George? Is he ill? What did he have to say?"

"You can ask me yeself, Mary...I'm right here," George said as he entered the room with Ambrose close behind.

Mary stared at the tall, thin young man entering the room with her husband and continued crying.

George hastened to her side and Mary stood and fell in his arms. He stoked her hair as he said, "Ah Mary...I didna mean to worry you, but there was no time to send a packet if I wanted to take advantage of the opportunity to come to Virginia. It was so sudden."

Mary pushed George back with one arm and looked into his eyes. "Then tell me truthfully...ye're not bringing bad news of my sisters."

"Nay, Mary, There's no bad news...our sisters are fine. They're with Robert's wife, Anne, and they're quite well...of course, they send their love."

"Then why...how did you get here...I mean...why were you on

this ship with the Royalists? Have you suffered badly from ye're ordeal?" Mary peppered as she studied her brother's face.

"I'm fine now....Mary. However, I will admit....I did become a mite peckish for a time...and thought I'd might starve....'twas no picnic."

"You still haven't answered my question. Why were ye traveling with the Royalists?"

Ambrose put his arm around Mary and said, "Mary, let's give George a little time to answer ye're questions. He's only just arrived."

"Aye, ye're right, Ambrose. What am I thinking?" she replied in a serious tone.

Mary backed away from her brother and examined his physique. "Ye've lost so much weight. We must do something about that. I'm sure ye're all hungry." Mary glanced at Maria as she entered the room and gave her a beaming smile. "'Tis my brother, after all, Maria."

"I see Mam.....how wonderful."

"Prepare these men a bowl of stew while I finish the bread." Mary directed Maria, then glanced back at her brother, "I must look a sight with this flour all over me." She wiped her face with her apron and continued to give directions. "Henry, Jr...see to ye're Uncle's things. George come sit by me and we'll talk while you and Ambrose eat."

"Whoa...there's me older sister again...always with the orders," George grinned as he and Ambrose moved toward the table while Maria prepared their food.

"Mary's certainly good with directions," Ambrose chuckled. "She can create order out of mass chaos. You ought to see her during a hog killing. Everyone runs when she starts barking out orders."

"Now, Ambrose....you know that's not true. I just try to make the most use of everyone's time. After all, it isn't every day that others provide so much help to us. 'Tis important for all to work in order to take advantage of their assistance."

"'Tis true, Mary. And no one can ever be accused of wasting time at our house on hog killing day. Ye'll be able to see her in action soon, George. We plan to kill our hogs in a few days if this weather holds up."

"Then that will be something I look forward to," George said and smiled at Mary. "I hope I have many days watching my sister Mary in action."

Mary blushed and smiled back at her brother.

The house was still. George could not sleep his first night at Mary's. He sat in the warm Parlour and stared at the fire. The events he experienced on Assateague Island continually played through his mind keeping him awake.

Why did Richard die and I survive? But most of all...why did I relent and allow my friend's corpse to be desecrated so we could survive. Will I ever be able to forgive myself? Mary, ye'd never have given me such a warm welcome if ye knew what I had done...and Anne...sweet...sweet Anne...ye'd never be able to forgive me...when I can't even forgive myself...I've probably lost ye forever...

George bent down and covered his face with his hands and wept.

God forgive me for what I have done!

CHAPTER THIRTEEN

February, 1650 -Accawmacke

February brought warm weather to Accawmacke so Joanne and John Custis invited a few friends to their plantation to meet and welcome Col. Henry Norwood to the Eastern Shore. George was anxious about attending the gathering. He knew questions would be asked about their experience and he was not sure how much information Col. Norwood planned to share.

As Ambrose, Mary and George entered the hall of John Custis' house, they heard, as usual, Col. Scarburgh's loud voice dominating the conversation. "Ye're lucky to have met with a few friendly Indians...or we wouldn't be visiting with you today."

A short, portly gentleman dressed in a camlet coat glittering with lace of gold and silver was sitting in the Parlour on a straight backed chair near the fire. He responded to Col. Scarburgh's statement, "You're mighty right about that...I know when the ship left us on shore...I never felt so forsaken in my life."

"I still do not understand why they left you," commented Joanne Custis. She wore a soft gray dress and was sitting across from Col. Norwood.

"That I didna know, either...all I can say is that those on board ship were mighty desperate themselves," Col. Norwood replied. He tapped his pipe on the fireplace mantel, lit it then gave a few puffs on the pipe before he continued. "At daybreak, we spied the ship under sail, heading for the Capes. I cannot express the amazement and confusion in our minds at being so cruelly left behind to fend for ourselves."

"I can only imagine....'" Mary commented sadly. She studied her brother's face as she spoke.

"How did ye survive without supplies?" asked Ambrose.

A servant added a log to the fire sending sparks up the chimney and Col. Norwood stared at the fire as he answered.

"After the ship disappeared from site, we decided to explore the land and my cousin Francis Cary, was still healthy so I sent him to survey our surroundings. He had a look around and came back to tell us we were on a small island with no inhabitants."

"How did ya' meet up with the Indians?" asked Ambrose.

"I'll get to that...but first...I must return to my cousin Cary...an angel must have guided him because he returned with a parcel of oysters."

"Praise be to God!" commented Anne Yeardley. "But how did you survive that snow storm?" she asked.

"We managed to forage a while by killing geese, ducks and other fowl which frequented the island, at least until the snow came upon us," George Willson added. He and Mary walked over and sat on a long bench placed against the wall.

"What did you use for shelter?" inquired Argoll Yeardley. "It has been fearsome cold this last month."

"We fashioned a couple of huts, one for the women and one for the the men...but as the days went by, it became colder and our food supply dwindled. Some even wished for death to ease our suffering. Then....death visited us as one of the women died....'twas then we reached our lowest point," Col. Norwood's eyes grew misty and he paused a minute before continuing.

He glanced toward George Willson and said, "Remember that day?"

The two men exchanged meaningful glances then George nodded knowingly and continued in a grim voice, "Death visited us frequently during that time. I lost my best friend, Richard Johnson," George's voice trembled when he said Richard's name. He paused a moment to regain his composure and stared at the flames in the fireplace.

Col. Norwood gave George a grateful glance. With tacit understanding, they had decided not to share the difficult decision about the dead corpses.

Ambrose watched the two men's brief exchange but said nothing.

"You still had not seen an Indian in all this time? Seems strange with the number of savages around here," Col. Scarburgh growled as he leaned against the fireplace mantel.

Col. Norwood frowned at Scarburgh, "Not a one was seen and we realized that we must have a new plan if we were to survive. Some of us still maintained a little strength so it was

86

decided our only recourse was to try to cross the creek and swim to the mainland about a hundred yards over rather than suffer a slow death from starvation. I was the strongest so I volunteered and cousin Cary..."

"That was noble of you," Joanne Custis interrupted. She smiled at Col. Norwood.

"Not noble, Joanne....'twas our only hope at the time," Col. Norwood replied. He smiled back at her and cleared his throat before continuing.

"Uhh...well...where was I....ummm..."

"You mentioned ye're Cousin Cary," John Custis offered.

"Aye...my cousin Cary labored hard for oysters to give me strength. While I cooked the oysters, Cary returned to tell me that he'd seen Indians walking on the mainland. Everyone still able to walk...rushed to see, but we were unable to discern any habitation on the mainland."

"I wonder which tribe they could have been...especially that far north?" Col. Scarburgh mused.

George said, "Later that same day, news came that Indians visited the women's hut and had given them shellfish. The Indians indicated they would be returning the next day."

"I must say...the Indians visit lifted our spirits, even those who had totally given up to the weight of despair," said Col. Norwood.

"Some in our group had become so desperate that they laid down with the intent never to rise again. Remember old man Grayson?" George focused his eyes on Norwood.

"Aye, I remember...'tis God's grace he survived," Col Norwood continued. "We waited with anticipation for the next day, but decided to have our guns ready in case the Indians proved to be enemies."

"Good idea," added Ambrose.

"To our despair....they did not return the next day and we were again disheartened," George retorted.

Col. Norwood then countered joyfully, "But alas, the following day, the Indians arrived with cheerful smiles and without any kind of arms or appearance of evil design. There were about twenty or thirty in all, men, women and children...wouldn't you say, George?"

"Aye, Sir," George answered. "It was a goodly number."

"They shook our hands and repeated the words *NY TOP* over and over which we assumed by their countenance to mean friend. I tell you we were quite ecstatic with happiness at our rescue," Norwood continued.

"They gave us ears of Indian corn...and the women...they showed compassion at the sight of our dead," George was overcome with emotion again and averted his gaze toward the fire.

"One of the Indians even presented me with a leg of a swan apparently assuming that I was in charge since I was dressed in this camlet coat with gold lace," Norwood laughed. "I gave the chief presents of ribbon and other items."

"Thank goodness for their kindness," Mary commented.

Col. Norwood nodded at Mary. "They stayed with us two hours and promised to return the next day with more for our relief and departed with the words, *Ha-na Haw* I never learned what the words meant."

"That night we thanked God for our deliverance," George continued.

"Did they return the next day?" Ambrose inquired.

"Aye, though later than they stated," George responded.

"Throughout the day, men, women and children brought bread and corn to our huts to exchange for truck we bought on shore, but if one of us had nothing to exchange, the Indians still provided them with bread," Norwood exclaimed.

"Humph, doesn't sound like any thievin' Indians I know," Col. Scarburgh countered. "By what name did they call themselves?"

"Kickotank, was the Werowance or Chief on whose land we stood."

"It had to be the Assateagues so far north, I ran a couple out of my tool outhouse last week....thievin' savages...they were probably trying to find what to steal from you," Scarburgh retorted.

"I doubt that...we had little truck with us...and they could have overtaken us at any time, weak as we were," Norwood said as he scowled at Scarburgh. "Least ways, by signs and gestures, we were invited to return to their country and since we saw no reason in all the carriage of the Indians on which we could ground any fear, we quickly departed with them....we really had no choice...we would have died if we remained on the island."

"That's for sure," George added. "Canoes were fitted to take us to the mainland where we were fed. Some of our group were so weak that they were unable to walk on foot through the woods. The King sent the canoes to carry us to the place of his mansion."

"You must have all been in terrible condition. 'Tis a wonder any of you survived," Mary observed.

"We were pretty desperate...I'll admit that," Norwood exclaimed.. "I digress....let me continue with our Indian encounter. First, we were taken to the house of the Queen. She was very charitable and generous. We were treated with courtesy, fed, and soon regained our strength so we were able to walk about a half hour to the King's mansion."

"You were at the King's mansion? What did it look like?" inquired Stephen Horsey.

"I was surprised at it's size. 'Twas made of mat and reed and about eighteen or twenty foot in breadth and twenty yards length. The roof was fast to the body with a sort of strong rushes," Norwood described.

"Did ya' go inside?" asked Amborse.

"Aye. The only furniture was several platforms for lodging, each about two yards long or more on both sides of the house and they were about five feet from each other. In the middle was a chimney with a hole in the roof for the smoke, but it was not very effective...a good deal of smoke remained in the house," Norwood laughed.

"How many houses were there?" inquired Scarburgh.

"I'd say about fourteen such houses, though the King's was twice as long as the others. He sat on a bank that was adorned with deer skins and finely dressed...with the best furs of otter and beaver I've ever seen," George commented.

"We stayed in one of the houses. We were fed again....first from a great wooden bowl filled with hominy...then we were allowed to take our rest. Afterwards, the King sent for me," Norwood said.

"Why did he send for you instead of the others?" Ambrose asked.

"I assume it was due to my dress and corpulent size," chuckled Norton. "He called me *Ny a Mutt*, which I have since learned means my brother. He compelled me to sit down on the same bank with him which I later realized was a great favor. He did not talk to me. Instead, he debated with his council, probably over our visit and what he was to do with us since they seem to be having a fierce argument. I can tell you, I was a mite worried as to what they would decide."

"As well you should've been. You can't trust savages," Scarburgh declared. "'Tis a wonder ye're still alive."

"I didna know about that...all I can say is that we were treated kindly," Norwood said as he glared at Scarburgh. "Now if ye'll let me continue...The chief tried to communicate with me...which was comical," Norwood laughed. "I had great difficulty understanding his gestures and body movements, but I must say...he was patient and diverted my difficulties into mirth and jollity. At no time during our many visits did I leave until he made me laugh with him...and I never understood why...but over the course of a few days...I managed to convey to him my intentions of reaching Accawmacke. Evidently, without our knowledge, he contacted Littleton's plantation and of course you know the rest of my story."

"Why would the ship leave you on the island in the first place?" John Custis asked. "That seems an awful harsh thing to do."

"Aye, 'twas a shock to us as well," Norwood replied. "We could not understand why and I didna know where the ship is now. It was a most troublesome sight that morning, seeing the ship at full sail, heading for the Capes...I just don't understand. The wind did change during the night. Mayhaps they feared another storm. All I can say now is by a gracious God, who helped us in our low estate and caused his angels to pitch tents round about them that trust in him, we are here now and able to give a faithful account of his miserable objects of his mercy in this voyage."

"Amen to that, Col. Norwood. God has been merciful to you both indeed," added Rev. Rozier who entered the room at the end of the conversation. "We're happy to have you among us today. Joanne, I'm sorry I'm so late, but I'm just come from Captain Roper's. I'm afraid he is very low and may not be with us much longer."

"I certainly hate to hear that," Ambrose said. "He's been a good friend to us all."

The men nodded in agreement.

Rev. Rozier continued, "I hate to ask you to repeat yourself...did I hear you mention a ship leaving you behind?"

"Aye, Rev., 'twas the *Virginia Merchant,*" Col. Norwood answered as George nodded. We still didna know why she left nor what happened to her."

"Then I believe I can shed some light on what happened to the ship. Some men came by the church today asking about our survivors. Of course, I directed them to Charlton and Littleton. They said they were from the *Virginia Merchant.* The battered ship arrived safely. However it was grounded in Jamestown. The governor sent out search parties for you as soon as he received word."

"Ah...thanks be to God that the others are safe. Did they inform you as to why we were left behind?"

"Aye, and there's a trial taking place in James City now because of it. Evidently, when the Captain arrived back on ship, he ordered the crew to set sail for the creek but they refused because the wind had come up and they wanted to set sail for the Capes. Of course, most of the officers were with you on shore so they easily overcame the Captain and locked him in his cabin. Then the crew took up anchor and sailed to James City where the ship was grounded. They tried to make their escape but all were captured and now they're on trial for mutiny."

"That explains it then. I never thought Captain Locker would leave us...not after his kind treatment on the ship," Captain Norwood declared. I must go to Jamestown at once to see about our friends and see if I can assist Captain Locker in this trial."

"Well, certainly not tonight, Colonel," Joanne Custis laughed. "Our meal awaits. We can discuss this tomorrow." Rev. Rozier, would you kindly bless our food," Joanne Custis declared.

"Aye, madam," Rev. Rozier answered as he and the other guests followed Joanne to the dining table.

After dinner the men continued to talk and smoke in the Parlour while Mary and the ladies visited in the hall by the fireplace. It was nearing dusk when Ambrose, George and Mary returned home. George did not say a word in the shallop and immediately went to his room when they arrived at the house.

Mary checked on Mary Jane then returned to the Parlour to talk with her husband, "I must say Ambrose, that story was pretty grim, but I'm most worried about my brother. He was so quiet on the way back. I believe something else is troubling him."

"He's been through a terrible ordeal Mary, and he lost a good friend as well. I'm sure that 'twas hard to deal with. He needs time to heal."

"Of course ye're right, Ambrose....I guess I worry too much."

As they walked to their bedroom, Mary reached out and grabbed Ambrose's arm to steady herself.

Ambrose halted and caught her with his other hand as well. "Are ye alright, Mary?" he asked with concern.

"Aye, I'm just a little unsteady on my feet, nowadays," she laughed as she patted her bulging stomach. Our son's grown quite a bit this month."

"Our son? Do ye believe it's a son?"

"He's active enough to be. I hope I will be able to give you a son this time Ambrose. I know you want one."

"Mary, I'll be happy even if 'tis another daughter. We already have a fine son with Henry, Jr. I'll be happy with either a son or daughter."

Mary smiled.

He said fine son. Ambrose, you are so kind. Henry, Jr. is not ye're son, but you think of him as your own. Thank God for providing me with such a wonderful man.

George lay on his bed and stared at the ceiling. Sharing the story of their survival had been difficult...it brought back so many feelings he was trying to forget. Being around Mary's family was helpful the last few days because they were always busy doing something, yet when he was alone...those horrible days on the island returned to his thoughts and he could not sleep...he knew he'd never sleep tonight...his emotions were too raw and images and smells of death so vivid. With his first glimpse of Col. Norwood...he was propelled back to the island and those terrible days.

I should have died....it would probably be better than living with this guilt. Why was I spared? I should have died with Richard....what makes my life any more precious than his? Their deaths were not a miracle....we only told ourselves that because we were so desperate. Oh Mary, what would you think of me if you knew the whole story? What would anyone think of me? I dare not tell anyone....not even Anne...she'd never understand....'tis useless to think of a future with her...she'd never forgive me...how can I live with this guilt?

CHAPTER FOURTEEN

April, 1650 Eastern Shore, Virginia

Before dawn on April 10, 1650, the church bell at Hungar's Parish rang out indicating an emergency. Word of a fire at Argoll Yeardley's plantation quickly spread throughout the community. Ambrose and George joined neighbors fighting the fire, but even with all their help, little was left of the Yeardley's home.

"At least no one died in the fire," Commander Yeardley said as he viewed the blackened shell of his home.

"And we managed to save ye're drying barn," remarked Stephen Horsey.

"Aye, and we'll have a tobacco crop to ship," Yeardley said as he embraced his tearful wife's waist. "We'll need it to recover from this loss." He looked into his wife's eyes and said, "We'll build an even grander house Anne....didna worry...I'll replace everything."

"I know, Argoll...'tis just hard to see all we built looking like this," she said with tears in her eyes as she gazed dejectedly toward the smoking ruins.

"Where will ye be staying, Argoll? We might be able to salvage some items and we can certainly help you move," Ambrose declared.

John Custis said, "They'll be staying with us...it will be nice to have my daughter with me again...at least while they rebuild."

"Aye, 'twill be like old times," Joanne Custis added as she smiled at her daughter and walked toward her. She took Anne's hand and gave it a gentle squeeze and continued, "We need to do some planning anyway for the wee one that will be here soon."

Ambrose said, "Argoll, I imagine we need to let things cool down first...but we'll be back to help you salvage what you can."

"Ambrose, I appreciate ye're offer...but everyone has done enough. I didna think there is much to salvage and my servants can certainly handle what's left." He then addressed the crowd, "Thank you all for coming so quickly.....without ye're help, we'd have lost much more."

The people began to gradually disperse. Stephen Horsey walked with Ambrose and George toward their horses.

"What do you think caused the fire?" George asked Stephen.

"They believe it was from the fireplace. The fire started in the Parlour."

"It appears Argoll has plans for a big house," George commented.

"Aye, he's been talking to his brother-in-law, John Custis, Jr., about adding on to his home. From what I hear, John has some right fancy ideas...but now that he has to build a completely new house...I didna know what he'll do. The Custis family's had quite a few visitors of late....with Col. Norwood and his friends. They'll have more room now since Norwood left for James City. I hear he's staying with his cousin, Gov. Berkeley."

"He's still extolling the virtues and kindness he received from the Indians, I'd imagine," Ambrose chortled.

"Aye, I'm sure that's why Gov. Berkeley addressed the Court last week," Horsey acknowledged.

"What did he say?" inquired Ambrose

"Believe it or not, he praised the Indians living here, particularly the Laughing King and reminded everyone how they refused to engage in that last bloody massacre in James City a few years back. Then he ordered that no land could be taken from our Indians without the knowledge of the full court and if the court didna agree then the matter should be sent to James City."

"I didna believe it...all transfer of Indian land must be approved by the court...but that seems to be a great hindrance."

"I agree. Nonetheless, that's what Gov. Berkeley declared. Scarburgh's fit to be tied over his statement. Col. Norwood must have made a strong impression on Berkeley about the kindness of Indian's here."

"Well, I agree they should be treated fairly, especially the ones who helped you, George." Ambrose said.

George nodded in agreement.

Ambrose continued, "However, I didna fancy going to the Commissioners whenever I want to buy more land. I have plans to extend my plantation further this year after delivery of my crop...that is if we have a good crop....'tis never a surety."

"That's for certain. That reminds me. I will be traveling back to England with my crop this year...will ye be going with yours?" Stephen asked.

"Nay, we'll have the wee one and I didna want to leave, Mary just now. George and Col. Norwood's difficulties on their trip disturbed Mary and she hasn't been able to rest much since hearing of them. I didna think 'tis a good time to travel to England."

"Sarah was quite upset too. I told her that no one can predict how safe a trip will be. Still, it didna ease her worries. We just have to put our trust in God to see us through."

"Aye, I said the same to Mary...and we'd best be getting on our way...she's probably worried about this fire," Ambrose laughed as he mounted his horse. "I didna want to mark our son with her worry."

"I'll certainly second that. I've given her worry enough with my adventure. She's been like a mother hen around me ever since I've arrived," George chuckled.

"God bless you, my friends!" Stephen shouted and his horse trotted toward his home.

While Ambrose and George were at the Yeardley's fighting the fire, Mary's contractions started. Maria wanted to send for the men immediately, but Mary refused, not wanting to disturb them while they fought the fire. Barbary, the midwife, was sent for. However, she had not yet arrived and Mary was pacing the floor.

"Miss Mary, I really think you ought to rest. The bairn may come before Barbary is here."

"Nay, Maria...I cannot rest...not yet. I'm sure it will be a while. The pains are not close," Mary said as she stooped to roll a walnut to Mary Jane.

"Whatever ye say, Miss Mary. Would you like me to send for ye're cousin, Priscilla? I didna think she would be at the fire."

"She's too far away. I'm sure Barbary will be here soon enough."

As if on cue, the two women heard a knock at the door.

Maria opened the door, and Barbary rushed through, talking rapidly as she entered.

"Mary, I'm sorry I'm so late. I was with Mrs. Wise and thought her baby would never come. What are you doing up? How far apart are the pains? Is Ambrose here? No, I expect not, he's probably at the fire...where's Henry, Jr.?"

Mary stopped pacing and smiled with amusement as Barbary peppered her with questions.

"Barbary, I've never seen you in such a flurry. I'm fine. You know this isn't my first 'lyin' in'. What brought all this on?"

"I'm sorry, Mary. I guess I do sound rattled. 'Tis Mrs. Wise's mother...you know how she is...no one can ever do anything right when it comes to her daughter. She stood over me the whole time...telling me I was doing everything wrong. You'd think this was the first time I was a midwife."

"I'm sorry. It sounds like ye've had quite a day. Sit down, Maria will make you some tea...I'm sure it will be a while."

Barbary stared at Mary, "Mayhaps I need to check you first."

"Nay, I've been through this before...'tis not yet time. Would you like something to eat?"

"Well, I could use a rest for a minute...and mayhaps a bite of something. I can't remember when I last ate. The last three days have been very busy," Barbary declared as she sat on the bench by the table. She smiled at Mary Jane who was sitting on a quilt, playing.

The child clapped her hands with glee as she stood up and walked toward her.

"Mary Jane is really growing up. It seems like only yesterday she was born. She certainly looks like you with that beautiful dark hair."

"I think she looks more like me Mum and my sister Anne.. I wish Mum was with me today. She loved children and would certainly enjoy seeing her grandchildren," Mary declared with a voice choked with emotion.

Maria returned with a hot cup of tea and a bowl of stew. "What did Mrs. Wise have, a son or daughter?"

"'Twas a daughter. You should have seen her husband. He was beside himself with excitement...with this child being their first."

"And how's Mrs. Wise?" Mary inquired as she sat down beside Barbary.

"Doing quite well. Though to hear her mother, you'd think she was at death's door...she constantly talked about how pale and drawn Mrs. Wise looked and what a barbaric life she had here. I tell you Mary, she is the fourth Royalist I've met and as far as I'm concerned they could all go back to England. They're always fussing about our uncivilized life here and how could we ever live like this...I've had all I can take of their complaints."

Mary frowned, "I hope they grow to love the Eastern Shore as we have. 'Tis hard to adjust when all you can see are the difficulties here. Mayhaps in time they will change their minds."

"Didna get your hopes up...especially where Mrs. Wise's mother is concerned. I know she plans to return to *civilized* England and away from all these savages." Barbary laughed and took another sip of her tea.

Suddenly a strong contraction enveloped Mary's body and she stiffened until it passed. Afterwards she gave a long sigh. "I had hoped that Ambrose and George would return before this wee one came, but now I'm beginning to have my doubts."

"Aye, Mary. Let's help you to the bedroom."

Barbary supported Mary's arm as they walked out of the Parlour. "Mayhaps we can send for the men. Is Henry, Jr. still here? When he came to get me, he was in a panic and I thought he was returning home after I was notified."

Maria picked up Mary Jane and followed them to the bedroom as she replied, "Aye, he returned. We sent him to check on the stock and feed the chickens. He was beside himself sitting here with his mother and seeing her in pain."

"Good idea. Mary, don't you want to send him for your husband and brother? I'm sure they'd want to be here."

"Nay, no sense them waiting and worrying. They"ll be here soon enough."

When Ambrose and George returned home, they were welcomed by a jubilant Henry, Jr.

"Papa, I have a brother...he needs a name. Mum wanted to wait for you first."

"A brother...you mean ye're Mum had the bairn? I should have been here. How is ye're Mum? Where is she?"

"She's sleeping now, Ambrose, and she is quite well," Barbary reassured him. "We wanted to send for you but Mary insisted that you were needed to fight the fire."

Maria asked, "Would you two like something to eat? I imagine you didna have anything all day. Was the Yeardley's house spared?"

"Nay, Maria. The fire started in the house and it was completely destroyed. Still, we saved the rest of his plantation except for a couple of sheds near the house. I would like something to eat but I want to see Mary first. Where's Mary Jane?"

"Mary Jane is sleeping." Maria answered.

"Well, I'd love some victuals while Ambrose checks on Mary...something smells mighty good." George declared.

Ambrose walked into the bedroom and gazed at his sleeping wife with her arm curled around his dark-haired son.

A son....you were right Mary. You gave me a son. Welcome to the world little man.

Ambrose reached over and put his little finger close to the child's hand and the infant grabbed it instantly.

Mary opened her eyes and gave Ambrose a contented smile. "What do ye think of ye're son, Ambrose?"

"Tis a handsome lad indeed and very strong. He has a mighty grip. What shall we name him?"

"I'm been thinking about that and you know my oldest brother Thomas died in the war. Could we name him after my brother and my father and call him Thomas Edward?"

"Aye, Mary. I remember. That sounds like a fine name, Mary. Well, Thomas Edward Dixon...what do ye think of ye're name?" Ambrose asked as he gently lifted him from Mary's arms.

Thomas let out a loud squall when his father moved him from the warm bed. On hearing the cry, Maria, Barbary, George and Henry, Jr. rushed to join them in the bedroom.

"Papa, does he have a name yet?" asked Henry, Jr.

"Aye, son. I'd like you all to meet Thomas Edward Dixon, my second son."

Mary watched Henry, Jr. and was delighted to see his beaming face.

Barbary spoke softly, "'Tis a fine name, Mary and Ambrose. If ye'll excuse me, I think I'll return home and try to rest some before the next 'lyin' in'."

"Thank you, Barbary," Mary said as she watched her leave

the bedroom with Maria trailing close behind.

Mary asked Ambrose, "What happened at the fire?"

"Their house is gone but the rest of the plantation was spared. Argoll and Anne will live with her parents until they rebuild. The best news is that no one died in the fire."

"That is good. At least, Anne has her Mum nearby."

George smiled at Mary and said, "You have a fine son and I'm sure our father and brother, Thomas, would be proud of their namesake, Mary. You need to rest...and I think I'll have some more of that good stew I smell in the kettle."

"Henry, Jr." Mary said, "Go tell Maria to prepare your Papa and George's dinner while I talk to ye're Papa a minute."

Henry, Jr. left the room and Ambrose leaned over and kissed his wife.

"Ambrose, you are a kind man and a wonderful father to my son Henry, Jr. I know it meant a lot to Henry, Jr. when ye said Thomas was ye're second son. It's hard being an orphan. I want you to know that I trust ye're judgment about his future."

Ambrose caressed Mary's head and fingered her hair before speaking. "Henry, Jr is a fine young man, Mary. He was such a small lad when we married...he does feel like my own son in a lot of ways. I'll always treat him as my own."

"Oh Ambrose, that eases my mind considerably. Of course, I'll still worry, but at least he won't be alone. You are too good to me."

"What is all this somber talk about being alone. Are ye feeling ill? Should I ask Barbary to return?" Ambrose asked, suddenly alarmed.

"Nay, nay, Ambrose. 'Tis only me worrisome nature...I've lost so many good friends and I know how if feels to be alone."

"Mary, as I vowed to you when we first married...I love you and I'll do anything for you. As long as I live, ye'll never be alone. Now you must rest."

Ambrose walked out of the room and Mary stared after him.

Oh Ambrose, I wish I could say those three words you want to hear...but I can't...at least...not now...I still love Henry....How can I love two men at the same time?

CHAPTER FIFTEEN

Spring 1650, Eastern Shore, Virginia

Ambrose was in his favorite place on the cool porch smoking his evening pipe when he saw Colonel Coulbourne approach on horseback.

"Halloa, Colonel, good to see you," Ambrose stood and greeted his friend. He placed his pipe on the porch railing.

"Good to see you too," Col. Coulbourne replied as he dismounted and tied his horse to the hitching post.

Col. Coulbourne was a hardy, robust man, who carried himself with an air of distinction. He had a grayish black beard that he frequently stroked with his right hand. When he reached the porch, he shook hands with Ambrose and declared, "Ambrose, I received word that you wanted to discuss the building of my house."

"Aye, Colonel. I'd like to start building right away while I have time."

"Tis a mighty generous gift ye're giving Maria with a new house and I thank you for it." Col. Coulbourne placed his other hand on top of their clasped hands as he spoke.

"You both deserve it Colonel and it's the least I could do for Maria. She's been more like family than a servant...we'll miss her. You treat her right or ye'll have me after you," Ambrose laughed and walked toward the door.

"No worry about that," Ambrose. "She's a good woman and I'm lucky she's to be me wife."

The two men entered the house to quite a commotion. Henry, Jr. was tickling Mary Jane as she lay writhing and squealing with delight while Maria was applying butter to Mary's burned hand.

Ambrose said, "Mary, what happened to ye're hand?"

"Nothing that bad...I'm just clumsy...I burned it a bit when I tried to retrieve the bread from the oven."

"'Tis just a mild burn, Mr. Dixon." Maria commented.. Her

back was to Ambrose. She turned to face him and saw Col. Coulbourne at his side. She almost dropped the butter, but managed to compose herself and declared, "Why, Colonel....I didna expect to see you!!"

"Ah...I s'pose not. Ambrose sent word for me to drop by. He needs to start building at once if we wed next month so I thought 'twas no time better than the present and here I am," he chuckled.

Mary said, "And we're glad to have you visit, Sir. Maria, I'll take care of the bread. You three go to the Parlour. Mayhaps it will be a little quieter there and you can discuss house plans."

"Are ye sure Miss Mary? What about ye're hand?"

"I've had worse." Mary replied as she tapped Henry, Jr. on the head and ordered, "Henry, Jr, stop teasing ye're sister and take her to the hall. You two need to quiet down some while I finish this meal."

George Willson joined the group while Henry, Jr. pulled his protesting sister by the hand toward the hall. George stared at Col. Coulbourne a moment then said, "I'm sorry sir. I don't believe we've ever met."

Mary frowned. "Oh George, I forgot ye didna know Col. Coulbourne. Col. Coulbourne this is my brother, George Willson, newly arrived from England."

"Newly arrived you say? What part?"

"Cranbrook, Sir...south of Canterbury."

"My home's in Somersetshire, England. I'm not sure I have much family left there now though. Do you have any news to report since the King's execution?"

"England's in a bit of unrest...that's why I decided to try my lot in Virginia."

"Aye, same reason I came here...too much of having to take sides...one didna know who to trust...there's none of that here...not so far as I've seen anyway. I hope our Mother country's troubles stay there."

Ambrose said, "I hate to interrupt Colonel. But we'd best be discussing ye're house while there's a little quiet time...'tis hard to come by around here with the wee ones."

"I imagine so....still, I love hearing their laughter...mayhaps one day, Maria and I will be able to enjoy children's laughter at our house," Col. Coulbourne said with a wink, then laughed when he saw Maria's beet red face.

"I think we'd best have a house first, Colonel," Maria said as she led the way to the Parlour.

Col. Coulbourne grinned, "George, I'd love to talk with you more, but it appears we have this house business to discuss now. Are you staying here with ye're sister?"

"Aye, Sir. We'll talk another time. Congratulations to the two of you," George commented as he shook Col. Coulbourne's hand.

"Thank you, George," Col. Coulbourne responded warmly and added "Now what do you have planned for us, Ambrose?" He followed Maria and Ambrose to the Parlour.

"Would you like some tea, George?" Mary asked as she watched him seat himself at the table.

"Nay, Mary...not now...but is this a good time to talk? I've had something on my mind for a while that I wanted to discuss with you."

"Certainly, George. Is it anything serious? Have you a maiden you wish to marry?" she teased as she gingerly removed bread from a pan with one hand and placed it on a wooden plank in the center of the table. Then she grabbed a knife to cut the bread.

"Nay, nothing like that...'tis something far more serious."

"Oh?" Mary stopped cutting the bread and stared at brother. "Serious? I thought ye said everything was fine with my sisters. What's troubling you?"

"Well, I probably used the wrong word when I said serious...it's nothing dire...it's just that....uh...well...I had a strange experience in London after the King was executed and I wanted to talk to you about it."

"An experience? What ever do you mean by that?" Mary sat down beside George on the bench.

"I'm explaining this poorly. Here's what happened. After seeing the gruesome sight of the King being executed, I had to walk to clear my head."

"You saw his execution? Oh...that must have been horrible. You never mentioned it before now."

"It's not something I want to remember," he replied. "But that's not what I wanted to talk about."

"Then what is it, George? I can't imagine anything any more

serious."

"Not serious really...Mayhaps, I need to explain a little first. You know, during the war, I had to fight in the King's Army because of his order, nonetheless, I often felt that I should have been fighting with Parliament's Army instead. But I saw too much brutality perpetrated by both Armies and I wanted nothing more to do with either, especially after the King was executed and I didna know where to go. I was quite confused until I met them...they seem to be the solution."

"Solution...saw them...who are you talking about?"

"The Children of the Light...or as some people call them Quakers. Have you not heard of them? George Fox is their leader."

"Children of the Light....Quakers? I heard the name Quakers. I've heard nothing good about them....Joanne said they were crazy, immoral and dangerous people. How can you talk about them as having the solution?"

"Please listen to me, Mary. What you say about them is not true at all. I spent some time with the Quakers. At first, Richard and I joined them to hide from Parliament's army. It was not safe in London for any of the King's former soldiers after his execution, even though we no longer intended to fight."

"I didna imagine it was. I worried about ye."

"Of course we had an another motive for joining with the Quakers, yet they welcomed us into their homes. Since they were obviously not Royalists; we had a haven until we could make further plans. While with them, I often heard George Fox talk and what he said made sense."

"What did he say?"

"I can't speak as well as him..but he said that God dwells in the hearts of his people not in Churches, or rituals and that we are to follow our own Inner light. We see truth only in our Inner light."

"I didna understand, George. What is this Inner light?"

"We must spend time in silent prayer with God. He will speak to us through our Inner light."

"But what about the Church, George...and our ministers? Do they guide us to this inner light?"

"Nay, Mary. All people are equal in God's eyes...everyone has their own Inner light and must seek it for themselves. I had trouble understanding his words until my experience with the Indians after I arrived on Assateague Island."

"What do you mean, George?"

"I did not understand how everyone could be considered equal...since we have King's, Lords and gentlemen who are better. But after I saw how brutal they were during the war...how could they be better people? I heard the Indians were uncivilized savages, a people to be feared. But the treatment we received by these so-called savages on the island was always kind and caring....better than I received from many Lord's and Generals in the war. There must be an Inner light in everyone or these Indians could not know kindness."

"I'm still confused, George...still...I like what you say about everyone being equal in God's eyes. However, this new religion sounds dangerous. Why are so many people against it?"

"Think about it...if everyone is equal in God's eyes...then why do we need Church leaders when we can find God in our own Inner light. For that matter, why do we need Churches. George Fox always preached in the open countryside. He said we didna need buildings. A Church is the fellowship of people in whose life Christ lives."

"This is so much to think about....give me time George. I'm still very confused."

"Aye, Mary. I understand. Granted, I was confused at first too. But somehow, the more I heard George Fox talk...the more I liked what he said. I only ask you to be silent and listen to God speaking to you."

"Aye, George...I'll try."

Henry, Jr. walked in the room with Mary Jane trailing behind. "Mum, I think Mary Jane is hungry. She keeps trying to eat her blocks."

"Oh, my little one's," Mary laughed. "Come to me. Mayhaps, everyone's hungry. I need to see if Col. Coulbourne would like to stay for dinner," Mary said as she led her children to the other room.

George remained seated as he watched Mary leave the room.

She probably thinks I've gone mad. How will I ever help her to understand what I experienced? This is such a new and strange idea to her. All I can do is pray that God leads her to her own Inner light...and Anne...will she think I'm mad as well?....I must say something about my feelings in my next letter...she was so concerned about me in her last letter...mayhaps there's a chance for us yet...but could she forgive me for what I have done?...what was it Mum said...time heals all wounds...and I have a deep wound that needs to be healed. I must be patient and let God heal me...I must wait on God.

George finally stood and followed Mary and the children into the Parlour.

Mary asked, "Col. Coulbourne, won't you join us for dinner? Henry, Jr. killed a deer this morning and we're having fresh venison stew tonight. Maria made a great apple pie."

"That sounds too good to pass up, Mary and the smells coming from the kitchen is persuasion enough. I believe I'll stay to partake of a meal with you. I can't get enough of Maria's pies."

"When the two of ya' get married we'll be missing her cooking, that's for sure," Ambrose added as he removed the boards from the pegs on the wall used for the table and placed them on supporting trestle legs. He set the table by the window.

"Where is ye're land, Col. Colbourne? Where didna plan to build ye're house?" Mary inquired.

"My land's up at Naswattucks creek...350 acres...I'm between Nicholas Waddilow and the creek."

"That's some good land ya' have there, Colonel and ye'll be happy come harvest time that ye're so near the creek and 350 acres will make a good start." Ambrose said.

"To hear my servants talk, ye'd think 350 acres is all I need...they complained all winter as we cleared land. At least they had a good roof over their head. I built my drying barn first and they stayed in that all winter." Col. Coulbourne sat down on the bench by George.

"How many servants did you have, Colonel?" George asked.

Mary sat trenchers in front of the men as they sat down. George carried the vat of stew to the table. Maria followed him with a loaf of bread.

Col. Coulbourne reached for a slice of bread and answered, "I brought seven indentured servants over, five men and two women. I know I'll need more acreage for tobacco since it really uses of the land so I hope to purchase more land after this crop is sold."

"You already planted ye're crop and built ye're barn? You didna believe in wasting any time!" Ambrose exclaimed.

Col. Coulbourne smiled at Maria who was helping Mary ladle the stew into bowls. "I had my reasons....but I wanted Maria to help plan the house she'd live in."

Maria returned his smile.

"How considerate Colonel!" Mary exclaimed.

A little embarrassed by Mary's remark, Col Coulbourne changed the subject. "Have you had any trouble with the Indians around here lately, Ambrose? Edmund Scarburgh said he's had quite a bit of stock killed...and is worried about an uprising."

"I'm not surprised that he'd say such a thing, but the Indians around us have been peaceable...and generous I'd say. If he'd fence his stock instead of letting them run wild and forage for themselves, he lose a lot less beef. I'm afraid, the Indians believe animals running wild are fair game and Col. Scarburgh has a way of riling the Indians. He'd like them all dead."

"Why does he hate them so much?" George inquired.

"I didna know. His land does border Indian property and I imagine the Indians consider his property hunting grounds...he probably has more theft going on than most of us. He's always trying to figure out ways to catch them stealing...said many times that he wish them all dead....the Indians call him the 'Conjurer."

Henry, Jr., who had been listening intently, asked, "What's a Conjurer, Papa?"

Ambrose laughed, "Something ya' didna want to be, son. Let's stop all this talk of Indians...'tis time to bless this great meal with good friends."

Everyone bowed their heads while Ambrose prayed, "Father, thank you for this meal and all the joys you brought us. Bless Maria and Col. Coulbourne in their future marriage...and most of all, thank you for keeping us safe and well...Amen."

"Amen" George added.

Maria and Col. Coulbourne married in late May at Hungar's church. A huge crowd attended the wedding. The wedding feast was held at Col. Coulbourne's new home afterwards. The house was not particularly large but many people admired the solid construction completed by Ambrose.

The roof was shingled with cypress. Partitions of the plantation dwelling had been first covered with mud, then whitewashed with lime since it was found in large quantity on the Eastern Shore due to the mass of oyster shells in the soil. The walls in his home were scaled with riven boards and wainscoting lined the partitions.

The Dixon's and George Willson did not return home until late in the evening. Thomas and Mary Jane fell asleep before they reached home. After Mary settled them in their bed, she joined George, Henry Jr. and Ambrose in the Parlour.

"This house will seem awful strange without Maria, won't it, Mum?" Henry, Jr. asked.

"Aye, son. I didna know how I'll manage without her."

"You won't have to wait long. I bought an indenture last week to replace Maria. She will be here next week if ye can manage till then."

"Oh thank you, Ambrose. I didna know....ye've said nothing about replacing Maria. I was not sure...." Mary's voice trailed off.

"I wanted her to be a surprise."

"Who is she Papa?"

"Her name is Betsy Johnson. I bought several indentured servants last week for the tobacco crop. One was Betsy's younger brother, Benjamin and I thought they might want to stay together so I bought Betsy as well. She is only seventeen and her brother is fourteen. Their parents were Royalists who were killed in the War. Her uncle, who's still in England, arranged for their journey on the *Virginia Merchant* for their safety, but they had no means of support when they arrived so they were indentured."

"I remember Betsy." George remarked. "She's a sweet girl...always watched out for her brother."

"Well if you approve...then I approve," Mary said as she smiled at George and her husband. "I only hope she knows a little about taking care of wee ones because our two certainly wore me out today."

"Papa, what does indenture servant mean?" inquired Henry, Jr.

"It means someone stays and works for us to pay off their

debt. Then when they are trained perfectly and can do the job without direction, they leave....just like Maria."

"I wish Maria was still here. I miss her."

"We all do...but at least she's not far.....we can still visit her," Mary reassured her son.

"When?" Henry, Jr. asked excitedly.

"Let's give her some time without us, son....but I promise you, it won't be long," Ambrose laughed. "I miss her too."

CHAPTER SIXTEEN

Spring and Summer, 1650 Eastern Shore, Virginia

In the spring, tension escalated on the Eastern Shore as rumors of an impending Indian attack spread throughout the area. On July 25th a council of war was held at William's Ordinary to discuss the rumors. Ambrose and George attended the Council. The Commissioners present were Commander Argoll Yeardley, Esq., Stephen Charlton, Thomas Johnson, Obedience Robbins, Captain William Roper and John Stringer.

Captain Roper, still recovering from his recent illness, was pale and drawn. All the Commissioners sat at a table facing the patrons. Several witnesses were called to report what they heard regarding the rumors. Robert Berry, an Indian trader, testified first. After he was sworn in, Commander Argoll Yeardley began questioning the witness.

"Robert, It has been reported that you heard a rumor about a possible Indian uprising. Please tell us what brings you to this conclusion."

"Well...as ye all know...I do a lot of trading with the Indians...I've come to trust a few. Not all of them are scoundrels ye know...despite what ye hear from others." Berry glared at Col. Scarburgh as he spoke. A few soft chuckles were heard in the room.

"Go on...tell us what ye heard."

"Well...about 10 or 12 days ago, an old Indian fellow...name of James Ornaw, who has always been truthful with me....least ways...I never caught him in a lie...well Sir... he came to my house and said that the Indians were not good...so I asked him why? Well...he answered that they always talk naught. He said that Gingasgoynes Indians were not good and the English were not wise in letting King Tom know what we did because he told the Gingasgoynes what he knew and heard. I asked him why...and old Ornaw said he heard that the Gingasgoynes planned to poison the English."

Gasps of astonishment and whispers filled the crowded

room.

Berry continued, "Well...I told old Ornaw I didna believe him. Old Ornaw asked me why I didna believe him? Then he said that the Indians will come when the moon shined all night...King Tom said they'd come when the moon changed. Well, I told old Ornaw I didna believe him cause the bayside Indians sold me their corn."

Berry took a moment to peruse the people in the room and gave a wry smile. It was obvious he enjoyed the attention.

Yeardley stared hard at Berry and asked, "What did Ornaw say to that?"

"Well, Old Ornaw....he looked angry at me for doubting him and all and he declared loudly....they sold their corn for truck. They had to pay Indians to come over the bay which they hired to fight against the Englishmen! Well, I saw how agitated he was and I asked him what he thought we ought to do. Well Sir, he looked all serious and advised me to leave my house and said if he had more that came with him...that he'd help me but if we stayed, we'd all be killed. I asked him again if he was sure and he declared loudly that they'd come in mayhaps two or three days."

Loud mumbling spread among the patrons in the courtroom and Yeardley pounded on the table in an attempt to silence the crowd.

Col. Scarburgh shouted, "If this is true...we must man our arms and attack at once!"

"I agree," Captain Roper responded weakly. He was still not well from his recent illness, but was determined to attend the meeting.

"Let's listen to the other witnesses first before we go off half-cocked." Argoll retorted. "Is that all you have to report, Robert?"

"Aye, Sir."

"Well, bring in the other witnesses," Argoll ordered.

Two strong black slaves were brought in. After they took their seats, Argoll asked "Phill, I understand you have knowledge of an possible Indian attack. Tell us what you know."

"Aye, Sir....I 'heered' something...I 'heered' King Tom say that he carried roanoke to the Nanticoke King for tribute...so that after the tribute was paid...then they'd come and poison all the wells so that would lessen some of the Englishmen."

"I didna know why we're sitting here listening to this," Scarburgh declared. "Those savages could be attacking our plantations now!"

"Edmund, we need to seek the truth in this matter before we plan an attack," Obedience Robbins calmly stated. "Now did you hear anything else, Phill?"

"Nay, sir... that's all I 'heered'."

"And you, Domingo....what did you hear?" Yeardley asked of the other slave.

"I 'heered' the same thing, Sir, but I also 'heered' that the King of Gingoteague and the King of Matchateague intended to fall foul upon the English, and that they had all consulted together. Only the King of Kikotank did not consult with them."

"Is that all ye know Domingo?" Argoll asked.

"Aye, Sir."

"Well...you two are dismissed," Argoll faced the other Commissioners seated at the table and said, "Gentlemen, I believe we need a little more verification as to the truth of all this before we plan an attack on our Indians here. They've always been a peaceable bunch and I'd hate to stir up needless trouble until we're sure."

Nathaniel Littleton added, I agree, "They've never caused any acts of violence around here...mayhaps a little thievery," he added as he observed Col. Scarburgh's face turning red with anger. "But thievery is not violence and didn't the Laughing King warn us of the attack on Jamestown in '44. Without his warning, more would have been killed...and of course we can't forget the kindness the Assateagues gave to the survivors of the *Virginia Merchant*."

Stephen Charlton nodded, "I'm in agreement to verify the information. There's always been talk among our Indians here, but never war talk."

Col. Scarburgh was sitting on the edge of his seat then stood and pounded on the table...."What about those savages that killed Fisher and his son last year? Didna forget that!"

"You know King Debedeavon acknowledged that and immediately killed two Indians and sent them to us as reparation along with roanoke and beaver skins," John Stringer responded.

"Col. Scarburgh's right though...They did kill and God forbid that I should ever take an Indian equal for a white man. The idea galls me...still," Obedience Robbins shouted.

"I agree...that was a murderous act but it was not warring against us...'twas just a few prowling Indians," added Thomas Johnson.

It was hot in the small room and Argoll Yeardley wiped his face with a handkerchief while he thought a moment about the testimony, then continued, "Fisher and his son were on the Laughing King's land...too far from Accawmacke. I hesitate to start a war with our Indians unless we have more than rumors to go on."

Captain Roper commented, "Remember Gov. Berkeley ordered last spring that the Eastern Shore Indians should be treated with kindness. Suppose we send some men to their villages to talk among the Indians and find out the truth of the matter....I'm sure a little rum will loosen a tongue."

Pockets of soft laughter came from the people observing the exchange between the men.

Col Scarburgh stood and shook his fist again, "Tarnation man...are you crazy? They may be planning their attack right now. Our citizens should be prepared!"

"Col. Scarburgh's right...we should be prepared but I agree...with you Yeardley. Let's keep a cool head and mayhaps we should send some men to seek the truth in the matter." Robbins added, "Of course, we should order all men to keep arms with them at all times while we wait and defend ourselves if necessary."

"I agree with Robbins," Thomas Stringer nodded his head.

The other commissioners agreed.

"Then it is so ordered," Yeardley declared.

Col. Scarburgh, red-faced in anger raised his fist again and declared, "I didna understand, you men...we didna have time to waste...I truly believe we should attack...all these savages should be killed...you can't trust a one of them." Scarburgh stomped out of the room still ranting and raving.

The Commissioners dismissed the hearing and many of the people stood and made their way to the exit.

George Willson looked at Ambrose and said "I see what you mean about Col. Scarburgh hating the Indians."

"He does have a bitterness toward the Indians but he may be right...I didna like what I heard today. Berry's a pretty reliable fellow. He does a lot of trade with the Indians and has many friends among them and if they are giving him a warning....then mayhaps there's something to it...either way...I plan to keep my arms close by...I'm afraid I've been a little lax of late...you never know what an Indian's thinking."

"It's hard to imagine the Indians attacking after my experience...they saved my life when we arrived. 'Twill be hard for me to kill an Indian," George commented.

"If you'd seen half of the things I have, you wouldn't have any trouble. Mary's going to be upset when she hears about Big Tom being involved. She took care of his son after his wife died."

"She did what?"

"Aye, 'twas a year after she and her first husband arrived...quite a story." Ambrose stood and pulled his pipe from his pocket before continuing.

"'Twas before Big Tom was King of course. He and his wife were near Henry and Mary's house when his wife suddenly gave birth, but she had troubles. I guess Big Tom knew Henry was a doctor so he went to Henry's house to get help for his wife."

Ambrose paused to take a long drawl on his pipe. "Anyway, Henry wasn't home so Mary tried to save her life...the woman died but the bairn was healthy. Big Tom left his son with Mary while he took his wife's body home. He came back a few days later to get his son and brought, pelts, corn and lots of supplies to Mary. He's been devoted to Mary ever since. She'll never believe that he'd harm a white man."

"That's is quite a story. I wonder why she never wrote me about it."

"Guess she felt ya' wouldn't understand. There's a lot of people think like Scarburgh...didna care much for the Indians 'round here. If you'd seen those people massacred in James City in '44, you'd feel the same way. They killed and scalped every man woman and child...took infants from their Mum's arms and bashed their brains against a tree...then burnt the houses and killed all the stock."

"But everyone said that the Indians around here have always been peaceable."

"Aye, the ones in Accawmacke have mostly been peaceable but I still didna trust them. I went on a quite a few forays when I first arrived in Accawmacke and after the '44 massacre, no matter how peaceable they are....I just can't trust 'em and I plan to keep watch around my place...we best be returning home now. Hearing all that talk about poisoning wells makes me nervous. I think I'd better put a watch on my well 'till things calm down a bit."

CHAPTER SEVENTEEN

November, 1650 – Eastern Shore, Virginia

The remainder of summer and fall went by without any further difficulty. The men sent to talk to the Indians returned with a mixed report. Numerous Indians were becoming angry over the increasing number of settlers acquiring land and pushing them further north. However, the men were never able to verify a specific plan to poison wells or attack the English. The Commissioners urged the citizens to remain vigilant.

George was due land from the headright he earned by journeying to Virginia. After the harvest, he asked Ambrose for guidance in finding land to patent. The two men spent a breezy fall day touring the area near Ambrose's plantation in a newly built sloop. Hundreds of geese flew overhead in the clear blue sky. The fresh clean air, filled with the fragrance of many wild flowers, was different from the foul smells George experienced in London. He was so overwhelmed by the sights and aroma that he exclaimed, "'Tis like a paradise!"

"Aye, that it is," responded Ambrose. "I've grown use to it... sometimes forget the beauty of Accawmacke...'tis true...'tis like a paradise...a paradise where a man can make a fortune."

"There's certainly no shortage of fowl in Accawmacke," George added. "Or other wild life for that matter."

"Nay, we are very lucky. The only thing I could do without is the incessant insects. They can almost drive a man mad at times, especially on a hot summer day. We've put in a pretty good day scouting for ye're land...what say we stop by the Ordinary for a pint of ale?"

"Sounds like a great idea to me. Mayhaps we can check to see if a packet has arrived from my sisters or Anne. I'm sure that would please, Mary."

The sloop pulled along side the pier. George climbed out and tied the boat to a post. Ambrose followed him toward the Ordinary. As they approached the small log building, they noticed several men outside talking among among themselves in an angry and agitated manner.

"What could be the cause of that?" Ambrose wondered a loud. "Looks like trouble."

George recognized Stephen Horsey but not the other tall, thin man with long hair tied behind his back. Stephen and the unknown man seemed to be involved in an intense discussion. Ambrose noticed that Stephen's face was white and the veins stood out in his forehead as they approached.

Stephen stared at Ambrose. His eyes flashed with anger as he declared, "Have ye heard what Parliament has done now, Ambrose? They're determined to break us."

"Nay, we've been out since sunrise...what's the news?" Ambrose asked.

"Well it seems they think we're all criminals and plan to punish us," Stephen shouted and pointed toward a ragged paper attached to a post next to the Ordinary.

"What?...ye're not making sense. What did ya' mean criminals?" inquired Ambrose in a tone of rising anger.

"They just posted it, straight from James City."

George walked over to the post and put his hand above his brow to block the sun. He squinted his eyes as he skimmed the notice.

Act Oct. 3, 1650: Whereas in Virginia, and in the Islands of Barbadas, Antego, St. Christophers, Mevias, Mounsirat, Bermuda's, and divers other Islands and places in America, ... which are and ought to be subordinate to, and dependent upon England; ..... and ought to be subject to such Laws, Orders and Regulations as are or shall be made by the Parliament of England........

"Well, what's it say?" Ambrose scowled.

"Here's what Stephen's talking about," George said as he read aloud, "*....and every the said persons in Barbada's, Antego, Bermuda's and Virginia, that have contrived, abetted, aided or assisted those horrid Rebellions, or have since willingly joined with them, to be notorious Robbers and Traitors, and such as by the Law of Nations are not to be permitted any manner of Commerce or Traffic with any people whatsoever; and do forbid to all manner of persons, Foreigners, and others, all manner of Commerce, Traffic and Correspondency whatsoever, to be used or held with the said*

Rebels in the Barbada's, Bermuda's, Virginia and Antego, or either of them...."

A quick wave of anger swept across Ambrose's face. "What? This can't be true! Are they trying to ruin us?"

"That part about us being traitors....that will make ye're blood curl," sneered the tall man.

George whistled. "I can't believe they'd say such a thing."

"Nor I, George, " Ambrose added gravely in a voice full of despair. He looked at Stephen. "Surely this is not true...there must be a mistake."

"I'm afraid not, Ambrose." Stephen said, his voice was filled with emotion. "A ship filled with Royalists from England arrived two days ago in James City. An official packet from Parliament was delivered to the Governor and they sent a messenger over this morning with this notice. I watched him post it. I can not believe that England thinks so badly of us."

"What will you do with ye're tobacco crop, Ambrose?" George asked. With this embargo, who will you sell to?"

There was silence for a brief time as each men contemplated their situation. Finally, Ambrose gave George a sad and discouraged glance as he retorted, "I didna know, George...this will hurt us...but more than that...what will it mean with our relationship with our mother country? We're Englishman...same as everyone else in England...not traitors...we didna even fight in their blamed war."

"Aye, that is what concerns me the most. We are English citizens...same as them...how could they speak of us this way?" Stephen added in a bitter tone.

"Well, if they reject us...mayhaps we should reject them as well," the tall man exclaimed.

"Now that's an idea!" Stephen retorted with a laugh.

"Reject England," George exclaimed in astonishment. "Nay, England is home."

"Ah, George...ye're only newly arrived in Virginia. Mayhaps you will change ye're mind after ye have lived here a while. Virginia is more home to me now than England but I've always considered us a part of England," said Stephen Horsey. "Still, welcoming all those Royalists here has certainly created a dilemma for us. We need a solution to this problem...what say we discuss it over a pint of ale?"

The four men entered the crowded Ordinary filled with livid colonists who were energetically arguing over the notice.

In November more Royalists arrived on the Eastern Shore, which strained the food supplies for the winter. Two months later, an additional ship filled with Scottish prisoners banished from England arrived and threatened the stability of the colony.

The colonists of Virginia were in a furor over the treatment they were receiving from England. In an attempt to diffuse the emotional state of the Eastern Shore and improve morale, Col. Yeardley called a public meeting to discuss what to do with the new prisoners. During the meeting, colonists vehemently proclaimed their displeasure with the continual impositions England placed upon them, but no new constructive ideas to solve the problem were brought forward. The Commissioners ordered the prisoners to be indentured among the citizenry of the Eastern Shore. Feelings were still strong so after the meeting, most of the men gathered in Hungar's Ordinary to continue the discussion.

"I didna like the Commissioners decision," commented an elderly gentleman with a beard. He took a slug of his ale before continuing, "I hadn't planned on taking anymore indentures this year...seems we're being forced to care for our country's rejects."

"Aye, and I'm tired of England taking advantage of us," agreed another pock-faced man.

Ambrose nodded his head in agreement. He took out his pipe and filled it with tobacco, then spoke. "Have you noticed that these prisoners seem to be mighty destitute? They've arrived with only the ragged clothes on their back...none have bag or baggage. I wonder why they're not better prepared, especially since they left the continent for good? Surely, they had family at home who could have helped them."

Stephen Horsey sat down beside Ambrose with his tankard of ale and said, "I acquired one of the prisoners as an indenture last week when he first arrived....and I asked him that very question. He had quite a woeful tale."

"What was his story, Horsey?" George queried.

"Well...as ye've heard...Cromwell defeated the Scottish defenses at the Battle of Dunbar in September but evidently he wasn't content with the victory. He went on to ransack Edinburgh and other Scottish towns and cities and take control of the country south of the Highlands."

"I guess he wanted to ensure they wouldn't continue to fight...I see nothing wrong with that," commented a man dressed in a red doublet.

"Twas what he did next that was so brutal. After the battle, Cromwell's forces rounded up around 5,000 Scottish prisoners and embarked on a 'march of shame.'"

"What didya mean...by 'march of shame'?" Ambrose asked.

"That's the name the Scots called it. My indenture told me that he was forced on a brutal 8-day, 118 mile march south to the English city of Durham with virtually no rest and with no food or water, other what could be scavenged. The prisoners were driven the first 28 miles to Berwick without even stopping during the night."

"That's unbelievable!" exclaimed George in an anguished voice.

"What was the purpose of being so cruel? They'd had their victory," shouted a man in the back of the room.

Stephen nodded and continued, "My apprentice said that of the estimated 5,000 who started the march only around 3,000 were left at the end when they reached their destination at Durham Cathedral and Castle on September 11, 1650."

"Only three thousand left...'tis hard to imagine" Ambrose responded.

"Durham Cathedral seems a strange place for a prison," an old man sitting next to George commented.

"I agree...'twas only a makeshift prison...and the conditions the Scots were kept in was appalling," Stephen added. "With virtually no food, clean water, or heat, disease spread and the Scots died at an average of 30 a day, then reached over a 100 a day toward October. By October 11, only 1600 of the original 5000 prisoners remained."

"Whewww....these prisoners have been through quite an ordeal," Ambrose declared quietly.

"I'll say...my young apprentice said it was extremely cold

during the winter and they were desperate to create some heat to reduce the death toll. Sadly, they were forced to strip the holy Cathedral bare of all wooden items, including pews, and even the organ. The only item that remained was a clock embossed with a carved Scot's Thistle...and they couldn't bring themselves to burn it."

"Did Cromwell just forget about them?" George asked.

"I have no idea...two months later, only 1400 of the 5,000 prisoners were still alive when nine hundred were sold to the Colonies, mainly Virginia, Massachusetts and Barbados. The other 500 were forced to serve in the French army."

"Well...'tis no wonder they are so bitter...I guess I'm willing to take them on as indentures. They've been through enough suffering," Ambrose stated.

"I agree with ye, Ambrose but with this embargo our country's placed on us...'twill be difficult to manage," Col. Coulbourne countered.

"Aye," many of the other men shouted in unison.

The bad news from England and the impending threat of an Indian attack overwhelmed the colonists and their emotional state was reaching a boiling point. On February 16, 1651, the Commissioners ordered all free men to meet at Walter Williams to consider the peace and safety of the parish.

Walters William's house was much larger than most, with a Parlour chamber, porch chamber and a hall chamber. Even though there were several chambers, the rooms were still rather small. The men met in the Parlour, however it soon filled to capacity and late-comers were forced to stand outside the room in the hall and porch chambers.

Commander Argoll Yeardley began the meeting by asking Rev. Rozier to lead them in prayer.

".......God bless these men gathered here today as they make decisions about the future of our colony. Keep us safe and guide our actions and words. Amen."

Commander Argoll Yeardley opened the meeting. "Thank you Rev. Rozier and thank you men for coming today. As you know we've much to discuss so we shall start immediately. I'm sure ye're all aware of the Act from England forbidding trade with Virginia."

Many Ayes and Boos permeated the crowd. After the comments diminished, Argoll continued.

"It is my belief that this Act was created because we welcomed those who sided with our late King with open arms...and no matter whose side you may be on...I feel we could do nothing less...especially hearing reports of the atrocious treatment of many of our friends in England."

Shouts of affirmation rang out and Argoll paused until the men were again quiet.

"Still...this leaves us in a predicament. Parliament considers us traitors and refuses trade with us. We must remedy this situation. I propose we send a packet immediately to Parliament to work out a compromise so we will again be recognized by England as a trade partner...after all, England is still home and our mother country...no matter her troubles."

"I agree...but how should we approach Parliament?" inquired Nathaniel Littleton.

"Why don't we send ye Col. Yeardley?" a man commented.

"He needs someone to go with him," Col. Scarburgh added, obviously wanting to be included.

"Well, I propose Nathaniel Littleton go," Ambrose declared. "He has a cooler head than anyone...we need someone like him to talk 'nice' to Parliament if we want a compromise."

Laughter sprinkled through the room.

"Well, I guess if the Commissioners vote on this proposal...then we'll be your messengers to Parliament, right Nathaniel?"

"Aye, Argoll." Littleton replied.

"Let's vote. All Commissioners in agreement to this proposal, say Aye."

All the Commissioners agreed and Argoll continued, "Now since we'll be representing everyone here. I know I'd like to hear ye're thoughts about a compromise. The meeting is open to comments."

The rest of the meeting was spent in discussion. It was quite late when it ended and the men dispersed to their respective homes, still concerned about their future.

In March 1651, Nathaniel Littleton and Argoll Yeardley returned to the Eastern Shore with a document to be signed by the freeman residing in their community. It was dated the 11th of March, the day before the ratification of the Articles of Surrender drafted by Parliament. The document read:

We whose Names are subscribed; do hereby Engage and promise to be true and faithful to the Commonwealth of England as it is now Established without King or House of Lords."

During the next thirty days, the signatures of one hundred and sixteen of the people on the Eastern Shore were secured including Ambrose Dixon, Stephen Horsey and Col. Coulbourne.

CHAPTER EIGHTEEN

April, 1651 Eastern Shore, Virginia

Meetings continued throughout the winter among the people on the Eastern Shore and worries about an Indian uprising mounted.

Ambrose and George completed the spring planting so they decided to stop by the Ordinary late one afternoon for a pint of ale and check on further news. When they neared the quay, they noticed three men in front of the log building. Two of the men had knives and were whittling as they leaned against the building and talked quietly. The third man, with long braided hair, was squatting in a crouching position and stared at the water while he smoked his pipe. He stood up as Ambrose and George approached.

"Why, Toby, Richard, John...what are you men doing here on such a good work day?" Ambrose greeted the men. "George, I didna know if ye have met these men or not but they are three of the best Indian fighters around, Toby Norton, Richard Vaughan, and John Robinson. I've been on many an Indian foray with them...especially after the '44 massacre...I trust them with my life."

"Nice to meet you gents." George declared as he shook their hands.

"You haven't answered my question. What brings ye here today? Is something amiss with the Indians?"

"I guess you can say so, Ambrose. Col. Scarburgh sent word to us this morning to meet him here. Didna he send for ye?" Vaughan replied.

"I wouldn't know it if he did. We've been in the fields since sunrise. Why where ye sent for?"

"Scarburgh says those Indians north of his land are up to something...you know how he's been complaining all year about them stealing from him. He's lost considerable beef, hogs and tools so he's asking for our help." Vaughan continued.

"I don't see how the four of us can be much help. We'll certainly be outnumbered," Ambrose commented as he pulled out his pipe.

"There's more men. John Dollings, Richard Bayley, Tomlin Price, Richard Hill and a few others are inside and more on on their way. Scarburgh wants us to capture or kill the King of Pocomoke." John Robinson added.

"Ye don't say. Capture him....What good will that do? Probably just rile them all."

"Scarburgh says that he's the leader of that conspiracy to poison our wells...so he figures if we take away the leader...then the Indians will back down," Toby Norton responded as he put the piece of wood he was whittling in his pocket and the knife in his boot. Then he stood up straight and said, "Well, gents...shall we go in and hear more about these plans. I'd like to wet my whistle."

Ambrose and George returned home late that evening. When they entered, Mary was sitting with her sewing basket in her lap. She could tell by Ambrose's face that something was troubling him but decided not to ask.

I'm sure he'll tell me in time. I hope it's nothing too serious...I have my own news for him.

"I imagine you men are hungry," Mary greeted them with a beaming smile. "Betsy, get them some of that good venison you made...and check to see if we have any pastry left."

"Aye, Mam...right away."

Betsy quickly ladled the venison into two bowls and set the long board that served for a table on the supports. She grabbed two pewter cups from the shelf and filled them with ale and set them by the bowls.

Mary continued to stitch one of Ambrose's shirts while Mary Jane and Tom played with some wooden blocks nearby.

Ambrose glanced around the room a minute before he asked, "Where's Henry, Jr?"

"Out at the stock pen...he said that we should have that new calf soon and he's keeping an eye on old Susie in case she has trouble."

"Smart boy, always thinking...I'm glad I put him in charge of the stock," Ambrose declared as he gave Mary a peck on the cheek.

George reached down and picked up Tom. He tossed the

child in the air and caught the laughing boy with his hands. Mary Jane looked up, stood and began pulling at George's shirt and shouting, "Me...Me...Me."

Ambrose bent down...and pulled the delighted girl in his arms and hugged her close, "You must wait ye're turn, Mary Jane...life is like that...you have to wait ye're turn."

Realizing that Ambrose was not going to toss her like Tom, Mary Jane began squirming in his arms so Ambrose began to tickle her. She squealed with delight.

"Ambrose, between you and George, those two bairns are becoming quite spoiled," Mary laughed.

"Didna you know Sis, that's what an Uncle is for...to spoil nieces and nephews," George replied as he sat Tom back on the wooden floor.

Tom started to cry, loudly and Mary said, "See that's exactly what I'm talking about." She placed her basket on the floor, picked up her son and tried to console him as she gently rocked back and forth in the straight backed chair.

George sat on the bench and Betsy placed a loaf of bread in front of him. Her hand accidentally touched his as she placed the pan of warmed venison beside the bread. Betsy quickly pulled her hand away and he smiled at her. She returned his smile with one that lit up her face.

Ambrose stood and carried Mary Jane with him to the table and noticed the interchange between Betsy and George before he sat down but said nothing.

"Sis, this is a mighty fine meal, but didna you say something about pastry?" George asked with his mouth full of bread.

"Aye...Mr. George," Betsy replied. "I'm sorry...I forgot."

Ambrose laughed and Mary gave him a strange look.

"What's so funny, Ambrose?"

"Nothing, love...just something I thought about," he said with a chuckle.

Later that evening, Ambrose and Mary sat alone in the Parlour, soaking up warmth from the fireplace. Even though it was April, a cool ocean breeze chilled the air.

Ambrose stared at the dancing flames, then reached for

Mary's hand. She smiled at him and gave his hand a squeeze. Ambrose rose and stood at the fireplace with his back to her.

"Mary, I have something to tell you but I didna want you to worry."

Mary gave a sigh, "I was afraid of that...I knew something was bothering you. 'Tis it more bad news from England?"

Ambrose turned around and faced Mary. "Nay, not this time...'tis Scarburgh."

"What is that man up to now? I'm sure it's in regard to the Indians."

"Ye're right...but you know how skittish everyone's been since last summer when we heard all those rumors. Mayhaps he has a solution."

"What kind of solution? Kill all the Indians?" Mary laughed.

"Not quite as severe but I know that according to him that would be his ultimate solution," Ambrose chuckled.

Ambrose returned to his chair and sat down by Mary. He took her hands in his and looked into her eyes.

"He's called up about fifty of the best Indian fighters and plans to attack and capture the King of the Pocomoke."

"And I guess ye're one of the fifty?" Mary declared in despair. "But why capture the King?" she said as she pulled her hands away.

Ambrose stood and began to pace, "Col. Scarburgh said that the King is leader of this conspiracy against the English and he feels if we capture him then the others will back down."

"What do the Commissioners say about his plan?"

"I didna know, but Scarburgh said we can't wait on the Commissioners to approve it because we are in danger now. I admit, I have my doubts about his plan but most of the men said we need to do something...waiting for an attack like this is infuriating. I'm afraid to leave you and the children, alone. I've seen what Indians do when they attack."

Ambrose sat down again and took Mary's hand in his and stroked it gently.

"But fifty men, is that enough? Won't it be dangerous with so few?" she asked softly.

"It will be dangerous, but we didna plan an attack on all the Indians...we just want to capture one King."

Both Ambrose and Mary were silent for a few moments. She suddenly grasped his face with both hands and stared into his eyes as tears flowed down her cheeks. "I didna know what I'd do if anything happened to you, Ambrose."

Ambrose was startled at her response. He stood and took her into his arms. She rested her head on his shoulder.

Could it be that Mary really cares for me? Dare I hope she loves me? How can I upset her like this?

Ambrose hugged her tightly.

They stood together for a few moments, then Mary spoke softly as she remained in his arms. "I have something to tell you Ambrose. I hope ye'll be happy."

"What is it, dear one?"

"We are to have another bairn."

Ambrose pushed Mary away from his chest but still held onto her arms. He gave her an astonished look as he exclaimed with excitement, "Another bairn...Oh, Mary. You make me the happiest man alive...another bairn....that makes four. I never thought I'd have such a family."

"But that means...we need you to stay safe. I mean it, I cannot manage without you."

Ambrose released her and solemnly declared, "Aye, Mary. I understand but at the same time...I must go with these men to keep my family safe."

Mary sat down and paused a moment before responding.

"I know, Ambrose...I know." She turned her head and stared into the fire. Tears flowed down her cheeks unchecked.

Oh, God...you have brought this man into my life...now please take care of him. I cannot lose another person I care about.

CHAPTER NINETEEN

April, 1651 Eastern Shore, Virginia

Ambrose Dixon, with forty-eight other Indian fighters, met at Edmund Scarburgh's house before dawn broke on April 28, 1651. Ambrose asked George to remain home with his family to keep them safe. After ensuring that all the men had adequate arms and ammunition, Col. Scarburgh marched the men toward the Pocomoke Indian village bordering his land.

The smell of light smoke from numerous fires drifted and floated above the small village as they approached quietly on foot with the hope of a surprise attack. It appeared they would be successful...as no one in the village was stirring.

Scarburgh pointed toward the main lodge in the village that was probably the King's abode. He signaled Toby Norton, Richard Baily and John Robinson to go first, the other men followed close behind. Half the men moved to the left and the other half to the right encircling the village. Edmund gave the signal and the men began firing all at once.

The startled braves, rushed out for their bow and arrows and other weapons, only to have them slashed from their hands as soon as they reached them.

"Watch it Vaughan," Ambrose shouted as he fired at a brave aiming an arrow at Vaughan's back. The brave was hit in the arm and his bow and arrow fell to the ground as he grabbed his useless arm with his other hand.

Ambrose noticed a matchlock near the brave as he fell.

What's a matchlock doing here? 'Tis against the law to sell guns to the Indians. Good thing we surprised them. No telling what would have happened if they'd used them against us.

Very few braves were able to retrieve their weapons in time to retaliate. Soon the scene was complete bedlam as the braves resorted to hand-to-hand fighting with clubs and anything they could find but the Colonist's fire power, sabers and long hunting knives prevailed, injuring many of the Indians. The small village was soon overtaken.

After the valiant braves were restrained, Scarburgh brought two men to the center of the village and bound them back to back with their neck and heels in chains.

"Well men, I'd say we have been successful," Scarburgh boasted. "Mayhaps this savages will think twice about attacking an Englishman. What do you say we take a few of these hot-headed braves and mayhaps some of these winsome maidens and children back with us along with the King? I didna know about you but I could use a few more servants....and while ye're at it.....break every bow you see. We didna want those remaining think they can follow us."

"Aye, Col. Scarburgh and it'll lessen their numbers some," Thomas Johnson added.

Ambrose observed the crying young children, trembling young girls and humiliated King and braves in the village. He thought about his own children. A young woman sat propped against a stump, her young infant, still clasped in the woman's arms, was wailing; she was dead from a musket wound to her head. Two children, a boy and a girl around eight years of age lay face-down in the dirt, bleeding profusely from gunshot blast in their backs. An old man slumped against a tree, held a broken bow. His face was partially blown away.

This isn't fighting...'tis slaughter. I certainly didna want to kill women or children nor make slaves of these people...I only wanted to stop them from killing my family. Edmund can take all the servants he wants...I'll not be a part of that.

Ambrose walked to the edge of the settlement. He recognized a young brave who had frequently traded with his family. The Indian always brought something special to give Henry, Jr. Now, he lay dead on the bloody ground, his face toward the sky.

Several of the Indian fighters drifted among the Indians and chose captives, chained them together and with the point of their gun, pushed them toward the center where the bound King proudly stood.

"March them back men, it appears we'll be home in time for dinner," Col. Scarburgh scoffed.

After the men returned to Scarburgh's house, most of them quickly dispersed, but some remained to bicker over the Indian

134

servants.

After Ambrose left Scarburgh's house, he took his sloop out on the Chesapeake and stayed alone on the water for two hours.

Word of the Indian raid spread throughout the Eastern Shore and many grew worried of the Indian Nation seeking revenge. The Commissioners immediately reacted and ordered the sheriff to arrest all the men who participated in the raid. They remained in the custody of the Sheriff until they posted bonds or appeared in person at James City to answer the Governor and Council on May 21st.

Ambrose was arrested as well as many of his close friends, including Thomas Johnson, Richard Vaughan, John Dollings, John Robinson, Toby Norton, Richard Bayly, Richard Hill, and Tomlin Price. In total, all fifty men were taken to James City to be prosecuted.

Three days later, Argoll Yeardley and William Andrews were sent to prosecute the defendants. A boat, well stocked with provisions and manned by three men, was placed at their disposal while Yeardley and Andrews remained in James City for the trial.

After Ambrose's arrest, Mary was frantic.

"George, what can I do to help him? They took him to James City. I wouldn't worry so much if he was taken to court here where people know him."

"I agree, Mary...but I didna know how ye can help. Have you talked to the other wives? Surely the Commissioner realizes what a devastating blow it would be to have fifty of our substantial citizens imprisoned."

"Ye're right George. How can they take fifty men away from our community. Tomorrow is Sunday. I'll talk to the other women after church. Mayhaps we can persuade the Commissioners...they might intervene."

It took a week, but the Commissioners relented and a representative was sent to James City to discuss the charges against the men.

Finally, by June, all the men except Col. Scarburgh and

Thomas Johnson were released and all charges were dropped, but because the Commissioners were concerned about possible revenge by the Indians, William Andrews sent one hundred arms' length of roanoke to Onecren of Pocomoke; and twenty arms' length of roanoke to the Indians who were chained neck and heels. They also sent ten weeding hoes to the King of Metomkin.

After further investigation, even Col. Scarburgh and Thomas Johnson were found innocent of the charges. A statement was made that they acted as careful and honest men ought to have done.

CHAPTER TWENTY

October, 1651- Eastern Shore, Virginia

The raid only worsened the bad feelings between the Englishmen and the Indians on the Eastern Shore. On October 9th the county was again divided into military precincts and commanders were appointed. Another raid was planned, but this time it was initiated by the Commissioners.

The Commission ordered twenty-five horses and mares, with saddles and bridles, to be provided by the planters. If enough volunteers did not appear, men were to be pressed into service by the sheriff. They met on the following Monday afternoon at three o'clock at the house of Richard Bayly, of Nuswattocks. Each man brought a pound of powder, with shot and bullets and rations for a week with him. They were armed with pistols, carbine and short sword and authorized to take such arms and harness from the planters, wherever they happened to find them.

George and Ambrose assisted in the massive raid. Mary met them on the front porch when they returned home. She was holding Mary Jane in her arms and peered anxiously at her husband's face before asking, "Did everything go as planned?"

"Aye, Mary. There's no cause for alarm this time."

"Thank goodness....ye're both safely home. I was so worried. Was anyone killed or hurt."

"Nay, our show of force intimidated the Indians and no lives were lost, and only a few belligerent Indians were injured. I may be wrong but I didna believe we'll have to fight them anymore," Ambrose exclaimed as he whisked Mary Jane from her mother's arms and whirled the astonished child around in the air. The child's dark hair flew around her head like a halo and she clapped her hands with excitement.

"I certainly hope you are right and I'm glad you went with the Commissioners blessing this time. I thought I might never see you again after the last raid."

"Are you saying, you'd miss me?" Ambrose smiled as he set

his daughter down on the floor. He pulled a shiny rock from his pocket for the child to examine. She immediately threw it across the room and chased after it.

"Oh, I might miss you some," Mary teased. "Though with the number of children we have now and this next one that will soon be here, 'tis hard to tell if anyone's missing."

"You should have seen ye're husband, Mary," George said. "He's becoming a regular hero to a lot of men around here. He saved Horsey's life this time."

"I'm just glad the two of you are home...I've had my fill of raids."

"Me too, Mary. I'd rather be planting and that's saying something because my true passion is building boats. I heard an interesting piece of information about our old friend Col. Scarburgh."

"Not again. What 's he up to this time?"

"Wait till you hear this, Mary. You'll never believe it." George grinned as he stood by the blazing fire to warm himself.

"It seems that our Indian hater, Col. Scarburgh, despite how much he hates Indians, has all the while been trading guns and ammunition to them."

"Nay!" Mary exclaimed. "Where did you hear this?"

"Obedience Robbins told me Scarburgh's ship, the *Sea Horse*...you know the one I built for him last year. It was seized by the New Netherlands government in Delaware Bay. The Dutch aren't too happy about the trade block Parliament instigated last year and have been attacking English ships. Anyway...when they boarded the ship they discovered a large quantity of arms and ammunition. The skipper said that it was for trade with the Indians. Of course, the Commissioners ordered Scarburgh arrested again and taken to James City."

"Oh my, that man never ceases to amaze me as to what he will do. I wonder if he'll get out of this situation as he has everything else. Have you heard anything about what is happening in England with the Dutch War and all? I'm so worried about my sisters. It seems that our great country will never be the same."

"Col. Yeardley received a packet last week. He said Charles the Second, who should be declared our King, invaded England, but was overthrown at Worcester in September. He managed to escape. One day, mayhaps he'll regain his throne."

"Aye, we can always pray for that...it appears we're had nothing but trouble with Parliament in control...but for now I 'spect you two would like a meal. Betsy will you see to that while I check on little Tom? I imagine he's hungry as well."

"Where's Henry, Jr.?" Ambrose asked.

"The usual place...taking care of our stock," Mary said over her shoulder as she left the room.

"That boy sure takes his duties seriously," George declared.

"That's true, George. But he needs to eat sometimes. I'll see if I can pull him away long enough to eat. I need to check and see how well he's taking care of the stock anyway," Ambrose said as he put on his hat and walked toward the front door.

Henry, Jr. was rubbing down Mary's horse Rascal when Ambrose approached him. The boy was now thirteen and tall for his age. He smiled expectantly as Ambrose drew close.

"Son, I appreciate you working so hard, but you need to come in and take a meal once in a while."

"I'm almost done, Papa. Rascal likes a good rub down in the evening and I wanted to finish my chores before I came in."

Ambrose walked around the pen and stopped from time to time to observe. "Ye're doing a great job taking care of the stock, Henry; couldn't have done a better myself and that new calf is really growing. He'll probably be bigger than the last one at this rate."

"Aye, Papa. I wanted to ask you about our last calf...seeings we have the new calf...would you be interested in selling off the last one? As you said, she's a bit on the small size but she'll probably make a good milk cow."

"Well, I really hadn't thought about selling her...why do you ask?"

"Do you know a negro by the name of Anthony Johnson?"

"Aye, he belonged to William Bennett but bought his freedom sometime ago. He settled on Pungoteague Creek. How do you know him?"

"He came by today and asked if we'd be interested in selling that calf. He's in need of a milking cow because he and his wife will have a bairn soon."

"I did hear something about him marrying. How does he intend to pay for it?"

"He said he had roanoke...at least enough to pay for that calf. I figure the calf is worth about twenty roanoke. He said Mr. Bennett allowed him a lot to plant and he sold truck off it."

"He did...well I'll be. Sounds like he's a hard-working negro. Alright then....if he can pay for the calf...I'll sell it to him."

"Could I take the calf to him tomorrow Papa? He was most anxious to have it soon...said if he didna hear from me tomorrow...then he'll go look at someone else's cow."

"I didna see why not. Just be sure ye take care of all your chores and tell ye're mother before ye leave. Seems ye're learning to be a good trader as well. Now let's go get us something to eat."

"Aye, Papa. Let me put away this brush and I'll be right behind you."

That boy never ceases to amaze me. He's a smart lad. I need to see about getting him some more book learning though. No telling what he might do with a little more book learning.

After Mary and Ambrose left the room, George remained behind with Betsy.

"Something certainly smells good, Betsy," he commented. "What have ye cooked up for us today?"

Betsy gave George a huge smile. "Chicken stew, Mr. George...it was my mothers specialty. I didna know if it's as good as hers but I tried."

Tom set the board for the table while Betsy filled a bowl to the top with chicken stew.

"If it taste anything like it smells...it should be great. You mentioned ye're mother but Mary said your parents were killed in the war. How were they killed if you don't mind me asking?"

"I didna mind the question, Sir...but I'm not sure I have the right answer. I was at the Church when it happened. All I know is that when my brother returned home from Church, our house was only ashes and we found our parents and little brother and sister all dead." Betsy paused and glanced away before continuing.

"My brother and me ran to a neighbor and she told us that

some Parliamentary soldiers were at the house making a racket that morning and when they left, they set the house on fire. I didna know if my family died from the fire or they were killed first. My neighbor, Mrs. Simpson couldn't tell me more because she ran and hid in her basement after she saw the soldiers."

"That must have been a horrible experience. Do you know why they were targeted?"

"Nay, but my father worked as a Clerk in the Court. Mayhaps that's why."

"What did you do after you found them since you no longer had a home?"

"We ran to our neighbor, Mrs. Simpson's house and stayed with her until my Uncle could come for us. He was fighting with the King's army. Since we lost everything in the fire, he arranged for our indenture to the Colonies. He thought the soldiers might kill us too if we remained in England." Betsy could no longer control her tears.

George pulled her into his arms and held her tenderly against his chest while she cried on his shoulder. "I'm sorry Betsy. I didna mean to upset. Ye're safe here now."

Betsy regained control of herself and pushed away from his arms. "I'm sorry Mr. George. I didna know what came over me...'Tis hard to talk about their death. You won't tell Miss Mary will you?"

"Nay, Betsy. I won't tell her, though I'd doubt she'd care. She understands grief for family herself...but I won't tell her. Can I help you with anything before they return?"

"Well, you could get those pewters mugs from that shelf," she laughed. "They're kind of hard for me to reach. My Papa kept telling me I'd grow taller, but it doesn't seem to be happening."

George walked over to her and stretched his arms behind her head to reach the shelf, forcing Betsy to press back against the wall. Their bodies briefly touched sending strange, enjoyable signals to their brains. They both pulled a part as if shocked and stared into each others eyes for what seemed like an eternity. Mary's voice penetrated the silence as she walked down the hall so George hurriedly placed the pewter mugs on the table.

"This wee one's hungry and getting heavier everyday. Tom, little man...you best be walking soon. If you grow any heavier...ye're Mum won't be able to carry you," Mary chuckled. She looked around the room and asked "Where's Ambrose?"

"Here, my love," Ambrose replied as he sauntered in the door with a grin on his face.

"You seem to be mighty happy for some reason," Mary declared.

"Who wouldn't be happy with such a wonderful family?" Ambrose exclaimed. "God has truly blessed us!"

Henry, Jr. entered the room. Mary looked around at all the members of her family and smiled.

Aye, Ambrose....we have been blessed. God has truly blessed us.

Ambrose rose early the next morning. He had an urge to spend some time on the water alone to think. Since George would be attending to the fields and Henry, Jr. planned to take the calf to Anthony Johnson, Ambrose decided to take his new sloop out to check her sea worthiness.

It was fall, and nature put on a show. He stood on the porch a minute to admire the view. A gentle breeze blew, colorful leaves fell to the ground like snowflakes while busy squirrels darted playfully among the leaves creating rustling sounds as they gathered nuts for the coming winter.

Ambrose followed the well-trodden trail to the quay. His boots crunched the autumn leaves making a quiet walk impossible. A bald eagle, startled by his approach suddenly took flight, squawking loudly in protest, as he soared above the marshes. Ambrose reached the pier and climbed into the sloop and pushed away into the still water.

Another bald eagle suddenly appeared in front of him and swooped down from the sky with talons stretched. He dove at the clear water then flew up again with a large fish in his strong talons. Ambrose watched the huge bird land on a nearby mud bank and tear the fish apart with his beak.

The call of geese flying overhead penetrated the quiet while a large Egret stood in the tall grass of the marsh and stared as the sloop glided by....annoyed at his presence.

After about an hour on the water, Ambrose decided to head for Hungar's to acquire a few supplies and check to see if he had a packet from his factor in England. When he neared the quay at

Hungar's, he noticed a large assemblage of people crowded in front of the Ordinary.

He climbed on the pier, quickly tied the boat to a post and walked toward the congregation of people.

Ambrose spotted his good friend Stephen Horsey, "Halloa Stephen...what's this all about...has something happened?"

"Aye, Ambrose. Parliaments at it again....always creating problems," Stephen replied as he angrily pointed at a parchment nailed to a post near the Ordinary.

"What could it be this time? Weren't they satisfied with that Oath of Allegiance we signed last year and the tax of forty-six pounds of tobacco they saddled on us?"

"This time they're meddling with our local government. They appointed Richard Bennett, Thomas Stegg and Captain Claiborne, commissioners and if that wasn't enough...they have a new Act forbidding goods, wares or merchandise, to be imported into England except by English ships...We can't ship our goods in Dutch ships anymore!"

"I guess our hope of remaining free from England's trouble with the Dutch are dashed. I thought we were far enough away...seems I was wrong," Ambrose replied with a grim expression on his face.

"'Twill be a problem...since we have so many Dutch living in Accawmacke. John Custis was here a while ago and he was fit to be tied. He has many Dutch friends and ships almost exclusively on their boats. Even if we export all our goods on English ships...there's the danger of the ships being seized like Scarburgh's was. He sure got himself in a dilemma this time, didna he? Imagine him of all people, trading guns and ammunition with the Indians."

"I couldn't believe it myself...guess it shows you never know about a person." Ambrose replied. "What say...let's you and me grab a pint of ale? I'd like to hear more about these new Commissioners."

Two months later on Christmas Eve, little Sarah Anne Dixon was welcomed to the Dixon household, increasing the children of Ambrose and Mary Dixon to three, Mary Jane, Thomas and now Sarah. Henry, Jr. was ecstatic to have another sister. "Now, we're even....two boys and two girls," he said.

"She looks just like our sister Elizabeth with that tinge of red hair," George Willson remarked.

"I thought so too, George... she's like a gift from Heaven," Mary said.

"I didna care who she looks like, but she's one of the most beautiful bairns in the world and I dare anyone to say different," challenged Ambrose as he gently cradled the small infant in his arms.

CHAPTER TWENTY-ONE

Winter and Spring, 1652 – Eastern Shore, Virginia

Col. Scarburgh was finally released from the charges placed against him concerning his ship the *Sea Horse* and immediately made attempts to take back his ship from the Dutch. He ordered depositions to be taken of his men so he could bring the matter before the Northampton Court and the Governor and Council of James City. After much legal maneuvering between the lawyers and Governor of James City and the Dutch, the ship was recovered.

By January, 1652, Colonel Scarburgh, obviously angered with all the troubles he had encountered in Accawmacke, made preparations to leave, indefinitely. He sold at least four ships to William Bunton of Boston, Massachusetts, and still filled with ire for the Dutch, he left Accawmacke. Edmund's abrupt departure from the colonies raised considerable talk among the people of Accawmacke.

In March, 1652, Captain Dennis arrived at James City and demanded the surrender of the Colony to Parliament and Governor Stone was removed from his position. The colonists, realizing their dependence on England for necessities of life felt they had no other choice and offered no resistance. Articles of capitulation were ratified on the 12th of the month.

The articles of capitulation provided that the Colony of Virginia was subject to the Commonwealth of England but the submission should be considered voluntary. The privilege of having fifty acres of land for every person transported to the colony was continued and the people of Virginia would be allowed free trade according to the laws of the Commonwealth.

Burdened by wearisome taxes and the loss of such a prominent citizen as Col. Scarburgh, people gathered daily to discuss the situation. One of the meetings, resulted in a protest being drawn up on March 30th signed by Stephen Charlton, William Whittington, Levin Denwood, Jonathan Ellis, Jonathan Nuthall and Stephen Horsey. When Ambrose heard about the document, he was worried about his good friend's involvement and potential consequences he might incur from Parliament by signing it.

Stephen's wife, Sarah, greeted Ambrose when he arrived at the Horsey plantation to discuss the document.

"Why, Ambrose...what brings you out here so early? No problem, I hope?"

"Nay, Sarah...Mary and the children are fine. You might be interested to know that we named our new bairn, Sarah...after Mary's sister," he added.

'You did...well as you can expect..seems a fine name to me. How many children does that make now...two, three?"

"Four counting Henry, Jr."

"My, you certainly have a growing family...we'll be having another soon...that will make four for us as well when you count my first three. Well, where are my manners...standing here at the door with you...come on in...I 'spect you've come to see Stephen."

"Aye, Sarah.....is he about?"

"He's down at the drying barn with the two boys...checking on the tobacco leaves...I'll send little Sarah for him. Would you like some tea while ye're waiting?...the kettle's warm."

"Aye, Sarah...I would."

"I'll fetch some of those good sugar pastries little Sarah made too. My daughter is turning out to be a good cook."

"Just like her Mum, I'm sure."

"Oh, get on with you now," Sarah replied as she raised her hand in protest and chuckled as she ambled out of the room.

Stephen arrived a few minutes later and greeted his friend warmly. The two men sat opposite each other by the fire as Sarah brought in tea and some cookies and set them on the table between them. She left the two men to talk alone.

"Stephen, I guess you know why I've come. I read the letter you signed and it appears to be pretty strongly worded...I'm worried about the consequences you might receive from Parliament."

"Do you not feel we are overly burdened by these taxes as well, Ambrose?"

"Aye, 'tis true....that's why everyone appointed the six of you to draft a letter...but here....I wrote it down so I could remember the words... in the letter you wrote:

....Ye County of Northampton to be disloyal and sequestered from ye rest of Virginia. Therefore that Law which requireth and injoineth taxation from us to be arbitrary and illegal forasmuch as we had neither summons for election for Burgesses nor voice in their Assembly (during the time aforesaid) but only the Singular Burgess in September, Ano., 1651, We conceive that we may lawfully protest against the proceedings in the Act of Assembly for public Taxation which have relation to Northampton County since ye year 1647."

"What is wrong with the wording, Ambrose? 'Tis all true. We've had no voice or representation in the election of Burgesses and therefore no voice in the decisions they make in taxing. When you add those exorbitant freight rates and even diminished price on tobacco, 'tis hard for our small planters to make a living."

Stephen's face grew red and he stood. He began to pace and suddenly exclaimed, "The tax is illegal....we've had many a meeting about this subject. '*Tis taxation without representation*...that's what it is...and not right. We should have a voice in the way we are governed. We are English citizens and must demand our rights!"

"I agree," Ambrose nodded. He stood and grasped Stephen's arm. "But 'tis you I'm worried about, dear friend."

Stephen gave Ambrose an astonished glance then sat back down in the chair.

"But why...'tis not everything in the letter only what you as well as the majority of the citizens voiced in our meetings? We only wrote what you directed," Stephen declared.

"Aye, ye're correct...and we will stand together in this and you know I'll back you with me life, Stephen. 'Tis only my worry that there are only six signatures on the letter...and yours is one of them. We should have required everyone to sign this letter...to show our resolve. The six of you should not receive punishment for something required by all the citizens."

"Ambrose, you worry too much my friend. The letter states that we are only representatives of the people. That should be sufficient. As for having everyone sign it, there simply isn't time. We needed to have this letter ready before the delegation from Parliament leaves this month if we hope to receive an answer soon."

"Ye're right, Stephen. I guess there is no choice. Send the

letter. Parliament must pay some heed to our complaints. Their taxes will destroy us and we should have a voice in our government, but if ye're in need my support when we have their answer, dear friend....ye know I'll be there for you."

"Aye, Ambrose. I know...and thanks for reassuring me."

The two men continued chatting amicably. It was late afternoon before Ambrose returned home.

CHAPTER TWENTY-TWO

Spring 1652 – Eastern Shore, Virginia

George, Ambrose and Mary attended the wedding of John Custis, Jr. and Elizabeth Eyer at Hungar's church. It was a pleasant day so almost everyone on the Eastern Shore turned out for the occasion.

"Doesn't Elizabeth look beautiful, Mary?" Joanne Custis asked. Mayhaps we'll have more grandchildren soon. I was worried that my son would never settle down."

"Aye, Joanne. I hope you have many grandchildren. Where do they plan to live? Will they still remain with Argoll?"

"Nay, John wanted a place of his own so Argoll leased a parcel of his land to him. They've built a small cottage for now but only until John can purchase property of his own. It shouldn't be long. John has a knack for getting things done...just like his father," Joanne smiled as she watched her husband in serious conversation with Col. William Coulbourne, Ambrose and Rev. Francis Doughty.

Rev. Francis Doughty was the new pastor of Hungars parish, replacing Rev. Rozier and though still an Anglican he was considered by some as a supporter of the the Nonconformists. He no longer used the Book of Common Prayer.

"What do ye think of Rev. Doughty, Joanne?"

There was a slight pause in Joanne's manner before she answered, as if she were unsure of what to say. She frowned when she finally replied, "I'm not sure, Mary. His approach to the service will take some time adjusting to but overall I like him. He has a great sense of humor and I understand he resided in the Netherlands for a while. Have you talked to poor Ann Eaton lately? I feel so sorry for her. She has certainly had bad luck with husbands."

"Aye, I see her from time to time. Life has really dealt her some blows after losing two husbands, then Rev. Eaton abandoning her like that and returning to England."

"Good riddance I say, he left the poor woman nearly

destitute after he gambled away her inheritance."

"She deserves better. My first husband, Henry was her guardian after her husband died. He tried to discourage her from marrying Eaton, but could not convince her otherwise. Her mind was made up."

"In matters of the heart...I'm afraid 'tis hard to dissuade the afflicted," Joanne laughed.

Mary looked at her brother who was chatting with Betsy. "Ye're right, Joanne...sometimes the heart knows best."

After the wedding dinner, Ambrose and Mary enjoyed a cup of tea in the evening as they set on their porch watching the brilliant sunset over the marshes.

"Ambrose, have you notice that George seems to be paying Betsy quite a bit of attention?" Mary asked.

"Aye, Mary...I think it's more than that...I'd say we might expect him to have a talk with us about her indenture pretty soon."

"What do you think of Betsy?"

"She seems a right smart girl and kind hearted. I think she'd make a good wife."

"I do too, Ambrose but I really hate to lose her. She's been a lot of help and quick to catch on to how I like things done."

"Mayhaps I can find you an older servant next time so we won't have to lose one so quickly. I know 'tis hard to keep training a new servant."

"Oh that reminds me, Ambrose. You remember the negro Henry Jr. sold that calf to...the one that bought his freedom from William Bennett?"

"Aye, what about him?"

"He and his wife Mary's house burned to the ground and they didna have anything left. I think we ought to help him some way....they're mighty hard workers and do anything for someone in need. We need more like him."

"Mary, that's a grand idea. Bennett always talked about what a good man he was...and how he managed to earn enough with that little plot to buy his freedom. It amazed Bennett. I think we could get some people around here to help. I'll mention it to Argoll. Mayhaps he can talk to the other commissioners and they can help."

As the sun was going down, Ambrose and Mary watched George Willson approach their quay in the sloop. "I wonder where he has been so late in the day?" Mary commented.

"Alex told me there was a packet from England for George at his store. He went to retrieve it."

"I hope it's from my sisters. We haven't heard from them in months."

George climbed onto the deck and quickly approached Mary and Ambrose with a determined expression on his face. When he drew closer, Mary sensed something was wrong.

"What is it, George? Is there bad news from our sisters?"

"Aye, Mary very bad. Our sister-in-law, Anne, has been accused of witchcraft and they fear she will be arrested any day."

"Witchcraft? Not sweet Anne! How can that be?"

"Many people in Cranberry have been accused as well. I must return to England at once to see what I can do. I checked with Alex and there will be a ship leaving for England in two days."

"Oh George. I hope you can do something. Surely Anne's friends will come to her defense. She has helped so many."

"I hope so, Mary. She is well-loved...that's for sure...but I feel I must be there to help."

151

CHAPTER TWENTY-THREE

July, 1652 Maidstone, England

George did not arrive in England until late June and by the time he reached Cranbrook, his sister-in-law had already been arrested along with others and taken to Maidstone to be tried. All assizes were held in Maidstone since the town was located in the center of the county. After a short visit with his sisters, George took the stage to Maidstone with the intention of talking to Anne before her trial. His sisters, Sarah and Elizabeth begged to join him but he feared for their safety, since many people felt that close family members were often witches as well.

Maidstone was a market town but the streets were more crowded than usual. People from all over England and all walks of life were in the small village, intent on observing the trial. George had difficulty finding accommodations. All the Inns, even the Star which had been a Royalists haven during the Civil War was overflowing. He walked up Gabriel Hill to Bell Inn but the crowd standing at the entrance gave him concern.

Mayhaps they're just conversing. I should at least check and see if they have a bed.

As he walked in, a portly man checking in to the Bell Inn was peppering the frustrated landlord with questions.

"Have ye seen it?"

The landlord was frantically trying to accommodate as many lodgers as possible and he stared at the annoying man asking the question a few seconds before answering, "Nay. 'Tis all I can do to take care of visitors...no time to chase down rumors."

Another tall man, standing nearby overheard the exchange and commented, "I've seen it. 'Twasn't much to see, though...hardly seems enough to have magical powers."

"Well, I heard it bewitched nine people. Must be something to it!" shouted another. "I hope I didn't come all this way for nothin'."

"Where'd ye see it?" chimed in another rosy-cheeked man

with a bulbous nose. He wiped his forehead with his handkerchief before he spoke again. "I've come from London for the very purpose of seeing it."

"'Tis at the Swan on High Street....just a short distance from here...I'm heading there meself if anyone wants to join me," added a chubby, red-haired man with an equally red beard. "Mayhaps someone will buy me an ale for me troubles."

The portly man standing by the landlord said, "Sounds like a fair bargain...I'll join ya'." Then he faced the landlord and asked, "Could ye hold that bed for me, good man? I'll return shortly."

The landlord frowned. "Nay Sir...as ye can see. There are many others who want lodging...I'm not holding it while ye traipse off on a stupid 'look see.'"

The red-haired man growled, "Didna mind him....you can probably find a room at the Swan. 'Tis a better class of people there anyhow...come, they might move it soon. Court is tomorrow so we'd better see it now or ye might not have a chance to later."

The red-haired man bounced back and forth on his feet as he contemplated the prospect of free ale.

"Well, lead the way, man...I certainly want to see it before it's moved."

Other people mingling in the room joined the two men as they left and the Bell Inn finally became quiet. The landlord took a handkerchief from his waistcoat and wiped his sweating brow. He glanced up at George and asked, "Are ye in need of lodging, Sir?"

George answered, "Aye.....and I also need information. Do ye know much about this court case tomorrow?"

"I didna know much...been busy here...but I heard eighteen people have been accused and there was something about a piece of flesh given to one of the women by the devil that gave them powers. That's what they were talking about just now. All a bunch of rubbish if ye ask me. But whatever it is...it sure has this town in an uproar. We've never had so many people wanting rooms or beds."

"Eighteen people ye say...you wouldn't happen to know if there were any from Cranbrook, would you?"

"Aye, there were several from Cranbrook. I didna know what has been taking place in that town but it appears witchcraft has taken hold. The piece of scorched flesh came from a woman in

Cranbrook."

"Did you know what they're accused of?"

"Nay, what's it to you?" The landlord inquired with a questioning look. "You seem mighty interested. Didya know one of the accused?"

"I'm just curious. I've traveled through Cranbrook from time to time...no particular reason," George replied cautiously. Now what about those accommodations?"

"All we have left are shared beds...I can put you in with old man Harris. He shouldn't be troublesome...especially after he's had a bit to drink. He won't be in the room till late tonight and then he'll sleep for ten hours."

"Well, if you have nothing better....that'll do."

After George paid him, the landlord gave him the key.

"Wonder what that was all about?" the landlord said aloud. "Strange people in town today...but this trial's certainly good for business."

Another man with his wife and three children in tow passed George as he walked toward his room. No one was in the room as the landlord stated. George sat his bag down but took little notice of his surroundings. His mind raced as he tried to develop a plan of action.

The trial's tomorrow...I must see Anne somehow...how could I abandon her like I did. I'm to blame for her troubles...I love her but I left her alone in England...but..I had no choice...or did I? Mayhaps I should have made an attempt to move her to Virginia.

George's thoughts returned to Betsy and he grew even more tormented.

Anne has never given me any indication that she cared for me...why should I continue to hope? Oh 'tis useless to dwell on...Anne needs my help and that's all that matters. Mayhaps I can see her at the gaol now without attracting too much attention.

George rushed out of the room and into the street. He began walking deliberately toward the prison, his thoughts on Anne.

I must see you today. This madness must end...but what can I do to stop it...and will I have time?

"Where you off to in such a hurry mate? Someone chasing ya'?"

George glanced toward the direction of the voice from a

155

shabbily dressed man lounging in front of the Louse Tavern lodging house. Several other disreputable men sat on the stoop of the dingy Tavern or under it's grimy windows watching the crowded street.

Where am I?...I've walked too far...I must be more careful...what was I thinking?

Ignoring the man's question, George turned and walked back up High Street and tried to disappear in the mob of people filling the town. Eighteen people accused of witchcraft was too enticing to miss and the town buzzed with excitement.

As dusk fell, George finally reached the public gaol in the center of town but from the conversations he overheard in the crowd, he learned that Anne and the other women from Cranbrook were being held in the Lower Court house in High Town so he altered his course. The massive crowd surrounding the building prevented him from nearing it. Since it was now dark, George decided to return to the Inn and make another attempt to see Anne the following day. He dejectedly walked back to the Inn.

When he reached his room, George was thankful it was empty. Exhausted, he collapsed on the bed and stared at the ceiling.

How could I have left them in England? This probably wouldn't have happened if I'd been here. I've been so selfish....I should have stayed here to protect them...Oh Anne...how ye've had to suffer....first Robert's death...now this....

George drifted off to sleep but woke with a start later that night when the other boarder, his bed-partner, entered the room. The man smelled heavily of liquor. George turned with his back to him and pretended to sleep. The man stumbled to the bed and sat on the other side. A loud 'thunk' was heard as the man's boots hit the floor and after a few minutes, his loud, drunken snores, pervaded the small room. George's thoughts returned to Anne as he tried to develop a plan of action.

I imagine she'll be well-guarded at the trial. My only chance is to see her in the gaol before Court so I should leave early. At least, now I know where she's being held. I wonder if she has a Councilor to defend her. Anne...dearest one...I should have brought all of you to Virginia when I had the chance.

George was unable to sleep the remainder of the night. At

first light, he hurriedly dressed and set out for the Lower Court house. Vendors were setting up their wares in the Market Square. George had not eaten since arriving in Maidstone so he bought some bread and cheese, then sat down on a bench in front of a store. Though still very early. the streets were already filled with people milling about and preparing for the day. He studied two women across the crowded street. They were absorbed in a conversation accompanied with many quick gestures and appeared to be having an argument.

Finishing his meal, George continued his walk toward the lower Court. This time, he was able to reach the entrance. A coach suddenly appeared and three men quickly disembarked. George pushed forward and shouted, "Sire, may I have permission to visit my sister-in-law, Anne Willson." One of the men, obviously a member of the council looked kindly at George and said, "There's no time. The trial is to begin shortly."

"Then may I have permission to attend the trial. I am her brother-in-law and her only relation here."

The man paused but a moment, reached out and grabbed George's arm and said, "Aye, you may attend. She seems to be a good lass and I hope she will be found innocent of these charges."

Once in the building, the man directed George to an empty room with chairs and benches. Presently, more people flowed in to the small room, crowding the small chamber. The constable entered next and moved some chairs and benches around. A few minutes later, the Councilors arrived and George recognized the gentleman he encountered earlier. After the men conversed a moment, one of the Councilors said something to the constable and he disappeared from the Chamber.

A few minutes later, low mummers broke out among the assemblage of people as the door opened and the constable returned, leading six shabbily dressed women, bound by chains and without shoes into the room. Several guards were on either side and behind the women to prevent their escape. People in the crowd stood while others shifted in the seats trying to secure a better view.

George searched the women's faces for Anne and gasped when he saw her. Anne's stringy hair partially shielded her face as she bowed her head as if in prayer. She wore a brown, ragged dress that appeared to be stained. George's emotions overwhelmed him.

Oh Anne, what has become of you? You were once so beautiful, cheerful, kind and full of life. How could I think of loving anyone else? How could I ever forget you?

George whispered, "Anne...Anne, I'm hear," as he tried to gain her attention without annoying the guards. Either, she did not hear or chose to ignore him because her head remained bowed and she never turned around.

Another door on the other side of the room opened and the Judges appeared and moved to the remaining table. George took little notice of them as thoughts raced through his head.

Oh, Anne....How can I help you? Am I too late? I should never have left...but I can't think about that now...I must have a plan.

George was so deep in thought he did not realize the trial had started and the charges were being read against the women until he heard Anne's name spoken.

"Anne Willson: relect of deceased Robert Willson of Cranbrook in the County of Kent at a special Court of Order held at Maidstone, County of Kent on the 30th day of July for the County of Kent before Judge Sir Peter Warburton and his Associates Justices of the said Court was indicted and arraigned for that of not having the fear of God before thine Eyes, through the Instigation of the Devil, thou hast forsaken thy God & covenanted with the Devil, and by his help hast used and practiced on the 20th of January 1652 witchcraft upon the child Mary Elizabeth Walcott; whereby the body of said child was hurt, afflicted, wasted and tormented until she died on February 1, 1652. for which according to the Law of God, and the Law of this great nation thou deservest to die. To which Indictments the said Anne Willson pleaded not guilty and for Trial thereof put herself upon God and her Country."

George watched closely for any reaction from Anne, but she continued to stand with bowed head as if she was oblivious to her surroundings.

Judge Warburton asked, "Anne Willson are you aware why you have been summoned and do you understand the charge of which you have been accused."

Before she could answer, one of the women fell writhing to the floor, screeching and crying dolefully. Pandemonium broke out in the court room as several people rushed to the exit while others pushed and shoved closer.

Someone shouted. "'Tis the devil...make way...he'll kill us all...make way...didna look at her!"

George was knocked to the floor during the melee and feared he might be crushed. He rolled under a bench and lay there until order was restored by the guards, then he rolled out from under the bench and returned to his seat. The woman remained on the floor between the Councilors and Judges but was now softly crying. The constable advanced toward her and with the help of another guard lifted her to a standing position.

Judge Warburton spoke, "Ann Ashby, if you are unable to control yourself...you will be removed. Are you able to control yourself?"

"I will try, Sir but Rug sometimes controls me and...."

"Rug? Who is Rug?"

"'Tis the mouse-like spirit that controls me...Sir."

Judge looked at her with astonishment. He stared at her Councilor and said, "Try to help Miss Ashby control herself...is that understood?"

Her Councilor nodded at the Judge.

"Now, Anne Willson, I'll ask you again. Do you understand the charges against you?"

Anne raised her eyes and looked at the Judge and softly said, "Aye, I understand, Sir." She quickly bowed her head again.

Ann Ashby started mumbling to herself so the Judge quickly asked, "Call the first witness against these women."

The Councilors called the name of Elizabeth Walcott. A young woman arose from her seat and was sworn in. Elizabeth was fashionably dressed in a salmon colored gown with a high neckline. A sheer scarf knotted into a collar around her shoulders. Her voluminous while sleeves were fastened back with a covered button and long white gloves covered her hands. Her dark hair draped gracefully over her shoulders. She smiled coquettishly at the the Judge.

"Mrs Walcott, in your own words, please tell us what you know about this...uh...hum...these charges against these women."

"Aye your Honor. I will be happy to. Last year, I was with...uh....how do I say this...well, I was in the family way...and well...I planned on Sarah Williamson to be my midwife to attend me. You see, she has been a dear friend of the family forever and delivered all the Walcotts....and...."

"But how does that have anything to do with the proceedings, Mrs. Walcott," the Judge interrupted.

"I was coming to that ye're Honor. When.....the time of...well...if I may be indelicate...my 'lyin in'...she could not be found...so naturally, I had to have someone...so I called Anne Willson...I simply had no other choice...I regret it to this day," she lowered her head as tears filled her eyes.

"I know this is hard, Mrs. Walcott...but do proceed."

"Well....Anne brought Mildred Wright with her....she told me Mildred was learning midwifery.....and everything went fine at first....my child Mary Elizabeth was born....we named her after me....you see."

"I see," the Judge said gently. "Continue."

"Mary Elizabeth was a beautiful child. Everyone thought so....but then....that witch, Anne Willson took her away from me," she sobbed and glared at Anne.

"How did she do that?" the Judge asked.

"Why Sir.....immediately after Mary Elizabeth was born, Anne Willson, held my baby and proclaimed, "Oh what a beautiful child.....and everyone knows that's the words of the devil in her......so he can take my child......Sarah Williamson and the Parson told me so.....Oh, my Mary Elizabeth," she moaned. "And a few moments later,....Oh 'twas horrible," Mrs. Walcott began to sob. "She....she....Mary Elizabeth began to tremble and turn blue......she struggled to breathe...she only lived a week. She was perfectly healthy when born but those women killed her....they all killed her....they're in league with the Devil!" she screamed.

Anne Willson looked up at Mrs. Walcott with a blank stare for a brief minute, then bowed her head again.

Ann Ashby mumbled louder. Apparently excited by the Mrs. Walcott's scream, she suddenly exclaimed "'Tis the Devil in her....'tis the Devil....have mercy!"

The Judge shouted, "Silence! Councilors, let's have Miss Ashby speak. Mayhaps that will silence her."

Mrs. Walcott sat back down and the Judge began to question Ann Ashby.

"Ann Ashby, what do ye have to say regarding the charges?"

"'Tis Rug, Sir....my spirit given to me by the Devil...Rug. I pass him from my mouth to the mouth of anyone I want to control The devil gave me and all them," she pointed to the defendants, " a piece of meat...you seen it...it gives us power over anyone we touch...why Anne Martin and Mary Browne...they's pregnant with the Devil's child....the Devil gave us power." She fell to the floor again and began kicking and screaming obscenities.

The Judge shouted, "Constable, remove this woman.....now!"

The guards scrambled to subdue her while chaos broke out among the observers. Many stumbled over the fallen as they attempted to leave the Chamber. George backed against a wall and remained there until the room was again quiet.

The Judge said, "Councilors, have Anne Willson and Mildred Wright been pricked for pain or blood?"

"I believe so your Honor but I can not say for sure and I do not know the results," one of the men said.

"Well, have it done again, today! Prick all of them! We'll continue this trial afterwards."

The Judges stood and left the room; the five remaining prisoners were led out by the Constable and guards and the Councilors followed.

George's heart was breaking as he watched Anne trudge slowly out in chains.

"They've already been pricked....the Judge should get on with this....'tis a waste of time," a seedy, old woman said to the elderly man next to her as they left the room.

George hesitated. He was unsure if he would be allowed to return if he left.

I know they'll never allow me to see her now. I'd better stay here. Mayhaps I'll have an opportunity to speak on her behalf.

George remained in the warm chamber alone and tried to decide what he could say to help Anne. Having received little sleep last night, exhaustion suddenly overwhelmed him. He leaned his head against the wall in the warm Chamber and promptly fell asleep.

CHAPTER TWENTY-FOUR

July 30, 1652 Maidstone, Kent County, England

George was not asleep long. He was startled by a noise and glanced up and saw the Councilor who helped him attend the trial walking toward him. "Hensley was right. He said he thought you were still here. Didn't you say ye're Anne Willson's brother-in-law?" asked the Councilor.

"Aye," George said as he stood and tried to clear his head.

"Good...good...mayhaps you can help. Come with me. We didna have long."

George followed the man out of the chamber toward a locked door with a guard standing beside it.

The guard glowered menacingly at the man.

"He's with me...now open up. I have a right to speak to her."

The guard begrudgingly unlocked the wooden door and the Councilor walked in a dark, tiny room with George following close behind. Anne was sitting on the floor in a corner of the room. She looked up, then gave a gasp and put her hands in front of her face."

"Nay, George...nay....ye mustn't see me like this."

George rushed over, bent down and put his arms about Anne. She trembled beneath his touch.

"Anne....Oh Anne...How did this all happen? Why are they accusing you of this?"

"'Tis no use, George. Go.....leave me...I have no life left to fight for."

"Nay, didna say such a thing, Anne. I'm here we'll fight these charges together," George looked at the Councilor and asked. "Pray, what can I do to help?"

"You've already helped. Your sister-in-law has been silent since she arrived in Maidstone. I can not help when she won't talk to me."

George looked back at Anne and asked, "Why won't you talk to this man, Anne? He is the only one who can help ye? I didna understand."

"Because I want to die," she moaned. She started to cry inconsolably.

"Nay, Anne. I know you have done nothing wrong. I know you did not kill that child....'tis nonsense. I believe the Judges think so too."

"You didna understand," she replied between sobs. "It does not matter that I am innocent. They all think I am a witch. They have pricked me...and tested me...but still say I am a witch. I can no longer be a midwife. If they find me innocent, there will be many who still believe I am...I will starve and so will your sisters...they will beat me and set dogs on me....leave England, George...take ye're sisters with you...I would rather die now than face a slow death of torture the rest of my life!" she screamed and pushed him away.

George reached out and gently brushed her hair with his hand and pulled her close. She relented and fell crying in his arms.

"Well, I guess I know now why she wouldn't talk to me."

"But what do we do now...you heard her...she is innocent."

"I'm afraid there's not much. She's right...even if she's found innocent and returns home, many will still believe her guilty. I'm afraid, these charges will haunt her the rest of her life. But that's beside the point...I need to defend these charges and save her life now. We'll deal with other problems later. Do you know anyone who will come forward to challenge the charges? Particularly someone of import?"

"I've been away in the colonies for the last few years and of course I'll speak for her but I know she has friends in Cranbrook."

"You would be of no use since ye've been away. They will only say she was afflicted by the devil after you left. But her friends in Cranbrook should help. It worries me though...why haven't they come forward before now?"

"Then what can we do! She's innocent!" George shouted.

"We could plead the belly. I know she's not with child now but while they check her, it could give us some time to find persons who will vouch for her."

"Then do it. I'll return to Cranbrook at once to find someone."

"Aye, it may not be as easy as you think. Few want to be involved when there is talk of witches in fear of being accused themselves."

164

"Surely not, when they know she's innocent."

"I wish you the best...but I have my doubts. Be quick about it...we have little time. Once they discover she is not with child....then there is no stopping sentencing."

"I'd like to wait until after the trial. She may be freed."

"Wishful thinking, I'm afraid. But that should be soon enough. It will take a few weeks for them to discover my little ruse. If we do manage to get her freedom, take your family to the colonies. She's right. They'll have no future here."

"Aye, and thank you, Sir. What is your name? How will I find you again?"

"Graham...Hugh Graham's the name...and yours?"

"George Willson. My brother Robert Willson, Anne's husband is dead from the wars."

"Sorry to hear that...well be quick about it...they'll come for her any minute to prick her again...silly busy, that."

"Aye, Sir." George gave Anne a last hug and kissed her on the cheek." He stood while the Councilor Graham knocked on the door.

The Councilor led George back to the chamber to ensure he was admitted, then left him there. George sat on the nearest bench and stared ahead.

Anne, oh....dear love....I hope we can save you. God be with you!

A few people entered the room and were talking quietly among themselves.

"Once they're found guilty...I hope they burn 'em....you know that's the only way their blood won't be inherited by family...least ways that's what me Mum said, " commented a wizened old man.

"I'd like to see them being roasted...'twould be a sight to remember...best way to stop this evil," the woman beside him commented.

George stared straight ahead as he tried to understand their hate.

God, you know Anne has done nothing wrong. How can you allow this to happen? Why do these people have so much hate for someone they do not know?

A few more stragglers came into the chamber. A door opened and the Councilors returned followed by five of the

165

women. Ann Ashby was missing. Doors opened and the Justices took their seats at the table. Anne Willson searched the room for George and caught his eye, then bowed her head again.

Judge Warburton asked, "Councilors have the women been pricked to see if they are witches?"

"They have your Honor."

"And what are the results...none of the women cried out in pain nor had a loss of blood."

"Have there been any other tests performed on these women to determine if they are witches?"

"Aye, your Honor. Anne Willson was asked to repeat the Lord's Prayer but could not do so without leaving out words. A black mark was found on Mary Browne that did not bleed. Ann Ashby could not recite the Lord's Prayer without shrieking. Anne Martin did not have pain or have a loss of blood when pricked, Mildred Wright could not recite the Lord's Prayer without leaving out words and Mary Read has a teat under her tongue."

The Judge sighed and asked, "Do you have more witnesses accusing these women?"

"Aye, your honor."

"Continue with the witnesses."

George watched his sister-in-law and grew despondent as witness after witness accused the women of being witches. As the stories unfolded, it became increasingly evident that Sarah Richardson and the Parson were behind the charges against Anne.

What has she ever done to them to cause so much hate...especially the Parson? The answer must be in Cranbrook. I hope I have time to find out and someone to come forward for Anne. God please help me find a way to help her.

The trial ended before dusk and the Judge studied the five women a few minutes, then consulted with his associates.

Finally he faced the women again, "Constable, please bring Ann Ashby in."

The Constable left and brought in Ann Ashby. His hand was grasped tightly around her arm. She was mumbling to herself.

"Ann Ashby, Ann Martin, Mary Read, and Mary Browne, the Court finds you guilty of being witches and not having the fear of God before thine Eyes, and through the instigation of the Devil, thou hast forsaken thy God and covenanted with the Devil, and by

166

his help hast practiced witchcraft on various sundry persons and animals. You are therefore sentenced to be hanged."

Ann Ashby screamed and fell to the floor.

The Judge ignored her and continued, speaking rapidly above her rantings, "Anne Willson and Mildred Wright the Court finds you guilty of being a witch and not having the fear of God before thine eyes, and through the instigation of the Devil, thou hast forsaken thy God and covenanted with the Devil, and by his help hast practiced witchcraft the 20th of January 1652 upon the child Mary Elizabeth Walcott; whereby the body of said child was hurt, afflicted, wasted and tormented until she died on February 1, 1652. for which according to the Law of God, and the Law of this great nation thou deservest to die. You are therefore sentenced to be hanged."

Several of the Councilors rose and began to speak all at once.

The Judge shouted, "One at a time gentlemen."

"Your Honor, I would like to plead the belly for Anne Willson, Sir."

"Same for Mildred Wright."

"And the same for Ann Ashby, your Honor"

The Judge said, "I expected as much, but you do know that if they are not found to be with child, then they will all still hang."

"Aye, your Honor the Councilors replied in unison."

"They're no more with child than I am," the shriveled old man next to George, muttered under his breath. "Should have burned them all....but they need to go on with the hanging and stop these Devil women before it spreads."

George was devastated.

Guilty....sentenced to hang...it sounds so final. I must get out of here...I can't breathe.

George stood and tried to move ahead of people slowly filing out of the chamber, as they tried to observe the women for the last time.

When George reached the street, he stopped an inhaled deeply, then exclaimed, "What can I do? How can I save her? Oh, God give me the answer....do I have enough time?"

People nearby stared at him as if he had gone mad so George composed himself and began walking briskly toward the

Bell Inn to make plans for his return to Cranbrook.

CHAPTER TWENTY-FIVE

August 1, 1652 Cranbrook, Kent County, England

George Willson's sisters, Sarah and Elizabeth, were extremely upset after he told them about Anne's guilty verdict. They cried incessantly the remainder of the evening while trying to make a list of up-standing people who might come to Anne's defense. George woke early the next morning, refreshed and with renewed determination to visit as many people as possible on the long list before nightfall. Anne had lived in Cranbrook all her life and as a mid-wife, she had many friends. It should be an easy task convincing them to assist her.

By late evening, George found, only two people willing to write letters and most discouraging of all, no one agreed to go to Maidstone to speak on Anne's behalf. When he returned home, his sisters were still tearful. They prepared a meal for him which he devoured with relish since it had been a full day since he'd eaten.

Elizabeth was in her room. Sarah, his eldest sister, sat companionably with George and quietly watched him eat for a few minutes. She asked, "Do you think the letters will be enough?"

"I didna know but 'tis the only chance we have."

"Ye're in love with her, aren't you George?"

George almost choked on the piece of bread he was chewing and Sarah began beating him on the back as she said, "I'm sorry...I didna mean to choke you."

When George recovered, he stuttered...but..How? Did I say something to give you that impression?"

"Nay, 'tis not what ye said. Anyone could see how you looked at her...even when she was married to Robert."

"I tried not to let it show...how could I love my brother's wife...I feel so guilty about my feelings."

"He didna notice and I'm sure she didna. They were both so much in love with each other. But he's gone now...you shouldn't be ashamed of your feelings for her. I imagine 'twas hard on you though. Anne loved no one else but Robert and was very distressed after he died. It was difficult living with her that first year after Mum died and Anne was so sad and full of grief herself."

"I'm sorry, Sarah. I should have been here for you."

"George, you couldn't. You were in the military...but I *was* surprised when you wrote you were in Virginia. I thought you'd at least come back home to say good-bye before leaving England."

"I wish there had been time. I was planning to go to Virginia anyway and could not pass up the opportunity to go and also receive payment for the trip."

"Your letters helped Anne overcome her grief. We all looked forward to your packets but Anne was in high spirits for days after we received them. I think she's fallen in love with you too."

"Thank you for telling me that Sarah. It means a lot to me that my letters made her happy...speaking of Virginia, while I return to Maidstone with these letters of support, I want you and Elizabeth to remain here and pack. When I bring Anne back, we're all going to Virginia."

"I didna understand!" Sarah exclaimed.

"You know there's nothing for you here...I have a little land now and Ambrose will help us build a house. I want you with me in Virginia. Pack only what you need on board. We'll ship the rest."

"But this is our home, George. We can't leave just like that. I'm a teacher...what will the school think?"

"Sarah, with all that has happened and after meeting all your so-called friends today, I'm afraid ye'll have a formidable time overcoming this if you remain here. Anne's Councilor warned me about the problems ye'd face. He said, even if the Judge changes his mind and Anne receives her freedom, the accusation of being a witch will never leave. Anne is aware that she will no longer be able to return to her profession as a midwife and you may not be able to be a teacher. Many people believe witchcraft is spread to other family members."

"Oh George, surely not. The people of Cranbrook have known me all my life."

"Didna forget, these same people knew Anne too and still they were prevailed to go against her. Talk of witchcraft frightens people and causes them to act in strange, dangerous and cruel ways."

"Mayhaps ye're right. Anne did suffer a lot of abuse from

people she thought were her friends before she was formally charged. I didna realize they'd be fearful of Elizabeth and me too. But are you going back to Maidstone alone? Elizabeth and I thought we'd travel with you this time. We want to see Anne."

"Maidstone is very crowded and a dangerous place with all the attention this witchcraft trial has received and I will be busy doing everything I can to free Anne. In all likelihood, you will not be allowed to see her. I was not even allowed to see her until the Councilor intervened and I will not have time to watch after the two of you. Why didna you send her a letter and some of your great pastries? I'm certain she will appreciate that more."

"Oh, I didna realize we'd be a burden. Ye're right. We're just so worried about her but gaining Anne's freedom is of more import and you should not be distracted from that purpose by attending to us."

"I hope to leave tomorrow afternoon, if possible. I still plan to see Sarah Richardson and the Parson. I believe if they withdraw their complaints, the other accusers will withdraw their accusations as well."

"Good luck....especially with Sarah Richardson. She truly hates Anne. She's jealous because so many women preferred Anne as their midwife and she spread lies about Anne for years. When the Parson started preaching about witches, he added fuel to the fire. Sarah embellished her stories with signs of witchcraft. That's what started all this witchcraft business against Anne. I'll go tell Elizabeth now so we'll have our letters ready." Sarah left George and he continued his meal. His thoughts returned to what his sister told him.

Anne enjoyed my letters. Dare I hope she loves me too? Mayhaps 'tis not too late for us. Oh God! Please help me save her!

George had a fresh start the next day. He immediately called on Sarah Richardson. After talking with her briefly about dropping her complaints, she all but threw him out of her house so he moved on to see the Parson.

He walked up five steps and knocked on the massive door of the Parson's residence.

"May I help you Sir?" a tall woman dressed in dark black

greeted him at the door.

"I'm here to see the Parson. Is he available?"

"I'm sorry, Sir. He is indisposed due to a sudden illness. He will be unable to see you today....mayhaps you could try tomorrow."

"Ill ye say?" George exclaimed. "I'm afraid it can't wait 'til tomorrow...are you positive he won't see me? It's an urgent matter I wish to discuss with him...a life depends on it."

"I'm sorry, Sir. There is no possibility of seeing the Parson. As I said, he is quite ill."

"I see," George said.

The woman quickly shut the door and George stood a minute as he tried to decide what to do next.

'Tis probably useless seeing him anyway. It seems minds are made up against Anne in Cranbrook. I need to head back to Maidstone. Mayhaps the letters I have will be sufficient. The Judge seemed to think kindly of Anne.

CHAPTER TWENTY-SIX

Summer, 1652 Eastern Shore, Virginia

The English and Dutch were now at war; tensions and relationships between the Dutch and Englishmen on the Eastern Shore of Virginia became strained. Many Dutch had settled in Accawmacke years before and were now prominent citizens, essential to the community's growth, but they became fearful that violence might be inflicted on them.

In an attempt to resolve the growing discord on the Eastern Shore, the Commissioners directed a resolution declaring that the Dutchmen who resided in Accawmacke and Northampton Counties were obedient to the State of England and should be respected as good citizens.

Obedience Robins, Edward Douglas, William Andrews, Thomas Johnson, John Stringer, William Jones and Sir Whittington signed the resolution.

Ambrose returned home with a packet for Mary and told her about the resolution.

"I hope this brings some ease to our Dutch friends here," he declared.

Mary nodded her head in agreement but she was only half listening while she broke the seal and tore open the packet. This was the first packet she had received from George since he had abruptly left for England. She pulled out the letter enclosed and began to read, then gave a loud gasp of astonishment.

"What does the letter say, Mary?" Ambrose asked anxiously as he picked up his son Thomas.

"'George says that he did not see Anne when he reached Cranbrook because she was taken to Maidstone for trial along with many other people from Cranbrook. They've all been accused of being witches!"

"That's unbelievable. I thought you said Anne was a

midwife. How could anyone honestly believe she's a witch?"

"I didna understand it, Ambrose. Anne is one of the kindest people I know. The thought of her being accused of being a witch is unbelievable. George says he is going to Maidstone to see what he can do to free Anne from the charges. He wrote this letter in June and should be there by now. Surely, he can convince the judges and bring her back. This is lunacy. I think the people in England have gone mad after our King was executed."

"It appears so. I hope their madness does not affect us here. We appear to be acquiring new people in our town everyday with strange ideas. Stephen was telling me that Rev. Doughty has been discussing the possibility of witches here."

"Witches here? That's as preposterous as believing Anne is a witch. We know practically everyone here. There are no witches among us." Mary stared at George's letter. "I hope George is successful and his next letter brings better news."

"I do too, Mary. We must pray for his success."

Mary's horse, Rascal, threw a shoe so Henry, Jr took the horse to Mr. Andrews, the farrier, to be replaced. While he waited in the dark shop, Henry, Jr. watched Tom Cottingham, the farrier's apprentice, work the bellows. Tom was about Henry, Jr.'s age.

"Tom, run get some more charcoal so this fire doesn't become too cold...fill the slack-tub too," the farrier ordered.

Tom headed for the pile of blackened branches and logs that were coaled and began breaking them up with an axe. A cloud of thin, black fine dust covered Tom from head to toe.

Henry, Jr. backed away and laughed, "You could stand next to that pile of black charcoal and no one would be able to see you!"

"I'd like not to be seen sometimes," Tom replied. "Especially when I make a mistake and get chewed out."

Tom took a load of coal in, grabbed the bucket and ran for the creek. Henry ran after him.

"Let's go for a swim!" yelled Henry, Jr. as he kicked off his boots and started removing his clothes.

"Nay, Master Andrews would have my hide," Tom replied as he filled the bucket to the brim with water. All of a sudden, Tom jumped in, fully dressed, and disappeared under the cool water. He came up completely wet with his white face shiny clean. "Mayhaps he won't fuss too much if I get that dust off a minute...it makes it hard to breathe sometimes."

Henry jumped in beside him with a huge splash. The boys spent a moment splashing each other in fun before Tom climbed out. "I need to get back or I'll surely be whipped."

Since the day was hot, Henry stayed a little longer and floated in the cool water. After a while he climbed onto the bank and put his clothes and boots back on. Tom was back at the stack of charcoal breaking the wood into small pieces, again covered from head to toe in black dust. He stopped chopping a minute to look at Henry. "I won't be trying that again. I thought Master Andrews was surely gonna kill me with the whip this time."

Henry looked closer at Tom's back and saw red streaks of blood on the back of his shirt.

"Henry...you out there boy?" the farrier called. "Ye're horse has been shod."

"Thank you, Sir. My father said he'd come by and settle with you later. He has some tools that need to be repaired too."

"Sure, boy. Run along now and leave Tom alone...he's got work to do."

Henry climbed on his horse and set out for his parents plantation.

Ambrose was mending the gate when Henry approached the stock pen. "Did Andrews have time to shod Rascal?"

"Aye, Papa. I told him ye'd settle with him when you brought the tools."

"Good."

"Papa, you knew Tom Cottingham's father didna?" Henry commented as he dismounted.

"Aye, Henry. George Cottingham was a good man and a fine Indian fighter. He died shortly after Tom was born...left Tom an orphan since his mother died when he was born. The boy had a guardian until last year when he became Andrews' apprentice. Why yc asking about him?"

"I saw Tom today helping Mr. Andrews...he sure is hard on Tom."

Ambrose stopped and studied his son's face. "Did something happen to Tom while ye were there?"

"Well, I didna actually see it...but Tom jumped in the creek when he went to get water...just to get all that dust off...he didna stay in the water long. Seeing how it's so hot, I stayed at the creek awhile and when I went back to get Rascal...I saw Tom again out by the coal stack and he'd been beat."

"Beat, ye say. How do you know?"

"He told me. He said Mr. Andrews like to killed him and I saw a lot of blood on the back of his shirt."

Ambrose stared off into the woods toward the farrier's house and said, "I hate to hear that...George wouldn't like his son treated like that. I was glad to hear Tom was learning a good trade but I know Andrews is hard on his servants...I didna think he'd be so hard on his apprentice...but son, there's not much I can do about it. He belongs to Andrews. 'Course, if he's too hard on him...we can bring it to the Commissioners ears, but to ease your worries...mayhaps I'll try talking with Andrews sometime."

"Thanks Papa."

"Now, get to your own chores...it seems ye've been a little remiss with duties yeself today."

"Aye, Papa."

CHAPTER TWENTY-SEVEN

August, 1652 – Maidstone, England

When George arrived in Maidstone, he immediately set out for Councilor Graham's house to give him the letters from Anne's friends. Excitement in the air of the small town was palpable. As he walked the streets, he was amazed by the number of people in the town intent on witnessing the hangings.

"They're getting off too easy, if ye ask me. They should be burned at the stake. Anyone with sense knows that's the only way to kill witches," a crusty old man said to two elderly women sitting on the stoop in front of a house.

George frowned and rushed on.

Oh Anne...they didna know what they're talking about. I hope these letters free you.

It was nearly dark by the time George reached Councilor Graham's home. He anxiously banged on the massive door with his fist. The door creaked open and a man, with a sneer on his face, appeared in the doorway.

"What's the meaning of you banging on the door like that so late and disturbing the Master?"

"I must see Councilor Graham immediately! 'Tis a matter of life and death and he's expecting me!" George exclaimed loudly.

"Well, the least ye can do is be civilized. There's no sense in all that racket. Now whom do I say is calling?"

"Tell him 'tis about Anne Willson. I'm her brother-in-law!"

"Anne Willson, the witch...or I should say accused witch? The Master doesn't believe there are witches you know."

"Aye, man...now let me see him!"

"Certainly. He said he was expecting someone. Come in...come in."

George entered the house as the man directed.

"Wait here, while I inform the Master," said the man as he disappeared behind a door.

The hall was huge and elegantly appointed. Eight large

portraits of stern-faced men graced the walls. George was studying the nearest portrait when Councilor Graham entered followed closely by the man who greeted George.

"Quite impressive, isn't he? None of them are related to me...this is my wife's estate. They're supposed to be Lords or something. I often wonder what they'd think of my practice of defending witches. I'm not too popular among the citizenry of Maidstone that's for sure...sometimes I think they'd like to burn me at the stake," he laughed. "But enough of that...you have some letters for me...I hope."

"Aye, I have some letters of support...but no one would come here themselves. Just as you said, they were afraid of being implicated."

"At least you have the letters...hopefully that will be sufficient. Do you have them with you? We've no time to waste."

"But I thought you said Anne had to be examined first."

"Come, we'll discuss this business in the Parlour. Matthew," Graham directed his butler who had been patiently waiting. "Bring us some ale."

"Aye, Sir. Right away."

George followed Graham into a massive room filled with heavy oak furnishings.

"Anne has been examined and found not with child," Councilor Graham stated as he sat in a padded chair nearest the fireplace. "Her hanging is scheduled for August 25th along with all the other women."

Startled by Graham's explicit declaration, George stood a minute to compose himself before he sat in the matching chair directly across from Graham and proclaimed angrily, "That soon! I thought you said that the Judge seemed to be in sympathy with her."

Graham tried to ease George's anger and spoke calmly, "I still believe he is sympathetic toward her but you must understand...he's receiving pressure from the officials and towns people to execute the sentences quickly. I've run out of options so your letters have come at an opportune time. The only chance is for her to be pardoned by Parliament. Do you have the letters with you?"

"Aye, they're here." George replied as he removed a packet

from his vest and handed it to Graham.

The Councilor quickly opened the packet and began to peruse the letters.

"These are good. I know these two men and they are well respected by many. We have no time to waste. I must show the letters to Judge Peter Warbutton immediately. He's in Cheshire right now. Where are you staying? How can I reach you?"

"I'm came directly here and have yet to arrange for accommodations."

"Well, likely as not, with the number of visitors here, you'll not find anything available...especially tonight. However, I'm not without contacts. I'll arrange for your lodging tomorrow. You can stay here tonight."

The butler entered the room with two tankards of ale.

"Matthew, see to George's needs, he'll be staying with us tonight...and prepare him some of that fine stew. I don't imagine you took time for dinner?" Graham asked as he looked at George.

"Nay, I appreciate the offer but is there any chance of seeing Anne?"

"Not tonight...but I'll take you tomorrow before I leave and make arrangements for you to see her while I'm gone. Mayhaps it will lift her spirits some."

The butler said, "If you'll come with me Sir?"

"Aye," George said as he stood and followed the butler out of the Parlour.

Early the next morning George and Councilor Graham went to the gaol on High Street in the Center of Town. Anne and the other women were transferred there after they had been found guilty. George followed the Councilor as he entered the gaol where Anne was being held with several other women.

It took a few moments to find her in the dark, oppressive room. She was seated alone in a corner, a waif of the former beautiful women she had once been. George gasped at the change in her appearance and rushed over to embrace her. Anne was startled by his action and at first tried to push him away.

"Nay, nay George. You shouldn't be here. I told ye I want to die."

179

"Oh, Anne...please didna say that," George cried in anguish. "You have so much to live for...I have good news. We are trying to obtain ye're release."

"Nay, George. I have no life outside this place. I told you before," she paused to catch her breath. Clearly this effort to speak was exhausting her in her weakened condition.

"I thought about what you said and that is why I plan to take you and my sisters back to Virginia with me. The people in Virginia will not know of your accusations. You can start a new life there. You must not give up."

"He's right, Anne," Graham interrupted. "I've letters of support for you. I plan to take them to Parliament. They should pardon you. You must not give up hope."

Anne focused on George and Councilor Graham with her large brown eyes that loomed even larger in her sunken cheek bones. "George, I can not run away from these accusations. They will follow me to Virginia. It will only cause trouble for you and ye're sisters if I go back with you."

"But I cannot live without you! I've always loved you. There I said it." George exclaimed.

Anne stared at him in astonishment for a brief moment then pushed him away. "You didna mean that George," she muffled a cry. "I was married to ye're brother. You cannot love me."

Ignoring the presence of Graham and all the other people in the crowded room, George continued, "I've loved you from the first moment I saw you, Anne. I didna want to and would never had let you know my feelings if Robert were still alive...but he's not here and I am. I want you to be my wife but first we must overturn this conviction."

"Nay, George. I admit I do care for you but...love? I didna know what love is anymore."

"How could you know when ye're locked up in this disgusting place!" George declared. He frowned as he glanced around the room. "Once you are released....you can decide about marriage but you must take better care of ye'reself or you won't live long enough to find out ye're true feelings."

Councilor Graham stood quietly waiting while George stated his love for Anne but he knew he needed to leave soon to catch the afternoon stage to Cheshire. "I don't mean to rush you

George, however, we must be on our way soon or I will miss the coach and I need to make arrangements if you hope to see Anne while I am gone. As for you, Anne, do what this young gentleman says. I understand you have eaten very little since you've been here. You must eat more and regain your strength. I believe these letters will obtain your release. Don't give up."

Anne looked up at the Councilor and for a brief moment gave him a flitting smile. "I guess I haven't made ye're job easy, have I?"

"'Tis true...I've had more cooperative clients. Will you promise to eat? My cook prepared some things for you."

"Aye, since you went to all that trouble, I'll try a little."

"Good. I'll leave you two alone a moment while I talk with Mildred Wright. These letters should help her as well since she was only assisting you in the birth of the child." Graham walked over to a disheveled woman sitting nearby with her knees clasped against her breast and they began to talk quietly to her.

Anne studied George's eyes and said softly, "You must forget about me, George. I have no future beyond these walls. The accusations will follow me wherever I go. I've seen what happens to those accused of witchcraft even if they are freed. You do not understand how cruel people can be. I will only be a burden to you."

"Nay, Anne...oh, sweet Anne. You would never be a burden. I only wish I could take you away from all this now," George declared with exasperation as he glanced around the dismal room with half-starved, whimpering women.

He pulled Anne in his arms and she rested her head on his shoulder.

Councilor Graham walked over to George and said, "George, I'm afraid I must insist that we leave now if I'm to travel to Cheshire today."

"Aye, ye're right...and your journey is of paramount importance," George said as he released his hold on Anne.

George stood and Anne slumped back into her corner and stared at the two men.

"I'll return as soon as I can Anne and we can talk more," George stated.

She nodded at him, then looked away.

George continued to watch her as he backed out of the room, then he turned and followed Graham. A guard opened the door and the two men rushed out of the building. "I've sent word to the gate-keeper that you should be allowed to visit her while I'm gone George, and I gave him a few coins to encourage his cooperation."

"Thank you, Sir. How can I ever repay you for helping Anne?"

"Setting her free will be thanks enough," he replied as they walked rapidly toward the coach. "Thank goodness for my wife's estate or my practice of defending witches would leave me completely bankrupt. It doesn't make me a very popular Councilor. I believe it is shameful what is happening to these poor innocent women and mind you, one day everyone will realize it. Why I'm not even allowed to have knowledge of the witnesses against her! 'Tis a travesty of justice."

They reached the coach just as passengers were boarding.

"Well, I guess this it is," Graham declared. "Oh, I almost forgot your accommodations. Take this letter to the owner of the Bell Inn. He's a good friend of mine and he'll find you a bed."

"The Bell Inn...I've stayed there before. Thank you, Sir...for everything," George said gratefully as he shook the Councilor's hand. "And good luck with the Judge."

"I will need all the luck I can get," the Councilor said grimly as he followed the last passenger onto the coach. "Take care of Mrs. Willson while I'm gone. At least try to get her to eat something before she starves to death or this will all be in vain."

George watched the coach depart then began walking to the Bell Inn.

The letter from the Councilor to the owner of Bell Inn was very helpful and George was given a room and bed to himself but George was unable to sleep. His thoughts were on Anne and doubts of Graham's success filled his head.

What will I do if he cannot persuade Parliament to pardon her? Could I help her escape? But even if she escaped from the people...how will I ever get her on a ship to Virginia? 'Twould be impossible.....but I must try somehow. Tomorrow when I visit the prison...I'll check to see how well the prisoners are guarded.

All night, George tossed and turned as he tried to come up with a plan to free Anne. He rose at dawn and set out for the prison with high hopes of seeing her again. A new gate-keeper was on duty when he arrived at the prison and would not allow George admittance.

I'll just have to wait until the other gate-keeper arrives. He's the one Councilor Graham made arrangements with.

George surveyed the prison and the many people filling the dusty street. The gaol was near Market Square where farmers, fishmongers and bakers were busy stocking their stands with today's fresh ware's. He walked over to a stand filled with pastries and bread manned by a young boy. George bought some gingerbread and sat down on a nearby bench while he ate it. Two well-dressed women walked by and he overheard snatches of their conversation.

"They should be burned at the stake....'tis the only way to ensure their evil dies with them...but I wish however they died...it should be done soon. I didna like being near them."

"Did ye make the witch bottle like I said?...'tis the only way to be safe."

"Aye, I filled it with rosemary, pins and red wine just like ya' said and sealed it with the red candle wax. I said,

> *Pins, needles, rosemary, wine;*
> *In this witches bottle of mine.*
> *Guard against harm and enmity;*
> *This is my will, so mote it be!"*

"Did I do it right?"

"Aye, where did you put it?"

"Behind a chest by the fireplace."

"That's good...the fireplace is the first place a witch will try to get in your house but you might want to make others to put by the doors and windows. With so many witches nearby in the prison...we can't be too careful."

The two women walked out of ear range and George stared after them.

How could they believe such nonsense and fear sweet Anne?

183

She will never be safe here with people like them around. I must see if there is a way I can help her escape. Then I'll take her to Virginia.

George returned to the prison. The same gate-keeper was still on duty so he knew there was no point in trying to gain entrance but he decided to observe the guards to determine if there was a possibility of extricating Anne from the prison. At mid-morning, a new gate-keeper came on duty and George tried to gain entrance but was again refused. He decided to remain to watch the prison and activities surrounding it the remainder of the day. When dusk fell, George returned to the Bell Inn, dejected but filled with resolve to free Anne.

George returned to the gaol each day for two weeks but was never allowed admittance, even when the original gate-keeper arrived. He became more depressed with each passing day as the people of Maidstone continued to blame every death or illness on the witches held in the gaol. The hysteria grew to a fever pitch. Additional guards were placed around the prison because of the mounting tension in the town.

He stood outside the prison along with many other people. Sometimes prisoners were allowed to obtain exercise and air on the walkway and he hoped to catch a glimpse of Anne. George stared at the additional guards with disgust.

The extra guards will make it impossible for me to help her escape and what has happened to Councilor Graham? He should have been here by now.

"Have ye seen any of the witches, yet?" a young boy standing beside George asked his friend.

"Nah, I'm didna think they let them out? But I heard the scaffold was built yesterday. Let's go see it."

"Where?"

"On Gallows Hill, of course....just outside of town on Penenden Heath."

The two boys dashed off and George decided to follow them.

If Councilor Graham doesn't come back in time, mayhaps there's some way I can rescue her when she's taken to the gallows.

The thought of Anne and the gallows, suddenly

184

overwhelmed George and filled him with anxiety. He had to halt a minute to catch his breath.

Oh God...how has it come to this? Anne being hung. I can not fathom it...but I must not give up. God will help me save her....Oh God, give me a plan to save her.

George regained his composure and continued his walk toward the gallows. As the grotesque image of the large scaffold came into view, George forced himself to study the structure for any vulnerabilities. A platform surrounded by a railing stood in the center of the heath. Each of the gallows consisted of two uprights and a cross beam with a hook for attachment of the noose. A ladder was secured to the side for the women to climb on the platform.

I must apprehend her before she reaches the top. I see no other way. Once she is on the platform, it will be impossible. Oh God, please give me a plan.

George spent the rest of the day studying the scaffold but did not come up with a course of action other than to attempt to snatch Anne from the guards while she was being transported to the gallows.

Mayhaps I could pay some lads to cause a disruption to distract the guards. But then what would I do? I'm only one person and I'm not likely to find anyone to help me.

He left the scaffold in deep despair and headed back to his lodgings. When he arrived at the Bell Inn, the owner saw him enter and called out to George, "Sir, I have a message for you....'tis from from Councilor Graham."

CHAPTER TWENTY-EIGHT

August, 1652 – Eastern Shore, Virginia

Stephen Horsey visited Ambrose's plantation in late August. Ambrose was in the carpentry shop and saw the sloop arrive so he walked out to meet him.

"What brings you this way Stephen?"

"Well, I was at Hungar's today and Mountney had this packet for Mary and I knew she was worried about her sister-in-law so I thought I'd deliver it."

"Mayhaps it's from her brother. Mary's been hoping for some news. But how's your problem with the Commissioners? Are you still not paying taxes and tithes?"

"They're on my back about the taxes thats for sure. But they're getting nothing from me until we're given representation in the legislature and voting rights to elect our Governor. That court is made up of a company of asses....you know they're threatening to put me in the gaol as well as require me to pay a hefty fine of tobacco."

"I heard something like that. What do you intend to do?"

"I plan to stay one step ahead of them as long as I can," he laughed. I'm not supporting those villains with any of my hard-earned money. Maryland's looking mighty interesting about now."

"But how could you leave all ye've built here?"

"It'll be a hard decision, mind you...and I'm just talking right now...but if they keep pushing me....well I didna know what I'll do. Several other people feel the same way. They're tired of all those new regulations the Commissioners keep imposing on us. Did you hear what happened to that negro Anthony?"

"Nay, what happened?"

"Seems the Indians from the Town of Oanancocke aren't too happy. They came to court the other day and were complaining about how they've been pushed off their land on Pungoteague Creek...And would you believe the court sided with them and ordered that no man could locate on the north side of Pungoteague

Creek unless just compensation was given the Indians and acknowledged by their chief. Poor Anthony Johnson was trying to increase his holdings after he bought all those indentured servants, he even has a couple of negro slaves and he wanted to patent some of that land near his plantation but now he can't unless the Chief agrees."

"That's unfortunate. I like Anthony."

"I tell you, Ambrose, those new Commissioners are making life intolerable around here." Stephen's temper was rising and his face grew red.

"Have ye heard anything back from England about the protest we sent Parliament?"

"Not a word, far as I can tell. It's like we're not even important enough for them to address our complaints. I feel England is only interested in using us to pay debts with all these taxes they try to collect."

"It certainly appears so....but at least there have been no reprisals against you or the others who signed. I was concerned about you my friend."

"I know ya' were, but the protest had to be sent. We have to stand up for our rights just like any other citizen. I think that's what hurts me the most...England does not seem to consider us citizens. We're being treated like we're not part of England and basically ignored until they want money."

"True....I wish I knew what else we could do. I hate being in discord with Parliament. I fear it will not benefit us."

"I agreed, Ambrose, but I see no other choice before us...they seem to be intent on taxing us without mercy."

"Well...it appears we'll not solve the problem for now and I 'spect I'd better get this packet up to Mary. She's anxious for news."

"Right...I'm sure she is. Didna you say her sister-in-law was accused of being a witch?"

"Aye, Anne was not only accused but taken to Maidstone for a trial."

"Makes me glad I'm here...even with all our problems when I hear something like that. I hope George can help her."

"I do as well. 'Twill be hard on him if anything happens to Anne. Why don't you stay for dinner? I'm sure Mary'd love to see you."

188

"Some other time, Ambrose. I told Sarah, I wouldn't be away long and she tends to worry. Tell Mary I hope I brought her good news in the packet," Stephen hollered back as he walked down the path to his waiting sloop.

Ambrose watched him leave the dock then walked toward his house. Mary met him at the door.

"Was that Stephen? I thought he'd come in and visit."

"Nay, he stopped by to deliver this packet. He thought ye'd want it as soon as possible since we're worried about Anne."

"That was nice of him," Mary said as she wiped her hands on her apron before taking the packet. She walked to the chair by the fireplace, sat down, broke the seal and began to read.

"Oh, Ambrose. Anne has been declared guilty of being a witch and sentenced to die by hanging. What can we do? I wish I was there. Oh, poor Anne...poor Anne," Mary's lips trembled and tears trickled down her cheeks.

Ambrose rushed over and took Mary in his arms. He caressed her head as she cried. Mary Jane and Thomas, had been playing with a puppy. They began wailing along with their distressed mother.

"Mary, dear sweet Mary, there is nothing we can do for Anne now but pray. George is there at least. Mayhaps he will be able to stop it," Ambrose said as he stroked her hair.

Mary finally gained some control over her tears. She bent over and picked up little Tom and held him close while Ambrose comforted his daughter.

"Mary, we cannot control what happens to us but we must trust in the Lord to get us through these trials."

"I know, Ambrose...but 'tis very hard sometimes...but I'll pray...we'll all pray for Anne."

CHAPTER TWENTY-NINE

August 23, 1652 – Maidstone, England

It was dark, but George left immediately for Councilor Graham's house after receiving word he had returned. He was warmly greeted by the butler this time and led into the Parlour.

"Please wait here, Sir," the butler requested. "I'll inform Master Graham that ye're here."

George took a seat by the fireplace and only had to wait a moment before Councilor Graham entered. He shook George's hand and said, "I have good news, George. Judge Warburton has agreed to take a petition to Parliament for the immediate pardon of Anne and Mildred. He said he never believed there was strong evidence against the two of them, but since other Judges were involved in the verdict, the only way they can receive a pardon is by Parliament."

"That's great news! But why aren't you in London. Don't you have to take his decision to them. She is scheduled to be hung in two days."

"Considering the time frame, Judge Warburton decided to address Parliament himself. He should be there now."

"I hope they agree with him."

"They will. I have no doubt. Judge Peter Warburton is a well-respected Judge. You should have Anne home soon."

"I hope you are right Sir, and thank you again for ye're assistance."

"How is Anne? Is she eating?"

"I didna know. I have been unable to see her since you left. I tried everyday but the gate-keeper refused to let me in."

"Why that scoundrel! And I gave him money too. Well, we'll see her tomorrow. He can't refuse me...and you can tell her the good news. We need to celebrate. I'll have Matthew bring us some ale."

George stayed until late that night. He returned to the Bell Inn filled with excitement about Anne's release.

George rose early the next morning and arrived at Councilor Graham's house just as dawn broke. The two men rode in the Councilor's carriage to the prison. When they reached the gate-keeper this time, he immediately allowed them in but Graham stopped before entering and said, "George, you go on up to Anne and tell her the good news. I'll join you in a moment. I'll think I'll have a *nice* discussion with the gate-keeper about why he denied you entrance."

George grinned and rushed up the steps to Anne's cell. As his eyes adjusted to the dark room, he saw Anne lying on the floor in the same corner. He felt like crying out when he saw her. She was so emaciated.

"Anne, I'm back sweet one."

Anne's eyes were closed but her eyelids fluttered when she heard his voice. She spoke softly, "I thought you'd changed ye're mind."

"Never dearest....I was denied entrance....I wanted to see you...Oh Anne!"

George leaned down and carefully drew Anne into his arms. She was nothing but skin and bones....and weak as a kitten. George stroked her hair and looked into her eyes.

"Dearest one...I have good news. Councilor Graham has been successful. Judge Warburton is going to Parliament to have you and Mildred pardoned. You will be free soon."

Anne stared at him with glazed eyes. She did not appear to understand.

"Oh Anne, what has happened to you? No matter...we'll take you home soon."

"Nay, George...I want to die here."

"Oh Anne...please love...please didna say that," George's voice broke.

Councilor Graham arrived and saw George and Anne in the corner and frowned. He walked over to Mildred and spoke gently to her, Mildred began crying and hugged Graham. After a few minutes, he stood by George and said, "How is she?"

"Not well, Sir. Not well at all. I hope we aren't too late."

"I convinced the guard to let you remain here 'til nightfall. I need to return home in case word comes from Parliament."

"Aye, Sir. Thank you."

Graham left and George continued to hold Anne. He coaxed her to eat a little soup and he held her close throughout the day, gently whispering in her ear his undying love for her. At dusk, the guard forced him to leave.

George raced to the prison the next morning but was denied entrance again.

"But Councilor Graham arranged for me to stay with her."

The gate-keeper laughed. "No one visits with the witches today. This is hanging day."

"Nay, she is to be freed. We will receive her pardon from Parliament. It's only a matter of time."

The gate-keeper chuckled again. "Parliament ye say. The witches must have strong powers. I've had no word from Parliament. The witches will hang today."

"Nay....Nay!" George yelled.

I must see Councilor Graham. He'll stop this....he can stop this....

George ran to the Councilor's house and pounded on his door.

The butler recognized George and allowed him to enter.

"Sir...Master Graham is not yet awake. Can this not wait?"

"Nay, Matthew. They plan to hang Anne today. The Councilor needs to stop this."

"I understand Sir. I'll alert Master Graham."

George paced the large hall while he waited. A few minutes later, Graham appeared in his robe.

"What is this you say about hanging Anne today?"

"That is what the gate-keeper told me. He would not allow me entrance. I thought you said that the Judge is addressing Parliament. Will they not postpone the hanging until they hear from Parliament?"

"I'd hope so. I thought I made that clear. Let me dress and I'll see what I can do. Matthew, prepare George some breakfast while he waits."

"Aye, Sir. Come with me to the dining room, Mr. Willson."

George followed the butler, but he was so anxious, he could not eat. Thirty minutes later Councilor Graham appeared and said, "Let's head for the gaol. Matthew, send a messenger for me at the prison if I receive a packet or anyone wants me for any reason."

"Aye, Sir, I will."

When they arrived at the prison, Councilor Graham argued with the gate-keeper for some time while George paced the street in front of the gaol. The crowd around the prison was tremendous and George was frequently jostled as each person tried to see 'the witches.'

After a time, Graham walked over to George and said, "I couldn't convince them to wait. We can only hope that Parliament's order will come in time. They will not allow you to visit today either but of course they have to let me in. However, if I spend time with Anne, I will be unable to consult with anyone who might delay the hanging. I believe it is more imperative that I work for a delay so I need to leave to do that. Do you want to go with me?"

"Can I help by going with you?"

"Nay....there's nothing you can do. Why don't ye stay here? There's a chance the gate-keeper will relent and allow you to see Anne."

"Aye, then that's what I'll do."

Councilor Graham left George and headed for the Lower Court House.

Oh Anne....dearest one....I'm here. How can I let you know? What can I do?

George walked around the prison several times and prayed that he would see Anne on the walkway. But she did not appear. He pleaded with the gate-keeper to allow him entrance but to no avail. Around mid-morning, two wagons with many more guards arrived. A large group of people began to congregate around the wagons which were parked side by side with the backs facing the prison gate.

"We'll see them now. Get ready for some excitement," chuckled an old man as he nudged George's arm.

"They better be in chains....or they'll fly away," shouted a stern-faced woman.

"Did ya' bring ye're garlic, Marge?" giggled a young woman as she looked at her friend.

"Aye, she smells bad enough to ward off all kinds of evil," laughed a young man. The younger girl stuck her tongue out at him.

This is madness...this can't be happening. Not to my Anne. Oh where is the Councilor? She should be freed and we should be on our way to Virginia.

George glanced around desperately with the hope that Councilor Graham's carriage would suddenly appear.

Four boys pushed George as they tried to maneuver closer with a basket of rotten vegetables and rocks. George blocked their path as best as he could but they simply went around and found a gap somewhere else, allowing them to reach the front of the crowd nearest the wagons.

Suddenly the door opened and the guards lined the sides of the wagons, making a path and blocking anyone from getting close. Two guards came out of the building, followed by the accused witches, Anne Ashby, Mary Browne and Anne Martyn. Their hands were tied in front of them with a cord. Anne Ashby was mumbling and tried to bite one of the guards.

"She's a wild one. Better watch out....she'd fly off if'en she could," shouted a burly man in the crowd.

Mary Browne was screaming. A guard was dragging her by the cord that tied her hands.

"Reckon she didna like this much. Can't do evil when ye're all tied up," laughed an old man.

Anne Martyn was very docile but crying.

"Look at that last one I fear the quiet one's most....don't know what they're thinking," the woman next to George mumbled as she pushed her elbow against his side.

When the women reached the wagon, a guard picked up each one like a sack of potatoes and threw her on the wagon bed where two others guards stood ready to chain them to the sides. After the three women were chained, the wagon slowly pulled away from the gaol with soldiers on horseback surrounding it. Immediately, the young boys began throwing rotten vegetables, fruit and rocks at the women. Anne Ashby was hit by a rock. She fixed her eyes on the boy and snarled at him.

"Watch it boys...she's putting a spell on ye." cried an old women.

195

The boys, frightened by her reaction, picked up their baskets and pressed backward into the crowd, tripping and falling as they pushed. Many people trailed after the first wagon, reducing the size of the crowd enough so George could move closer to the remaining wagon. Again, his eyes searched the people behind him feverishly looking for any sign of Councilor Graham.

Please God. Bring him here with the order to stop her execution. There's so little time left.

The door creaked open again and two more guards left the building. Mary Read followed the guards. Her eyes darted as she searched the crowd.

"She's the one had the teat on her tongue....I seen the teat...she's belongs to the devil and should be burned," cried a old woman.

A chant of "Burn her...Burn her...Burn her," began to resound in the mass of people, who grew more excited and distracted them for a brief moment from the next women leaving the prison, Anne Willson. She was so weak, the guards were almost carrying her. She was thrown on the wagon like the other women.

George groaned when he saw her treated so harshly. He tried to catch her eye but she had them closed and seemed to be praying. A guard pulled her up to chain her to the side but her legs gave way and she collapsed.

"Bring me a chair," he shouted.

A tall man across from George laughed, "Not a very powerful witch now, 'ere ye?" The crowd joined in the laughter.

A chair was brought out and Anne was tied to it then tied to the sides of the wagon with a cord.

Mildred was the last women to leave the building. She was crying inconsolably. She saw George and screamed, "I thought he said we'd be freed."

"I'm sorry, Mildred. I thought so too," he replied.

A man next to him, studied George a minute, then said, "What do you mean by that? We can't free these witches. Are you some kind of fool? You're probably a witch too." The man turned briefly to tell someone else what George said. George realized the danger he was in and tried to melt into the crowd and become invisible.

The assemblage of people followed the wagon to Gallow

Hill, about a mile out of town. Rocks, vegetables, dung and other filth was thrown at the women as the wagon moved through the street. George trailed behind the main part of the crowd, glancing back frequently for Councilor Graham's carriage.

The first wagon had already reached the gibbet and the three women were in the process of being escorted to the platform. Anne Ashby was snarling and trying to bite any guard near her. She stood on a small stool with a noose placed around her neck. Her arms were tied above the elbow to her sides with another cord, leaving her hands free to pray. She kicked at a guard who was trying to tie her skirt and legs. The other two women were placed in the same positions as Anne Ashby.

The crowd was in a frenzy....shouting taunts at the helpless women.

"The Devil is waiting for you."

"Ye'll be in hell soon."

When the wagon carrying Anne Willson reached the platform, the two women who could stand were forced to climb the ladder. Anne was too weak to stand so she was lifted out of the wagon, still tied to the chair and placed on the platform. A noose was placed around the two women's necks and they were tied like the other three. Anne was placed, still tied to the chair, under the remaining noose. A guard placed a white cap atop each woman's head. George panicked and frantically searched for Councilor Graham's carriage.

OH GOD! THIS CAN'T BE HAPPENING! WHAT CAN I DO?

The executioner stood at the front and center of the gallows and the crowd grew quiet.

The chaplain placed a piece of black silk on Ann Ashby's head and she grew strangely quiet as he did so. He proceeded to read her sentence "Ann Ashby, the Court finds you guilty of being a witch and not having the fear of God before thine Eyes, and through the instigation of the Devil, thou hast forsaken thy God and covenanted with the Devil, and by his help hast practiced witchcraft on various sundry persons and animals. You are therefore sentenced to be hanged. The sentence is to be carried out today, August 25, 1652. Do you have anything to say?" She spat in his face and shouts rang out.

"She's of the devil."

197

"Rot in Hell, you witch."

The chaplain wiped his face and moved on to Ann Martyn.

After placing the black silk square on her head he said, "Ann Martyn the Court finds you guilty of being a witch and not having the fear of God before thine Eyes, and through the instigation of the Devil, thou hast forsaken thy God and covenanted with the Devil, and by his help hast practiced witchcraft on various sundry persons and animals. You are therefore sentenced to be hanged. The sentence is to be carried out today, August 25, 1652. Do you have anything to say?"

"I'm innocent, Father,' she screamed. "I'm innocent."

"I'll pray for you my child."

He placed the square of silk on the heads of Mary Read, Mary Browne and Mildred Wright and read their sentences as well. Each one declared their innocence and he prayed with them. When the chaplain reached Anne, he placed the silk cloth on her hair and said, "Anne Willson the Court finds you guilty of being a witch and not having the fear of God before thine Eyes, and through the instigation of the Devil, thou hast forsaken thy God and covenanted with the Devil, and by his help hast practiced witchcraft the 20th of January 1652 upon the child Mary Elizabeth Walcott; whereby the body of said child was hurt, afflicted, wasted and tormented until she died on February 1, 1652. for which according to the Law of God, and the Law of this great nation thou deservest to die. The sentence is to be carried out today, August 25, 1652. Do you have anything to say?"

"She looked up at him and said, "Pray with me."

The Chaplain, "Certainly child." He put one hand on her hair while she clasped her hands in prayer and they prayed silently together, while tauts continue to ring out from the crowd.

When they finished, the executioner ordered the guards to cover the women's heads with the white cloths. Two guards lifted Anne Willson's chair up so the noose could be placed around her neck. Another guard adjusted the noose while the guards held the chair in the air. Guards stood behind each of the other women. A hushed anticipation fell over the crowd. The executioner gave a command. The stools were kicked from under the women and the two guards released Anne Willson's chair. It fell loudly onto the deck and the rope grew taunt around her neck.

George fell to his knees in anguish as shouts filled the air from people surrounding him.

"Praise God....they are dead."

"May you all rot in hell where you belong!"

Tears trickled down his cheeks as he covered his face with his hands. After a few moments, he stood and slowly walked away, not able to bear hearing the hateful words emanating from the crowd. Suddenly, he picked up his pace and began running from the horrible scene.

Why....oh why God? Why could you not save her? She was to be freed. Why was she punished so?...She is innocent.

He saw the Councilor's covered carriage approaching and hailed the driver. The driver recognized him, halted and George walked over.

"Is Councilor Graham inside?"

"Aye,"

George opened the carriage door and the Councilor asked, "I came as soon as I heard the hanging was to take place. I still haven't heard from Parliament but hoped to force some kind of delay."

"Ye're took late. It is done," George cried.

"Ah, George, I'm so sorry. I feel sure Parliament would have pardoned her. Come, get in. We'll return to my house."

"Nay, I need nothing from you now. Do you know what they plan to do with her body? I'd like to take her back to Cranbrook for burial."

"Oh lad, I'm sorry. That's not possible. It has been decided that all the witches will be burned."

"She's not a witch. Didna call her that!"

"Aye, George.... Are ye sure ye won't return home with me?"

"Nay, I must return to Cranbrook. My sisters are waiting to hear." George closed the carriage door and continued walking toward Bell Inn.

CHAPTER THIRTY

September, 1652 Eastern Shore, Virginia

The clang of the church bell reverberated throughout the town announcing the marriage of Anne West, daughter of Anthony West and Col. Charles Scarburgh, son of Col. Edmund Scarburgh.

A large crowd attended the wedding feast afterwards since it was such a pretty day. Colorful leaves cluttered the ground on this fall day and young children threw them at each other as they darted about among the tall trees.

Anne was dressed in a beautiful fitted blue bodice with a deeper blue skirt. On her head she wore a wide-brimmed straw hat with blue ribbons. Charles sported a red coat over beige knee breeches and a beige vest with a powdered wig adorning his head.

"Don't they make a handsome couple." Mary commented to her cousin Priscilla as they sat next to each other on blankets while their youngest children napped.

"Aye, I like Charles. He's not nearly so pompous as his father." Priscilla Willson responded.

"Mind if we join you two?" asked Joanne Custis. She was carrying a blanket and a basket. Her very pregnant daughter-in-law followed close behind.

"We'd be glad to have you join us Joanne," Mary answered with enthusiasm.

"Thanks, Mary. Elizabeth needed a place to rest. She's been feeling poorly."

Elizabeth Custis gave a weak smile and sat down on the blanket her mother-in-law spread on the ground. "I may never get back up again but I could use some rest. This belly takes some getting use to."

Mary and Priscilla looked at each other and laughed.

Mary said, "It does at that but after the third time...it kinda becomes a normal way of life."

"There won't be a third or even a second time if I have anything to say about it," Elizabeth grumbled.

Joanne frowned at Elizabeth's announcement and the air suddenly grew tense.

Mary tried to change the subject and pointed to the children playing with Henry, Jr., "Isn't that Andrew's apprentice, Thomas Cottingham, with those children? I'm surprised he allowed him a little time away. He works that boy awful hard."

"The way I hear it, Mr. Andrews is mighty liberal with his whip on all his servants and apprentices," Joanne added. "There have been quite a few complaints against him to Commissioners. Several of his servants have tried to run away. 'Course there's not a lot the Commissioners can do since it's the owners right to correct his servants."

"There are better ways of correcting without resorting to the whip all the time," Priscilla said curtly.

"I agree," Mary added, "Joanne, there's something I wanted to talk to you about. I didna know about you, but I taught Henry, Jr. all I'm able. He needs more education than I can provide. We planned to send him to England before the war. We dare not send him now with the unrest there. You have grandchildren and many others in our community do as well. Several boys like Anthony West's son, John, my Henry, Priscilla's son and your little Argoll, to name a few, would benefit from a school here. What do ye think?"

"That's true, Mary. Like you, Ann and Argoll wanted to send Argoll, Jr. to England and decided against it. It's still too dangerous."

"I mentioned the idea to Ambrose and he agreed. He also said that he and Stephen Horsey were planning to patent additional land next month and could donate a parcel for a school."

"That's great! I'll talk to John and Argoll about it. Mayhaps the Commissioners will send for a teacher."

The women continued to excitedly discuss the potential for a school.

When a ship from England bearing George Willson and his sisters, Sarah and Elizabeth, arrived in Accawmacke the following month, the plans for a school were put on hold. Mary was ecstatic with the arrival of her family. However, the news of her sister-in-law's death put a damper on the joyous reunion.

Sarah and Elizabeth quickly adapted to the routine in the Dixon family. Their assistance in the daily chores provided a welcome relief for Mary, but George's usual cheeriness was waning. Anne's death weighed heavily on him and he frequently spent time alone.

"Has he talked to you much about Anne's death?" Mary inquired of her sisters one morning while they were preparing breakfast.

"Nay, Mary...very little. I believe he blames himself for some unknown reason. Parliament overturned Anne's and Mildred's convictions, but by the time word reached Maidstone it was too late...." Sarah said in a trembling voice.

Mary hugged Sarah, "'Tis tragic what happened to Anne and we'll never understand why...I'm so happy ye're all with me now...away from those horrible people who treated her so badly."

"We are too," added Elizabeth. "Anne's death was very hard on George. When he returned from Maidstone, he simply said he was too late. He never even shed a tear...just said it like it was a fact...and wouldn't add any details."

"We tried to talk to him about her death," Sarah said. "But he refused and told us to quit pestering him. Did ye know that he was in love with Anne?"

"Nay, she was his sister-in-law...how could he be in love with her?" Mary gave Sarah an astonished look.

"I always suspected, but George told me so himself when he was trying to free her from the gaol," Sarah said.

"You never told me that," Elizabeth said.

"I didna see any point in telling anyone after she was dead...'twould only bring more heartache."

"That explains why he hardly said a word on the ship...just kept to himself. I wish I knew how we could help him," said Elizabeth.

Mary added, "I do too, Elizabeth. I believe all we can do is pray that God will help him see he was not at fault."

"I think he's turned his back on God. I never see him pray anymore. He use to pray all the time...especially after he met those Quakers, remember Sarah?" Elizabeth asked.

Sarah nodded.

"You know...shortly after he arrived here, years ago, he

talked to me about meeting some Quakers. Actually, we had a long discussion about them. I admit it was quite a confusing conversation. I didna understand what he was talking about. He mentioned something abour an 'Inner light' I must have discouraged him because he never spoke of the Quakers again." Mary set her childrens' porridge in front of them.

"I've heard some about the Quakers in England...not anything good, though. They're always being arrested for something...particularly their leader, George Fox. I saw him once before we left. He was rather disheveled in appearance, wore leather breeches if you can believe it. He was very tall and thin...and preaching to a group of people while standing on a rock...strange person he seemed to me," added Elizabeth "But I listened to him for a few minutes and I was spellbound. I remember the things he said made a lot of sense at the time."

"Some of my students had Quaker parents. They seemed nice enough...not dangerous people like they were described at church," Sarah added.

"Well, all I didna care what religion George chooses so long as he goes back to his old happy self," Mary declared. "I just wish I knew how to help him. But speaking of school...you are a blessing from heaven Sarah. We've been talking about the need for a school here in Accawmacke and I'm sure the Commissioners would like to have you as the teacher."

"A school? Oh how wonderful. I thought I'd have to give up teaching forever."

"Not with the number of wee one's being born around here," Mary laughed.

CHAPTER THIRTY-ONE

Spring and Summer, 1653 Eastern Shore, Virginia

After a difficult winter, spring was welcomed by everyone in Accawmacke. Rev. Doughty suggested a picnic after church one day in April and the event drew a large attendance.

After his sermon, Rev. Doughty said, "I have a very important announcement to make. I have it from a reliable source that Gov. Stuyvesant of New Netherland is trying to convince the Narragansetts to attack us."

A collective gasp came from the congregation.

"Who is this reliable source, Rev. Doughty?" questioned Commander Argoll Yeardley.

"Chief Uncas of the Mohegans. You know he has been our friend for many years."

"Aye, but how did he learn this? The Mohegans and Narragansetts are not exactly on speaking terms," Ambrose remarked. "In fact, I'd go so far as to say they were avowed enemies."

Rev. Doughty appeared distressed at Ambrose's comment. "I'm sure Chief Uncas would not mislead us. He only has our best interest at heart."

"I've a mind to believe Chief Uncas," Col. Scarburgh. "I've never trusted the Narragansetts."

"Ye've never trusted any Indian," Stephen Horsey said.

Pockets of laughter broke out in the congregation and Col. Scarburgh frowned at Stephen.

Rev Doughty continued, "Believe him or not.....I feel it would be prudent to protect ourselves."

Argoll Yeardley stood up and declared, "Ye're right Rev. We'll have a meeting tomorrow at Hungars to discuss this situation. Meanwhile, I'd advise everyone to be on guard and report any Indian who looks suspicious."

Ambrose walked out of the men's door of the Church and overheard Thomas Johnson whisper to Col. Coulbourne.

"'Tis not only the Narragansetts we should be worried about but many of the Dutch citizens living right here in Accawmacke. Who knows where their sympathies lie?"

Ambrose remarked, "Thomas, I didna think we should distrust people we have known for years. Let's give them the benefit of the doubt."

"Ye're being naïve, Amborse. The Dutch are not to be trusted...mark my words," Thomas Johnson replied and walked toward his sloop waiting by the quay.

Rev. Doughty's announcement restrained the festive mood of the people. Many decided to return home to protect their property rather than stay for the picnic. The Dixon family remained. Mary and her sisters were spreading a quilt under a tree when Maria Coulbourne approached them. Mary Jane and Thomas ran toward her, screaming with delight.

"How are my sweet wee ones?" Maria said as she hugged the children in her arms. "I've certainly missed you."

"We've missed you too," Mary declared. "I feel like my right arm is gone. How has Col. Coulbourne been treating you?"

"He is such a dear...never complains and loves my cooking."

"I'm sure he loves ye're cooking because we truly miss it." Mary looked at her sisters, "Sarah, and Elizabeth...you have never tasted apple pie until ye've had Maria's apple pie."

"I wouldn't quite say that, Mary...but I came over to give you some good news."

"Oh tell us the good news...we could use some after what Rev. Doughty just reported," exclaimed Sarah.

"Well...let's say in a few months, Mary Jane and Thomas will have someone else to play with."

"You didna mean it?" Mary cried. "Ye're going to have a wee one."

"I never thought it would happen for me again, but...what can I say," Maria affirmed.

"Oh Maria...how wonderful! You will really have a family again."

"Aye, Mary...sometimes I guess there is a lot of darkness before the dawn...I've had my share of darkness, now I'm happy it is finally dawn."

The Commissioners met the following day and decided to send some men among the Indians to investigate the rumors about the potential attack. A week later, word came from James City that Gov. Stuyvesant also heard the rumor and became concerned. He sent two of his officers to negotiate a treaty with Gov. Bennett of Virginia and seek protection for the Dutch citizens to avoid any reprisals against them. But Governor Bennett informed the men that he did not have authority to negotiate any arrangements with the Dutch and the matter would have to be referred to England.

During the meeting, another matter was discussed. The ship, *The Fame of Virginia,* owned by Royalist and Accawmacke citizen, Walter Chiles, had been seized by Captain Richard Husband on the grounds that Captain Chiles did not have a license. The Court ordered the ship to be released but Captain Husband had already taken his prize and sailed away. The Commissioners ordered the citizens of Accawmacke to reimburse Captain Chiles for his loss.

Commissioner Captain Thomas Johnson became enraged at the order and walked out of a meeting. He refused to continue the discussion. Instead he sent word to the community that the citizens should meet in Dr. George Hacke's old field the first Saturday in June where he would read aloud the orders of which he disapproved.

Ambrose met with Stephen Horsey and Captain Johnson in the Ordinary at Hungar's a day prior to the called meeting.

"How many do you think will show, Ambrose? Ye're probably heard more talk than I have," Johnson asked.

"I'd say all the older settlers are behind you, Captain. They consider you a hero to take on the other commissioners."

"That's good to hear. One never knows exactly what others are thinking."

"I'm glad ye stood up to them. These Royalist's fancy they can come here and take from us with all their fees and taxes. 'Tis time someone stopped them. We need to be preparing for an Indian attack, not arguing over how much money they want."

"Aye, that's what I thought. Sometimes, I think these new citizens think we're only here to provide for them...haven't seen much hard work from the lot."

Col. Edmund Scarburgh walked in and spied the three men deep in a heated discussion; he walked over to join them.

"I see things haven't changed much since I've been away. Still talking about those savages, I see."

"I saw ya' at church, Col. Scarburgh...it appears ye've returned at an opportune time if this rumor about the Indians is true. When did you get back?" Horsey said as he stood and shook Scarburgh's hand.

"Arrived about a week ago...and as far as the Indians go..I've always maintained to kill them or drive them out. It's the only way to solve the problem."

"The Indians aren't the only problem this time, Colonel. Those Commissioners would take everything we earned if they could," Horsey added.

"I thought they backed off on those taxes, what has changed?" Scarburgh inquired.

"Tis not the taxes this time," Horsey growled. "They want us to reimburse Chiles for his boat that was seized."

"Reimburse him? Since when is that a responsibility of the people? No one came to my aid when my ship was seized."

"I agree, Edmund. And that's exactly why I walked out of the meeting. I feel for Walter Chiles and all but it's the responsibility of the Governor, not the people to reimburse him. I've called a meeting tomorrow to discuss it at Hacke's field."

"I'll be sure to be there. We must put a stop to those money grabbing commissioners. They'd break us if they could," Scarburgh growled.

It was late morning by the time Ambrose, George and Henry, Jr. arrived at the field where over a hundred people were assembled, angrily discussing the events that had transpired.

"This should be interesting," Ambrose commented as he dismounted his horse."

"Aye. I'm sure Captain Johnson is glad to see the support for his actions," George added.

"Why is everyone so upset, Papa?"

"Well, son...there comes a time when a man has to stand up for his beliefs and passion fuels the fire in a man's blood. That's why they're angry. I just hope everyone stands together so we can forge some change and emotions don't get out of hand," Ambrose said as he studied the number of men with matchlocks in the crowd. He spotted Stephen Horsey waving at him to come over.

"Papa, I see Tom Cottingham over there. Could I go talk to him? I don't see him much. Mr. Andrews always has him working."

"Sure son. I'm surprised Andrews let Tom come. I'm sure he'd like some company," Ambrose responded as he looked in the direction Henry, Jr. pointed. Tom was sitting on the wagon of Mr. Andrew's oxcart.

When Henry, Jr. reached the oxcart, he asked, "What are ye doing over here, Tom? Everyone's in the field."

"Mr. Andrews told me to come with him but made me stay by the wagon. He said I might learn how men are supposed to act but I sure can't learn much sitting on this here oxcart. Just between you and me I think he was afraid I might catch a few winks while he was gone."

"Ye're probably right. I didna think he's a very generous with his breaks from work after the last time I visited. But speaking of learning, have ye heard about the schoolhouse they're planning to build? My Aunt Sarah's going to be the teacher."

"I heard a little about it but what's that to me?"

"I thought mayhaps Mr. Andrews would let ye go and we can see each other more."

"Now why would he do that...seeing's how I'm apprenticed to him to learn the blacksmith trade? When would I have time to attend? I work all day for Mr. Andrews."

"I guess ye're right. I don't imagine he'll let you go."

"I wouldn't mind going though. Miss Susan, my guardian's wife after my father died, taught me how to read some and I can write a little, but I could sure use more learning in sums. Mr. Andrew didna know much sums and he says everybody cheats him out of what he's due."

"Mayhaps he'll let you learn sums so you can help him with his accounts."

Tom laughed, "I didna think he'd trust me either, especially if I knew more sums than him....'sides, he never let me leave during a work day."

"I have an idea. I'll teach you. I can come by in the evenings and teach you sums."

209

"I...I didna know about that. I didna know what Mr. Andrews would think about that...he probably consider that wasting time."

"I'll have Papa talk to him. Mayhaps, he could convince him to let me come by."

"I guess there's no harm in ye're Papa asking," Tom smiled at Henry, Jr.

A loud whistle interrupted their conversation and both boys glanced in the direction of it's source. Captain Johnson was standing on a large tree stump preparing to speak. Stephen Horsey gave another loud whistle in an attempt to gather the assemblage closer.

Finally, silence fell over the crowd when Captain Johnson began talking. "I guess you've all heard something about why I've called you here today."

Some of the people nodded their heads in agreement while others shouted "Ayes."

"I have the resolution here that our commissioners wish to adopt and I think I best read it to you. But first I'd like to inform you of its purpose. Many of you have already heard...Col. Chiles was falsely accused of not having license from England and his ship, *Hopeful Adventure,* was seized and sailed away by Capt. Richard Husband. As restitution for Col. Chiles loss, the Commissioners proposed assessing the inhabitants of Northampton and Accawmacke to pay...." Capt. Johnson halted as the rest of his speech was drowned out by shouts from the people surrounding him.

"What do they mean by making us pay for their mistake?"

"I'll not pay a pence."

"Nor will I."

The men in the crowd continued shouting angrily so Capt. Johnson stepped down from the stump since he could not be heard among the crowd.

Stephen Horsey excitedly took his place, "I said it once before and I'll say it again...the Commissioners are nothing but a company of 'Asses and Villains' and I'll not pay one pence toward this debt. I'll not pay their taxes either. Who wants to join with me?"

"Aye...Horsey, I'm with ye," Col. William Coulbourne added.

The throng cheered their approval. Anger was on the face of

210

the each man and discussions continued well into late afternoon on how to protest the Commissioners orders.

The citizens became more defiant and continued to hold gatherings about the Commissioners actions. This infuriated the governing officials. As the citizens meetings became more frequent, the Commissioners became alarmed and felt they needed assistance from James City to quash what they thought was quickly becoming a revolt. Evidence was collected to bring the leaders to justice. Men who had not taken part in the protest were upset at the turn in events and tried to defuse the situation. They drafted a petition which denied that the gathering was a revolt but instead a mere misunderstanding between the Commissioners and protesters regarding reimbursement for Col. Chiles ship.

Word arrived in July that James City responded to the petition and a large gathering assembled at Hungar's Ordinary to discuss the results.

"It appears Governor Bennet believes we're traitors," Stephen Horsey growled. "He's declared us scandalous and seditious and is coming here to determine punishment himself."

"Is that so?" Ambrose declared. "What didya suppose the punishment will be?"

"Well...for one thing, we'll not be allowed to hold office. I was ordered to leave the last meeting and there's talk of fines," Stephen Johnson complained.

"But we were only holding meetings...they can't stop meetings...'tis not right," Col. Coulbourne commented.

"I didna believe they're concerned about what is right...all they want is more money from us...but they'll not have more from me...I'm leaving," Col. Scarburgh added.

"Where will ye go?" Ambrose asked.

"Out of their money hungry grasp...that's for sure," Scarburgh replied wryly.

On July 29th, complaints and seditious acts were laid before the court. Captain Thomas Johnson, considered the initial instigator, was fined five hundred pounds of tobacco and bound over to keep the peace. Stephen Horsey was ordered imprisoned and fined three hundred pounds of tobacco. By the time the Governor arrived Col. Scarburgh was not to be found. Peace was restored. But the bitterness toward the Commissioners remained among many on the Eastern Shore and began to fester.

CHAPTER THIRTY-TWO

1654 Eastern Shore, Virginia

A light drizzle fell as Ambrose's servants glided his shallop toward Hungar's Church. Ambrose, Mary, Henry, Jr., George and Mary's sisters, Sarah and Elizabeth all rode in silence while the crew guided the craft toward the quay. Only a medley of sounds from the chirping, winged, insect world, aided by the distant cry of geese disturbed the quiet. Everyone's thoughts were focused on the sad event they were attending. Elizabeth Custis, the young bride of John Custis, Jr., died shortly after giving birth to their first child, John Custis, III.

The crew maneuvered the shallop next to the pier. Ambrose and George climbed on the decking and assisted the ladies.

Mary straightened her dress over her bulging stomach and looked toward the church while she waited on her sisters. She located her friend, Joanne Custis in a group nearest the church. Joanne was dressed completely in black and a young lady standing next to Joanne held an infant.

When her sisters joined Mary on the deck, they walked the path leading to the church while the men followed close behind.

"I wonder who will raise the poor bairn now? 'Tis quite a burden for a young father," Sarah commented.

"I'm sure Joanne will be of great assistance to her son," Mary responded. "She was so looking forward to her grandson's birth. I imagine John's sister will also help. John is lucky to have family with him."

"I wish we had been here to support you when Mary Margaret died." Elizabeth said.

Mary looked affectionately at her sister.

Oh if you only knew the countless days I wished the same thing, Elizabeth. My family seemed so far away doing those first years in Accawmacke but each experience made me stronger. I see that now.

"You'll be here for this wee one...'tis all that matters now,"

Mary said as she placed her hand on her stomach.

Mary and her sisters approached Joanne to offer their condolences. Joanne suddenly reached out and pulled Mary in her arms.

"Oh, Mary. I can't believe it. Oh my poor son. He loved Elizabeth so much. His heart is broken and I didna know how to help him."

Mary hugged Joanne and patted her gently on her back. "Time will ease his pain, Joanne. But we will pray for him. Only God can heal his broken heart."

Joanne released her grasp on Mary and said, "You're right of course, we must leave it up to God." Joanne focused her attention on the woman holding the infant behind her while she dabbed at her wet eyes with a handkerchief.

"This is John Custis, III. Isn't he a beautiful child? But he'll never know his sweet Mum." Tears began to flow down Joanne's cheeks.

Mary reached out and quietly held Joanne's hand until she regained control of her emotions. Then all four ladies walked toward the church for the funeral service.

Rev. Doughty began the service by saying many wonderful things about Elizabeth Custis but his demeanor changed toward the end of the funeral sermon when he became quite animated and shouted loudly, "We have evil among us...and we must find and stomp out this evil wherever it exist! Evil has taken this fair lady from among our midst. I tried in vain to help her but 'twas too strong...and evil overcame her...and took her life. We must not let this continue. Pray with me and help me seek out the evil in our community before the devil claims another life!"

Mary watched Joanne to see her reaction to Rev. Doughty statements. Joanne's face was beet-red and full of anger as she stared ahead. Mary looked over at John Custis and his son but they were seated in the men's section and she only had a view of the back of their heads.

After the service, Mary and her sisters filed out of the church. Joanne remained behind. After a few minutes Joanne left the church and appeared distraught. She walked toward her family without saying a word to anyone. Rev. Doughty exited from the men's door. The congregation walked directly to the nearby cemetery where Rev. Doughty made a few more brief remarks then closed in prayer. He invited everyone to the Yeardley's plantation for the funeral feast. Joanne and her family quickly left the cemetery.

Mary walked beside her husband as they approached their waiting shallop. Ambrose grasped Mary around the waist and supported her arm as they went down the steep embankment.

"Ambrose, did ye notice how upset Joanne seemed to be about what Rev. Doughty said at the service?"

"Aye, Mary. John Custis did not seem to like Rev. Doughty's statements either. I wonder what he meant by evil took Elizabeth's life."

"I'm not sure, Ambrose but there must be more to her death than we know."

"Mayhaps we'll learn more at the Yeardley's," Ambrose added as he assisted Mary in boarding.

A few minutes later, their shallop joined many others at Argoll Yeardley's large plantation in Old Town Neck on Mattawoman Creek. Make-shift tables filled with mounds of food surrounded the house. A large number of the people in the church attended the feast and were milling around and conversing quietly. Mary and her sisters approached Ann Yeardley, John Custis' sister, the hostess to offer their assistance.

"Thank you, Mary...but I believe everything is under control for now. However, Mum is inside if ye'd like to talk with her. She's quite upset at what Rev. Doughty said and refused to come out. I can't believe he voiced such accusations at Elizabeth's funeral."

"Accusations? What do ye mean?" Mary inquired.

"Why he practically blamed poor Elizabeth for her own death."

"But why would he blame Elizabeth for her death, I didna understand," Mary asked.

"Because Rev. Doughty thinks Barbary is a sorcerer."

"What? 'Tis preposterous...whatever gave him such an idea. Barbary Window is a fine midwife. How can he call her a sorcerer?" Mary exclaimed.

"Let me try to explain. Elizabeth was healthy until a couple of months ago when she developed a cough. Barbary gave her some herbs to cure it but they did not help so Mum sent for Dr.

215

Hacke. "

"I'm sure Barbary did the best she could but she is only a midwife."

"That's what Mum thought and that's why she sent for Dr. Hacke. But Dr. Hacke saw how sick she was and immediately started bleeding Elizabeth everyday. She continued to grow weaker and became feverish."

"I'm not surprised...my Henry never wanted to bleed because he didna feel it helped," remarked Mary.

"Of course, we were all frantic with worry and sent for Rev. Doughty to pray for her. Both Rev. Doughty and Dr. Hacke were attending her when Dr. Hacke mentioned that the herbs Barbary gave Elizabeth may have made her sick. Rev. Doughty became very angry and started saying Barbary was a sorcerer and full of evil and Dr. Hacke did not dispute his words."

"Oh poor Barbary!" cried Sarah "How could she go against those learned men."

"But why did Rev. Doughty blame Elizabeth?" inquired Mary.

"Rev. Doughty began visiting Elizabeth daily, praying over her and continually telling her she must fight and reject the devil within her but poor Elizabeth was so sick and confused. She argued with Rev. Doughty and begged to see Barbary. This only made Rev. Doughty more angry and determined to rid her of the devil. Mum, Papa and John didn't know what to do. They finally decided it was best for Dr. Hacke to continue his treatment but Elizabeth just grew weaker everyday. It was too much for her when little John was born. She never recovered from his birth and died a few days afterwards. Rev. Doughty told Mum it was because she would not reject the devil within her...and Barbary was a witch."

"Oh...how terrible. This witch talk...'tis nonsense. It was God's will....we must accept it."

"I agree and so does Mum but Rev. Doughty upset her greatly when he spoke at her funeral."

"Do you think it would help if I talk to Joanne?"

"I wish you would, Mary. Mayhaps she'll listen to you."

"I'll go to her immediately," Mary said and walked toward the Yeardley house with determination.

Mary found Joanne sitting alone in her Parlour whimpering

quietly. She stood for a moment unnoticed, trying to decide what to say to console her friend. Joanne realized Mary was standing in the doorway and greeted her, "Oh Mary, I am so glad ye're here. I know I should go outside and talk to our friends but I'm so overwrought right now...I can't force myself to see them. I didna know what to say to everyone after what Rev. Doughty said."

"Anne told me all about it and I would be distressed too," Mary entered the room and sat in the chair across from Joanne. "He had no right to say such things about Elizabeth. There was no evil...only a tragic death."

"We didna know how to help poor, Elizabeth. She grew weaker every day...I worry if we did the right thing by allowing Dr. Hacke to bleed her...she kept asking for Barbary...I just didna know what to do." Joanne's voice trailed off as she began to sob inconsolably.

Mary reached out and took Joanne's hand.

"We'll never understand why God allowed Elizabeth to die...I know you did the only thing you knew to help her and no one can be faulted for her death. It was just her time. Didna allow Rev. Doughty's words to concern you."

Mary stayed with Joanne and attempted to console her until nearly dusk.

CHAPTER THIRTY-THREE

Fall, 1654 Eastern Shore, Virginia

In late August, the community built a small log schoolhouse near Hungar's church and Sarah Willson was immediately hired by the Commissioners as the schoolmistress. The first classes would begin after the harvest. Sarah was thrilled for the opportunity to teach again. After a materials arrived for the school, Sarah and Mary spent a day preparing the classroom.

"Mary, this will be quite different from my classroom in England...the task of being totally in charge of all the students is a bit daunting,"

"Aye, I'm sure it is...but remember....without you...they might receive little education. 'Tis too dangerous for our children to travel to England now...I'm thankful you are here and I'm sure other parents feel the same. Do you have an idea of how many will be attending?"

"The Commissioners said there should be fifteen...but we'll have to see who shows up next week."

"Henry, Jr. is certainly looking forward to school and it won't be long until Mary Jane is of age. I wish Jonas Jackson could attend. His mother and I were close friends before she died and I know she would have wanted it for him but now that he's apprenticed to Henry White, I doubt he'll be allowed to attend. The same is true for Tom Cottingham."

"I believe Henry, Jr. has a plan for Tom Cottingham," Sarah laughed. "He told me that he plans to teach him sums in the evenings."

"Did he?" Mary laughed. "I wonder when he'll find time to do his chores? But, seriously...I wish there was a way we could help our orphan children. I'm sure they will not be allowed to attend school."

"I know Mary. 'Tis a hard life for orphans."

Mary suddenly stood and grasped her back. "It appears, I'm about to add another future student for you Sarah. This wee one appears to be coming soon."

"How soon?" Sarah gasped.

Mary laughed, "We have plenty of time but I 'spect we'd better go home for now and Elizabeth will have to help you finish here."

"Oh, Mary...didna worry about that. Let's take you home. Do you want me to send for Dr. Hacke?"

"Nay, Barbary has been with me through all my bairns and she needs our support now more than ever. Send for her."

"Aye, Mary."

There was a flurry of excitement when Sarah and Mary arrived home. Henry, Jr. set out to find Barbary while Elizabeth went to the field to notify Ambrose and her brother George. Despite her protests, Sarah ordered Mary to rest. Betsy began boiling water while Sarah gathered quilts and prepared the crib in Mary's bedroom.

Mary laughed as her excited sister collapsed in a chair beside her. "Sarah, you must relax. 'Twill probably be a few hours...ye should know that. You assisted Anne many times."

"Ye're right, Mary. But I guess I'm a little more worried since Elizabeth Custis funeral and all. I don't want anything to happen to you."

"Sarah, there's no reason to worry. I've never had problems before and I didna expect any problems now."

"I hope you won't this time, Mary....but I like to be prepared."

Henry, Jr burst into the room and shouted, "Miss Barbary is on her way, Mum. She said she'd be right behind me. Do you need me to get anyone else? What about Papa and George?"

"Elizabeth has sent for them, Henry, Jr. You just need to calm yeself, now. Have you eaten?"

Sarah, stood. "I forgot...the food. Betsy, let me help you. I know everyone will be wanting something. Mary what about you?"

"I might try a little of that stew I smell, Betsy."

"Aye, Mam," Betsy replied as she pulled a bowl from the shelf. "What about you Master Henry?"

"Aye, Betsy, I'll have some too."

Mary grimaced as another contraction came over her.

Henry appeared frightened so Mary patted his hand. "I'm fine Henry, Jr. Don't worry." She brushed a wayward lock above his brow to the side of his forehead.

He smiled lovingly back at her.

Everyone looked toward the door as they heard Ambrose, Elizabeth and George enter the house.

"Mary, what is this I hear? Is it time?"

"Aye, Ambrose. Don't fuss so. I'm fine. They shouldn't have sent for you so soon. I'm sure ye've much work to do. But now that ye're here, you might us well join us in this meal. Betsy, will you see to them?"

"Aye, Mam."

When Barbary arrived a few minutes later, she urged Mary to bed and she finally relented. Sarah and Elizabeth stayed with Mary and Barbary while the men remained in the Parlour and prepared for a long wait ahead. But only two hours later, crying could be heard coming from Mary's bedroom. All three men began pacing the floor at the sound and looked up expectantly when Elizabeth appeared in the doorway of the Parlour with tears streaming down her face.

"Twas a boy Ambrose...but....but...he was stillborn."

"Ahggg...gggg." Ambrose cried aloud as he fell into a chair.

"What about Mum...what about Mum?" screamed Henry, Jr.

Ambrose stood and exclaimed, "Is Mary alright?"

Elizabeth rushed to Henry, Jr. and embraced him, "She's fine...upset of course...but she's well enough."

"But why? What went wrong?" George questioned.

Elizabeth grabbed her brother's hand. Tears flowed down her cheeks as she spoke. "We didna know, George. Barbary did all she could. I watched Anne deliver many bairns and Barbary did nothing wrong...it 'twas the same as Anne would have done ...he....he...just did not live."

Ambrose regained his composure, "Can I see Mary?"

"Of course, Ambrose. I'm sure she wants to see you."

Ambrose followed Elizabeth into the bedroom. Mary was lying on the bed with the edge of a quilt grasped tightly in her fist. Her eyes were closed; tears crept slowly from under the lids and over her wan face. She opened her eyes when Ambrose entered and cried, "Oh Ambrose, I failed you. Our son has not lived."

"Nay, nay, Mary. 'tis not true...you didna fail...'tis only God's will. We must accept that." Sarah moved out of Ambrose way as he sat beside Mary on the bed.

Barbary was cleansing the bairn. She asked, "Ambrose would you like to see your son?"

"Aye, he said."

Barbary lifted the small infant and placed him in Ambrose's arms. His eyes became misty as he studied his perfectly formed son.

Ambrose placed the infant on the bed beside Mary and said, "He's a beautiful boy, Mary and we must name him. Did ye have a name in mind?"

"Before he was born, I thought about naming him after you Ambrose but now..."

"Aye, Mary. Then we should not change...we will name him Ambrose, Jr."

"But..."

"Mary, I didna know why little Ambrose, Jr. was taken from us so soon...but 'tis for God to know...not us...but with the name Ambrose, Jr....he will never be forgotten."

"Aye, Ambrose. His name will be as you say." Mary circled the infant in her arms and asked, "Could you leave us for a while? We want to spend some time alone with our son."

"Aye, Mary." the ladies said in unison and left the room.

Sarah sent for Rev. Doughty to make arrangements for the funeral. Barbary was gone before the minister arrived later that evening. After he left, Elizabeth asked, "I wonder why he asked so many questions about Barbary?"

"There's no telling," Sarah responded. "But I imagine 'tis not a good reason...I know he doesn't hide his hatred for Barbary."

George overheard their conversation and asked, "What kind of questions did he ask?"

"He wanted to know the exact words she said when the bairn was born and if I notice anything unusual about Barbary?"

George frowned, then a flash sprang to his eyes as he exclaimed with determination in his voice, "This will not happen again! He will not use this tragedy for his witching purposes. I could not help, Anne but with God's help I will help Barbary!"

"But what can you do?" asked Elizabeth.

George looked at her gravely, "I didna know...but I will not wait for him to act first. I must do something now."

The next day, George left early to visit John Custis and did not return until late that evening. Three days later little Ambrose, Jr. was buried in High Meadows beside Mary's infant daughter and Henry Pattenden, her first husband where many of her friends were buried. She stood between Ambrose and her son Henry, Jr. Ambrose held Mary around the waist and squeezed her hand tightly as Rev. Doughty spoke. "God take this infant, Ambrose Dixon, Jr. into your loving arms. The evil on this earth will no longer control him."

Mary stared at Rev. Doughty.

What does he mean? Evil on the earth will no longer control him. What evil controlled my son? He never took his first breath of life.

The prayer was said and the funeral ended. Rev. Doughty walked over to Mary and took her hand. "I hope you will help me wipe out this evil that took your infant from you," he said.

"What do ye meant? I didna understand," Mary asked as she looked into Rev. Doughty's eyes.

"We'll talk of it later, Mary. Now is not the time," he replied and patted her hand.

Ambrose put his arm around Mary's shoulder and said firmly, "Mary needs to return home now Reverend."

Ambrose led Mary down the path to their shallop. George and her sisters followed close behind.

When they reached the boat, Mary asked, "What did he mean by helping him wipe out evil, Ambrose?"

George said grimly, "'Tis his attack on Barbary...I think he plans to accuse her of being a witch."

"What? He can not accuse her of such a thing!" Mary exclaimed. "I must stop this at once...I must tell him..."

"Mary, I didna think there is much use in talking to him. I heard about this yesterday and immediately went to Rev. Doughty and asked him to withdraw his complaints against Barbary. He refused."

"But what can we do? Barbary's not a witch," Mary spoke to George, "This can't be happening again...not like Anne..."

"I plan to stop this atrocity, if I can Mary." George commented. "A petition has been signed by people who support Barbary. Ambrose gave me names of many neighbors who have come to her defense."

"Argoll informed me that Rev. Doughty is planning to accuse Barbary of witchcraft this week and is asking for a hearing. George wasted no time and most of the citizens of Accawmacke have signed," Ambrose added.

"Most of them...not all?" Mary exclaimed. "I cannot believe everyone did not sign."

"I'm afraid, Rev. Doughty can be very persuasive with his talk of witchcraft, Mary," Sarah added. "You ought to hear some of the things he's saying and when anyone dies, people want to blame someone for the death."

"I just hope we have enough names and the Commissioners listen to us," George stated with emphasis.

A week later, Barbary Winbrow was summoned to Court to answer charges of witchcraft. Mary remained home with her young children and waited anxiously to hear the results of the meeting while Ambrose, Henry Jr., George and her sisters attended the hearing to support Barbary. When the door opened and she heard happy chatter, Mary was relieved.

"Oh, Mary. I wish you had been there," exclaimed Elizabeth.

"What happened?" Mary inquired.

"Our brother, George, was eloquent in his defense of Barbary and the large number of people who signed the petition clearly impressed the Commissioners," Sarah declared.

"I think the fact that the charges were ludicrous had something to do with their favorable decision," George said.

"Don't belittle your effort, George. I doubt things would have gone well if you had not gathered all those signatures. I've heard of many stories of witches in Boston, recently....many people have been killed there for witchcraft," Ambrose added.

"I didna believe that will happen here. Some of the Commissioners drafted an order that anyone who made scandalous accusations against a person and could not prove it, then they would be required to pay a thousand pounds of tobacco."

"I'm so thankful. Knowing what we do about false accusations, I admit I was worried about Barbary," Mary said. But anyone knows, God is in charge of life and death.....especially when it comes to bairns. Mum helped me to realize that after Mary Margaret's birth. Our bairn's death was no one's fault. Little Ambrose is in Heaven with Mum and the rest of our family and I accept that God wanted him there for reasons only He knows. Now tell me everything and leave nothing out. But first, I must tell Betsy to finish dinner. We were waiting until ye returned home."

In their bedroom, later that evening, Ambrose watched Mary as she brushed her long dark hair in front of the mirror. He walked over to her and planted a kiss on the top of her head, then embraced her.

"Mary, you grow more beautiful everyday but I know all this was hard on you...yet I never hear ye complain."

Mary looked at him with moist eyes. Unmistakable traces of tears were on her cheeks. "I admit 'tis hard to lose our bairn....but..." her voice broke....she dropped her head and tried to continue. "'Tis useless to think about...God took Ambrose, Jr. from us for some reason and we'll never understand why...a part of me died with him...just as it did when I lost Mary Margaret....I know they're both with God and that does bring me some peace." Mary could no longer control herself. Her eyes flooded with sudden tears. She sat down and buried her face in the skirt of her gown and sobbed convulsively.

Ambrose pulled her into his arms. She lay her head on his shoulder and continued to cry as he tenderly stroked her back and tried to comfort her.

"Sweet Mary, I wish I could take the pain from ye're heart."

After a few moments, Mary regained control and said, "I'm glad you stood up for poor Barbary. No one should be blamed for our bairn's death, certainly not Barbary. I didna understand why Rev. Doughty hates her so much. Why does he see her as evil?"

"That I didna know but the situation disturbs me too. George told me a minister was one of the people who accused ye're sister-in-law Anne of being a witch. Mayhaps I should not say it, but it appears some of these *so-called* minister's of God give me doubt." Ambrose released Mary from his arms and began to pace.

"Rev. Eaton is a prime example. He married poor Anne, then gambled all her money away. I'm glad he left Accawmacke and returned to England. We didna need the likes of him here but he left poor Anne almost penniless."

"I agree, Ambrose. But who will give us guidance other than our ministers? What shall we do if we cannot trust them?"

"Mayhaps God speaks to us too and we are not listening."

"What do ye mean Ambrose?"

"Has George mentioned the Children of the light or the Quakers to you?"

"Aye. He said something about a light within each of us but I didna understand. He stopped talking to me about them when he returned from England. He hasn't mentioned them again and seems to have lost interest in almost everything."

"I know. George has been very solemn since he returned but it seems this witchcraft accusation by Rev. Doughty reinvigorated George. At least there was some good that has come from it. George and your sisters told me a little about the Children of Light on our way back from the courthouse today."

"What did they say?"

"Evidently, George went to a few meetings before he ever came to the Colonies and he said they didna believe in ministers. Instead they believe that everyone has the ability to hear God within themselves."

"But how, Ambrose?"

"I admit I'm confused too. But after our experience with Rev. Doughty, I would like to learn more."

"But aren't they in England?"

"That is what I wanted to talk to you about. George has been corresponding with several people belonging to Children of the Light in London. He received a packet the other day from a woman named, Lizzie Harris. She plans to visit Virginia and needed a place to stay so George asked if she could reside with us while here and I told him she could."

"Lizzie Harris? A woman? How old is she?"

"I believe she is young but I know little else. I was surprised too...especially about her being a young lady but George said that women are thought of as equals with the Friends."

"Equals? That's interesting. I believe I will enjoy meeting her. When will she arrive?"

"In a couple of weeks."

"That doesn't give us much time to prepare. I'll talk to Betsy and my sisters tomorrow. Mayhaps she can share their room."

"That reminds me of something else. With the number of people moving here since the War, our community has been hard-pressed to house them all. I've decided to build an Inn to fill this need. I believe Henry, Jr. is old enough to help me manage it."

"That sounds wonderful, Ambrose. I'm sure Henry, Jr. will relish the opportunity."

"With George here to assist in the tobacco plantation, I'll be able to expand the ship-yard. Mary, it looks like we have a great future ahead, especially now that we seem to be at relative peace with the Indians."

"God has been good to us....even in spite of our recent loss," she quickly added. "I'm curious about this woman, Lizzie Harris though. Do you think George is interested in her?"

"Nay. According to George, she's married and has a child. Lizzie Harris was the only one coming here. From what I understand, she's leaving her child and husband behind and coming alone to share her religious experiences with the people of Virginia."

"Coming alone? Lizzie Harris sounds like a very interesting woman indeed. I can not imagine leaving a child back in London with my husband. Mayhaps she wants to leave her husband."

"Nay, George said that her husband supports her visit. He's a Quaker himself."

"Hmmm...I guess we'll just have to wait and meet her before making any judgments....but 'tis hard to understand."

"I agree, Mary. That's why I offered our home for her visit. I thought ye would enjoy meeting her."

"I will indeed, Ambrose."

What kind of faith does this woman have? I can not imagine leaving my family and traveling to an unknown country alone. It was hard enough leaving my family as Henry's wife...and we were building our life together in America. I'll definitely enjoy meeting Lizzie Harris.

CHAPTER THIRTY-FOUR

1655 Eastern Shore, Virginia

Lizzie Harris arrived in Northampton by late spring of 1655. Her visit created quite a stir. The petite, dark haired woman around twenty-two years of age was always dressed in a plain black or brown dress with a simple shawl on her shoulders. She was not shy as one might expect from a woman so young. A couple of days after her arrival, the Dixon family sat by the fireplace to talk with their visitor while Mary Jane and Thomas played. Sarah was asleep in her crib.

Lizzie Harris suddenly asked George, "Where can a 'threshing' meeting be held?"

"A threshing meeting...what is that?" Ambrose inquired.

"'Tis a public meeting to separate the wheat from the chaff or those who accept us from those who didna." Lizzie replied tartly.

"Shouldn't ya' meet some of the people here first?" Elizabeth asked.

"'Tis not me I wish people to know....'tis God...I am merely a messenger of His love. There is no need of a building...a field will be fine," she continued.

"A church meeting outside? I never heard of such a thing," Sarah scoffed.

"Aye, God's church is not in a building, Sarah," Lizzie responded in a gentle voice. "God is within each of us...thy only need listen to his word. He will speak to each of us. There is no need of a bishop or priest to hear God speak."

Ambrose rose from his chair and placed another log on the fire before he declared, "No bishop, that's interesting. From the ministers we've had around here lately," Ambrose voiced trailed off as he looked at Mary then continued, "I'd like to hear more."

"And thee will, Ambrose," Lizzie smiled at him. "I'm sure God wishes to speak to thee."

"But how do we hear God? Does he speak? I'm confused," Mary stated.

"Aye, Mary...through the 'Seed of Light' within each of us. We need only be quiet enough to listen," Lizzie stated softly.

Little Thomas was trying to climb in his mother's lap but fell to the floor instead. He began crying loudly. Mary bent over, picked him up and laughed, "I'm afraid there's not much quiet around here. I believe it's time I put these wee ones to bed."

As she left the room, George said, "Lizzie, mayhaps we should meet in a smaller group at first."

"I believe that would be best, George," Ambrose added. "No offense to ye, Lizzie but I imagine some people would like to meet you first. I'm sure Rev. Doughty might complain about ye're visit."

"I'm a guest in thy home, Ambrose and I'll abide by thee wishes but I feel a concern to witness for God's truth soon," Lizzie declared.

"Aye, I understand. We'll arrange a gathering this week," Ambrose smiled at his guest.

"Then, if thee will excuse me, I'll retire," Lizzie responded as she stood.

"So soon," Sarah asked. "'Tis not dark, yet."

"I would like quiet time to commune with God. Thank thee all for thy kindness," Lizzie smiled as she stood.

"After Lizzie left the room, Sarah exclaimed, "She seems nice enough. I admire her independence. I can't imagine traveling so far and leaving her husband and child in London."

"Seems unnatural to me," Elizabeth commented. "But I do like her...though what's with this talk of 'thy' and 'thee."

George added, "'Tis the Friends belief in plainness of speech. I heard George Fox speak about it. They believe that all people are equal. But I agree, Lizzie appears to be a remarkable woman indeed."

"'Twill be interesting to see how she's accepted here, especially by Scarbough," Ambrose exclaimed.

"Is he back for good? Does he not fear the court anymore?" George asked.

"I guess not. He was talking to Argoll at the Hungar's Ordinary last week. Horsey said he was interested in the High Sheriff position."

"I thought Gov. Bennett banned him from public office," George declared.

"I assume he hopes everyone forgot about that while he was away," Ambrose chuckled.

"With Lizzie Harris' visit and Col Scarburgh's return, I'd say Accawmacke is due for some excitement," Sarah laughed. "'Twill be interesting to say the least."

Friends and neighbors of the Dixon's met at Ambrose's house a few days later to hear Lizzie. The families of Stephen Horsey, Henry Vaughn, George Truitt, William Durand, Levin Dunwood, George Brickhouse, William Colbourne, Henry White, George Johnson, Thomas Price, and Thomas Leatherbury were in attendance.

Lizzie opened the meeting with prayer and said, "Friends, It may seem strange to some of thee that a woman should appear in so public a manner and bring my testimony but this is the work of the Lord at this day, even by weak means to bring to pass his mighty work in the earth, that all flesh may be silent, and the Lord alone may be exalted in them. Now I live, yet not I, but Christ liveth in me, and the life that I now live is by the faith of the Son of God."

"My coming here hath not been for my own needs, but in obedience to the will of God, for it was placed before me that I should come here to witness for God, whether or not thee hear or not and to lay down my life if it be required. The Lord hath given me peace in my journey and God hath given means that I have the great privilege to speak."

She paused and bowed her head in silent prayer for a moment, then continued.

"The Lord God hath opened to me that every man was enlightened by the divine light of Christ...if you love this light, it will teach you...the light is that which exercises the conscience towards God, and towards man. If you love the Light, you will bring your deeds to the Light, that the Light may prove them, whether they be wrought in God yea or nay: but if you hate it, it will be your condemnation, but I exhort thee, whoever thou art, as thou tenderest the good of thy own Soul, that thou love the Light which is the Life of Men, and embrace it, and love it with all thy heart, and with all thy mind, with all thy Soul, and with all thy strength."

George asked, "But what do you believe of man's laws?"

"To be plain, there is no Law to compel people to conform, if they show a lawful or reasonable excuse. Religion being an obligation...man is bound to God, and not to men's opinions."

An audible gasp was heard from someone in the group so Lizzie paused again and bowed her head.

She smiled and continued. "The Scriptures are clear in this point, for they say that the Law was not made for the innocent, but for wicked men. And do not the Statues say the same thing in effect, when it allows both a lawful and reasonable excuse. Behold our God is appearing for us, and they that be in the light may see him. God chooses the foolish things of the World to confound the wise, weak things to confound the Mighty. God has given me concernment to bring our testimony against that Anti-Christian law and oppression of tithes, by which many of the Servants of the Lord have suffered, and against the unjust of them, which hath come up since the days of the Apostles in the Apostacy, and set up by the commands and laws of men."

Several people in the small group nodded their heads.

Lizzie declared, "In the world are many encumbrances and entanglement, some on one hand, and some on another to draw the mind from God, so there is great need of holy zeal and diligence, in observing the time to wait upon the Lord to feel your strength renewed, to help through the many things and his power to strengthen and support, that in your families and all your undertakings you may be a good favor to the Lord, being guided by his wisdom to rule and order your children and servants, and He will give authority to stand over every thing thats contrary to his witness."

Lizzie bowed her head again. She sat silently with the group for a few minutes. Ambrose said, "Thank ye, Lizzie. I'm sure you have given us much to think on."

"Aye," Stephen Horsey said, then asked, "What do Friends think of predestination?"

Lizzie smiled at him, "God nor Christ never purposed love nor salvation to shut out the greatest number of mankind by absolute predestination. Everyone that will be a disciple of Christ Jesus must come into the self-denying life."

Several of the men nodded their heads and the discussion continued till early evening. Horsey offered his field as a site for a threshing meeting to be held the following week and plans were made by the women in attendance to provide a meal afterwards.

CHAPTER THIRTY-FIVE

Summer 1655, Eastern Shore, Virginia

A large curious crowd attended the threshing meeting. News of Lizzie Harris' visit circulated widely among the community and even some Commissioners, Col. Edmund Scarburgh and Rev. Doughty were in attendance.

"I wonder if she'll wear sackcloth and ashes like some do in London," Scarburgh laughed.

George frowned at him. "You should be more respectful of her, Col. Scarburgh. She's done no harm you."

"She's nothing but one of those foolish Quakers. I heard plenty about them when I was in Boston," Scarburgh retorted. "I don't know what all the ruckus is about her."

A hush came over the crowd as Lizzie started to speak.

"Love the Lord thy God with all thy heart, and thy neighbor as thyself...so shalt thou come to feel the plant which the Lord's right hand hath planted in thee, to grow up, if thou lovest it. For he that sows to the flesh, shall of the flesh reap corruption. But he that sows to the Spirit, shall of the Spirit reap Life Everlasting and Joy and Peace, which shall never be taken from them. Be obedient unto the Light of Christ in thee, thereby thou mayest come to witness victory over all that which hath availed from thee the pure seed of God in thee."

"And as we abide faithful unto the Lord, we know that we shall all sit down with Abraham, Isaac, and Jacob, where none shall make us afraid, though ten thousands rise up against us, yet shall we not fear what man can do unto us, for our God is on our side, Who then can be against us? who works all our Works in us and for us continually; who never ceases to administer daily, refreshment unto his own Seed in us; For this know assuredly that the Lord is come to look for Fruit. The Lord moved me to come to thee to bear witness against the idol shepherds...the word of the Lord hath come unto me...to go cry against the foolish prophets that preacheth lies in my name; for when men do undertake either to

Inform or Correct others in matters of Religion, it ought to be done in Truth and Righteousness, from that inward Principle of the divine Life, whereby good men govern their Actions, and where that Principle rules.

It is likely the high-flown Churchmen that make a trade of religion will not like this discourse; but I cannot help that, it is the widows mite cast into the treasury; I am sure I have no enmity in my heart against any of them, but do desire well for them; Gods love is universal to mankind; For God is Love, and they that dwell in God, dwell in Love; I heartily wish that they would understand and practice this, it would soon put an end to Differences in Religion. It is a Duty incumbent with every true Christian, to shew those that they love, their mistakes; it were uncharitable to let people alone until their own folly corrects them. Now unto all you young people, sons, daughters, apprentices, men or maid servants, all that are convinced of God's truth...let not your minds wander, neither look at the vanities in this world, for Christ's kingdom is not of it, nor to be found in pride, wantonness, and lust of the flesh, the fashions, customs, and friendships of this world, for the devil is the king of pride.....”

As Lizzie spoke many among the crowd began to nod their heads in agreement...but Rev. Doughty's face became beet red. After she finished speaking, Rev. Doughty rushed over to the Argoll Yeardley and began loudly shouting, “This is blasphemy. We must drive this woman from our community.”

Edmund Scarburgh joined the two men. “I could have told you that before she ever started. These Quakers are nothing but trouble.”

Ambrose and George noticed the animosity from the Commissioners toward Lizzie and said, “I think we'd better take Lizzie home now.”

George nodded. Despite her protests, they escorted Lizzie to the waiting shallop where Mary and her sisters were waiting.

“Lizzie, I believe ye're words caused quite a reaction around here,” Mary laughed.

“'Tis God not me, Mary. I only speak God's words.”

As the shallop left the pier, everyone on board watched Col. Scarburgh and Rev. Doughty point and angrily shout at Argoll Yeardley who stared at them with a frustrated expression on his face.

The brief trip home was silent. Everyone seemed to be deep in thought about Lizzie's speech and the events that had just taken place.

After the family arrived at the house, Lizzie and Mary's sisters immediately went to the bedroom to change clothing while Mary, Ambrose and George walked into the Parlour where Betsy was entertaining the children with hand shadows. Mary warmly greeted her excited children with hugs and kisses as Ambrose sat in his favorite chair by the fireplace and gazed at the smoldering fire. After a time, he spoke sharply.

"George, I must be plain spoken. I fear for Lizzie's safety. Some at the meeting...especially Rev. Doughty and Scarburgh appeared quite angry."

"Aye...I agree. But I didna believe it matters much to Lizzie. Once the calling is felt...it can not be denied," George replied.

When Betsy heard this, she quickly lowered her head so no one could see the tears that sprang to her eyes.

Mary gasped and released her children as she exclaimed "What do ye mean? Have you experienced a calling?"

Betsy pulled Thomas in her arms and glanced up lovingly at George as he spoke.

"I didna want to tell you till I was sure...but I've felt God calling me for some time...and I can no longer deny it. Lizzie plans to leave next week to minister in Maryland and I will go with her when she leaves."

"But George...I thought you planned to build ye're own plantation nearby. I never dreamed..." Mary's voice broke as she stared at her brother.

Elizabeth overheard their conversation as she entered the room, "I plan to go with her as well."

"But...but," Mary stammered.

Ambrose went to Mary's side. He put one arm around her as he shook George's hand with the other. "I must admit, George. This doesn't totally surprise me. I suspected something was on ye're mind. 'Tis good that ye'll be with Lizzie...but I admit I'm taken back by you, Elizabeth," he added as he looked at her.

""Twas only today that I finally decided," Elizabeth responded. "I've been talking to Lizzie since she's been here...and today...well, I can't explain it but I felt God's call to learn more. I can only do that if I travel with Lizzie and George."

Lizzie and Sarah had quietly joined the family group and Lizzie smiled when she heard Elizabeth speak.

She spoke softly, "God does indeed work in mysterious ways. I believe we should all pray for his guidance in this endeavor. Will thee join me in prayer?"

Everyone in the room bowed their heads as Lizzie began to speak. Mary leaned heavily against her husband.

God, I didna understand...I've only had my family with me a short time...and now ye're taking them away...God, please keep them safe and if it be ye're will...bring them back to me.

Later the same evening, Ambrose and Mary were alone in the Parlour. Mary was sewing a patch on one of Henry, Jr.'s shirts.

"Ambrose, what do you make of the things Lizzie says?"

"Well, Mary...Lizzie does have strong words. I agree with what she says by man being compelled to follow God's word not man's opinions. Stephen Horsey and I have said much the same thing. Did you see Rev. Doughty's face when she talked about high-flown churchmen? She really upset some people today," Ambrose laughed. Then he became solemn as he spoke. "Over all, I believe she is right. When I read my Bible, I often feel as if God is talking directly to me. Mayhaps, we should all listen more to what God is trying to reveal to us as individuals."

"Didna you think that is what she means by listening to our 'Inner Light'? I often feel the same way when I read my Bible...but I never thought about it before now...and sometimes I feel God's closeness when I am most frightened...mayhaps that is my 'Inner Light as well," Mary added.

"I believe this young lady has much to teach us. I imagine we'll learn quite a bit before she leaves us."

"Aye, Ambrose. I 'spect ye're right."

A week later, Elizabeth, George and Lizzie left for Maryland but not before Lizzie held several more meetings at Ambrose's house. Ambrose, Mary and many of their friends were 'convinced' of the Friends of Truth faith and became leaders in the small community. Impressed by the commitment of up-standing citizens such as Ambrose and Col. Coulbourne, others attended the meetings and joined in the belief. Those who embraced the religion sat in silent meetings for worship waiting in holy expectancy 'to hear what the Lord spoke to them.'

The meetings were without any pre-arranged form. The important thing was to seek to be obedient to the Spirit and to be in union with it as much as possible. Out of the quiet waiting there often came some vocal ministry which was meant to help others in their worship or in their daily life and activity.

As the number of 'convinced' citizens grew, dissension began to develop in the community. Rev. Doughty scorned those 'pulled into the sin of iniquity' and frequently complained to the Commissioners about citizens who refused to pay their tithes. The Commissioners became angered when many of the 'convinced' citizens stopped paying taxes as well citing that the Commissioners were not acting in the best interest of the County.

Ambrose and Stephen Horsey, as usual, heard Col. Scarburgh's loud voice as they entered the Ordinary.

"'Tis a crime that woman was ever allowed to come to Accawmacke...I told you, the Quakers were nothing but scoundrels...this Lizzie Harris is like a plague to our county."

Scarburgh took another slug of his ale and noticed Ambrose and Stephen as they walked in, "There's the men responsible for bringing her...I never thought I'd see the likes of such good Indian fighters as you two being swayed by a woman."

"What harm has she done to thee, friend Edmund?" Ambrose asked.

"DONE TO THEE! FRIEND EDMUND? You can no longer even talk correctly." Scarburgh stood and shook his fist as he continued to shout, "I'm COLONEL Scarburgh to you.....the High Sheriff of Northampton and I expect you to address me as such!"

"God's Inner Light has convinced me that we are all equals and should be addressed as such," Ambrose responded defiantly as he braced himself for assault.

"Inner Light, I'll show you Inner Light!" Scarburgh exclaimed as he moved from behind the table where he had been sitting.

239

Argoll Yeardley stood and blocked Scarburgh's path and said, "Edmund, no need for this altercation...we must address this matter civilly...in the courts. I'm sure Dixon and Horsey will relent once this Quaker woman has been driven from our midst. Of course they realize that all mankind must have leaders."

"Leaders, mayhaps...but not rulers!" Stephen Horsey exclaimed. "You need only look to what happened in England to rulers!"

A gasp emanated from the people listening in the crowded room at Stephen's comment.

"Men, men...let's be reasonable," said John Custis. "As Col. Yeardley said, the matter of the Quakers will be taken up by the Courts. I'm sure we need to leave it in their worthy hands. Stephen, you and Ambrose share a pint of ale with us. Cooler heads must prevail."

"Nay, John. I believe I've lost my taste for ale," Ambrose responded. As Ambrose and Stephen left the Ordinary, they heard Scarburgh exclaim, "Those were two good Indian fighters....I never thought I'd see the day when they'd change so....but they've been deluded by this Quaker plague among us."

CHAPTER THIRTY-SIX

Fall, 1656 Eastern Shore, Virginia

George, Elizabeth and Lizzie Harris returned home to Accawmacke in 1656 in a triumphant mood with the news that William Fuller, acting governor of Maryland, after hearing Lizzie speak, was convinced and now considered himself to be a Friend.

"God has a fertile field in Maryland and I feel compelled to return there as soon as possible," George exclaimed. "The people are ready for the Holy Spirit to work in their lives."

Mary stared at her emaciated brother and said, "Before thee return, thou must fatten up some, George. When did you last eat?"

Elizabeth laughed and punched her brother on his arm. "I told you she'd notice right away. Mary, we constantly reminded George he must eat but he always forgets. Sometimes, he'd go without eating for two days because he was so intent on ministering to the people."

"Their needs are greater than mine," he replied.

"George has a fervent calling indeed," Lizzie added. "We reminded him frequently that he is of no use to God if he becomes weak in body."

"It seems ye'll need someone to keep thee from starving," Mary commented.

Betsy was quietly waiting while the family greeted each other. She smiled at Mary's comment. "Would you like me to serve ye're meal now, Miss Mary?"

"Aye, Betsy. I'm sure 'twill not be too soon for George," Mary responded.

As the family settled around the table, Ambrose blessed the food and said, "It sounds like Maryland is much more accepting of Friends than Accawmacke has been."

"What makes you say that, Ambrose?" George asked.

"The court has made laws against Friend's meetings in Virginia so we've had to hold our meetings in secret. But since William Robinson was known as a missionary and was entertained by Henry Vaughan, his visit could not be kept secret. Vaughan was arrested last week and Robinson was ordered back across the Bay. I'm afraid the Commissioners will be ordering thee to leave as well, Lizzie."

"I plan to leave soon anyway, Friend Ambrose. 'Tis time for me to return to England."

"Leaving so soon, but it seems, ye've only just arrived," Sarah said.

"God has placed a concern on my heart to return home to England and I must obey, Sarah...but I will not forget thee. I'll write and send books and I'm sure other Friends plan to follow my visit. They will not be discouraged by these new laws."

"How can they make laws against simply meeting? We do no one harm," Elizabeth asked.

"That's not what, Scarburgh believes, Elizabeth. He calls Friends of Truth, a plague," Ambrose commented.

"A plague....what can he fear from us?" George stated vehemently. "We only speak God's truth."

"I'm afraid, 'tis much like a fear of witchcraft, George. People fear what they do not understand," Lizzie replied and smiled at him.

George nodded, knowingly.

"I guess it's time I share my news," Elizabeth declared. "I plan to return with Lizzie to England."

"What? But why?" Mary exclaimed.

"God has placed a concern on my heart to learn from George Fox. Lizzie and George heard him speak and I feel I must do the same so I can become a better disciple for God's ministry."

"But will you return to the Colonies?" Mary pleaded.

"I didna know, Mary. 'Tis up to God."

"God will take care of Elizabeth, Mary. Thee must commit her to God," Lizzie added.

"I know, Lizzie," Mary said with misty eyes. "It's just so sudden...but...I will accept God's will for thee," Mary reached out and squeezed Elizabeth's hand.

Elizabeth smiled at Mary then looked at George. "The only thing I fear is that there's no one to take care of George. I'm afraid he might starve," she laughed

"God will take care of me, Elizabeth. Thee need not worry

242

on my account." He glanced at Betsy who was standing behind Ambrose. She gave him a look of pure adoration.

Mary watched the subtle exchange between them.

Betsy will complete her indenture in a few months and free to marry. Mayhaps we won't have to worry about George for long. I need to discuss this with Ambrose.

Mary smiled at her brother.

At the end of the week, George and Ambrose escorted Lizzie and Elizabeth to James City so she could travel on the next ship to England. Lizzie reassured them that other Friends of the Truth would soon follow her to the Accawmacke. They stopped by the mercantile on their return home where George picked up a packet he received from friends in Maryland. As Ambrose guided the sloop away from the wharf, George broke the seal and began to read the letter.

"Ach.....I must go to Boston to help them. Mayhaps my return to Maryland should be delayed."

"What happened in Boston?" Ambrose inquired.

"Two Friends of the Truth from England, Elizabeth Fisher and Ann Austin, have been imprisoned. All their property was confiscated and their books burned. No one has been allowed to even visit them until recently and they were found half-starved. A Friend bribed the gaoler with five shillings a week so he can at least provide them with food. Our Friends are suffering in Boston. I must go to help."

"Thy must pray about this George. Let God put the concern on ye're heart first. We should not go against God's wishes or we might place an obstruction in His purpose."

"'Tis hard to wait when their needs are so great...but thee are right. I must let God guide my path. I will pray as thy suggest."

Ambrose expertly maneuvered the small craft among the marsh grass and a flock of ducks next to them, suddenly took flight, protesting with loud squawks at being disturbed.

Ambrose watched the ducks fly off, then said, "Even when we hear bad news, we should never forget that we are truly blessed in this country and must share with others. I need to start building my Inn soon so our Friends of the Truth who come to visit us will have a safe and welcome place to stay. I fear that some in Accawmacke will not readily invite them into our community."

"Aye, I'm sure thee are right. Especially, our commissioners. I hope they will not resort to imprisonment."

"I do too, George. But some have great hatred for Friends."

A few months later, news spread throughout Accawmacke of the impending wedding of John Custis to the wealthy thrice widowed, Alicia Traveller Burdett Walker. The wedding was the event of the year but the Dixon's probably would not have attended since Friends had an aversion to all frivolities. However, their long standing friendship with his parents Joanne and John Custis prevailed and they decided to go to the wedding.

Mary sat in front of her mirror as she wound her hair in a bun and stared at her reflection. Dressed in black, she appeared to be attending a funeral rather than a wedding.

Ah how times have changed. How silly I was in the past over so many vain things.

Mary glanced through her dresser to find something to tie up her hair under her rochet. Her eyes fell on a ragged ribbon with many colors. The edges were frayed and colors faded but she immediately recognized the treasure and her eyes became misty. It was the ribbon her family gave her before she came to the Colonies. Her thoughts flooded with memories of Cranbrook, many years ago.

Oh Papa....Mum....I still miss ye as much as ever. Will this pain never leave? So much has changed since those cherished days in Cranbrook.

Mary fingered the ribbon.

Dare I?

She hesitated a moment more, then quickly picked up the ribbon and wound it around the bun. She secured it tightly at the nap of her neck. Next she placed her plain rochet on her head and studied her reflection in the mirror.

No one will see it...and I'm sure God will forgive this slight indiscretion in dress.

Mary stood and glanced down at her protruding tummy. Well, little one...We're ready and I guess 'tis time I told Ambrose

244

about thee. I wonder what ye'll be this time. I hope ye're another son. Mary's eyes misted again as she thought of their stillborn child, Ambrose, Jr. and she dabbed at them with her handkerchief.

I didna know what's the matter with me. I'm being so silly today.

She studied her face in the mirror and pinched her cheeks.

I must stop this silly crying. Everyone's waiting for me.

Mary took a deep breath and stood tall. She paused another moment, then left the room.

"Aahh, Mary. I'm so happy to see you here," Joanne Custis commented as Mary approached her friend. "I was not sure ye'd come with this new 'religion' of yours. Everyone says you no longer attend events."

"'Tis true, Joanne but thee friendship is still very important to us."

"Thee...thou...Oh Mary, what is this outlandish way you speak nowadays....it seems quite cumbersome....will you not come to ye're senses and return to the Church."

"It may appear cumbersome to others, Joanne and I do slip frequently in my conversation. However, God does forgive my mistakes and I'll never turn my back on the Truth," Mary replied tartly.

"Oh, Mary...didna mind a grouchy old woman on such a joyous day. I meant nothing by it...I'm just glad ye're here."

"And I as well," Mary said warmly as she hugged Joanne.

Joanne looked in the direction of her son, John as he talked seriously among a group of men. "Alicia may not be as young and beautiful as sweet Elizabeth was but I'd say my John has done quite well for himself."

"Aye, John is fortunate," Mary commented softly.

"After all, Alicia is the wealthiest woman in all of Accawmacke....but....," Joanne paused. "Well, how do I say it...I didna expect any more grandchildren from the likes of her," Joanne chuckled.

Mary blushed at Joanne's frank remark and changed the subject, "I heard a rumor that Rev. Doughty plans to wed Ann Eaton. 'Tis it true?"

245

"Aye, and none too soon I imagine. Her last husband left her with little to live on. Mayhaps she'll have more success in this marriage."

"I hope so...Ann has had a difficult time. Her father left her quite wealthy but after her marriages, to Rev. Cotton and especially Rev. Eaton, well..."

"Hopefully, she will have more success in a marriage to Rev. Francis Doughty. He's a widower himself and does have some property. Would you help this old woman in the church, Mary? I believe 'tis time to sit a spell."

"Certainly, Joanne...but you are not old."

"Tell my bones that," Joanne laughed.

Mary supported Joanne's elbow as the two women walked toward the women's entrance of the church.

At the next Friends women's meeting, George and Betsy announced their intention to wed. Quaker tradition required that the couple be investigated by both the women's and men's meetings. A week went by while the women investigated and discussed the couple's marriage plans. Once the women approved, George and Betsy announced their plans at the men's meeting. They were again investigated and approved. However, an interval of time was still required for any member to object to their wedding before plans could be finalized. It was a joyous day at the Dixon house when George was finally able to report that their marriage had 'passed the meetings.' A date and time was immediately set for the wedding.

On the day of their marriage, people entered Ambrose's house quietly and sat in silence. Almost an hour went by before William Coulbourne stood and ministered to the small group as he frequently did in other meetings. A few more members stood and shared ministry as well. Just as the meeting appeared to be drawing to an close, George and Betsy, who had been seated, facing each other, stood and took each other's hands.

George spoke first, "Friends, I take Betsy Johnson to be my wife, promising through divine assistance to be unto her a loving and faithful husband until it shall please the Lord by death to separate us."

Betsy smiled at George and said, "Friends, I take George Willson to be my husband, promising through divine assistance to be unto him a loving and faithful wife until it shall please the Lord by death to separate us."

Everyone present signed a document witnessing the marriage and all set back down while the document was read by Ambrose.

"These are to certify whom it doth or may concern, that George Willson and Betsy Johnson did in the presence of us whose names are written, the day above written, take each other and declare themselves to be man and wife, the said George, taking the said Betsy by the hand, said in the presence of God and of you who are here met together, Friends, I take Betsy Johnson to be my wife, promising through divine assistance to be unto her a loving and faithful husband until it shall please the Lord by death to separate us; the said Betsy taking the said George by the hand, said in like manner, Friends, I take George Willson to be my husband, promising through divine assistance to be unto him a loving and faithful wife until it shall please the Lord by death to separate us."

Ambrose returned to his seat and another customary period of silence occurred. Gradually, people began leaving the Dixon's home.

Since their house was not yet completed, George and Betsy went immediately to the Inn Ambrose had recently opened and shared a wedding supper with family and friends. People continued to visit them at the Inn each day for two weeks while their house was being built.

Upon it's completion, George and Betsy set up housekeeping in their new home and returned visits to those with whom they wished to remain associated. A special visit to Ambrose and Mary Dixon occurred in January, 1657. Betsy was with child and she excitedly shared the news with Mary.

"We will have our two bairns close to the same time," Mary exclaimed to Betsy as they prepared dinner.

"When will thee 'lyin in' occur?" asked Betsy.

"In May, when will thee?"

"'Twill be in July," Betsy answered. "I hope we'll have a son."

"I didna think it matters much to me any more what we have...just as long as my bairn is healthy," Mary said.

"I hope we will still be here for my 'lyin in''

"Why, where else would thee be?"

"George feels compelled to return to Maryland and I will go with him. When he returned the last time, I was worried about him."

"Well, he must stay here for thee 'lyin in'....'tis too dangerous for thee otherwise. I need to have a good talk with my brother," Mary said in a serious tone.

In May of 1657, Ambrose and Mary's fifth child and third daughter, Elizabeth Maria was born and after Mary talked with George, he complied and remained in Virginia until their daughter, also named Elizabeth was born.

George spoke at the next meeting and related that God had placed a concern on his heart to return to Maryland and witness among the people there. The new parents left September, 1657 with their one month old daughter.

George's sister, Sarah moved into their home while they were away since it was closer to the school house.

CHAPTER THIRTY-SEVEN

1657-1658 Virginia and Maryland

Quaker, William Robinson, visited the Eastern Shore of Virginia in the later part of the 1657. Thomas Leatherbury donated some of his land and Levin Denwood with William Robinson's help, built a ten foot square meeting house for the Friends. William Robinson left to join other Friends in Massachusetts.

In spite of the persecution of some members of the Society of Friends, Maryland soon became a safe haven for many Quakers as the message of the Inner light appealed to many former Puritans who had become disillusioned.

Toward the later part of the year, George, Betsy and their daughter Elizabeth returned home with exciting news. Betsy was again with child.

"'George was insistent that we return home for my 'lyin in'," Betsy said to Sarah as she unpacked while George directed the unloading of the shallop. "We've had to live in some difficult situations, sometimes barns, even sheds became our place of abode. One month, we even lived with the Assateagues. I can tell thee, 'tis good to be back in my own home. I was not looking forward to having my 'lyin in' in the wilderness."

"I imagine not...I'm happy he was wise enough to bring thee home," Sarah declared. "It will only take me about a week to gather my things and move back to Mary's house."

"Nay, Sarah. Please stay with me. I didna believe George will remain this time. He plans to go to Boston and I cannot convince him otherwise. I would appreciate thy company. I didna want to be alone," Betsy implored.

"George plans to go to Boston? Will he be back in time for ye're 'lyin in?"

"I didna know Sarah. God has given him a concern for the Friends in Boston. We have heard many bad reports and he feels that he must go. I guess 'tis up to God whether he makes it back in time."

"I need to talk to my brother. He should not be away from thee at such a time."

"Please don't Sarah. I didna wish to dissuade him from God's work. But thy must see why I wish thee to stay."

"Aye, I will remain here as long as George is away. Thee should not be alone."

Sarah and Betsy joined George in the Parlour. He was stacking wood next to the fireplace.

Sarah gave her brother a hug and said, "I'm glad to see thee. This is a wonderful home but at times it has been a little lonely."

She pushed George away from her and studied him for a few minutes. "Betsy, thou has been good for George. He's not as thin as before."

Betsy laughed, "'Tis not all my doing. Everywhere we went, Friends were worried about him so they were constantly feeding him. Even the Indians gave him an abundance of food."

George smiled, "I'll have to admit. I've eaten some mighty strange food...especially when we lived with the Assateagues."

"That must have been quite an experience," Sarah commented.

"Oh it was," Betsy groaned.

"But thee have to agree. They were kind. In fact, I'd have to say that compared to how some of our own people treated us, we were treated better by the Indians."

"I would agree with that," Betsy added. She glanced away quickly to hide the tears filling her eyes.

"I'm sorry to hear thee were treated badly," Sarah said. "Didna I hear that Maryland had a Religious Toleration Act? I thought they'd be accepting of Friends."

"Many were but there's always some who do not understand us and sadly they were usually the officials in charge," George said. "I wonder if we will ever have true toleration for our beliefs."

"At least, the Act gives us some hope," Sarah added.

George, Betsy and Sarah visited Ambrose and Mary a few days later. Ambrose and Mary's children were excited to see their

Aunt and Uncle and it took some time before Mary was able to settle the children down so she could visit with her brother and his wife.

"When do thee plan to leave?" Ambrose asked George as Mary returned to the Parlour.

"Next week," George replied.

"But George, wouldn't it be better to wait awhile?....at least until thee bairn is born," Mary implored.

"Mary, we should not dissuade George if God has placed this concern on his heart," Ambrose stated quietly.

"Thee are right, of course...but does he have to leave so soon?"

"God's time is not our time, Mary. I must obey his will," George added.

Ambrose walked over to the fireplace where he kept his tobacco on the mantel and began filling his pipe. "Tell us about thy experiences in Maryland, George. I hear the people are more accepting of our beliefs there. 'Twas good news indeed when thy returned with Lizzie Harris and reported of Captain Fuller's convincement to our beliefs. But thee said Fuller is acting Governor...what does that mean?"

"When I left, news arrived that Captain Fendall has returned. He has an agreement to be restored as Governor."

"What will that mean for our Friends settled in the Maryland?" Mary inquired.

"I hope they will still be accepted...but I'm not sure. Hopefully, Governor Fendall will not be antagonistic toward them. Why do thee ask?"

"It has been difficult for us here in Virginia. Our Commissioners didna accept our beliefs. Stephen Horsey has often mentioned that mayhaps we should move to Maryland," Ambrose replied.

Mary stared at Ambrose with astonishment. "Move to Maryland? But I thought Stephen was only planning such a thing...I never thought thee would consider moving. How could we leave everything we've built here?"

"We may not have a choice. The Commissioners are discussing laws against our meetings and imprisonment for entertaining visitors of Friends on the Truth. I do not wish to leave

251

but we can not give up our beliefs," Ambrose emphatically declared.

"I always hoped our distance from James City provided us some freedom from their restrictions...but it seems that the laws have now come to us. It will be hard to leave but I trust thy judgment, Ambrose," Mary acceded.

"Let us hope we have a place to go to. I thought Maryland would be the place since Gov. Fuller was a Friend but now with the news of a new Governor...I'm not so sure."

"Thee will have to trust God to provide the place, Ambrose," George added.

"Aye, George...we'll seek God's guidance."

George left for Massachusetts a week later. George and Betsy's son was born in June, 1658, the same month news arrived that he had been imprisoned in Boston along with twenty-six other Friends of the Truth.

CHAPTER THIRTY-EIGHT

1659 Eastern Shore, Virginia

By March 1659, life became even more difficult in Virginia for the Society of Friends. The General Assembly passed a law prohibiting Quakers from entering the colony. They were described as *unreasonable and turbulent sort of people who daily gather together unlawful assemblies of people, teaching lies, miracles, false visions, prophecies and doctrines tending to disturb the peace, disorganize society and destroy all law and government and religion.*

Ambrose returned home to inform Mary about the law. He found her teaching their seven year daughter, Mary Jane, how to make bread. Mary Jane was covered from head to toe with flour and happily chatting with her mother as she stood beside her pounding dough. She gave her father a beaming smile when he walked in and gleefully exclaimed, "Look Papa, I'm making bread...Mum says I'm a good baker."

"I imagine thy Mum is right judging from the amount of flour on thee."

Mary studied her husband's face and realized that he must have something important to discuss with her so she said, "Mary Jane, I forgot to feed the chickens this morning. Would thee do that chore for me now? I'm sure they must be hungry."

"Aye, Mum. I'll go right now...I'll be right back." Mary Jane rushed over to retrieve the pail of chicken feed and ran out the door.

Ambrose smiled and stared after his daughter. "She's beginning to be some help for thee it seems."

"Aye...sometimes she is a lot of help...but thy face tells me thee has something to discuss with me Ambrose. Thy appears worried."

"Aye, Mary. I was at Hungar's and saw Stephen Horsey. He told me that the Commissioners made a law against Friends entering the colony and I'm afraid that law is just the beginning of

253

many more aimed at us."

"Why do the Commissioners hate Friends so much, Ambrose?"

"'Tis because of taxes, I'm sure. God has convinced me not to contribute tithes nor taxes to an unjust Church and Government. Stephen feels the same. He was even fined and threatened with imprisonment last week for not removing his hat in court. Stephen has patented land in Maryland and I feel we must do the same."

"Will we have to leave Virginia?"

"Mary, I know it is thy desire to remain in Virginia but I fear we may not be allowed to reside here much longer if we plan to have any normal life for our children. News has come that Massachusetts has banished long settled residents and all children and servants are being sold as slaves to Barbadoes. Such a law may be passed here. We must protect our children and servants."

"Children sold as slaves?" Mary asked incredulously. "I cannot believe it! How could they think of doing such a thing? We'll do as thy think best, Ambrose. When must we leave?"

"Soon, Mary. I wanted thee to know so thee could start preparing for our move." Ambrose sat down on the bench near the table and pulled out his pipe. He tapped it on the table and continued.

"That's not all I'm concerned about Mary. There's also been talk that Col. Scarburgh's planning an attack on the Assateagues. I'm sure he will request my assistance, but I will decline. After the experiences George had ministering to the Assateagues, God has convinced me not to war against them. I know Scarburgh will not be happy with my decision."

"Why does Col. Scarburgh want to attack the Assateagues, Ambrose?"

"The usual reasons. They've been forced further north and complained to the Commissioners. Some have attacked individual plantations and killed their stock." Ambrose filled his pipe with fresh tobacco then lit it.

"That man's hatred for the Indians runs deep. I wish Col. Scarburgh would understand that the Assateagues only want to be treated fairly."

"I'm afraid, he'll never understand, Mary, and he has convinced the Commissioners and Governor of an imminent

254

attack. He's assembling a company of men, horses, sloops and other weapons in preparation for war with the Indians."

"But surely our Governor Matthews has not agreed to war?" Mary sat down on the bench opposite Ambrose and reached for his hand.

"He not only agreed but also wrote Maryland's Governor to request assistance. Gov. Matthews suggested that it was an opportune time to awe the Nanticocks and Wiccocomicos so they neither aid nor receive the Assateagues while Scarburgh attacks them on the seaside."

"There are so few of them around here now, especially after the smallpox killed so many last year. Why is there a need to attack them?"

Ambrose took a long draw from his pipe before answering. "Thy knows Col. Scarburgh would like to kill all the Indians around here. He's threatened to do so many times."

"Aye, but I always thought it was only talk. I never thought he'd tried to really carry out his ambition."

"Oh I almost forgot. This is from thy brother," Ambrose reached inside his doublet, pulled out a packet and handed to his wife.

Mary stood and walked to the window for better light as sh quickly tore the seal. She sat in the chair beside the window and began to read the enclosed letter.

"He has been released and will be returning home!" Mary exclaimed.

"How soon?" Ambrose stood and walked toward his wife.

"He sails for James City this week. But this letter says when the men were released, they were flogged through three towns and put out at the limits of the colony to fend for themselves. He must be in very poor health after such an experience. I must go to Betsy and take care of their children. I'm sure she'll want to meet his ship. Oh Ambrose...this is great news. Mayhaps we'll all go to Maryland where we'll be safe."

"Ah Mary. I hope so...I certainly hope so," Ambrose said. He placed his pipe on the windowsill and took Mary in his arms.

Sarah traveled with Betsy to James City where they

remained at an Inn for a few days, waiting on the ship carrying George home. When they received news of its arrival, they hired a carriage and rushed to meet him. Sarah and Betsy searched the faces of the exiting passengers, but almost did not recognize George when he appeared. He was extremely emaciated; his dark hair was nearly all gray and he walked with a limp. Betsy had difficulty holding back her tears as she stared at her husband from a distance.

"Oh Sarah....he must have suffered terribly," she cried.

Once George spied them and walked toward the carriage. Betsy climbed down and met him halfway. She threw her arms around his neck and he held her close for a moment, then asked, "Where are my children?"

"They're with Mary. I thought it best to first meet thee alone," Betsy replied.

Sarah walked near them and added, "We weren't sure about thy health after reading the letter, 'Tis good to have thee home. Thee has been through a terrible ordeal."

"Aye, I have, but minor in comparison with others," George said. He paused and glanced back toward the ship.

"We have a carriage. Where is thee baggage?" Betsy inquired.

"I have nothing but what I'm wearing," George responded. "We were thrown out of Boston with only the clothes on our back."

"Oh, George....how did thee survive?" Betsy cried.

"Through the kindness of strangers and other Friends. Let's be on our way...I'm anxious to see my children," he continued.

As they rode in a carriage to the Inn, George related news of their Friend William Robinson, who arrived in Rhode Island from Virginia.

"'Robinson wrote the magistrates and tried to obtain our release but he was unsuccessful so he and Marmaduke Stevenson traveled to Boston. 'Tis a miracle that he and the other Friends arrived safely on their small craft. They arrived on fast-day and attempted to speak to the congregation in a church but were arrested along with little Patience Scott. She was only eleven years of age."

"They arrested an eleven year old girl?" asked Sarah incredulously.

"Aye, they also arrested Mary Dyer, who is quite aged. But they were released and everyone but Patience was banished. All were ordered to leave the courts jurisdiction in two days or be put to death. Robinson and Stevenson set out for Salem and held meetings in the woods. Mary Dyer went to Rhode Island. But later they met and being convinced by God to continue their ministry in Boston, they returned. Some citizens of Boston heard they were returning so they were met by an angry crowd and constables and immediately taken back before the magistrates. The magistrates sent them to jail."

"What happened to them?" Betsy asked anxiously.

"The next day was Sunday so the Minister of the Church where Robinson tried to speak, preached a sermon urging the magistrates to remove the curse of the Quakers presence from the country."

"What did the magistrates do?" Sarah asked anxiously.

"They didn't have to do anything. The Governor heard they were in jail and passed the sentence of death upon William Robinson, Marmaduke Stevenson and Mary Dyer."

"Oh Nay...Nay," Betsy cried.

"What happened then?" Sarah exclaimed.

"Well, by then, I was released, as well as others who had been arrested with me. We all gathered outside their prison window with the hope of coming up with a solution to assist them. I must say, there was quite a crowd. All brave souls. When Robinson saw the number, he began to preach," George laughed.

"I imagine that angered the Governor," Betsy commented.

"Aye, but it angered the Minister more. He called a number of people to the church and preached another attack against Quakers and the Governor ordered two hundred soldiers around the gibbet where they were to be executed. The Governor also ordered drums to be beaten loudly so Robinson's, Stevenson's and Mary Dyer's words would be drowned out."

"No one could get close?" Sarah asked.

"'Twas difficult but some managed. Those that witnessed the event said all three walked hand in hand, with joy on faces."

"God bless them!" Betsy exclaimed.

George continued, "It was said that someone remarked to Mary Dyer that she should be ashamed walking hand in hand with two young men and she answered, "No, this is to me the greatest joy I could enjoy in this world."

"Bless her," Sarah declared.

"Were they not even allowed to speak before hanging as 'tis the custom?" Betsy asked.

"Robinson and Stevenson were given a few moments to speak, despite the Minister's protest...then they were hung."

"Oh Nay!" cried Sarah.

"Mary Dyer was next. She stood bound and blindfolded on the ladder with the halter around her neck when a shout rang out that she had been given a reprieve."

"How did she get a reprieve?" asked Betsy.

"Her son interceded for her."

"Did they stop the execution?"Sarah inquired.

"They took off the halter and asked her to come down but she refused and said, she was there willing to suffer as her brethren did, unless they would annul their wicked law. But the officers pulled her down and took her back to prison. Last I heard she was escorted out of Boston."

"But Robinson and Stevenson did not receive a reprieve," Betsy declared.

"Nay, but God used their death to win many others to Him. Before I left, I was reassured that several people who watched their execution were so impressed by the two mens' calm and joy, that they were convinced and are now Friends of the Truth. God's Truth will always prevail."

George wanted to return home immediately to see his children but Betsy insisted they stay a few days in James City while he recuperated from his ordeal. Sarah visited a Friend in James City while Betsy took care of George at the Inn and gave the couple some time to be alone.

Betsy encouraged George to rest during the day and she frequently shopped while he was napping, One day she was at the market searching for food to 'fatten' George up. She was bartering with a merchant over bread when two women, who were obviously Royalists accosted her.

"What do you mean by waiting on the like's of her ahead of us?" one of the women exclaimed to the merchant.

"I'm sorry, Mam. I didna see you." the merchant said. "Wait a moment madam while I take care of this lady."

"But why?" Betsy asked. "I was here before them."

"Please madam....didna make any trouble." he exclaimed.

"But....but..." Betsy stammered.

"But what....woman," the Royalist woman asked. "Are you daft? Didna you hear him? Move out of the way!" she continued as she poked at Betsy with a parasol.

Betsy lost her footing and landed in a box of apples. Several people laughed while she tried to stand up. Finally, a man in a plain black suit assisted her.

"Serves the Quaker right!" the other women retorted.

"What's she doing here anyway? We have a law against Quakers," exclaimed a man standing nearby.

Betsy was mortified and thanked the man who helped her. She briskly walked away.

When she reached the Inn, a crowd of people were clustered around the entrance.

"I wonder what this is about," she said aloud to herself. She tried to go around the group of people but heard her name being called. She looked up and saw George being forced out the door by two soldiers.

"Ye need go no further Madam," the constable said. "Ye're husband is hereby arrested for violating the law. Ye're both Quakers and as such are prohibited from entering the colony of Virginia."

"But...we're residents of Virginia. Not visitors."

"That is of no matter. You are not welcome here and ye're husband is being arrested."

Two soldiers grasped George's arm and forced her to go with them as he tried to talk to Betsy. She stared after him in dismay. Then began to scream, "You have no right to treat a citizen of Virginia in such a way. We are residents of Accawmacke County and have been for many years. I thought the law was for visitors."

"That I do not know, Mam. I was ordered to arrest George Willson who entered Virginia illegally and I have completed my task. Take up your complaint with the magistrate."

"Go home and inform Ambrose, Betsy," George shouted as the soldiers pulled him away. "He'll know what to do."

Betsy set out to find Sarah. It was early evening by the time

259

she found her and told of the events that had taken place, Sarah hugged her sister-in-law and said, "Don't worry Betsy. We'll straighten all this out. But I don't imagine there's anything we can do tonight. We'll have to trust that God takes care of him and see the magistrate at first light. Come we must plan how we will obtain his release. Mayhaps my friend can help."

The next morning, Betsy and Sarah were allowed to visit George. The dungeon was a miserable place, dark and dank with no window for light. They brought some victuals for him but were allowed to stay only a brief time. Afterward, they set out on foot for court but were immediately turned away.

Betsy cried, "What can we do, Sarah? How can we obtain his release? He hasn't even seen his son."

"I didna know Betsy. Let's try to visit him once more. We can at least provide him with more food."

They went to the market and bought some bread and a number of pastries then returned to the gaol but were not allowed to see George. Betsy begged and pleaded but to no avail.

Sarah gave the jailer some money to take the food to her brother but had little hope that he'd actually receive it.

As they left the gaol, Betsy cried, "Oh Sarah, I'm afraid he will starve if we don't get him released."

"Aye, I'm concerned too. He's in no condition to remain in the gaol. But we need Ambrose's help to get him released. We must return to Accawmacke and inform him of the situation."

"I will not leave my husband, Sarah. Thee saw how ill he was. He might... he might...die," Betsy stammered.

"Aye, I understand. Thy should stay here and see to his needs. I'll return home and inform Ambrose."

George sat alone in the dismal dungeon and tried to come to terms with his situation. He studied the room once his eyes adjusted to the darkness; he discovered that there was no window to let in light or cooling breeze. Some straw was on the floor, obviously intended for bedding.

God I accept my circumstances...but Oh, God...how I wish I could see our children. And please protect Betsy...she does not deserve this worry.

George was startled by a noise and realized it was simply a rat busily investigating something quite foul-smelling in the corner of the room. George could not move about much because he was secured by a short chain to an iron post in the floor.

As he sat on the stone slab, he reflected on his life. Thoughts of his miserable days on Assateague Isand when he first arrived in the Americas suddenly filled him with dispair.

God, if this is punishment for my past transgressions? Then I accept it willingly.

George lay on the straw mat and tried to focus on happier times but his mind kept returning to the lowest points in his life when he was forced to sup on the corpse of other human beings and when he was unable to free Anne.

God...I am but a rank sinner and not worthy of your love. But please God...didna make my family suffer for my mistakes.

After many hours went by, George finally slept.

CHAPTER THIRTY-NINE

Jan. 1660 Accawmacke/Northampton County

Ambrose set out for James City immediately to try and gain George's release. Stephen Horsey traveled with him. When Ambrose, Stephen and Betsy arrived at the gaol, they discovered William Coale, another Quaker from Maryland, had also been imprisoned with George.

Once they entered the gaol where the two men were being held, Ambrose and Stephen were overcome by a rancid smell. Little air circulated within the small room. George and William Coale were secured to the floor across from each other. Betsy brought some food in a basket. She set it on the floor and kneeled down to hug her husband.

Ambrose spoke first. "George I want thee to know we'll do everything we're able to obtain thy release."

"I know thee will Ambrose but after my experience in Boston, I feel little can be done. As Lizzie Harris said, people fear what they do not understand and if 'tis God's will that I remain in the gaol. I will do so willingly to further His Cause."

"Amen, Friend George. We will remain here as the will of God," William Coale added.

Betsy squeezed George's hand, "What can I do to help thee endure? Can I bring thee anything?"

"Some parchment and pen to write would be good," George replied. "I would like to share my thoughts with my Friends."

"We'll see to thou need immediately," Ambrose declared.

"Has the gaoler given thee victuals I sent?" Betsy inquired.

"Nay, I've only received what thee has brought on thy visits," George replied.

Betsy began crying, "Oh, dear husband....how can I help thee?"

Ambrose spoke quietly, "We've given the gaoler some coin and provisions for thy nourishment...hopefully thee will receive what we have provided."

"God will sustain me," George said as he pulled Betsy to him and stroked her hair. "Didna worry dear one...God will sustain me."

They heard a commotion at the entrance to the room and gaoler stood in the doorway.

"That is all the time...ye're allowed. Be off with ye now."

Betsy sobbed and cried, "I cannot leave thee like this."

George looked at Ambrose and said, "Please take Betsy back home. She needs to be with our son, not staying here worrying about me."

Ambrose nodded.

George pushed Betsy from him and the gaoler grabbed her by an arm as he tried to pull her from the room.

Stephen intervened and grabbed the gaoler's other arm and bent it behind his back, "Take ye're hands off her or I'll break this arm."

The gaoler frowned but relented.

Stephen relaxed his grip and Betsy stood unaided. She wiped the tears from her eyes with the corner of her apron and said, "I'll return as soon as I can dear husband." Then she turned and walked out of the room. Stephen followed.

Ambrose said, "We'll do all we can to get thee out of here, George."

"I know, Friend Ambrose. But we must do God's will...if 'tis his will that I remain...'tis not thy fault. His truth will prevail."

Ambrose stood for a moment. He glanced around the oppressive room then reluctantly left and followed Stephen down the hall. A stern expression settled on his face as he walked in silence, tortured by George's fate.

Ambrose, Stephen and Betsy returned to the Tavern after their visit to the gaol totally despondent over the situation. Betsy was so distraught, she asked to be excused and went immediately to her room while the men went to the Ordinary to discuss the situation.

"We could try to gain an audience with the Governor tomorrow, Ambrose. I always felt Gov. Matthews was a fair and reasonable man."

"Aye, and mayhaps we need to employ a Councilor to work

on George's behalf."

"That is probably all we can do....besides finding someone who will ensure that he receives adequate provisions. That dungeon is a ghastly hole."

The next morning, Stephen went to Governor Matthews house and was informed that he was ill and would not be receiving visitors. With some difficulty, Ambrose managed to retain a Councilor for George. Few wanted to come to the defense of a Quaker. The Councilor gave them the name of a woman who would furnish provisions for a fee. Around noon, Stephen, Betsy and Ambrose returned to the gaol but were turned away.

Betsy burst into tears. "I fear he will never come home, Ambrose. George has hurt no one. Why are they doing this to him?"

"I didna know, Betsy. I wish I could understand why they fear us so much."

There was nothing left to do but return to the Inn. As their carriage approached the tavern, they noticed several horses tethered to the horse rack.

"It appears there are more visitors. I hope it doesn't mean trouble," Stephen declared as he assisted Betsy from the carriage.

A large congregation of men were assembled inside and were in a heated discussion.

"Who will lead us now?" shouted one of the men.

"That I do not know...evidently no provision was made if he died."

"We need to send a packet to Parliament right away."

Ambrose approached the Inn Keeper and quietly asked. "Has someone of importance died?"

"I'll say, 'twas Governor Matthews...died just this morning....they said he went to sleep and never woke up."

Ambrose gave the man an astonished look. "Surely not!"

"Are ye calling me a liar?" the Inn Keeper responded in a robust voice.

Several of the gentlemen conversing, glanced in the direction of the Inn Keeper.

Stephen said in a calm tone, "Nay, nay. We're surprised ...that's all. We tried to see the Governor this morning and we were told that he was ill. We were evidently misinformed. Do thee know who will replace him?"

The Inn Keeper frowned. "That's what those gentlemen are discussing. As of today, we do not have a Governor."

Ambrose, Stephen and Betsy observed the men.

"I wonder what this will mean for George," said Ambrose.

"'Twill probably mean a delay in his release. I'm sure no one in the party will be interested in assisting a Friend at this time...they seem more bent on trying to determine who the next Governor will be."

Betsy's eyes filled with tears. Ambrose and Stephen realized she was quickly losing control of her emotions.

Ambrose put his arm around Betsy and said, "I suggest we retire to our rooms and discuss what we should do in light of this news."

Ambrose and George remained with Betsy another week in James City but George remained in the gaol and they were no longer allowed to see him. After much deliberation, Ambrose and Stephen convinced Betsy that it was useless to wait in James City until a new Governor was appointed. They encouraged her to return to Accawmacke with them to take care of her children and she reluctantly consented.

"'Tis one of the hardest things I've ever done to leave him there, Mary," Ambrose reported when he returned. "I gave the gaoler money to make sure he receives good provisions but since I was not allowed to see him, I'm not sure if the gaoler is doing as I asked."

"Thank thee, Ambrose," Mary said. "I know thee did everything possible."

"While I was in James City, I heard more news about Maryland."

"What news? Nothing bad I hope."

"Nay, only more encouragement for us to move there. It seems that many of our Friends are settling around the Annamessex River and I believe we should settle there as well. With all that has happened to George, I decided to patent land south of the river."

"Then 'tis final. We will be leaving Virginia...and our home?"

266

Mary asked in a trembling voice.

"I'm afraid we must Mary. Stephen heard the Commissioners plan to arrest us soon along with several other Friends for entertaining Quakers. He is moving there this spring and will be leaving in a week to construct his house. I plan to go with him to build ours. Life is becoming intolerable here and I could stay and fight the charges but I didna feel I'd be successful and I must consider our family and servants safety."

Mary looked into his eyes and said, "I know thee are making the right decision for us, Ambrose. We will move to Maryland as thee suggest." She studied her protruding tummy. "But 'tis my wish that this bairn will be born on Virginia's soil before we leave, like all our other children. Barbary has been with me doing all my 'lyin in' and I hope she will be with me this time.

"Aye, Mary. We will wait 'til then but I still must leave this spring to prepare our home."

Ambrose pulled Mary into his arms and held her close.

On January 29, 1660, Col. William Coulbourne was taken to court in Northampton County where he was charged with the violation of the law against entertaining Quakers. He did not deny the accusations and told the court he would continue to associate with them. The Court fined him a hundred pounds sterling and offered him the opportunity to have a meeting where he and his wife, Maria could renounce their errors but they refused.

George Willson remained in the gaol through the grueling cold winter of 1660. Betsy continued to visit him whenever possible. That winter, she realized that she was again with child.

CHAPTER FORTY

1660 Accawmacke/Northampton

With the hope of King Charles II's return to the throne after Cromwell's death, Sir William Berkeley was again appointed Governor of Virginia. Shortly afterward his appointment, a strict law was passed by the Virginia Assembly to suppress the Quaker religion. The Citizens of Virginia were not allowed to entertain Quakers and Commanders of ships bringing Quakers to Virginia were fined £100 sterling. Quakers were to be apprehended and committed to prison without bail till they provided security to leave the colony. Distribution of literature was strictly forbidden.

Ambrose and Stephen returned from Maryland in May, 1660 only to be arrested and taken to Court at Accawmacke along with Levin Denwood for nonpayment of church tithes. Rev. Teackle, who had taken Rev. Doughty place as parish minister, made the accusation against the men. All three were found guilty and fined.

As they left court, Stephen bitterly declared to Ambrose, "I see no other choice but for us to move to Maryland. They'll ruin us with these continual fines. I will not pay their tithes, nor their fines."

"Nor will I," Ambrose added.

"Then we must begin our move to Maryland before they confiscate our property."

"I agree. My plantation in Maryland is not quite complete but I didna feel we can wait much longer."

Utilizing shallops and oxen-drawn carts, Ambrose and Stephen Horsey as well as many other Friends residing in Accawmacke moved their households to Annamessex, Maryland. Stephen's move was completed that summer. In July, 1660, George and Betsy Wilson's second son and third child, William was born while George remained in prison. One month later, on August 15,

269

1660, little Grace Penelope Dixon, Ambrose's and Mary's sixth child was born to them in Virginia.

Charles II, who had kept his royal court in Holland, was brought back to Britain and took his throne in May of 1660. King Charles II pardoned all members of the Parliamentary Army and continued the Commonwealth's policy of religious toleration. He also accepted that he would share power with Parliament and not rule as an absolute monarch.

With the ascent of King Charles II to the throne of England. the leaders and many citizens in Accawmacke who had remained loyal to the Monarchy were overjoyed. The Protestants were no longer in control of the Government. The Eastern Shore of Virginia was again split into two counties, Accawmacke and Northampton. Accawmacke was the northern county and Northampton the southern portion of the peninsula.

In November 1660, before Ambrose's completed his move to Maryland, he along with other Friends were again summoned to court at Northampton to answer charges placed against them.

Col. Yeardley questioned Ambrose.

"Ambrose, it has been brought to the Court's attention that ye as well as Thomas Leatherbury, Henry White, Henry Vaughan, and Levin Denwood are reported to be in breach of the law concerning Quakers. What do ye say to this charge?"

"Aye, I acknowledge that I have had fellowship with Friends," Ambrose replied.

"Now Ambrose, ye have always been an upstanding citizen. Why must ye persist in this endeavor?" Col. Yeardley declared.

"I see nothing wrong with continuing my fellowship with Friends of long-standing. Many of whom are good citizens of Accawmacke," Ambrose replied.

Col. Yeardley frowned at Ambrose's statement. Then fixed his gaze on Henry Vaughan, "Henry Vaughan, you have been charged with transporting Quakers up ye Bay to be set ashore at Nuswattocks. What say you to the charge?"

"I have transported Friends in and out of Virginia." Henry

Vaughan replied.

"That's exactly what I'm speaking of...'tis in violation of the law against Quakers," shouted Col. Yeardley in exasperation.

Col. Scarburgh shouted, "Let's get on with this. You know they're all guilty."

Col. Yeardley stared at Col. Scarburgh. "Please be seated Col. Scarburgh. We will conduct this hearing in an orderly fashion."

Scarburgh frowned but sat down.

"We'll proceed. Call the witnesses against these men."

The trial continued for the rest of the day and into late afternoon. Finally the verdicts were read. All the men were found guilty and various fines were imposed. But further censure was deferred to the Governor of Virginia.

All the convicted men left Court with a resolve to complete their move to Maryland as soon as possible.

Most of the Friends of Accawmacke were settled on the Annamessex River in Maryland when Christmas arrived in 1660. George remained imprisoned in James City. Betsy refused to leave him behind in Virginia so Ambrose arranged for her and their three children to stay in James City with some Friends where she will be near the gaol and occasionally have the opportunity to visit her husband. Betsy's brother, Benjamin, having served his indenture, remained with her.

The Commissioners again summoned Ambrose Dixon, Stephen Horsey and many other Friends to appear before them in Court to answer charges, but the order was returned by the authorities as *non est inventus*. All the men had left Virginia and could not be found. In 1661, Col Scarburgh became Surveyor General of Virginia.

CHAPTER FORTY-ONE

1661 – 1662 Maryland and Virginia

Once Berkeley governed Virginia again, a controversy developed between Virginia and Maryland. The exact line between Virginia and Maryland was disputed for years, especially around the area of Watkins's Point. Eight square miles of the area was still claimed by Virginia but it was a difficult place for Virginia to reach and collect taxes. Knowing this, Lord Baltimore of Maryland encouraged settlement in the area with the hope of securing the land for Maryland.

On November 6, 1661, Maryland's Governor Phillip Calvert published an official invitation to all displaced Virginia Quakers to relocate to Maryland, where their religious beliefs would be accepted with open arms. Even though the land was in dispute, Friends from throughout the Colonies flocked to Maryland and the population grew rapidly, especially around the Little and Big Annamessex River territory.

This 'no-man's land' seemed a safe haven for many Quakers including Ambrose and Stephen Horsey. They soon completed their homes and began clearing the fields. At last, the small Friends refugees from Virginia, felt safe and began to establish their community.

Mary worried about her brother who remained in the James City prison. Letters from Betsy and George were welcome but she became more despondent with each letter.

"I do not believe they will ever release my brother," Mary said to Ambrose after reading her latest letter from George. Ambrose was sitting in his favorite spot on the long front porch smoking his evening pipe while Mary leaned against a post which supported the railing.

Mary continued, "I didna know how much more he will be able to endure the prison. Betsy says he is so thin and his skin is

273

covered with sores. She tries to help him but is often denied visits."

"I wish we could assist him somehow, Mary. But I didna know of anything else we can do but pray for him. Virginia's government has become increasingly hostile to Friends. I'm not even sure Betsy and her family are safe."

"I know, Ambrose. Thee was right to move us to Maryland. I only wish George and Betsy had the opportunity. I don't understand why Governor Berkeley won't release George and banish him from Virginia. That would be better than keeping him imprisoned."

Ambrose nodded. The setting sun shed its last rays through an elm tree next to the porch, casting a shadow on his face.

"Stephen said Gov. Berkeley is not happy about so many of Virginia citizens leaving for Maryland. There's some dispute between Maryland and Virginia now over the land where we now reside."

An alarmed look broke over Mary's face. She walked over and sat in the vacant chair beside him and asked, "Does that mean we'll have to move again?"

"Nay, Mary. At least, I hope not," Ambrose reassured her. "Horsey was appointed Surveyor General of the area and I've been appointed to assist him. We'll survey the land for Maryland and hope for the best. I'm sure Governor Calvert will support us. My only worry is that Col. Scarburgh owns some of the land that is in Maryland. I'm never sure how Scarburgh will react."

Mary glanced toward the stock barn and watched her son, Henry Jr. approach. "That's for sure. To be such a good friend in years past, he certainly is not very cordial to us now."

"'Tis hard for him to accept our belief. All we can do is pray for him to hear God speak to him and show him His Truth."

Henry, Jr. stepped onto the porch and declared, "Papa, we finished clearing that second field. It should be in good shape for planting this spring."

"That's great son. See, Mary, we'll have a regular working plantation in no time like I promised thee."

"Aye, Mary nodded. I never doubted thee, Ambrose. "Twas just hard to leave so much of our life behind."

Henry, Jr. leaned against the porch rail and smiled at his

parents.

"Henry, Jr. Did I tell thee I saw Tom Cottingham last week at Stephen's?" Ambrose asked.

"I always liked that young man. He had a difficult time as apprentice under Mr. Andrews," commented Mary.

"I did too, Mary. That's why I've continued to ask about him from time to time. I was surprised to see him here."

"Why is he in Maryland, Papa? Did Mr. Andrews send him here for some reason?"

A broad smile broke over Ambrose's face as he reported, "It seems we didna have to worry about him any longer. He's completed his apprenticeship and evidently making his own way in life. He and John Rhodes asked to hire a boat from me in exchange for 110 pounds of tobacco a day."

"That's good news," responded Henry, Jr.

"It certainly is. Mayhaps, his life will improve," Mary added.

"Aye, I heard Andrews tried to have him whipped by the Commissioners for swearing once."

"Did they whip him?" Henry, Jr. inquired.

"Nay. I think they felt sorry for him. They just gave him a warning. If he was heard swearing again, he'd receive twenty-one lashes and I never heard of any more trouble for him."

"That's good. He received enough abuse from Mr. Andrews," Mary said.

"Where's he staying?" Henry Jr. asked.

"I believe he's blacksmithing for Anthony West and staying with him a while."

"Then I'll have to drop by and see him...I'm glad he moved to Maryland."

"Well, I imagine thee both are hungry so let's see what we can find for thee dinner. Mary Jane's been busy cooking something special and I didna know what it is but I certainly appreciate the help."

"If it's anything like that last meal she cooked, then I think I might need to visit our neighbors for dinner," Henry Jr. laughed.

"I'll join thee," Ambrose chuckled.

"That was kind of a *strange* dinner," Mary tittered as they entered the spacious dining room.

Later that evening, Ambrose and Mary sat in the Parlour

with Henry, Jr. and Mary Jane as Henry, Jr. quietly read from the Bible. A flickering fire burned in the fireplace. Sarah and Thomas sat in front of the fireplace on a quilt listening to him read. Henry, Jr. halted his reading when they heard a carriage pull up outside. Everyone looked toward the front hall with anticipation, but Mary knew instantly that something dreadful had happened when their servant, Permelia, opened the door. Betsy appeared in the doorway with her three children. Her face was ashen and had a sad tale written on it. A terrible sense of doom fell over the household.

Mary rushed to her sister-in-law. "Why are thee here Betsy? Is there news of George?"

"Oh, Mary...oh...Mary." Betsy replied in an anguished voice.

"What is it? What has happened?"

Mary Jane summoned the servants and joined her mother at the door. She took little William from Betsy's arms. The child started squalling as Betsy thrust her arms around Mary and cried on her shoulder.

"Please Betsy...what is this about...what has happened?" Mary implored as she embraced her sister-in-law.

Ambrose joined the distraught women and added, "Aye Betsy, please tell us. Has anything happened to George?"

"They killed him...they killed him!"

Mary released her hold on Betsy and looked toward the Parlour as she tried to comprehend what her sister-in-law said.

George dead. It cannot be...it cannot be.....

Overcome by grief, Mary hung her head. Tears trickled down her cheeks and dropped off like rain drops. She sat down on a near-by chair to try and gain control of her emotions.

Permelia ushered the younger children into an adjoining bedroom. Ambrose reached for Betsy who was about to collapse and guided her to a chair. He asked, "What do thee mean...*killed him*? George did not receive a sentence of death."

"They might as well have sentenced him to death in that dungeon! Oh Ambrose...it was a horrible place...he never received enough food or water...and they'd never let him out. It was filthy. They even chained an Indian to the same iron post. All of it was too much and he died...he's gone, Ambrose...George is gone...my husband is with God now. At least, he'll have peace with God," Betsy wailed.

Mary regained her composure and walked over to Betsy. She pulled her into her arms and hugged her tightly. Betsy continued to sob for a few moments then Mary gently said, "Tell us what happened Betsy."

Betsy pulled away from Mary and dabbed at her eyes with the corner of her apron as she tearfully spoke. "There's nothing to tell really. I knew George was growing weaker every time I saw him but I always had hope. His skin even began to peel away where he was chained and I could see his bone. I begged the gaoler to send for the doctor but he said, George deserved to die..."

Betsy began to sob uncontrollably again and Mary sat beside her and held her sister-in-law's hand until her emotions were spent.

After a time, Betsy took her hand away and reached for her cloak. She pulled a letter from it and haltingly said between sobs, "On our last visit, he gave me a letter for thee. Mary, I didna have time to send it."

Mary accepted the letter and quickly broke the seal. She stood and walked over to the fire as she read aloud.

Dear Mary,

Sweet...sweet Mary. I doubt that I will ever see thee again. I didna dare tell Betsy. She has worried enough...I feel God is calling me home...and I am comforted. I only hope this reaches thee in time so Betsy will not be alone.

Have no concern for me...I will soon be in a better place and out of this loathsome existence here in this gaol. I am now chained with an ox chain to an iron bolt along with an Indian who is in prison for murder. As I sit here chained, I can say I have been treated with more kindness by Indians than I have by my own kind. And for my fellow Englishmen, all I can say is God forgive them for they know not what they do.

Mary, please take care of Betsy and my children. Betsy brought them to the prison one day but I asked her not to bring them to the dreadful place again. My only regret is that I will not be able to see them grow up and reveal to them God's truth but I know they will be in good hands with Betsy and trust that thee and Ambrose will guide them to acknowledge their Inner Light.

This is a hard letter to write but know that I will soon be with God in that glorious place where the Lord awaits me. Take care of my family and I love you all.

Thy loving brother,
George Willson

After Mary finished reading, Betsy wailed loudly. Mary encircled her sister-in-law in her arms.

Ambrose asked, "Betsy, I'm sorry but I must ask, what has happened to George's body? Where did they take it?"

"Benjamin's arranged for a sloop to carry him here. I knew George would want to be buried near thee. Benjamin will arrive with his body tomorrow. We had to argue with the magistrate for even that small request. They wanted to bury him in a paupers grave," Betsy replied in a voice full of emotion.

Mary held Betsy's hand and said, "Thee will have a home with us, Betsy...as George wished. I know it 'tis hard to see now but George's died for some reason known only to God. We must take comfort in that."

"I know, Mary...but"tis so hard to accept. George never hurt anyone...he didna deserve to die as the gaoler said."

Betsy's tears began anew and Mary held her close. Ambrose quietly said, "Nay, he didna deserve to die, Betsy."

George Wilson was laid to rest on Ambrose and Mary's plantation. A large gathering of Friends surrounded the gravesite to pay their last tribute of respect. After George's coffin was lowered into the grave, heads were bowed and a silent communion of the Friends was held. Sun rays poured through the leafless tree.

A faint voice from a woman dressed in a plain brown dress and simple rochet, was heard, "We stand at this grave in anguish as we mourn our dear loved one who is wrapped so closely in the bosom of earth. He whom we loved is not here. But mourn for the mourner, not for the dead; He is at rest, but we are in tears."

Silence again prevailed then several young men with long-handled shovels stepped forward and filled the grave. Other men came forward, took the shovels from their hands and bore his share in turn. When the grave rose above the turf, the crowd turned and slowly dispersed.

Ambrose stood at his grave for a few moments then said to Mary and Betsy, "George's death must be remembered. We'll build a meeting house beside his grave and call it God's Acre. All who pass will remember how he sacrificed his life."

CHAPTER FORTY-TWO

October 1663 – Accawmacke/Northampton

Even though the Commonwealth was abolished in England there was still much suspicion regarding Nonconformists. After an armed revolt by religious radicals in London, Quaker leader, George Fox was imprisoned. In an attempt to free him from prison, Margaret Fell, a long term Friend and benefactor of George Fox, came to his defense with a declaration given to King Charles II stating Quaker beliefs on peace. She stated:

"We utterly deny all outward wars and strife, and fightings with outward weapons, for any end, or under any pretense whatsoever; this is our testimony to the whole world...The Spirit of Christ, by which we are guided, is not changeable, so as once to command us from a thing as evil, and again to move unto it; and we certainly know, and testify to the world, that the spirit of Christ, which leads us into all truth, will never move us to fight and war against any man with outward weapons, neither for the kingdom of Christ, nor for the kingdoms of the world."

When news of the Peace testimony reached Accawmacke. Col. Scarburgh, who was now High Sheriff of Northampton, became enraged and voiced his opinion in the Ordinary at Hungar's.

"These Quakers stand aside and let others do their fighting. Where would they be if we hadn't killed and chased off those Assateagues? Now I hear that many have moved to the Annamessex and Manokin River and claim to be residents of Maryland. That's Virginia land they're settled on and everyone knows it. The Commissioners will back me. Who will join with me to repel their contempt for Virginia?"

"Aye, we'll drive those Quakers from our midst....I'm with ye," exclaimed the man sitting with him.

"And I, shouted another!"

"Count me in!"

Before he left the Ordinary, Col. Scarburgh rounded up forty horsemen and made plans to head for the Annamessex River Sunday October 11, 1661. The following morning the group rode to Stephen Horsey's plantation. A soldier pounded on his door.

When Stephen opened the door, he was astonished to see Col. Scarburgh seated on his horse with other residents of Virginia.

"What is the purpose of thee visit so early, Scarburgh? Thee has no jurisdiction in Maryland," Stephen commented

"This land is Virginia land and you know it Stephen and I demand ye swear allegiance to Virginia and come with us to answer charges against ye," Col. Scarburgh shouted.

"Virginia land? Thy know this is Maryland...and I'll do no such thing. Why the Governor of Maryland would have me hanged if I declared this land Virginia," Stephen emphatically replied. "I have a patent for this land from Maryland...not from Virginia and if thee will come inside I'll show it to thee."

Col. Scarburgh declared, "'Tis evident that by ye Lord Baltimore's bounds, he has no lands to the southwards of Watkin's Point...therefore you must subscribe to obedience to his Majesty's according to the Act of Assembly."

"Thee are wrong...if thy will not come inside...at least give me a moment to show my patent."

Stephen walked back in the house while Col. Scarburgh impatiently waited on his horse by the porch. In a few moments, Stephen returned with a parchment.

"Come see...I have a patent from Lord Baltimore for this land."

"I need not look at ye're fraudulent document. Lord Baltimore is mistaken. Swear allegiance to Virginia and you will continue to enjoy ye're lands and goods and his Majesty's Governor would protect you as his subject."

Stephen declared. "If I were to do as ye say, I would be false to the trust put in me by the Lord-Lieutenant of Maryland."

"There can be no trust where there is no interest. This is Virginia's land. You must answer the charges or we'll arrest you for contempt and rebellion."

"I will not. The Governor of Maryland will come soon after ye are gone and hang me at my door."

"Arrest this man and paint the broad arrow of confiscation

on his door," Col. Scarburgh shouted. "Your plantation is now government property of Virginia."

Two horsemen grabbed Stephen by his arms and forced him out the door while another man painted an arrow on the door. Seeing her husband so brutally handled, Stephen's wife, Sarah, rushed to the door with her daughter trailing close behind. "Col. Scarburgh, thee cannot do this," she screamed. "We are citizens of Maryland."

Col. Scarburgh laughed at her distress and kicked the sides of his horse. "Come men, we have more to do this day." The horsemen galloped further down the river.

Col. Scarburgh and the forty horsemen proceeded on to Ambrose's plantation on the south side of the Annamessex river. Ambrose was sitting on his porch smoking his pipe and talking to his neighbors George Johnson and Thomas Price when the group arrived.

Ambrose and his visitors rose to meet the assemblage. When Ambrose spied Stephen on horseback with his hands tied, he shouted at Col. Scarburgh, "What is the meaning of this intrusion? Why do thee have Friend Stephen trussed up in such a manner?"

"Friend Stephen, indeed. He is nothing but a rebellious scoundrel as you all are," Scarburgh laughed. "George, Thomas....it appears ye saved us the trouble of visiting your houses. I'm not surprised finding the likes of you Quaker rascals together. As I offered Stephen Horsey, I now offer you all the opportunity to swear allegiance to Virginia or come with us to answer the charges ordered against you."

"We are no longer citizens of Virginia, Col. Scarburgh, as thee well know. This is Maryland," Ambrose responded "And Stephen is not a citizen of Maryland either."

"Thee have no authority here." George Johnson expressed vehemently.

"And we will swear no allegiance to Virginia...as Friend Ambrose says...we are in Maryland."

Col. Scarburgh stared at Ambrose and frowned, "I thought you'd have more sense than this. But I see ye're nothing but a creeping Quaker and prater of nonsense. Arrest these men and paint the broad arrow about his door."

Several men dismounted and began walking toward Ambrose and his visitors when Mary appeared in the doorway. Henry, Jr. followed close behind with his matchlock.

Ambrose saw Henry, Jr. with the gun and quickly admonished, "Put the matchlock away son. There's no need for violence."

"But Papa...they have no right!" Henry, Jr. exclaimed.

"True son...but this will be worked out peaceably. We have no need for violence."

"At least, you still have some sense, Ambrose," Col. Scarburgh declared. He became aware of the men who dismounted and were standing in wait of his orders. Scarburgh shouted. "Well, what are you waiting for...arrest these men and paint the arrow...be done with it. We have others to visit this day."

Mary reached for her husband's sleeve and Ambrose turned. He managed to hug her before two horsemen roughly pulled him away. Tears were in her eyes as she watched Scarburgh's men tie Ambrose's hands and throw him on a horse. Two men pushed her aside as they painted an arrow on her door. All the horsemen left with Ambrose, Stephen, George Johnson, and Thomas Price.

Mary stood and watched until they were no longer in view.

Will this never end? Will we ever find peace again? Oh God....I do not understand.....Please take care of Ambrose....I cannot lose him....I cannot lose another one I love....and I do love him....I know now....I do love him....Please God...return him to me so I can tell him so...why didna I tell him before....Oh God...please bring him back...

After leaving, the Dixon home, Scarburgh continued to Henry Boston's home and again demanded allegiance to Virginia. Henry Boston did not refuse to swear allegiance to Virginia, but requested a day or two to consider so Scarburgh did not arrest him. Scarburgh ordered him to report to Virginia Commissioners the following week.

Col. Scarburgh continued his rampage on other Quakers houses. Seeing Ambrose and Stephen held as prisoners caused some of the men to agree to Col. Scarburgh's order and they swore allegiance to Virginia. They promised to return and pay taxes and fines so the Broad Arrow was not painted above their door. The next day, the Col. Scarburgh and his horsemen returned to Virginia with their prisoners where they were placed in the gaol until the next Court session the following Monday.

As Commander, Col. Yeardley was also Judge for the Court. he arrived early for the session and angrily addressed Col. Scarburgh as he approached. "What is the meaning of this? Who gave you the order to arrest these men, Scarburgh? The Commissioners certainly did not."

Col. Scarburgh was dressed for Court in his finest red doublet, gray breeches and plumed hat. He frowned and paused a moment before entering the log building.

"The men violated the law by not paying their fines. I am High Sheriff of Northampton, I didna need an additional order to arrest them," Col. Scarburgh replied. He walked to the center of the room and looked around. Seeing no others, he spoke more softly, "Yeardley, you know it's Virginia's land and we must make a stand or this blasphemous Quakers will take it away."

Col. Yeardley drew himself up and stared into Col. Scarburgh's eyes, "I know of no such thing, Sir. You well know that land is in dispute and since it borders ye're own land...I'm sure that is why you have interest. But I do not wish to start a fight with Maryland over ye're personal interest."

Col. Scarburgh glowered menacingly at Col. Yeardley and clinched his fist. The two men stared at each other for a few moments, but several Court visitors entered so Scarbrugh broke away from Col. Yeardley.

After the other Commissioners arrived and were seated at the table, Col. Yeardley said, "Bring the prisoners in."

Ambrose, Stephen and the other prisoners were brought into the Court room and led before the men. All were chained together.

"Why are these men chained? They are no threat!" Col. Yeardley exclaimed in exasperation. He stared at Col. Scarburgh for a brief moment then continued.

"You men have been charged with failure to swear ye're allegiance to Virginia and failure to pay fines due her....but it has come to our attention that you now claim to live in Maryland. Is that correct, Stephen Horsey?"

"Aye, Sir. We are all citizens of Maryland and as such, owe our allegiance to that colony," Stephen said with defiance.

"Aye. I understand..." Col. Yeardley said.

Col. Scarburgh stood and shouted, "They are citizens of Virginia, I tell you."

"Order, Col. Scarburgh...Order, I say. This Court will be conducted with order," Yeardley declared.

Col. Scarburgh sat back down and Yeardley continued. "The land on which all you men now reside is in dispute between Maryland and Virginia and until this dispute has been settled, I didna see that the Court can find you guilty of the charges. You are hereby released until the dispute is settled. But you may be charged again if the land is found to be Virginia's territory."

An audible gasp was heard among the observers and Col. Scarburgh stood with an fierce scowl on his face.

"Col. Scarburgh, release these men," Col. Yeardley ordered.

Col. Scarburgh motioned to the guards and they released the prisoners.

Ambrose and Stephen stared at Col. Scarburgh as they walked toward the door rubbing their wrists. The other prisoners followed them from out of the court room.

Once they were outside, the former prisoners gathered together to discuss what had transpired.

"Do thee believe Scarburgh will stop now?" one of the men asked.

"Nay, knowing him as I do....once Scarburgh has something on his mind...he does not soon forget," Ambrose declared.

"What can we do to stop him? I didna like being dragged to Virginia whenever he takes a hankering," one of the younger men announced. "I have more to do than waste time in their gaol."

Stephen said, "We should write the Governor of Maryland. He needs to put a stop to this."

"Aye, Stephen. That's a good plan. We'll draft a letter when we return home...now let's see about hiring a boat for Maryland," Ambrose said.

A day later, Mary was observing travel on the Annamessex River from her porch, as she had done everyday since Ambrose was so brutally taken from their home. She saw a small speck far off in the distance. Mary went to the steps and shaded her eyes with her hands.

Surely that is a shallop but I didna recognize it.

The speck grew closer and she could see several men aboard, but the shallop was still too far away for her to see their faces. Gradually, the shallop turned and approached their quay. Mary waited another moment to be sure...then she quickly ran down the steps toward the pier.

"Oh Ambrose...thee are home...thee are home!"

Ambrose climbed onto the decking and the men remaining on the boat laughed at Mary's excitement.

"It appears, thee will receive a warm welcoming," Stephen chuckled before Mary reached the dock. "I only hope I have the same."

Ambrose looked back at his friend and laughed. "I'm sure thee will Friend...thee are only recently wed."

Mary reached the boat and blushed when she saw the other men. She became embarrassed by her excitement in front of them. Mary searched Ambrose's face with loving concern.

"I was so worried, husband...especially after George's death," Mary tried to explain.

"No need to worry, Mary. The Court released us...and I believe we are safe...at least...for now."

The boat pulled away from the quay and Mary and Ambrose held hands as they watched it depart. They turned and began to walk slowly up the path to their home.

"Will Col. Scarburgh ever stop harassing us, Ambrose?"

"I didna know, Mary. Thee knows how much he hates Indians. I fear he now bears a similar hatred for Friends."

"But why?"

"That I didna know. I wish I did so we could resolve our differences...But 'tis good to be home. Have thee had any difficulties?"

"Nay, Ambrose...thee has trained Henry, Jr., quite well...and Ambrose I must tell thee something...I should have said it years ago..."Mary stammered. She stopped walking and turned toward him.

Ambrose halted and gave her a look of alarm at her serious tone. "What is it, Mary?"

"This experience...well....I've been thinking...that is...," she

287

continued to stammer.

Ambrose waited patiently and continued to stare at Mary.

Mary lowered her head a moment then looked him full in the face. Her eyes were filled with love and adoration as she said, "I'll just come right out and say it...I love thee, Ambrose...Please didna let anything happen to thee...I could not bear it!"

Ambrose grabbed Mary under her arms and gave her a bear hug. He lifted her off her feet and twirled her around in a circle as he gave a whoop. Mary laughed and exclaimed..."Put me down, Ambrose...whatever will the children think?"

Hearing the commotion, Thomas shouted, "Papa's home! Papa's home!"

Mary Jane, Sarah and Elizabeth ran from the house toward their parents.

When the children reached them, Ambrose sat Mary back on the ground and the children flung their arms around them tightly. They linked arms, encircled their parents and danced around them chanting, "Papa's home...Papa's home"

Ambrose looked into Mary's eyes and softly said, "Thee has made me the happiest man in the world, Mary."

"Thee may be a little happier, Ambrose. It seems I am with child again."

Ambrose hugged Mary to his chest. She lay her head on his shoulder and whispered in his ear, "This time I hope to give thee a son. I believe thee has enough daughters."

Ambrose laughed and the children laughed with him. He asked, "Where's Henry, Jr.?"

"At the shipyard with Tom Cottingham," Sarah replied.

"He and Tom are doing a great job," Ambrose said. "I'm glad Henry, Jr. became friends with him."

"He's not the only one who is good friends with Tom Cottingham," added Thomas. He smiled sheepishly at Mary Jane and she gave him a swift kick as they followed their parents toward the house.

"What do thee mean, son?" asked Ambrose.

Thomas glanced at Mary Jane before answering then said, "I just mean that Tom Cottingham is a good friend to others as well."

Mary Jane smiled and nodded at her brother.

After receiving many letters from Maryland citizens,

Governor Calvert became enraged by the harassment of Scarburgh so he visited Governor Berkeley at James City in the spring of 1664. After their meeting, Col. Scarburgh was ordered, along with other surveyors to go to Manoakin May 10th to confer with commissioners concerning the part of Maryland claimed by Virginia and if possible settle the boundary dispute. The disagreement over the line was still not resolved but the two colonies agreed to remain cordial and Scarburgh's forays stopped for a time.

CHAPTER FORTY-THREE

July, 1665– Annamessex River, Maryland

Ambrose stood on the long porch that expanded across the front of his home and surveyed his large plantation. Dixon's Lott...that was the name he chose after he patented an additional 550 acres. In addition to the original grant of 350 acres he received when he first moved to Maryland, he now owned over 850 acres, a handsome home, barn, and many smaller houses for servants, tools and other necessaries. He also had three indentured servants and five negro slaves. With the growth of his ship building business, surely his family was secure. Mary and Ambrose now had seven children. Alice Margaret Dixon, their seventh child was born February 14, 1664.

Seven, God's number. God has truly blessed us. This move was right for us....especially now that Scarburgh has halted his harassment for now. All we need is a schoolhouse for the children. They need a good education. Mayhaps I should bring this up at First Meeting when we discuss business.

Ambrose looked in the direction of the Meeting House that he and other Friends built on his property. The sturdy log building stood in the warm July sunshine with its doors and windows open, ready for meeting, amid a clearing and surrounded by many trees. The cemetery was located next to the Meeting House. A little further down the road was the small cottage he had built for Sarah and Betsy and Betsy's three children. Sarah tutored the children and Betsy earned a living as a seamstress for people in the area. Betsy's brother Benjamin was now married and lived nearby.

A dust cloud appeared on the road. Ambrose recognized Stephen Horsey's carriage approaching the Meeting House followed closely behind by Levin Denwood's.

Mary Jane appeared in the doorway. She was now seventeen and like her mother, had grown to become a beautiful young lady. Dressed in a simple black frock with a white apron, she had a small white rochet covering her dark hair.

"Papa, are thy ready for meeting? Mum sent me to find thee."

"Aye, lass," Ambrose replied. He put his hat on his head and walked back in the house to assist Mary with the younger children.

Sarah held her sister, Elizabeth's hand, and followed her mother to the waiting carriage. Mary was dressed in a simple, soft gray dress. She carried Alice, her infant daughter, while Ambrose followed close behind with Grace in his arms.

"Now where's Thomas and Henry, Jr.?" Mary asked as she glanced around the Parlour.

"Here, Mum," Thomas declared from the porch. He peered around the doorway. Henry, Jr. stood quietly beside him, dressed as Ambrose, in his tall hat and black coat.

"I guess we're all ready now, Ambrose," Mary said.

Ambrose smiled, removed his hat and kissed Mary on the cheek.

"What was that for?" she inquired.

"For being thee," he laughed.

The Dixon family climbed into the open carriage and set out for the Meeting House a short distance away. Henry, Jr. swung himself into the saddle and followed them on his horse.

"Seems a waste to take the carriage this short distance," Mary declared.

"With the number of wee ones we have...we'd spend all morning keeping them rounded up as we walked," Ambrose retorted.

"Ah, I suppose thee are right."

By the time they reached the Meeting House, the hitching posts were all full so they tied their horse to a tree. Stephen Horsey, stood outside exchanging greetings with other Friends. He waited for Ambrose to draw near the building.

"Halloa Ambrose and all thee wonderful little Dixon's," Stephen exclaimed loudly. Several men turned to look at Ambrose as he approached.

"Where's Sarah?" asked Mary.

"Already inside. She wanted to get out of this hot sun," Stephen replied.

"I didna blame her. Children follow close behind," Mary ordered as she walked toward the women's entrance.

"Did thee hear that the plague is rampaging again in England, Ambrose?" Stephen asked.

"Nay. How bad is it?"

"Much worse than last time according to the Captain of the *Elizabeth*. He arrived last week. I, for one am glad to be in Maryland right now."

"We must pray for them."

"Aye," Stephen retorted. Ambrose and Stephen followed the other men in the Meeting House. They sat on the other side of the partition separating them from the women. After a few irrepressible coughs and cries from children, an all-pervading silence fell over the Meeting House.

Only the whinny from one of the horses broke the quiet. Grace's head began to nod in the warmth of the small room. Mary reached over and pulled her head in her lap and Grace immediately went to sleep. The door remained open to provide a little breeze. Elizabeth watched a frog light on the porch outside and hop about.

Suddenly, Levin Denwood stood and leaned on the rail in front of him. He began to speak.

"A Holy Spirit dwells within us who watches all our evil deeds, and treats us according as we treat Him. If our heart condemn us, God is greater than our heart. If our heart condemn us not then we have confidence towards God. Whatsoever we ask....we receive of Him. Because we keep His commandments and do those things which are pleasing in His sight."

Levin stood quietly a moment more, then sat down and silence prevailed again in the Meeting House. After a few more minutes passed, Henry Boston stood and shared his testimony. The meeting continued in this fashion for another hour and half. The sun was rising high in the sky when the Elders clasped their hands and signaled that the meeting was at an end. Scuffling of feet could be heard as everyone shifted positions then as if on cue, the people began to stand and slowly move outside.

"Sarah and Elizabeth broke loose from their mother's hand and raced toward the carriage.

"See why we need the carriage, Mary," Ambrose laughed as he took Grace from Mary's arms. "We'd never catch those two."

"That's true," Stephen remarked. "I believe they could

293

outrun my mare and that's saying something. She's the fastest in the area."

"Would thee like to place a wager on that?" Ambrose asked.

"Gentlemen...how can thee speak of wagers...we're in front of the Meeting House. Didna thee gain anything for meeting?"

"I'm sorry, Mary. Thee are right. I forgot myself," Ambrose said as he winked at Stephen behind her back. Ambrose leaned over and whispered to Stephen..."We'll talk of this later."

Stephen smiled at Ambrose and waited on his wife, Sarah, to join him.

They boarded their carriages and went their separate ways.

A few days later, Ambrose rose early and rode his horse three miles to Stephen's house. The road to his house was lined with a dense forest of stately trees and sweet Indian grass bordered the lane. A wide porch extended across the front of the house. Ambrose dismounted and tied his horse to the hitching rail.

"Why Ambrose, what brings thee here so early in this morning?"

"I wanted to continue our conversation from the other day without Mary around?"

"What conversation?

"Thee wager on thy mare."

"Oh that...I was only jesting. Thee knows that the women would have our hides if we ever did wager."

"True but I have another idea."

"What idea?"

"I heard Gov. Robert Brooks, before he died, had some fox hounds and held several fox-hunts. I thought we'd start the same here. Our wives might condone a fox-hunt over a wager any day."

"Thee might be right. Sarah wasn't too happy when she heard about my comment after last Meeting. Come on inside. Let's see if Sarah can scare up some pie and we'll discuss it."

Ambrose followed Stephen into his spacious home. He waited in the hall while Stephen went to find Sarah. In a few minutes, he returned with Sarah close behind. She carried a tray of food and the two men followed her into the Parlour. Sarah set the tray on a small table near the fireplace between two chairs facing

294

each other. She poured a cup of tea and handed it to Ambrose before she spoke,, "Ambrose, "I'm certainly glad to see thee. How's Mary and the children?"

"She's well, thanks for asking. She sends her regards."

"I need to visit her soon. Seems there's never time for visiting anymore," Sarah lamented.

"Aye, seven children keep her busy as well. Mayhaps our plans can remedy the situation," Ambrose nodded at Stephen.

"Plans, what plans?" she inquired.

"Nothing serious, right now. We're just contemplating a way to become more social," Stephen responded conspiratorially.

"I'm sure," Sarah countered as she gave her husband a quizzical look. "Well....enjoy thy visit. I've chores to do."

"Thank you, Sarah," Stephen said and gave his wife a peck on the cheek.

After she left, Stephen asked, "Now what do thee have in mind about this fox-hunt?"

Ambrose walked over to a chair by the fireplace before answering. "I thought I'd purchase some fox hounds from Brooks and start having fox-hunts here."

"Does he have any for sale?"

"Aye. Coulbourne attended a hunt at Thomas Brooks plantation recently and he learned of their sale. I came here to ask thee to write a letter and inquire into the purchase."

"Certainly, Ambrose."

The two men continued to discuss the future fox-hunt. Before Ambrose left, a letter was drafted to Thomas Brook.

CHAPTER FORTY-FOUR

September, 1665, Annamessex River, Maryland

Ambrose and Stephen decided to set the time for the fox-hunt in September, after the harvest. Excitement prevailed in the small community as the day for the hunt approached. Mary had her servants and children scrub every inch of their house and with the assistance of neighboring women, a large repast was prepared for the event.

On the morning of the hunt a westerly wind blew across the land. Billowy clouds danced in the sky and geese honked overhead as they began their trek south for the winter.

"I hope we have enough food," Mary sighed as she carried a bowl of venison to a makeshift table on the side of her house." Mary Jane and little Sarah followed with trays of bread and cheese.

"Mum, I believe we have enough for twice as many people," Mary Jane responded.

"But...I'm sure the men will have big appetites after the hunt," Mary exclaimed.

"Then they'll have to find and cook their own food," Betsy declared as she approached Mary's house with two of her children. Sarah trailed behind, carrying Betsy's third child.

"Ah, Betsy. "Tis glad I am that thee and Sarah arrived early."

"What can we do to help?" Sarah asked.

"We have more food inside. Will thee be dears and help bring it to the tables?"

"Aye, Mary," the two women said in unison.

Tom Cottingham arrived on horseback and Mary Jane caught a glimpse of him as he dismounted. She immediately turned and walked back toward the house.

"Where are thee going, Mary Jane? I need thy help here," exclaimed Mary.

"I'll be back in a moment, Mum," Mary Jane shouted over her shoulder as she entered the house. She looked down at her gray dress, stained with food and frowned.

I must not let him see me like this....

Mary Jane rushed toward the bedroom she shared with her two oldest sisters. She threw off her dress and stared at her image in the small mirror above a chest. Streams of curly hair escaped from under her rochet and encircled her face. She walked over to the wash bowl and splashed water on her sweaty face and chest then dried with a cloth. She removed the rochet and brushed her long, dark curly tresses.

Mum would say I'm too vain but still.....

She twisted her hair in a bun and tied it neatly with a ribbon and covered her hair with her best rochet, trimmed with lace. Mary Jane stared at her image in the mirror and frowned.

This is silly....Papa and Mum will never approve of Tom Cottingham. He is not a Friend and they'll never allow me to marry him...but...Oh....what can I do...all I think of is Tom....

She sat on the side of her bed and contemplated her situation.

I must convince Papa and Mum somehow.

Mary Jane heard footsteps approach the bedroom. Her sister, Elizabeth, appeared in the doorway.

"Mum said, Thee are to return right now and help," Elizabeth declared. She observed Mary Jane's dress thrown carelessly on the floor and asked, "What are thee doing? Why did thee remove thy dress?"

"'Tis stained...tell Mum, I'll be there shortly...now leave me be."

Elizabeth stared at her sister for a moment then exclaimed, "I know...thee is changing because of Tom Cottingham. Thee knows he's not a Quaker....Mum and Papa will never approve."

"Leave, Elizabeth...please leave now," Mary Jane implored. "And please didna tell Mum or Papa," she pleaded.

"Aye, I'll keep thy secret...but thee best hurry. Tom Cottingham will leave soon to join Papa."

After her sister left, Mary Jane selected a pale gray dress and a white apron. She held the dress in front of her as she regarded her image in the mirror.

'Tis so dull. He'll probably not even notice me.

Mary Jane slipped the dress over her head; put on her white apron; and looked again at her reflection in the mirror. She pinched her cheeks and pulled a few tendrils of hair out from under her rochet.

'Twill have to do. It won't matter anyway....Elizabeth's right....Papa and Mum will never approve.

Tom was in the Parlour holding a huge tray of food when Mary Jane entered. Tom thought he had never seen so lovely a woman and the expression on his face, revealed his thoughts. He asked, "I wondered where you went Mary Jane? Did I offend you in some way? You left so quickly."

"Nay, nay." Mary Jane quickly responded. "Thee would never offend me Tom." She gave him a big smile and he beamed back at her.

Mary entered the Parlour and became aware of the interchange between Mary Jane and Tom. She stared at her daughter for a brief moment then ordered, "Mary Jane, our guests will be here shortly. Tom I'd appreciate thy help but mayhaps Ambrose needs thee assistance. Why didna thy check with him at the barn?"

"Aye, Mrs. Dixon. Whatever you say. I'll just place this on the table," Tom replied but he never took his eyes off Mary Jane while he spoke. Then he turned abruptly and walked out the door. Mary Jane followed him with a basket of bread.

Oh Mary Jane.....I'm so afraid thee heart will be broken...he is not a Friend of the Truth....I like Tom...but he is not a Friend...I need to discuss this with Ambrose.

Mary sat down in the straight back chair by the fireplace and reflected on her first love, and first husband, Henry Pattenden.

Papa did choose him for me.....and I grew to love him before I married...but we married with Papa's blessing. Ambrose and I can not bless this marriage...I want thee to marry one thy love....but we cannot bless a marriage with Tom Cottingham....what will Ambrose do when he learns of this?

Sarah entered and said, "Mary, I'm afraid we need another table to..." her voice faded away as she saw her sister sitting in the chair.

"Has something disturbed thee, Mary?"

Mary stood and faced her sister with a smile, "Nay, Sarah, I guess I'm being lazy and sat down for a moment. What did thee say about another table?"

By mid-morning, the Dixon plantation was alive with carriages and riders from the surrounding countryside. The people milled around and friendly greetings were exchanged. After a time, Ambrose gave the call to mount. A few young women joined the men in the hunt and they were assisted as they mounted their horses. Some of the horses were excited and had to be raced around the yard for a few minutes to release their energy.

Hunters tore through the woods, over logs and brooks and across fields of springy turf. It took all afternoon to finally unearth a fox but he soon disappeared near a stream and the hounds lost it's scent. The hounds ran hither and thither with their noses to the ground but to no avail. Finally Amborse blew the horn and called the hounds back.

Dusk was falling over the land as the hunters drifted back to the Dixon's house grumbling at their failure. After taking their fill of all the food, everyone returned to their respective homes by nightfall.

Later that evening, Mary and Ambrose sat in the Parlour discussing the success of the hunt.

"For the first one, I'd say all went well," Ambrose declared.

"First one?," Mary asked. "When do thee plan to have another?"

"Stephen plans to have the next one...probably in a couple of weeks...why do thee ask? Was it difficult for thee?"

"Nay, not with everyone's assistance but I would like a little time before the next one...but there's something I need to talk to thee about Ambrose."

"What is it, Mary? No problem, I hope."

"It may be...I'm not sure. Have thee noticed how often Tom Cottingham has been visiting lately?"

"Aye. Tom's a good lad. He's not caused any problems has he?"

"Nay...nothing like that....'tis just that our eldest daughter has become interested in him."

"What do thee mean, interested?"

"I believe she thinks of him as a beau."

Ambrose stood and walked over to the fireplace. He threw another log on the fire then turned to face Mary. "That does present a problem since he's not a Friend. Has she spoken to thee about him?"

"Nay...but I noticed her interest today."

"Then mayhaps, he does not feel the same way."

"I wouldn't count on that dear husband. He seemed interested as well."

"Mary Jane has a good head on her shoulders. She knows marriage with one outside the Friends is forbidden. Until she speaks to thee, I'd say let us not worry. She'll change her mind."

"I hope thee are right...but I'm not so sure...I do not want her to be disowned...and I have to admit I'm worried."

"We 'll pray that God's light within will reveal the Truth to her," Ambrose said. He sat down beside Mary, took her hand and gave it a reassuring squeeze.

"Aye, Ambrose...we will pray."

CHAPTER FORTY-FIVE

October, 1665, Annamessex River, Maryland

Mary Jane felt soft rain drops fall as she walked along the well-worn path to the creek. She needed time to think and filling the water pail seemed the best way to find time alone. It had been raining off and on for the past three days and the ground was completely saturated but she continued her trek along the trail.

Perhaps the rain will help wash away my shameful behavior. I need to find my 'Inner light.'

The harsh words Mary Jane had just flung at her Papa were still fresh in her mind, and left her shaking.

Why did I say such things? I've never before spoken to Papa in such a way. But I never expected him to react like that, especially over something that fills me with so much joy. Why won't he understand my feelings?

Gradually the soft raindrops changed to a stinging rain that pierced Mary Jane's skin and she began to walk faster toward her destination. Each stinging drop brought back her father's piercing words.

How could he accuse me of such things? My love for Thomas does not change my love for God. How can I make Papa understand?

In Mary Jane's haste to reach the creek, the bucket bumped nosily against her shins and she heard the crack of a branch directly ahead of her. She held her breath while she admonished herself for being so careless. Her father's reprimand echoed in her head, "Mary Jane, thee must learn to be more watchful. Thy head is too often in the clouds rather than on the task at hand."

She gave a sigh of relief as she watched a startled squirrel scurry down the path, leaving a half eaten nut behind.

"Little squirrel, thee gave me quite a scare but also taught me a lesson," she laughed aloud.

Their settlement was still new territory and very close to the Pocomoke Indians. Though they were friendly and often visited her family, she knew she had to be wary of other tribes traveling through the area.

A small trickle of water began to tear away at the beaver dam on the corner of the creek and the lower ledge of the dam broke. Water reached the banks and gradually spread over the saturated field but Mary Jane continued along the path unaware of the impending danger. Her dress was soaked and the hem of her skirt was trailing on the ground. The path was becoming slippery and Mary Jane realized she needed to walk carefully or she would slip. It would be hard carrying the water back on such a slippery walk.

This is silly. I should go back. I could just leave the bucket outside and the rain will probably fill it in no time...But then what would I say to Papa. I've disappointed him enough.

She began to think about Thomas again and a smile flickered over her face. Mary Jane recalled the anguish in his eyes the night Thomas related the story about his father's death. Since he was an orphan, he had been indentured. Later he was apprenticed to learn the blacksmith trade. From the age of eight, Thomas had never known a normal family life again.

Poor Thomas. He lost his father at such a young age. I'm sure that's why he followed us to Maryland when his apprenticeship ended. Our family has become his adopted family. If only he would become a Friend, then Papa would accept him. I must talk to Thomas about this but how can I see him when Papa has forbade it.

Mary Jane's feet suddenly slipped out from under her and she fell with a thud on the muddy ground. "Don't I feel silly now. I'm covered with mud," she exclaimed aloud.

She tried to stand, but gave a sharp cry from the pain she felt in her left ankle.

"Oh no, what have I done? How will I ever walk back on that slippery path with this ankle?"

Mary Jane looked around for a stick to brace herself and saw rushing water flowing over the hill in her direction. The Annamessex river had flowed out of its banks and was spreading rapidly over the field.

Mary realized that she was in a valley directly below the river where the water would be the deepest. Somehow, she must quickly run to higher ground but with her ankle would she be able to make it in time? She had to try.

"How foolish of me? It serves me right," she said as she frantically climbed to her feet. "I should not have spoken to father that way and run off in a such a huff."

Suddenly, Mary slipped again and her feet went out from under her. She slid on the slick mud toward the rising water. Panic rose in her throat as she tried to regain her footing...only to fall once more. She stared at the rushing water from the river headed toward her and froze in sheer terror.

Oh God...please help me...no one knows where I am...

Strong gusts of wind with rain began to pelt the house and Mary looked anxiously out the front window. Where has that girl gone? She should have been back by now.

"Elizabeth, where exactly did thy sister say she was going?" Mary inquired.

"I believe it was to the creek, Mum. She was going to get some water and she likes to think there sometimes."

"I didna imagine she can do much thinking in this weather. I wish she'd return."

"I'm sure she's fine, Mum. Mary Jane likes the rain."

Ambrose and Henry, Jr. opened the door and a blast of wind blew out the candle on in the hall.

"'Tis coming up a real blow out there," Ambrose exclaimed. "It appears we're in for a storm."

"Did thee see Mary Jane?" Mary asked.

"Aye, this morning...I'm afraid we had words about young Tom Cottingham. I thought she returned to the house."

"She did but she went back out and Elizabeth says she's at the Creek. I'm worried about her being out in this storm."

"We'll go search for her," Ambrose said as he put his hat back on his head. Come Henry, Jr."

"I want to come too," Thomas declared.

"Nay, Thomas. Stay here with thy Mum. She made need thee," Ambrose ordered.

After Ambrose and Henry, Jr. left. the wind grew more intense. Mary tried to remain calm but as the gusts became stronger, she became anxious.

After the rain stopped briefly, Thomas Cottingham took the opportunity to ride over the land he had purchased from William Planner a week ago. Heavy rain for the past week had prevented him from surveying his newly purchased property.

I actually have land I can call my own. I never thought it possible. Mayhaps now I can ask for Mary Jane's hand in marriage. I dared not approach Mr. Dixon before now.

By mid-morning, the rain started again and he knew he had to return home soon or be caught in the deluge. Most of the rivers and creeks were swollen and he was forced to pick his route carefully but he could not resist crossing Ambrose Dixon's land with the hope of seeing Mary Jane. As he neared the Crane creek, he saw a girl walking along the creek bank.

Is that Mary Jane? What is she doing out in this weather?

Suddenly, she seemed to slip and fall. At the same moment, he spied water flowing across the field above her.

The river's overflowed its banks and she'll be trapped.

Thomas kicked the sides of his horse and the horse galloped toward Mary Jane. Mary Jane tried to stand but fell again. She appeared to be frozen as she stared at the approaching water.

Thomas raced toward her and shouted, "Mary Jane...grab my hand."

Mary Jane was startled by his shout and looked in his direction. She tried to stand again and braced herself with a stick. As Thomas drew close, she reached out ready to grab his extended hand. He grasped her arm tightly and threw her indelicately across the front of his horse just before the water reached where she had been lying. Thomas kicked his horse's sides and raced to higher ground. Once they reached the safety of an incline, he called gently to his horse, "Whoa...Spirit....whoa..." The horse slackened his pace and finally came to a stop. Thomas threw himself out of the saddle and assisted Mary Jane off the horse. Then he took her in his arms. She trembled from fright as he held her. They stared at the flood waters now covering the field below them.

"Oh Mary Jane...Thank God you are safe! I feared so when I saw you lying there," Thomas exclaimed.

"Thank God, thee came to my rescue, Thomas," Mary Jane

responded with a touch of shyness.

Realizing the intimacy of their position, Mary Jane broke away from Thomas' hold and turned to face him. "'Twas foolish of me not to realize the danger."

Lightning flashed and the rain pelted them as they stood. Both were soaked. Thomas' dark locks were plastered against his forehead and Mary Jane's long hair whipped in the wind covering her eyes. A look of unutterable love flashed across his face and Thomas impetuously pulled her into his arms again. This time she did not pull away and Tom gradually tightened his clasp on her until the pressure was almost painful.

Suddenly, Tom turned her to face him. "Mary Jane, I can no longer remain silent. From the day I first saw you, I've had no moment, sleeping or awake, when your face has not been before me."

He paused a moment, then stared into her eyes, "I love you and I want you to be my wife and I can not let you go from me until I hear with your heart and lips that you love me."

Thomas' words swept over Mary Jane like at torrent. She felt her love for him rise up to answer his expectant lips as he tilted his head toward her in anxious waiting.

She leaned forward and he finally bent down and pressed his lips against hers...but she abruptly drew away and slumped against him in despair. Thomas cried out, " What is it Mary Jane? I know you love me? Why can't you tell me? Have I been rash?"

"Nay...nay!" cried Mary Jane. "I love thee Tom...when thee came upon me...I have truly loved thee for so long...Oh Tom!" Mary cried as she pushed him away in anguish. "'Tis Papa! He will not allow us to marry...thee are not a Friend. He will not allow me to marry in discord."

Relieved that she had not out right rejected him, Thomas gathered her in his arms as the rain intensified. "Is that all that troubles you?...Then I will become a Friend...I will do anything for you," he said quietly and gently kissed the top of her head.

She pushed him away and studied his face, "Nay....Thomas. Thee mustn't say such a thing. Thee cannot simply become a Friend by saying so...Thee must hear God through thy Inner Light."

He grasped her arm and said, "But...but...Mary Jane...you are my love and my very life....I want to give you my all. I now have land and soon a home to provide for you."

"But it cannot be...at least not now...Papa....Papa!" Mary Jane started to sob.

The wind howled as Thomas asked in anguish, "What must I do?"

Mary Jane continued to cry.

Thomas dropped his arms to his side and he said bitterly, "Then you must not truly love me if you will not marry me."

Shouts penetrated through the noise of the storm before she could answer. Ambrose and Henry, Jr. approached the young couple.

"Mary Jane, thee Mum is worried. Where have thee been and what are thee doing out here with him after I forbade thy meeting?"

"Papa...Papa...Nay...Nay...Thomas saved my life! I hurt my ankle and I would have been swept away by the flood if he had not saved me!"

"What? Well, I owe thee my thanks, Thomas...I'm sorry if I have misjudged...but we must return home immediately," Ambrose shouted above the wind. "This storm is becoming worse and thy Mum is worried. Come with us Thomas. Thee needs shelter. I didna believe I've ever seen a storm so bad."

Before they reached home, large branches were blowing off the trees from the ferocious wind. Blinding flashes of lightning forked across the sky, and peals of thunder reverberated across the land. When they reached the house, Henry, Jr. and Thomas took the horses to the barn, while Ambrose carried Mary Jane into the house. They were soaked to the skin. Elizabeth and Mary helped Mary Jane change into dry clothes.

"I didna know why thee chose to go out in such a storm, Mary Jane. Thee had me worried. Was that Thomas I saw with thee? Didna thy Papa tell thee not to meet with him again?" Mary peppered as she undressed her daughter.

"Mum, please...let me answer," Mary Jane begged. "Thee have it all wrong. It was not raining when I left and Thomas...well Thomas saved my life."

"Saved thy life. What do thee mean?"

"I fell and hurt my ankle when I was by the creek. I was almost overcome by the flood water from the river when Thomas suddenly arrived and saved me."

Mary sat down on the bed beside her daughter as she realized the import of her words. "Oh Mary Jane, to think we almost lost thee."

Mary embraced her daughter and held her for a few minutes. Then she abruptly stood. "We must thank Thomas. He has brought thee back safely. Dry thy hair with this cloth. Thee must not become chilled. I'll get cloths for thy ankle," Mary said as she left the room.

Sarah sat down by her sister.

"Did he really save thee...like a knight saves a lady in distress?"

"Aye, he did."

"Oh how wonderful and heroic," Elizabeth added.

"That is not all that happened....but thee mustn't tell Mum or Papa..."

"What? What else?" cried Sarah.

"We won't tell," cried Elizabeth.

"Thomas asked me to marry him," squealed Mary Jane.

"He asked thee to marry him...but...but...thee cannot. He is not a Friend of the Truth."

"I know," Mary Jane lamented. "But I do love him so...I must find a way."

"But what can thee do? Papa will not allow it...the elders will not allow it...thee will be disowned," Sarah exclaimed.

Thomas remained with the Dixon family since the storm continued to intensify outside.

Around nightfall, they heard a loud crash as a large oak snapped and fell near the front of their house. Ambrose became concerned and suggested everyone remain together in the Parlour till the storm abated.

"Do you think this could be a hurricane, Mr. Dixon?" Tom Cottingham asked. Some of the Indians told me about a hurricane occurring some years back. Many villages were destroyed by the vicious wind."

"Could be, Thomas. I hope it does not become any worse."

The strong gusts soon changed to a continuous howling

wind that threatened to drown out all conversation. Lightning and thunder was almost nonstop and sheets of rain pelted the house. Alice and Grace cried continuously. Mary sat on a quilt near the fireplace and tried to console them in the dark house. A loud crack was heard at the front of the house. Ambrose stood and peered out the window.

"The porch has blown away," he said. "I hope the barn holds."

Other cracking sounds continued as sheds surrounding the house gave way to the wind. Two hours went by and the wind and rain suddenly began to die down. A silence developed over the land. The rain stopped.

Ambrose walked to the door and peered outside, "That's strange...I can see the moon and stars above. This must be the quiet time, the Indians spoke about that happens in hurricanes," Ambrose said. "Mary, I'm concerned that this house may not hold up...and that flood water is awful close....I'd feel safer in the Meeting House...'tis more solidly built and on a rise. We have little time now. Thomas, Henry, Jr., help me saddle the horses. We can ride in the wagon to the Meeting House. Mary, have the children ready to leave as soon as we're back with the wagon."

Mary ordered her older daughters to gather quilts and place them by the door while she gathered food and candles. She put some food supplies in a basket. Everyone quickly climbed on the wagon when Ambrose arrived. Thomas and Henry, Jr. carried the blankets and basket and threw them on the back of the wagon. They grabbed hold of the sides of the wagon while Ambrose sped toward the Meeting House. The wind began to pick up again before they reached the building. Several carriages were seen around the Meeting House but no horses were visible.

Ambrose, Tom Cottingham and Henry, Jr. helped Mary carry the children inside while Mary Jane, Sarah and Elizabeth carried the blanket and basket.

Several other families were inside. The room was pitch black so Mary lit a candle and looked around. She called out, "Betsy...Sarah...are thee here?"

"We're here, Mary," Sarah answered.

"Thanks be to God," Mary exclaimed.

Ambrose shouted to Mary above the howling wind, "I need

to get the servants and our negroes."

"Oh Ambrose...please be careful," Mary screamed.

Ambrose raced out the door and boarded the wagon as the rain beat down. Mary stood anxiously at the door of the Meeting Horse watching him ride away in the darkness.

"Mum, we need to shut the door," Henry, Jr. said as he pulled his mother inside. Grace reached out for Mary and she picked the crying child up and held her against her cheek.

The cracking of tree branches could be heard outside. Time seemed to drag as Mary waited for Ambrose to return.

Oh God...please take care of Ambrose...please protect him.

"Listen, Mum...I think I hear the wagon," Thomas shouted.

Ambrose appeared in the doorway followed by their servants and their five negro slaves.

"Praise be to God...thee are safe!" shouted a man in the back of the large room.

"What about the horses, Papa?" Henry, Jr. asked.

"I released them. Hopefully, they'll make their way back to the barn," Ambrose shouted above the wind.

A loud snap was heard and a tree penetrated the roof of the Meeting House. Rain fell through the gap, soaking those under the opening in the roof.

"We need to pray that God will protect us through this night," Ambrose declared.

"Amen to that, Ambrose," someone said.

Members of the church huddled together in family clusters as the howling wind strengthened.

"We'll all blow away," cried a woman.

"God save us!" shouted a man. "We are in thee Hands."

Rain pummeled the shuttered windows. The younger children cried and screamed while their parents prayed.

The Meeting House creaked and groaned under the pressure of the wind. A loud bang was heard and a tree branch broke through a window.

Three hours went by before the winds began to slowly subside, but the torrential rain continued the remainder of the night. No one slept. Finally, morning arrived and streaks of sunlight filtered through the closed shutters. Shuffling noises were heard as the people stood and made their way toward the doors. A couple of the men opened the men's door and went outside.

Ambrose approached the exit and stepped over a huge tree partially blocking his path. He surveyed the devastation. Henry, Jr. followed him out.

"'Tis good we left the house," Ambrose remarked as he pointed toward what resembled only a small shed where his house once proudly stood. Several trees had fallen over the bedrooms, crushing them completely to the ground.

Some of the men began to appraise the damage to the Meeting House. Other than two large trees that had fallen over and sent the tree branches into the roof and window, the front of the Meeting House held up well. Ambrose walked to the back, then stopped and took in the site. The plain wooden cross stood undisturbed under a large oak tree where George was buried. Leaves still remained on the tree while all the remaining trees surrounding the grave had been knocked down, stripped bare and broken off by the wind. Two large trees near the Meeting House were pulled up by the roots and leaned precariously into the oak tree at the head of George's grave and thus prevented them from crushing the Meeting House.

Ambrose shook his head in disbelief at their good fortune. Henry, Jr. joined Ambrose at the back of the Meeting House.

"God was certainly with us last night," commented Henry, Jr.

"God and his angels," added Ambrose.

The Annamessex River, filled with flood waters, roared nearby. The water from Crane Creek, directly below Ambrose's house was edging slowly up the incline toward his barn. Numerous trees snapped off or were blown flat against the ground while the larger trees had been pulled up by their roots.

As more Friends filed out of the Meeting House, they meandered around in shock for a few moments then gradually departed for their respective homes on foot.

Mary stood at the door of the Meeting House with tears trickling down her cheeks. "Oh Ambrose. I fear what would have happened to our family if we remained in our home."

"Aye, Mary," Ambrose agreed. "Come with me...I want to show thee something."

Mary walked over to him. She was carrying Alice in her arms. Ambrose grabbed her around the waist and held her tight as they walked to the back of the Meeting House.

Mary stared at the undisturbed gravesite and the trees propped against the oak tree, "God was certainly with us last night, Ambrose."

Betsy emerged and searched the landscape for her cottage. "Sarah, we no longer have a home. What are we to do?" she moaned.

Suddenly, Ambrose exclaimed. "With God's help.....we'll build again. That's what we'll do! He kept us safe through this long night and He will not abandon us now!"

"Aye, Papa!" his children shouted.

Drops of rain started to fall again and Ambrose released his hold on Mary. He started walking with determination toward the barn. "I must see to the stock. Henry, Jr., take our servants with thee and see what food provisions thee can retrieve before the rain starts again."

Henry, Jr., Thomas and Tom Cottingham along with the servants hurried to the remains of the house while Mary, Betsy and Sarah urged the children back inside the Meeting House.

A few minutes later, Thomas returned to the Meeting House lugging the large black kettle his mother used for cooking.

"Mum....come look...thee still have the kettle," he shouted as he approached the building.

Mary went to the doorway and sighed as she watched her son struggle with the heavy kettle."

At least we'll not starve, not as long as I have something left to cook.

She looked toward the barn and watched Ambrose approach on horseback.

"'Tis that Rascal?"

"Aye, Mary. He's all we have left I fear. Mayhaps we'll find the other horses in the woods. We have three chickens, two milk cows and three or four hogs but the rest of the stock has scattered. I need to check on our neighbors and inform them of shelter at the Meeting House. Thomas, tell Henry, Jr. to try and repair the roof on the barn and the Meeting House as soon as possible...No telling how long this rain will continue. If it clears, try to salvage some of these trees for lumber for our new house."

"Be careful, dear husband."

"I'll return as quickly as I can, Mary."

Mary stood for a few moments watching Ambrose ride away on Rascal and her thoughts returned to the day her first husband, Henry brought the horse home for her.

Thee destroyed my garden....but now thee are all we have. We didna have much when we first came to America and we didna have much left now but we'll manage. God will be with us.

She gazed in the direction of her house at her sons diligently searching through the remains.

God will be with us.....

CHAPTER FORTY-SIX

November, 1665, Annamessex River, Maryland

Ambrose returned a few hours later with several women and children. He was soaked to the bone since rain began to fall again after only a brief respite. Mary met him at the door.

"Most of our friends survived, but like us...their homes were destroyed," Ambrose said as he entered the Meeting House.

"How are Stephen and Sarah?" Mary asked.

"Stephen Horsey's house is damaged but he will still be able to reside in his home. In fact, he offered to shelter Sarah, Betsy and her children until we can rebuild her house if they want."

"Thee said most of our friends survived. Were their any deaths?"

"Aye, those nearest the river. The flood waters swept them away. At least, they haven't been found yet."

"Mayhaps they fled to safety."

"I hope so, Mary...but...I need to return and help search for them. I only came back to guide these women and children to shelter. Their husbands stayed at their plantations to save what remains."

"Stay a moment to rest and eat a meal. Thy hasn't eaten since last night. We managed to prepare some stew before the rain commenced again."

"I'll stay a short time...but night will be here soon and we still have many missing."

Mary nodded and prepared him a bowl of stew. Ambrose looked around the room and saw straw mattresses lying on the floor. Food supplies were stockpiled in a corner of the room and dry clothing was stacked in another corner.

"Thee have been busy while I was gone. Were thee able to save much from our house?" Ambrose asked as he sat on a bench and ate the bowl of stew.

"Some...we have more items and food provisions in the barn. Our sons, Tom Cottingham and the servants managed to repair the roof on the Meeting House and our barn. At least we'll remain dry. They even built a shed to cover the kettle so we can cook outside when it rains."

"That's good. I wish this rain would let up so the flood waters would recede. Thou mentioned Tom Cottingham, is he still here? I thought he'd returned home by now."

"He asked to stay and help and I could not refuse. We need all the help available...he resides with Col. West and Tom said that the Colonel would have more than enough help. He asked me to tell you that if thy see Col. West to please tell him he was safe."

"I will...I'm headed in his direction next." Ambrose placed the empty bowl on the bench beside him and stood. "Well, I must be on my way if I'm to return by nightfall."

"Please be careful Ambrose."

"I will my dear but didna worry about me...pray for those still missing. This has been a fierce storm."

Ambrose grabbed his black, felt hat and pulled it over his head. He gave Mary a quick kiss on her cheek, then left the Meeting House.

Rain continued for eleven more days; making recovery from the hurricane difficult. Many plantations were destroyed, crops were lost, cattle, horses and other stock were swept out to sea by the flood waters. The Meeting House and other houses or buildings not destroyed by the storm, filled with victims seeking shelter. The Indians in the area were also severely affected by the storm. Some moved north and further inland.

When the rain finally relented, Ambrose immediately started construction on his house. Tom Cottingham remained with the Dixons and helped them rebuild. After two weeks, men from the surrounding community came by to take their families home. The Dixon family was the last family still using the Meeting House for shelter.

The Friends could not use the building to hold meetings while the Dixon's remained in it, but they were not deterred. They brought benches, barrels and chairs. They placed them next to the Meeting House and sat silently in an outdoor meeting waiting on God to lead them to testify.

316

As the meetings were held, Tom Cottingham usually went back to work on the Dixon's house. He had not spent time alone with Mary Jane since the storm. She'd barely spoken to him and appeared to be avoiding in him.

What can I do? She said she loves me. Why won't she talk to me?

By Christmas, the outer part of Ambrose's home was nearing completion. One afternoon, Ambrose was showing young Cottingham how to properly caulk when Tom abruptly asked, "Mr. Dixon, how did you know your house was not as safe as the Meeting House to remain in during the hurricane?"

"Because I built them both," Ambrose continued to explain. "When I built my house...I built it quickly because our family was under pressure to leave Virginia. I didna have a particular plan in mind...just shelter until I could provide more. When our wee one's were born and I needed more room...I just added additional rooms, here and there, no thought for a plan or design."

"But how was that different from the Meeting House?"

"Our community built the Meeting House. We talked and planned it together and came up with a design we all agreed on. We built the Meeting House according to that plan. Everyone did their best to complete the Meeting House in accordance with the original design. It made for a much stronger building."

Ambrose and Tom continued to work a few moments then Ambrose paused and stared off toward the woods.

"Thee might say a strong marriage is like a strong house."

"How so, Ambrose?"

"Well...when two people have the same beliefs and plan a life together, they marry. Their marriage will be strong since it is based on common beliefs."

Tom looked at Ambrose and nodded but not quite understanding. He thought about Ambrose's words.

Is that what Mary Jane was trying to tell me? She wants us to have the same beliefs so we'd have a strong marriage. But I said I'd become a Friend...why isn't that enough...what did she say..I must be a Friend by hearing my Inner Light. What the devil is my Inner Light?

"Mr Dixon, could you explain something to me...what's ye're Inner Light?"

317

Ambrose smiled. "Everyone has an Inner Light...'tis the way God speaks to us."

"God speaks to us? With words? How can that be?"

"Not with words and voices like ours...with God's voice. But we can only hear Him when we are silent and listening for him."

"Is that why you sit together silently in Meetings?"

"Aye, we're listening for God to speak to each of us."

The two men continued to work quietly, side by side, the rest of the evening. After dinner, instead of sitting with the others chatting about the day's events as he usually did, Tom walked toward the woods alone. He continued this pattern for the remainder of the week.

The following week, the Dixon family was sitting around a fire outside after dinner, when Ambrose announced they could move back into their house in two more days.

"Great, Papa!" Mary Jane exclaimed.

"'Tis wonderful news, dear," Mary added as the other children cheered and hugged Ambrose.

"The house is still not complete inside but at least we'll have more room than here," Ambrose said "So I didna want to hear complaints."

"I'll never fuss again," Elizabeth declared. "Not ever!"

Ambrose and Mary laughed at their daughter's declaration.

"I guess that means I should be leaving tomorrow," Tom Cottingham commented.

"We've certainly appreciated thy help, Tom," Ambrose said. "And I didna think I ever adequately thanked thee for saving Mary Jane's life."

At the mention of her name, Mary Jane blushed and walked toward the Meeting House. Tom watched her leave but did not follow.

The next morning, Tom was gone before anyone awakened. When Mary Jane woke, she joined her mother outside by the fire.

"I didna believe I'll ever marry," Mary Jane said as she flounced on the quilt near the fire.

"Why do thee say that, dear?"

"I didna understand men...and I didna think I care too."

"What has upset thee so, Mary Jane?"

"'Tis Tom Cottingham...he never even said good-by. I

318

thought he'd at least do that before he left."

"Thee has not been very cordial to him."

"But, Mum...thee said I could not marry him. I didna want to encourage him."

"That is still no excuse for thy rudeness. Thee hardly spoke to him for weeks...and he has been so helpful to our family."

"But Mum..."

Elizabeth joined Mary Jane and her mother. "Shall I start gathering our clothes for the move, Mum?" Elizabeth asked, excitedly.

"I think we can wait one more day, Elizabeth. Thee Papa said we would move in two days and it won't take long to pack. I'm afraid, we have very little left."

"It will be wonderful living in our on house again, won't it Mum?" Elizabeth exclaimed.

"Aye, Elizabeth...it will...it most certainly will."

CHAPTER FORTY-SEVEN

Spring and Summer 1666 - Annamessex River, Maryland

Much of Annamessex had recovered from the hurricane by spring and talk spread for a petition to be drafted to create a new county in Maryland. The idea was being discussed by several Friends as they congregated outside the Meeting House.

Ambrose approached the building with his family following close behind.

"Papa, isn't that Tom Cottingham standing beside Stephen Horsey?" Thomas pointed.

"Why, I do believe it is? I wonder what he's doing here?"

Tom Cottingham followed Stephen in the men's section before the family reached the Meeting House. Mary led her daughters through the woman's door while Thomas and Henry, Jr. followed Ambrose through the men's entrance.

Several people cleared their throats and coughed as they prepared for the silent meeting. A hush fell over the congregation as the elders indicated the beginning of the meeting. A half hour of silence passed then Henry Vaughn stood and began speaking. "The Lord's Power is with us and I truly desire to tread and walk in His Blessed Truth."

Suddenly, Tom Cottingham rose from his seat and began to speak.

"Through the Providence of the Lord, I am convinced God preserved me and many in this congregation from the ravages of the most recent storm. The Lord's power preserved us from hurt and I stand before Him now ready to receive His Truth with reverence. God has revealed to me that within the confines of this Meeting House, God has raised up a tabernacle of witness in this wilderness country and I would rather hear Friends within this walls than a priest a thousand times." Thomas paused for a moment then sat back down.

Moments went by as the Friends prayed silently. Henry Boston stood. He placed his hands on the railing in front of him and said, "God has truly given us a test and as Friends of the Truth, we have not been found wanting. We have witnessed the power of God and received the Truth that we may abide within. The Lord has born our spirits and enabled us to bear our burdens. Now we are in a tender season of God's love. I myself have through the Grace of God and the obedience of faith witnessed the Peace of God and am greatly concerned for the all the inhabitants of this land to have this same Peace." Henry closed his remarks and sat down. Silence prevailed again among the assemblage.

Ambrose rose, paused a moment, and said, "It is my belief that through strict obedience to the Inward Light and Guide of my soul to walk in the light...then I have the true test of guidance in the discovery of my actions to promote peace, goodwill, charity and benevolence for my neighbors, for such actions proceed from no other than God. It was a happy day when God opened my eyes and appeared in the Beauty of Holiness to my soul." Ambrose sat down.

Several other Friends spoke, men as well as women. Mary quietly shifted her position on the bench. Alice was asleep in her mother's lap. All at once, she gently lifted Alice and placed her in Mary Jane's arms.

Mary's cheeks were flushed as she stood and began to speak, "Religion is heart-work, the battle is an inward one, nothing counts but victory over sin, nothing but the inward possession of the Love of God. God visits you, the Voice of the Spirit calls you. Obedience will bring the Light and Truth into your inward parts, and you may be Redeemed of the Lord." Mary returned to her seat and took Alice from Mary Jane.

The meeting continued for another hour, then the Elders signaled the end of the meeting by clasping their hands. Friends, by common impulse, rose and unhurriedly shuffled toward the open doors.

Brief conversations followed on the grounds in front of the meeting house. Tom Cottingham searched the faces of the women exiting the women's entrance. His face beamed with delight when he saw Mary Jane and caught her eye. She smiled back and advanced toward him.

They stood facing each other for a brief moment, then walked together around the corner of the Meeting House to seek more privacy.

322

"Mary Jane, I understand now what thee tried to tell me. I listened to my Inner Light. Does thee believe me?"

"Aye, Tom. I believe thee."

"Then I will ask again. Will thee marry me?"

She answered with a touch of shyness, "Aye, Tom. I will marry thee if Papa and the Friends approve."

"Papa *AND* the Friends. I thought 'twas only ye're Papa's approval you sought...I mean..thee thought. I'm still not use to this language," he laughed.

"Do not worry...I didna see a problem," Mary Jane countered as she looked him full in the face. "Not after what thee shared in Meeting."

Thomas pulled her into the shadows of the Meeting House and held her close for a moment.

They were startled by her mother's voice impatiently calling, "Mary Jane, 'tis time to leave."

Mary Jane pushed Tom away and turned to leave. He quickly reached out and grabbed her arm and said, "One thing more, Mary Jane..."

Mary Jane stopped and glanced back at him. "I must go, Mum calls..."

Tom gazed at Mary Jane, his eyes filled with love, "'Tis just this Mary Jane. I know thee wishes to be married in a Friends Meeting and I wish this too...but..."

"Aye," she interrupted. "There is no question about that, Tom. Thee knows we must marry in Meeting."

"Aye, but...well could we not also be married by Henry Boston," he implored. "Thee has heard what others call Betsy and George's children because they were only married in Meeting. Henry Boston is a Friend but he is also Justice of the Peace and as such can marry us according to the Laws of Maryland. I do not wish our children to be called, bastards, Mary Jane," Tom said with an voice filled with anguish.

Mary Jane reached for Tom's arm, "I do not wish it either. I have seen the bitterness on Betsy's face when others have spoked the hurtful word. We will marry twice as thee say."

Mary's mother called again, "Mary Jane, come now or thee will need to walk home."

Mary Jane turned and dashed toward the waiting carriage.

"Here I am, Mum."

Tom stared after Mary Jane and was thrilled at the thought of her becoming his wife.

But will she ever be mine? Now I must pass the Friends approval. Who's approval will I need next? What course should I take now? I need to talk to Mr. Dixon.

Tom mounted his horse and trailed slowly after the Dixon's carriage. Once the carriage reached their plantation, Mary climbed down and took her children inside. while Ambrose and his sons continued on to the barn and began unhitching the horses. Tom Cottingham arrived at the barn and dismounted. He approached Ambrose.

"Friend Dixon, could I speak to thee for a moment?" Tom asked.

"Why, Tom Cottingham...I didna see thee ride up? What do thee want to talk about, son?" Ambrose inquired in a grave tone.

"'Tis a private manner."

"I bet I know what thee wants to talk about," Henry, Jr commented as he led one of the horses to the barn. "Tis about Mary Jane."

"That's enough son...boys take care of the horses while Tom and I have us a talk," ordered Ambrose.

Tom tied his horse to the hitching post.

"Come Tom. Take a walk with me." After they they moved some distance from the barn, Ambrose asked, "Now what's this about."

"Henry, Jr was right. I've come to ask for Mary Jane's hand in marriage."

"That doesn't surprise me...after hearing thee at Meeting today, I expected as much. Thee has heard thy Inner Light?"

"Aye, and I would like to become a Friend of the Truth. 'Tis like thee said, Mary Jane and I should be of one accord...I understand that now."

"Well son...I was impressed by thy sincere testimony, and I will give thee my blessing to marry my daughter...but what does she have to say?"

"She has agreed to marry me if thee and the Friends approve. But how do we acquire their permission?"

"Thee must ask at the Women's and the Men's Meetings.

They will discuss the matter and if agreed...thou will be free to marry."

"Do thy believe they will agree?"

"I see no problem...not if thee are sincere about being a Friend."

"I am sincere. I have a lot to learn but I am sincere."

"Then it looks like we'll have a wedding to celebrate soon. Let's go inform thy future bride," Ambrose laughed.

Three weeks later, Tom and Mary Jane's pending marriage passed both the Men and Women's Meetings. A wedding date was set for the 8th of July, giving Tom enough time to complete their home on the north side of the Annamessex River.

Early on the morning of the wedding, Mary Jane and Tom rode in a wagon to Henry Boston's house and in a brief private civil ceremony, they were wed according to the Laws of Maryland. On their way home, Tom suddenly pulled off the road and drove the wagon under a shade tree.

"Mary Jane, I can not wait any longer, thee are now my wife," Tom said.

Mary Jane gave him a perplexed look as he gently lifted her from the wagon and stood her on the ground. Then without waiting for a response, Tom took Mary Jane in his arms and passionately kissed her.

Mary Jane's bonnet fell from her hair, but she ignored it and reached up and clasped her arms tightly around his neck. Every fiber of her being rose to match his emotion. Reluctantly, their lips parted and Tom took her hands and placed them against his cheek then gently kissed each finger. They stood together for a moment enjoying their new status as man and wife.

"Mary Jane, this is the happiest day of my life....and I promise to take care of thee," Tom said in a voice filled with emotion.

"And I will devote my life to thee, Thomas," Mary Jane said. Her eyes expressed the love she felt for him.

Tom touched her cheek with his lips and the slight caress, light as it was, sent hot color surging over her face. Mary Jane said, "Oh Tom....I truly...truly love thee."

Tom took her in his arms again and gently lifted her onto the wagon. He picked up her bonnet and handed it to her. "Then let's get this second wedding over with so we can start our life together," he laughed.

Later that same morning, the newly wed couple sat facing each other in the Friend's Meeting. Nearly the whole community was in attendance.

Mary Jane wore a simple, white dress. Her hair was tucked neatly under a white bonnet trimmed with lace. Tom was dressed entirely in black.

After several Friends had given testimony, Tom Cottingham and Mary Jane stood and faced each other. Tom gently took Mary Jane's hands, cleared his throat and began to speak, "In the presence of the Lord and before this assembly, I take Mary Jane Dixon to be my wife, promising with Divine assistance to be unto her a loving and faithful husband until death shall separate us."

Mary Jane looked at her husband with eyes filled with love for a brief moment then said, "In the presence of the Lord and before this assembly, I take Thomas George Cottingham to be my husband, promising with Divine assistance to be unto him a loving and faithful wife until death shall separate us."

The Church clerk repeated their declaration before the Friends. When his last words died away, a deep, reverent grace filled the room as Friends silently prayed for the wedded pairs commitment.

Mary's loving glance fell on her daughter and she saw a joyous light in Mary Jane's eyes as she sat beside her husband on the bench. Tom's face equally revealed love and happiness for his bride. The Elders gave a signal and every Friend present signed the wedding document as witnesses of their marriage. When the Elders indicated the end of the Meeting, everyone filed outside to converse briefly.

The Dixon's left to complete preparations for the wedding dinner at their plantation where they welcomed all their Friends and Family.

In late afternoon on the day of the wedding after everyone had left, Ambrose sat on his porch smoking his pipe. His favorite fox-hound was lying beside him and Ambrose scratched his ear from time to time. Mary joined her husband on the porch and sat in her usual place beside him...the place where they frequently watched the setting sun and discussed the day's events.

The fox hound raised his head and watched Mary for a moment then lowered it and closed his eyes again when Mary sat down.

Mary rubbed her protruding belly and asked, "I saw thee talking to Stephen Horsey after the wedding. Did he have any news to report?"

"Aye, Mary. He said Gov. Calvert heeded our petitions and will create a new County here."

"A new county? What name has he given it?"

"'Twill be named Somerset County after Lady Somerset, Gov. Calvert's sister-in-law."

"Somerset County, 'tis a pretty name. I like it."

"Stephen is to be High Sheriff and Commissioner. He said I was to be appointed Surveyor of Highways."

"Thee deserve the appointment, Ambrose."

"'Twill take me away from the plantation some, but I guess 'tis a position that needs to be filled. But I didna know about the other office he mentioned."

"What office is that, Ambrose?"

"There's talk of me being elected to represent Somerset in the Lower House of the State Assembly...I'm not sure I wish to take that office."

"But why, dear husband? Thee would make a good and fair representative. I'm sure that's why there's talk of thee serving."

"I'd like to follow my neighbors wishes but I'd have to swear an oath to serve as Burgess...that is if I was even elected...and as a Friend, that I cannot do. I will not deny my faith by swearing an oath. What type of man would I be if I didna stand up for my beliefs? What example would I be setting for our children?"

Mary reached for her husband's hand and fervently said, "I love thee, dear husband.

Ambrose fixed his eyes on his wife and gave her a beaming smile. He turned toward her, and put down his pipe, took her other hand in his and stared deeply into her eyes, "I love thee, dear wife. Thee has given me a wonderful life."

327

Mary gave him a radiant smile, then leaned back in her chair and stroked her prominent belly while she looked in the direction of Mary Jane and Tom Cottingham's house on the north side of the Annamessex. "It appears our children will be starting their lives in a new county, Ambrose. I wonder if they'll have a good life?"

Ambrose gazed across his acreage and watched a crane, squawking loudly as it flew overhead. A squirrel rustled in the leaves nearby. The fox hound raised his head and pricked up his ears, searching for the source of the noise. Suddenly, the sky was filled with a myriad of red and orange streaks across the horizon as the sun set in the west.

Ambrose squeezed Mary's hand affectionately, "With God's help, I'm sure they'll have a great future Mary...with God's help...they will have a good and happy life in this great country...just as we have."

APPENDIX

CHAPTER ONE - The King required a man from every family to fight in his army. King Charles army was defeated in the Civil War. He was captured, tried and executed. The description of his execution is from a letter written by an spectator at the King's execution so it is fairly accurate. George Willson and Richard Johnson are fictitious characters created by the author. However, Mary (Willson) Pattenden Dixon lived on the Eastern Shore of Virginia and was assumed to be the sister of George Willson.

CHAPTER TWO - The family facts concerning Ambrose Dixon and his marriage to Mary (Willson) Pattenden is correct. Their first child Mary was born around this time, though the author added Jane to her name. Mary Willson had previously been married to Henry Pattenden and they had one son Henry Pattenden, Jr. (Mary's life with Henry Pattenden is depicted in the author's first book in the series, Ribbon of Love). Ambrose Dixon was a caulker by trade and became a ship builder. Henry (instead of the name John) and Joanne Custis owned a popular boarding house in London frequented by Royalists but left for Holland then the Eastern Shore with their son, John Custis II when their daughter Ann married Argoll Yeardley. There was a Priscilla Willson married to John on the Eastern Shore who may or may not have been related to Mary Willson. Barbary and Maria are fictitious characters but there was a Barbary Winbrow living in Accawmacke around this time.

CHAPTER THREE - Ambrose Dixon became a ship-builder on the Eastern Shore. Col. Edmund Scarburgh was a wealthy man on the Eastern Shore who hated Indians. Alex Mountney ran a mercantile store on the Eastern Shore. Stephen Horsey was a resident of the Eastern Shore and a good friend of Ambrose Dixon. The information on Finley and Col. Stone and the Religious Toleration Act is historically accurate.

CHAPTER FOUR - The family history in this family is fictitious.

However there was a Willson family in Cranbrook, England and general historic timeline events are accurate. John (Henry) and Joanne Custis were friends with Col. Norwood in England. Rev. Rozier was a minister at this time on the Eastern Shore of Virginia.

CHAPTER FIVE - The *Virginia Merchant* set sail for Virginia with approximately 350 passengers, Cavaliers and loyal supporters of King Charles. Col. Norwood and Col. Williams arranged the trip. The ship encountered the problems indicated in this chapter and arrived on the Island of Fyall. The events that transpired there are accurate according to Col. Norwood's journal, *Voyage to Virginia.* George Willson and Richard are fictitious characters created by the author.

CHAPTER SIX - Hog-killing was a major event and usually occurred in the fall after harvest. During this era, people thought that if a expectant mother's cravings were not met then it would 'mark the unborn child." A Col. William Coulbourn lived on the Eastern Shore around this time and he became a good friend of Ambrose Dixon. He married 1st a woman named Anne (last name unknown) and 2nd Margaret Cooper. There is no evidence that he married a woman named Maria. Literary license was used by the author creating their marriage. William Coulbourn was a non-conformist. He and his wife have never been proven as Quakers but leaned toward the Quaker faith as they. entertained the founder and apostle of the Society of Friends, George Fox, in their home and held a worship service with him upon his visit to Somerset in 1672. William eventually became High Sheriff of Somerset and was instrumental in negotiating a treaty with the Nanticoke Indians, Somerset County, MD. The name Maria did occur in the Coulbourne family in descendant lines but literary license was used by the author to further the story of the Dixon's servant.

CHAPTER SEVEN - Major Morrison and Captain Norwood, Royalists, planned a trip on the *Virginia Merchant* to the Colonies. Captain Locker was the ships captain. The events that took place on the ship are historically accurate and recorded by Captain Norwood in his narrative *A Voyage to Virginia.* George Willson and Richard Johnson are fictitious characters created by the author.

Tom Reason and John Smith are actual people who were praised by Col. Norwood for their heroic actions. The makeshift fire pit was created by the crew as described and Col. Norwood and other planters pledged tobacco to Tom Reason for his heroic action in raising a sail.

CHAPTER EIGHT - The events are historically accurate, Mate Putts was on the *Virginia Merchant* and offered the suggestion about ballast. Col. Norwood, Major Morrison with others were left on the island by the *Virginia Merchant.*

CHAPTER NINE - The story about James Hughes trial was taken from actual Eastern Shore Court records from the time. Sarah Williams was the widow of Michael Williams. She lived near Stephen Horsey and they later married. Stephen Horsey served on a trial of James Hughes as depicted and the Commissioners and signed a proclamation declaring Charles II King in December, 1649. He witnesses many wills according to Court records.

CHAPTER TEN - The events in this chapter are all historical accurate. Major Morrison, Col. Norwood were left on shore without provisions by the *Virginia Merchant.* The ship set sail after Captain Locker had promised to return the next day. George and Richard are of course fictional characters. Francis Cary was Col. Norwood's cousin and was with them on the island.

CHAPTER ELEVEN - The events in this chapter are historically accurate. Col. Norwood was among the survivors and later wrote about their experience in *A Voyage to Virginia* and their decision to eat the corpses to survive and Col. Norwood had was elected leader. Richard and George are fictional characters. The Kinkotanks saved the survivors. Jenkin Price led them to safety at Nathaniel Littleton's. Littleton owned a large plantation on the Eastern Shore as did Stephen Charlton and assisted the survivors as depicted in the story.

CHAPTER TWELVE - The events concerning Col. Norwood and his party and how they were found by Indians are accurate. Mary is thought to be the sister of George Willson who became a resident on the Eastern Shore.

CHAPTER THIRTEEN - The events described by Col. Norwood and George are historically accurate. The party left on the island included Col. Norwood and in order to survive, they fed off the dead corpse of those who died. Col. Norwood wrote of this experience in *A Voyage to Virginia by Henry Norwood, Coloniel.* Many more interesting details can be found in his account of the trip in his book

CHAPTER FOURTEEN - The Yeardley house burned in 1650. Col. Norwood lived with his cousin Gov. Berkeley for several months and Gov. Berkeley addressed the court of Northampton in April 1650 expressing how faithful the Laughing King Indians had been and because of their friendship during the massacre, "No land to be taken from them but what shall be allowed both in justice and convenience by the full court. And in case the Commissioners disagree in their opinion, that you refer the whole matter to be considered by a full court at James City." Mary and Ambrose had son, Thomas around this time.

CHAPTER FIFTEEN - The Children of the Light were called Quakers – Friends, and Friends of Truth – They believe in an Inner Light. Betsy Johnson and her brother Benjamin are fictional characters.

CHAPTER SIXTEEN - The events about the court hearing in this chapter were taken from actual Accawmacke court records. The names are taken from the court records.

CHAPTEEN SEVENTEEN - All the historical events regarding England and the Colonies are accurate. The transcripts of the Oct. 3, 1650 notice is accurate and angered the Eastern Shore residents. Nathaniel Littleton and Argoll Yeardley were assigned to negotiate with government officials and the document was signed by the Eastern Shore citizens.

CHAPTEEN EIGHTEEN - The names listed were all known as good Indian fighters on the Eastern Shore and Col. Scarburgh organized a raid on the Indians at this time according to court records from the Eastern Shore.

CHAPTER NINETEEN - The Indian raid took place and the court events following were taken from court records. All the names mentioned were in the Eastern Shore court records and the people mentioned were imprisoned and fined.

CHAPTER TWENTY - A second raid on the Indians was ordered by the Commissioners of the Eastern Shore. The ship seizure event related by Obedience Robbins concerning Col. Scarburgh appears in Court Records and it was discovered that he was trading guns to the Indians. Parliament appointed the men Commissioners further angering the citizens of Accawmacke. Sarah Dixon was born around this time.

CHAPTER TWENTY-ONE - The events concerning Col. Scarburgh are accurate. Captain Dennis came to James City and required surrender of the Colony to Parliament. This is the first document sent to Parliament concerning *"Taxation without Representation"* from Eastern Shore citizens.

The statement about the Northampton Protest was included in Ye Kingdom of Accammacke by Henry Wise as follows; *Whatever may be the claims of other sections of the country to priority of concerted remonstrance against Great Britain in the following century, whether the palm be accorded the adherents of the Mecklenburg Declaration, of the Fincastle Resolutions, or the people of Massachusetts, the first organized remonstrance against British Authority in the form of a protest against taxation without representation was made by the people of Northampton County, Virginia, March 30, 1652, antedating all the others by one hundred and twenty-odd years; and yet, not a single historian of our country has dwelt upon the importance of this Protest. It may be said that such a remonstrance, directed against local authority, is unworthy of the significance which the writer claims for it. And here let us ask, to whom was the Northampton Protest directed? Was it directed to the Commonwealth of Virginia? No. It was a direct protest against the authority of the Commonwealth of England, which, from March 12th, to April 30th, 1652, was represented by Parliamentary Commissioners, not chosen by the people, nor any section of the*

people of Virginia.
This document expressing the complaint of 'taxation without representation' was sent to Parliament 120 years before the famous slogan *No taxation without representation* was used in Boston in the 1750's but has not been recorded in many history books.

CHAPTER TWENTY TWO - John Custis, Jr. married Elizabeth Eyer around this time. His descendant Daniel Parke Custis, married Martha Dandridge who later married George Washington after her first husband's death. "It is a generally accepted fact that the Dutch were responsible for the introduction of slaves into Virginia in 1619. It was several years later before the first slave appeared on the Eastern Shore, and a decade had elapsed before slaves were brought to the peninsula. The first blacks in Accawmacke of whom we have any knowledge, were two free citizens of color, Anthony Johnson and his wife Mary. They were so highly thought of by the white inhabitants of the county, that, when, in 1652, they had the "misfortune to lose by fire after great service & etc.," after dwelling as law-abiding citizens in the county for over thirty years, they were exempted from paying taxes. While no blacks are mentioned in the census of 1623, the Johnsons must have lived there at the time. The descendants of these free blacks were for many years respected property owners and owned in addition to much land, a number of slaves." (from Nabb Research Center)

CHAPTER TWENTY-THREE - An Anne Wilson from Cranbrook was accused of being a witch. Her relationship to the actual Mary Wilson is fictional but she was sent to Maidstone to be tried with several others for her trial. (Assizes are trials) The events and names of the prisoners in the trials are accurate.

CHAPTER TWENTY-FOUR - Midwife's were often accused of being witches and even if found innocent, they were victimized. The trial events are fictional but typical for the time. Hugh Graham is a fictional character.

CHAPTER TWENTY-FIVE - Few people defended those of accused of being witches for fear of being accused themselves. Accusations occurred many times as revenge.

CHAPTER TWENTY-SIX - Dutch and English tensions increased on the Eastern Shore and the names listed in the resolution came from court documents. Tom Cottingham was apprenticed as a blacksmith. Andrews was a farrier on the Eastern Shore known for being hard on his indentures and apprentices.

CHAPTER TWENTY-SEVEN - The superstitions about witchcraft are accurate for the time period. Penenden Heath was a common place for hangings.

CHAPTER TWENTY-EIGHT - Stephen Horsey quit paying taxes and tithes around this time. The events concerning Anthony Johnson are accurate according to Court records.

CHAPTER TWENTY-NINE - The Cranbrook witches were hung August 25, 1652 on Penenden Heath. Anne Wilson's and Mildred Wright's charges were dismissed by Parliament but by the time the order reached Maidstone, they had already been hung.

CHAPTER THIRTY - Charles Scarburgh, son of Col. Edmund Scarburgh married Anne West, daughter of Anthony West. The Quaker religion was becoming popular in England. Sarah and Elizabeth are fictional sisters.

CHAPTER THIRTY-ONE – Rev. Doughty was the minister of Hungar's church around this time and involved in the charges against the Narragansetts. Chiles boat was seized as described and the Court gave the order for citizens to reimburse. Commissioner Thomas Johnson walked out of the meeting in protest. Col. Scarburgh returned around this time. The protest occurred in Dr. Hacke's field and the Court reacted as described with penalties to those who participated.

CHAPTER THIRTY-TWO - John Custis, Jr. wife died around this time. She and her husband had one child, John Custis III. Rev. Doughty began to mention witches in the pulpit. Barbary Winbrow is an actual character who was accused of being a witch on the

Eastern Shore. After her trial, the Commissioners issued the rule about falsely accusing people.

CHAPTER THIRTY-THREE - The schoolhouse and Sarah as a teacher is fictional. Ambrose and Mary had a child Ambrose, Jr. who died young....maybe not at birth. The information on Rev. Eaton is from court records. Elizabeth Harris, a Quaker, was the first to visit the Eastern Shore. This is a fictional account of her visit. Her speeches were taken from Quaker writings.

CHAPTER THIRTY-FOUR - Elizabeth Harris arrived around this time on the Eastern Shore. She also visited Maryland before returning home to England.

CHAPTER THIRTY-FIVE - Lizzie's speech has been paraphrased from Quaker writings around this time. Col Scarburgh, and other Royalists hated Quakers. Elizabeth Harris visited Maryland. A George Wilson, Quaker, appears in America around this time. The relationship as brother of Mary Wilson is fictional. Ambrose, Mary and many other residents of Accawmacke converted to the Quaker religion. It is not clear that Stephen Horsey was a Quaker but he was a Nonconformists and protested frequently with the Quakers.

CHAPTER THIRTY-SIX - The information about Quakers being persecuted is typical for the time. A George Wilson, Quaker, visited Maryland. His marriage as depicted here is fictional. George Wilson, brother-in-law of Ambrose Dixon, according to Ambrose's will, married Elizabeth Johnson but the relationship as described in the book are fictional. The Quaker wedding described is typical. Ambrose and Mary had their fifth child Elizabeth around this time. George and Elizabeth Wilson had three children.

CHAPTER THIRTY-SEVEN - William Robinson, Quaker, visited the Eastern Shore and the residents mentioned built the first meeting house as described. The Quaker, George Wilson went to Massachusetts where he was imprisoned with 26 other Quakers. His connection to the Dixon family is fictional.

CHAPTER THIRTY-EIGHT - The law against Quakers come from

court records. Ambrose was frequently brought to court for violation of the law against Quakers. The information about persecution of Quakers is accurate. George was finally released from prison and went to Jamestown were he was promptly arrested and thrown in a filthy dungeon. The information on Quakers, William Robinson, Stevenson and Mary Dyer is true.

CHAPTER THIRTY-NINE - George Wilson and William Coale continued to be held in prison. George wrote frequently from jail. Governor Matthew's of Virginia died abruptly in January and Virginia was without a Governor for this time period. The information on Col. Coulbourne is true.

CHAPTER FORTY - The historical information from England is accurate. The information on Ambrose, Stephen Horsey and Levin Denwood comes from Court records, Ambrose, Stephen and many other Quakers moved to Maryland during this time period.

CHAPTER FORTY-ONE - The statements on the disputed land between Virginia and Maryland is accurate. Gov. Berkeley was again Governor of Virginia. Gov. Calvert invited the Virginia Quakers to Maryland. Tom Cottingham contracted with Ambrose for the use of boat as depicted. George Wilson, the Quaker, died in prison in Jamestown. He wroted to many other Quaker and the letter includes some of his words from his letters. Jamestown was sometimes called James City. Ambrose built the first meeting house for Quakers in Maryland and called it God's Acre.

CHAPTER FORTY-TWO - The information on the peace document in England is true. The episode concerning Col. Scarburgh is true and described by him in Court records. All the men arrested were released. Gov. Calvert visited Gov. Matthews trying to settle the problem after receiving many letters from the Quakers in Maryland.

CHAPTER FORTY-THREE - Ambrose and Mary had their seventh child on this date. The description of the Quaker meeting is typical for the time. Fox-hunting was a popular sport in Maryland, even among Quakers, at this time. Thomas Brooks of Maryland brought foxhounds from England.

CHAPTER FORTY-FOUR -The fox-hunt described is typical for the time.

CHAPTER FORTY-FIVE – A hurricane actually hit the area of Jamestown Sep 6, 1667. The author took a little leeway on the actual date. The storm is considered to be the most severe ever recorded to strike Virginia. It lasted about 24 hours and was accompanied by violent winds and tides. "Approximately 10,000 houses were blown over, crops were beat to the ground, cattle drowned in area rivers and bays by a twelve foot storm surge. The foundations of the fort at Point Comfort were swept into the river. Twelve days of rain followed this storm across Virginia. Many accounts of the hurricane were recorded in the news and letters.

CHAPTER FORTY-SIX – Tom Cottingham, future husband of Mary Dixon, lived with Anthony West in Maryland. He bought from William Planner that was located across the river from Ambrose Dixon and was often found in Court records regarding business transactions.

CHAPTER FORTY-SEVEN - In 1666, the Government of Maryland created a new county from the area around Ambrose and other Friend's plantation and named it Somerset. Stephen Horsey became a Commissioner and was appointed High Sheriff. Ambrose was appointed Surveyor of Highways and elected to serve represent the Lower House of the State Assembly. However, there is no record of Ambrose serving. He more than likely did not serve because he would have been required to take an oath and Quakers did not believe in taking oaths. Tom Cottingham and Mary Dixon were married by Henry Boston July 8th, 1667. They settled on their land on the Annamessex River across from the Dixon's.

Ambrose and Mary lived many more years in the new county of Somerset Maryland. Their story as well as their descendants will be continued in the next book in the *Tapestry of Love* series.